# THE NAMEDROPPER

*Brian Freemantle titles available from*
*Severn House Large Print*

Time to Kill
Dead End
The Holmes Factor
The Holmes Inheritance
Two Women

# THE NAMEDROPPER

Brian Freemantle

**Severn House Large Print**
London & New York

This first large print edition published 2008
in Great Britain and the USA by
SEVERN HOUSE PUBLISHERS of
9-15 High Street, Sutton, Surrey, SM1 1DF.
First world regular print edition published 2007 by
Severn House Publishers, London and New York.

British Library Cataloguing in Publication Data

Freemantle, Brian
    The namedropper. - Large print ed.
    1. Identity theft - Fiction 2. Suspense fiction 3. Large
    type books
    I. Title
    823.9'14[F]

    ISBN-13: 978-0-7278-7678-2

Printed and bound in Great Britain by
MPG Books Ltd, Bodmin, Cornwall.

*To Charlotte and Will
And of course to Eliza Bunny,
with so much love*

I am indebited to Dr Matthew Dryden, MD, FRCpath, FRGS, for his medical guidance and advice on the sexually transmitted conditions discussed in this book. Any errors reflect my lack of understanding, not Dr Dryden's outstanding knowledge and patience in trying to prevent my making such mistakes.

# Author's Note

Divorce legislation differs from state to state in the USA. In a minority of states there still exists on statute books claims, not just for alienation of affection, but also for engaging in criminal conversation – shy, early American nice speak for adultery. North Carolina is one such state. Others include Hawaii, Utah, Illinois, Mississippi, New Mexico and South Dakota. If a divorce court jury in such states can be persuaded that a spouse's affections were alienated by he or she engaging in criminal conversation with a cited defendant, that defendant is liable for financial damages, sometimes punitive, that in recent years have exceeded a million dollars.

There are many law enforcement agencies that consider the phrase 'identity theft' to be nice speak for today's fastest growing crime in the developed world; dismissed by those who have not yet been affected by it to be a victimless crime because banks and financial institutions most often bear the cost of those against whom the fraud is committed. The

US Federal Trade Commission has estimated the annual profit of identity thieves in America to be $53 billion a year. British fraud protection services dismiss as a gross underestimate a 2002 Cabinet Office study estimating the UK cost at £1.3 billion a year.

# One

Harvey Jordan always chose an aisle seat, disinterested in looking out at ploughed clouds at 35,000 feet, so it wasn't until the plane banked over the sea for its customary descent into Nice that he got his first sight of the boat-sailed-and-propeller-spumed Mediterranean and, coming rapidly closer, the regimented squads of private jets parked at ease on their parade ground. As always on his arrival in such a familiar, welcoming environment, in which he could, unusually, *be* Harvey Jordan, there was the immediate and professional recognition of the easy and openly available opportunities spread out before him even before getting off the aircraft. Just as quickly came the objective refusal. As Harvey Jordan, the genuine name by which he had been christened and officially registered in St Michael and All Angels in Paddington forty years ago, this was forbidden ground, a positively prohibited working zone. He was legally – and therefore necessarily above suspicion – Harvey Jordan. And this was a vacation, even though he considered what he now did for a living more a permanent holiday than work.

But it *was* work and the living had been good, very good indeed. So far this year Jordan had operated twice in New York, once in Los Angeles and three times in London. Currently the profit was nudging £600,000 – with no irritating pre or after tax qualifications – and he'd already planned three new hits when he got back from France, which should comfortably take his income beyond the million. The only uncertainty was whether to try to fit in something else after that, which couldn't be decided until he got to the end of his carefully calculated schedule.

Jordan ignored the scrambling-to-stand bustle behind the business class separation the moment the plane stopped, smiling his thanks at the flight attendant's approach with his carry-on luggage, and instinctively allowed three of the other passengers in the section to disembark ahead of him. Just as instinctively he isolated the CCTV cameras inside the terminal, again immersing himself among the concealment of preceding arrival passengers. With no checked-in luggage to collect Jordan passed unchallenged through the customs hall, smiling expectantly at the time-consuming melee around the car rental desks. The Nice city bus left within minutes of his boarding and it cost a ten Euro tip for the driver to make an unscheduled stop directly outside the Negresco hotel.

The concierge smiled in recognition at Jordan's entry, took his luggage and assured him the pre-booked hire car was waiting in its parking space. The primed duty manager was already at the reception desk by the time Jordan reached it, the registration only needing Jordan's unaccustomed but genuine signature.

'Only staying two nights this time, Mr Jordan?' said the duty manager.

'Moving around, as always. I might ask to come back while I'm in the area,' said Jordan, who rarely made any long term commitment.

'There's always accommodation available for regular guests,' smiled the man in reply.

'I know,' Jordan said and smiled back. It was refreshing, and the purpose of his vacations, to be able to relax and be recognized for who he really was and not to have to constantly remember and react to the identity he had assumed.

# Two

That afternoon, as he always did upon relocating to different towns or cities no matter how well he already knew them, Jordan set out to re-orientate himself. Jordan operated to a number of self-invented and imposed rules, one of which was never to take anything for granted, no matter how familiar or predictable the situation or surroundings. Before quitting the hotel he put the intrusion traps in place in his sea-fronting suite, hanging his clothes with pocket flaps and trouser lengths arranged in such a way, and shirts in such an order in partially withdrawn or fully closed drawers, that he would have known instantly if they had been disturbed during his absence. Downstairs at the caisse he rented a safe deposit facility for the bulk of his money, genuine passport, standby Letter of Credit and emergencies-only – again genuine – credit cards: like most successful professional thieves, Harvey Jordan took the greatest care protecting his own finances and possessions. He'd lost everything, including a wife, once and was determined never to do so again.

The most necessary and basic essentials put into force, Jordan strolled into the town as far as the railway station, re-establishing its layout in his mind and isolating new constructions and shops since his last visit. He walked in a gradual familiarizing loop via the park to a corner cafe he'd enjoyed during a previous visit for coffee and pastries. Gazing out over the sun-starred water he calculated that it would only take three months – four at the most – for his last victim, a flamboyant, frequently gossip-columned London investment banker, to restore his credit rating. Harvey Jordan prided himself upon his Robin Hood integrity, always establishing the financial resources of those whose identity he stole and used. Another working rule was that, with only ever one exception, he never stripped them to the monetary bone, as he had been stripped with pirhrana-like efficiency. It had taken Harvey Jordan two years, after crawling almost literally out of the vomit-ridden gutter, to discover the identity of the man who had first stolen his identity and along with it his legitimate computer programming business. Then it took a further year, using the man's genuine identity, to recover financially everything, and more, of what had been taken from him. He hadn't, of course, been able to recover Rebecca. Or the bankrupt business. It was a matter of integrity, he reassured himself, that, having personally learned it the hardest way imaginable, he provided a very necessary lesson to those from whom he stole to never again be so careless with their personal details and information. It wouldn't, Jordan knew, be a defence if he were ever caught – which he was equally determined never to be – but he considered the money he took not so much illegally obtained as justifiable and well-earned tuition fees. If he didn't do it who else was there to teach them?

In the early evening Jordan drove the anonymous rented Renault to Monaco and ate at one of his favourite restaurants in the principality, a specialist fish bistro overlooking the harbour and the pink-painted royal palace, and afterwards climbed the hill for coffee and brandy on the Hotel de Paris terrace, watching the early arrivals at the casino. Jordan himself crossed the square just after ten and bought £5,000 worth of chips; on holiday, just as when he was following his chosen profession, tax exempting casino winning receipts legally proved his income legitimately came from gambling. He started out with chemin de fer, and at the end of an hour he was showing a profit of £1,500, which he much more quickly quadrupled at the roulette table.

Throughout Jordan remained constantly alert to everything and everyone around him, twice moving to a different position at the roulette table to prevent people getting close enough to either pickpocket or steal his chips, even though he was confident he would have instantly detected any attempt at either. The need, as always, was to avoid attracting attention. He was aware, too, of two unaccompanied women who had seen his success at the card table and were now attentively standing on the other side of the roulette wheel; he identified both – professional recognizing professional – as working girls. He decided against either this early on in his vacation. Because of how he lived, Jordan accepted that any permanent relationship – certainly another marriage – was impossible but sex was as essential as the best food and finest hotels during such periods of necessary relaxation. But Jordan preferred equally casual but uninvolving holiday romances to financial practitioners, no matter how adept. There was often an added frisson from amateur enthusiasm.

Jordan concluded his evening just before midnight with a profit of £2,500, the essential casino receipt confirming the gambling winnings for later tax submission proof, and a feeling of total satisfaction at his first, non-working day for three months. He decided it was an omen that aurgured well for the rest of the trip.

Which it proved to be.

As he drove the following day into the mountain hills to St Paul de Vence, he decided to extend his stay in Nice, to allow more time to re-explore the surrounding countryside, momentarily doubting his decision when he reached the

14

village which was full of too many milling, jostling tourists in very narrow streets. The uncertainty seeped away when he reached the Colombe d'Or to savour both the luncheon menu and the display of original Impressionist art. Jordan considered the small Chagall, protectively stored in one of his well hidden bank vaults, probably the best investment he'd ever made. Twice, once in London and again during his most recent New York expedition, he'd felt sufficiently confident of his specific Impressionist knowledge to have successfully passed himself off as an expert on the subject under two separately assumed identities.

Jordan telephoned the hotel from the Colombe d'Or to lengthen his stay in Nice and to alter the already confirmed reservation in Cannes – because Jordan never did anything even as mundane as moving from one place to another without guaranteeing the most appropriate accommodation – sure there would be no difficulty in his arranging either, which there wasn't. The years – and the period had been years, not months – over which Jordan had worked to protect and preserve his now near perfect existence was finally paying the highest dividends and it was a good feeling he wanted always to preserve.

That night's gambling was at the Beaulieu casino in which Jordan finished £4,800 ahead, which provided another useful tax receipt. An equally satisfying success was in confirming his previous night's judgement; there was a mutual facial recognition between both of them. She was the second of the two professionals he'd isolated in Monaco, tonight's simple black tube dress, the only jewellery a single rope of pearls, better showing off both her figure and blonde attractiveness than the earlier more full skirted red. She smiled at their initial eye contact and he briefly nodded back in acknowledgement. She made her approach – as Jordan had anticipated she would – when he was having his farewell brandy, after he'd cashed up.

'You gamble well,' she opened.

'Luckily,' Jordan qualified. 'How did you know I was English?' Such attention to detail was always important.

'You talked more in English than French to the croupier.' Her own minimal accent wasn't French.

'And you don't gamble. You didn't last night. Or tonight.' He wanted to establish his own awareness.

'Not at the tables.' She slightly moved the chair at which she was standing. 'May I join you?'

Jordan nodded, politely rising as she sat. 'You'd like champagne?'

'That would be very pleasant. My name is Ghilane.'

'John,' responded Jordan, gesturing for a waiter. It was the christian name of his most recent victim and that to which he was therefore most accustomed. It would have been unthink-able – amatuerish – to have given her his real name even though this was going to be the most fleeting of encounters.

16

'You are here on vacation, John?'

Jordan hesitated, while her wine was served. 'I enjoy the South of France.'

'So you know it well?'

'Well enough.' He wondered by how much the fulness of her breasts was helped by the uplift of her bra, but decided against paying to find out.

She grimaced extravagantly, pulling down the corners of her mouth. 'Which means I can't offer to show you places you haven't seen before?'

She was very good and very enticing, acknowledged Jordan. Refusing the heavily intended double entendre, he said, 'It's quite late.'

'Not too late to be too tired,' she misunderstood.

'I was thinking of you.'

'As I was, of you.'

'An hour from now only sad loss-chasers will still be here, without any money left. I don't want it to be a lost evening for you.'

Her face tightened imperceptibly but quickly relaxed, opening into a smile. 'You sure about that?'

'I'm sure.'

'I don't usually get a response like this: get so immediately recognized like this. I think we could have had fun together – more interesting fun than normal for both of us.'

'I'm sure we could,' said Jordan, meaning it but at the same time discomfited by her reaction to his rejection. He'd never known a hooker anywhere in the world – and he'd known enough in a lot of the world – who wasn't or didn't easily become a willing police informant to protect themself. Which, professionally again, he totally understood and accepted.

'You're right,' said Ghilane, looking briefly around her. 'It is late and there's a lot of desperately perspiring men around the tables. Maybe tomorrow night will turn out better.'

Jordan knew she hadn't given up and admired her for it. He touched her champagne flute with his brandy snifter and said, 'Here's to a more successful tomorrow.'

'But not with you?'

'But not with me,' echoed Jordan. It had been a passing, even entertaining interlude but it was time it ended.

'Perhaps I'll see you again? I'm often here or in Monaco.'

'I'm moving on tomorrow,' said Jordan, gesturing for his bill.

She shrugged, philosophically. 'My loss.'

'Both our loss,' said Jordan, gallantly.

Jordan's excursion the following day took him away from the coast, just beyond Mougins to where Picasso once crafted his ceramics, of which there were still a lot of photographs but with most of which Jordan was unimpressed, as he was with some, although by no means all, of the artist's various period experimentation, particularly Picasso's female genitalia obsession. The eating choice had obviously to be the Moulin de Mougins, even though Jordan knew the legend of Picasso settling bills there with sketches instead of cash to be untrue.

Jordan didn't hurry the short descent to the Carlton at Cannes, timing his arrival perfectly for a late lunch on the terrace, although as far back from the traffic-thronged promenade as possible, his placement perfect for when the heat went out of the day. He wasn't aware of her when he first sat, but almost at once registered the carefully page-marked but set aside book, as well as the solitaire engagement ring he conservatively estimated to be at least five carats overwhelming the surprisingly slim adjoining wedding band. She was remarkably similar to the blonde-haired, heavily busted girl who had called herself Ghilane, although younger, probably little more than thirty. There was a handbag too small to contain a cell phone, a protective, wide-brimmed hat on the same side chair as the discarded book, no longer necessary because of the table umbrella, the shade of which made it impossible for Jordan to make out her features. Despite the shade, she still wore sunglasses. She was already on her coffee, the single glass of wine only half drunk. Jordan smiled when she turned to look across the intervening four tables in his direction. He could see enough of her face to know that she didn't smile back but looked immediately away, towards the sea.

Time to move on from Impressionists, Jordan concluded. It really was developing into the sort of vacation he'd hoped it would be, as in previous years it had invariably proved to be.

# Three

Over months, eventually stretching into years, Harvey Jordan had learned every trick and manoeuvre to access, uncover and utilize the identity of unwitting victims, none of which had to be employed to discover all he needed to know about the blonde, disdainful woman. This was pleasure, an amusement to pass the afternoon, not work upon which he had to concentrate. Directly after making his deposit box arrangements and setting the intrusion traps in his suite, Jordan quit the Carlton to stroll along the Croisette towards the port to indicate his own disinterest, although frequently pausing to ensure that she was not coincidentally taking the same exercise behind him, wanting the intended encounter to be at his choosing, not by accident.

Using his knowledge of the hotel, he timed his return to the Carlton for the beginning of their afternoon tea service, confident that he entered the lounge without her awareness and gained a seat sufficiently close behind her to easily overhear the waiter address her as 'Madam Appleton' and to detect the American accent when she ordered. He was also close enough to see that the book in which she was now engrossed was *Pride and Prejudice*. Jordan declined tea himself, needing to be in position in the lobby. He didn't hurry selecting the right place, disappointed there wasn't an unobtrusive spot from which he had a complete view of the room-key pigeon holes as well as a sufficient warning of her approach into the lounge. He settled for the best available combination and hid himself behind the *Herald Tribune*, raising it higher at the first sight of her before she actually came into the reception area. He was doubly lucky as she did precisely what he'd hoped by going straight to the desk for her key, which Jordan immediately recognized to be at the suite level upon which he had his own, five rooms further along the same corridor; an unexpected but welcome bonus. Because he was not working and sought recognition, rather than his usual anonymity, Jordan had ensured his immediate acknowledgement by heavily tipping upon his arrival the valet parking supervisor at the top of the hotel's sweeping entrance into the underground facility, and so was greeted by name as he approached. Knowing from his previous visits that vehicle spaces were allocated by room number he gave that of the woman, not his own, shaking his head when the supervisor frowned as he looked up from his occupation list and said, 'That's Mrs Appleton's suite? She doesn't have a car here.'

'Stupid of me: not concentrating,' apologized Jordan, giving his own number.

Jordan drove contentedly along the Croisette in the direction he'd earlier walked, leaving the Renault in the underground public car park adjoining the port and choosing the restaurant with a first-floor overview of the marina and its yachts, reflecting upon what it had been so easy to learn about the dismissive Mrs Appleton. She was an abstemious American woman about thirty years old who liked classic English literature, with so few friends or acquaintances she didn't even bother with a cell phone, staying alone and without transport in one of the best hotels in the South of France, sufficiently wealthy to wear a five-carat diamond ring and be able to afford a beach-fronting suite, although unlikely to venture out too long upon it from the umbrella and sun hatted care she took to protect her complexion. And she was hopefully lonely or bored or both.

The ice maiden melted the following day, although initially only very slightly. But still enough. By the time she emerged from the elevator, just before eleven, Jordan had bought a paperback edition of Jane Austin's *Sense and Sensibility* from the English language bookshop near the railway terminus and was back, ensconced in the lounge, the book and its title positioned on the table in front of him to be obvious to anyone entering from the lobby; Jordan himself was once more hidden behind his raised newspaper awaiting her arrival. He kept the *Herald Tribune* uncomfortably high, his arms beginning to ache, until the coffee service began, thankfully lowering it to order and establish that she was deeper within the room, writing at an upright table. Whatever it was appeared to be a long letter, several thick pages, not a holiday postcard. She was wearing a bare shouldered day dress but with a matching patterned bolero, her book, wide-brimmed hat and sunglasses carefully beside her on the other chair. Better able to see her without the glare of yesterday's sun Jordan decided she was very much younger than the casino professional and her hair a much more natural blonde. The dark-rimmed reading spectacles it seemed necessary for her to wear added rather than detracted from her attractiveness. It was going to be an interesting distraction trying to establish whether she was a genuinely natural blonde. He'd give himself today, maybe going over into tomorrow; if there hadn't been sufficient progress by then he'd move on. Maybe, even, go back to one of the casinos to find the more approachable Ghilane.

Jordan waited until she finished whatever it was she was writing and was reading through it before rising to make his way out into the lobby, choosing a path to take him directly by her table. He did not look in her direction, nor was aware of her looking in his, and he was past before she said, 'Excuse me!'

The satisfaction coursed through him. 'I'm sorry?'

'Your book. You've left your book.'

Jordan frowned, turning to where he had been sitting. 'I have a call to make. I'm coming back.'

'I'm sorry ... I thought...'

The words were stumbled but she didn't colour with embarrassment. Closer he saw that she was

23

blue-eyed, so maybe she was genuinely blonde. 'Thank you. Will you stand guard while I'm gone?'

'I'm embarrassed.' She still didn't blush.

An east coast accent, the vowels hard, judged Jordan, expertly. 'You've no reason to be.'

Jordan continued on before she could reply, building in the time for his absence by going up to his suite and remaining at the window for a few minutes, watching the beach filling up beneath its parasols. From the attention with which the sunbathers were creaming and oiling themselves Jordan guessed it was hotter out on the beach than it had been the previous day.

She was waiting for his return, smiling up at once, her thick manila envelope sealed. It was automatic for Jordan to try to read the address but it was very positively turned against him, which would have made his interest too obvious if he'd tried harder. 'My book is untouched, as I left it,' he said and smiled. The spectacles were back in their case now, along with everything else on the chair beside her.

'I misunderstood. I'm sorry...'

'I'm not,' said Jordan, maintaining the momentum. 'Now we're talking instead of being on the opposite sides of the room from each other.' Standing above her he could see the dark beginning of a deep and enticing cleavage.

'I didn't intend to intrude, but...' she began again.

'I didn't think that you did,' Jordan stopped her. 'I think it was a fortunate misunderstanding.'

She shifted uncertainly, looking down at the only available chair full of her belongings.

Gesturing to where he had been sitting earlier, Jordan said, 'There's more room where I am. Let's have an apéritif there.'

'My things?' she said, making her own gesture.

'They can stay where they are. Or be brought to us if you want them.'

She hesitated. 'They can stay here.'

It was going to work, as it invariably did, Jordan decided.

Harvey Jordan, whose vocation was seduction in every sense and definition of the word, didn't hurry. He never did once the first barrier was breached. The initial isolation and pursuit of a victim was as much an orgasmic pleasure as its culmination, either sexual or financial, and he had a lot of mental foreplay to savour here. Remembering her half glass abstinence the previous lunchtime he chose a single glass – not even a half bottle – of champagne for their apéritif and distanced himself from her at the furthest end of the couch. He gave her his real name – Christian as well as family – and learned that hers was Alyce ('with a y, just to be different') and that it was her first visit to France. She hadn't yet felt confident enough to try the French in which she'd graduated, as well as in Spanish, both with A plus, from Smith college; she admired the ease with which he spoke French to their waiter, ordering the drinks and asking for the luncheon menu and for a table, not outside on the open terrace, but directly inside the better shaded floor-to-ceiling veranda doors which, still imposing his own pace, Jordan did without inviting her in advance. She accepted at once when he belatedly apologized for his feigned presumption. Jordan felt a fleeting jump of unease at her mention of the park-view appartment, because his last identity sting had been in Manhattan, quickly dismissed by the self-assurance that small though the island was, the likelihood of her knowing anyone with whom he'd had a chance encounter was remote, particularly after her reference to a weekend house in the Hamptons, which she preferred to the city. And he hadn't been using his own name then anyway. There was no reference to a job, or a profession, or to the husband who had presumably provided the diamond and the wedding band, and Jordan held back from any curiosity: it was a not infrequent reflection of his that so easily did he find it to encourage people to unprompted disclose their life histories that had he chosen a legitimate profession he could have lived well – although not as well as he did now – by setting himself up as a psychologist. Or an end-of-the-pier fortune teller, complete with crystal ball.

Jordan's restricted offering was well rehearsed and faultlessly delivered in the hope of encouraging further disclosures from her: he'd been fortunate with a family inheritance, which he'd used to develop a so far sufficiently successful career as a venture capitalist. It enabled him to travel extensively, although that freedom

26

brought with it personal restrictions, chief among them a difficulty in establishing permanent relationships; there had been someone, a few years earlier, with whom he believed himself to have been in love – although now he was no longer sure – but against whom he felt no resentment or disappointment for refusing to put up with his too frequent absences, and abandoning him for someone else to whom he believed, and certainly hoped, she was now very happily married. They still exchanged Christmas cards: last year's had featured a family photograph that included a baby girl. In reality it had been the drunken self-pity that Rebecca had refused to put up with. He'd seen the announcement of her second marriage in the *Daily Telegraph*. And the birth announcement. He certainly didn't feel any resentment against her walking out on him as she had; he'd have done the same in her circumstances.

'That's sad,' responded Alyce, although not offering an explanation for the wedding band now covered by her other hand.

'Not for Rebecca – that was her name,' further tempted Jordan. 'She's got a husband and a baby and a proper life, not someone whose existence is regulated by airline schedules.' Or, after the bankruptcy, the availability of a gin bottle, he remembered.

'Sad for you,' she insisted, still without volunteering more.

'But not today!' declared Jordan, briskly. 'Today I am on vacation and we're having lunch together and I am no longer lonely.'

27

Alyce hesitated and for the briefest moment Jordan thought she was going to change her mind and decline the belated invitation. Instead she said, 'No. Now neither of us are lonely.'

Jordan did order a whole bottle of wine, a grand cru Chablis, and took time consulting the menu with Alyce, who followed his recommendations. He'd seen a film version of *Pride and Prejudice* and speed-skimmed enough of *Sense and Sensibility* to maintain a conversation about Jane Austen and her books – his familiar, never-yet-failed technique now fully on track – and went easily into his well practised repertoire of fictitious venture capitalist and investment anecdotes. She laughed on cue but once more brought him up short after the third story by saying, 'Your experiences seem much more amusing than my husband's.'

'He's in the business?' queried Jordan, his stomach lurching.

'Wall Street. He's the Appleton of Appleton and Drake, the commodity traders.'

'Different sort of finance altogether,' insisted Jordan, the alarm receding. 'All far too clever for me.'

'And me,' she said as she smiled. 'I don't understand any of it.'

Thank God he hadn't gone on to his two New York inventions, Jordan thought. 'I've visited New York, of course. Great city. But I haven't done any business there.'

'I prefer the Hamptons,' she repeated.

She'd opened the subject at last! Jordan said, 'Is your husband joining you here?'

'No!' Alyce said, sharply.

'I'm sorry,' hurried Jordan, feigning the embarrassment to match hers earlier. 'I didn't ... forgive me...'

'Let's talk about something else.'

'Let's,' agreed Jordan, anxious to maintain his self-imposed schedule. 'Have you read Dumas?'

Alyce frowned, confused by such an abrupt switch. 'I tried him in the original French but ended up with the translation.'

'Which book?'

'*The Man in the Iron Mask*. What else?'

It was like winding a clockwork toy, knowing how it would respond when the catch was released. 'Have you any plans for tomorrow?'

The frown returned at the further apparent switch. 'No?'

'Will you trust me to take you on a mystery journey?'

'Should I?'

The first hint of flirtation, Jordan recognized. 'That's for you to decide.'

She made as if to consider it. 'I'll take the risk.'

'You'll need sun protection: something to cover your arms as well as oil or cream. Not the sort of hat you've got over there. A bill cap. A swimming costume, if you decide to swim. Bring one anyway.'

'Are those all the clues I get?'

'It's too many already.'

'I like mystery.'

'So do I.' She really was quite beautiful, Jordan decided.

*  *  *

Should he cool things down before things even got started? Jordan asked himself, observing the familiar precaution. He would certainly stage the promised, now inescapable excursion, but then move on further along the coast, which had always been the intention. But not with Alyce Appleton as a companion, which, objectively, she might not be persuaded or want to be anyway. Jordan had worked often and successfully in New York but knew there was no way his path could have crossed or intertwined with that of Alyce's husband. If they had, he would have immediately recognized her name, even before she identified her husband. And she was hardly going to mention him or his name when she got back to America. There couldn't be the slightest risk of any professional difficulty arising from her husband being in commodity trading, which really was a quantum leap from any company identity theft with which he might involve himself in the future, doubly so now by his knowing the name of her husband's firm. The more Jordan rationalized it, the more he accepted his concern at learning what her husband did had been exaggerated. Too early to abandon his pursuit of Alyce, he determined. Just something to keep in mind.

Jordan excused himself immediately after lunch, talking of prior arrangements that were going to keep him busy for the rest of the day and into the evening, sure he detected her disappointment at their not spending more of the day and perhaps dinner together.

'Don't forget what you'll need tomorrow.'

'It's a boat, right?'

'Maybe. You don't like the sea?'

'I told you I've lived in the Hamptons, remember?'

Lived, in the past tense, isolated Jordan. 'Much rougher there than here.'

'So I'm right!' she demanded.

'Wait and see.'

'What time?'

'Ten. I'll call you if there's any change.'

Not wanting to use those of previous expeditions, Jordan got the names of three new yacht charterers from the concierge on his way upstairs and fixed meetings with the two most convenient, both with boats available in the port. A man of instinctive attention to detail Jordan checked the following day's predicted wind strength and chose the twin-hulled catamaran instead of the older, mahogany-fitted single hull he would have preferred in calmer conditions. It took longer to decide the food and wine he wanted, even for a one-day charter than it did to choose between the two yachts. The departure was confirmed for ten o'clock, which meant he didn't have to alter their already agreed schedule. Jordan could easily have got back to the Carlton for dinner but guessed she would be eating there, so he ate again in the restaurant dominating the marina. From his balcony table he could easily see the catamaran he'd hired being prepared for the following day.

Jordan's 9 a.m. call was a test, to assess her tone.

'Is there a problem?' she asked at once

'None at all. I'm just checking it's still all right with you?' She'd been worried, prepared for disappointment.

'I'm looking forward to it.'

'You got everything?'

'Everything.'

'I'll see you in the lobby at nine forty-five.'

She carried a small duffel bag and wore jeans, a white shirt with a thin anorak looped around her shoulders, her blonde hair in a ponytail under the bill cap, confident without any make-up, and Jordan thought she looked good enough to eat and hoped he would be doing just that very shortly. He definitely wouldn't be moving on soon. He'd ordered a hotel car rather than bother with the hired Renault, pleased to see that the previously tipped crew of two men and one woman were already waiting for their arrival, the catamaran open and ready to sail.

As they cleared the marina on engine Alyce said, 'It's time I knew where we're going.'

'To see the cell in which the man in the iron mask was actually held,' announced Jordan. Her reaction was exactly the same as that of the two other women – one English, the other Australian – he'd taken on the same trip, hopefully this time with the same uncomplicated result of the previous two.

'*What!*'

'Alexander Dumas's story is based on fact. One of the fictions was that the mask was iron. It wasn't. It was black velvet.'

'I can't believe what you're telling me!'

The catamaran cleared the immediate harbour and the sails billowed out above them. Jordan said, 'Why don't you relax in the webbing between the hulls?'

'Because I want you to tell me what you're talking about! It's not really true, is it?'

'Totally true. What no one has ever established is his real identity, although he's buried as "M de Marshiel". He was a state prisoner, of Louis XIV. For forty years he was held in jails all over France. He died in the Bastille in November, 1703. Whenever he was moved, from jail to jail, he had to wear the velvet mask to prevent any-one ever recognizing who he really was...' Jordan waved his hand beyond her. 'And one of those prisons was on the Ile St Marguerite, where we're going.'

Alyce swivelled to look at the undulating smudge on the horizon. 'We're going to see the actual cell?'

'The actual cell,' echoed Jordan. It was going to work. It always had.

'I don't believe it!' she said again.

'You can use your schoolgirl French to read the memorial plaque. There's a pamphlet, too.'

'What horrendous crime did he commit, yet escape execution?'

'No one knows that, either. There's a lot of legends. One is that he was the Duc de Verman-dois, an illegitimate son of Louis, although on the face of it that's an extreme way to treat your own son. In his book, if you remember, Dumas copied Voltaire in suggesting the man was an illegitimate elder brother of Louis, fathered by

33

Cardinal Mazarin. There's also a lot of historical insistence that he was a Count Mattiolo, a minister of the Duke of Mantua, who tried to trick Louis during diplomatic negotiations and was punished with a totally unknown and unrecognized living death.'

Alyce shuddered. 'Kept locked up for forty years!'

'A non person for forty years, someone whose face was never again seen except by his jailers: there's even a story that he had to wear the mask before he was given food, so that even the jailers wouldn't know what he looked like. If he defied them and refused to put it on, he wasn't fed.'

Jordan thought she was remarkably agile, disembarking at the island, as she had been boarding the catamaran. She slowly read the memorial plaque and collected the pamphlet, and in the bare cell, which was very cold compared to the outside near midday heat, she shuddered again several times.

'Whatever he did, he didn't deserve what was done to him,' she insisted.

'It had to be bad.'

'It doesn't make any difference.'

By the time they returned to the anchored catamaran the crew had erected a sun awning. Alyce didn't refuse the champagne but stopped at the second glass of Chablis and didn't need any urging to eat the lobster with her fingers. They let the strongest heat go out of the day before swimming off the port fin, Jordan delaying his climb back on to the boat because of his momentary and too obvious excitement at seeing her, surprisingly unashamed, in the briefest of bikinis. When they got back to Cannes she said she wanted to walk back rather than call for the hotel car or a taxi, and did so almost immediately taking his hand, moving her fingers over his. She said she wasn't hungry when he suggested dinner but that the sea air had tired her and that she thought she'd go directly to bed.

'But not alone,' she added.

Jordan thought it was far more exciting than Ghilane might have made it discovering that Alyce was indeed a natural blonde. And very eager and proud to prove it.

They checked out of the Carlton together the following morning, Alyce leaving the American Express office in Cannes as her forwarding address for any mail and, despite the inevitable traffic congestion on the meander to St Tropez, once they got off the autoroute they managed to get to the Residence de la Pinade and their corner tower room in perfect time for lunch on the sea-bordering terrace, even after he'd organized the necessary safe deposit box. Held by the excitement of discovery they spent the afternoon in bed in fresh exploration and decided they didn't want the additional exertion of walking into the town in the evening. Nor to eat anything other than each other. She didn't enjoy the following day's bustle of the town or the clutter of polished Harley Davidson motorcycles looped like a necklace around the harbour edge so they escaped by taxi over the hill to Pampalon Plage, and the Tahiti restaurant, the first of several they visited over succeeding days –

judging the Tahiti their favourite – except for the day Jordan chartered another yacht, traditionally hulled this time, to sail the coastline to the car-free Iles de Porquerolles. That was the day – or rather the night, as they lay side by side, naked, recovering from their lovemaking – that Alyce suggested extending her vacation by another week and Jordan said he thought she should tell him about the status of her marriage.

'There isn't one,' she replied. 'Status or any longer a marriage. That day we met? The envelope? It was divorce papers I couldn't wait to sign.'

'I'm sorry, I shouldn't...'

'It's not important,' she said, dismissively. She looked steadily at him across their table. 'Mad at me?'

Jordan hesitated, searching for the right response. 'Tit for tat, to balance your betrayal?'

'Something like that. In fact exactly that.'

'Why should I be mad?'

'I used you.'

'You didn't make any secret about being married.'

She smiled. 'I started out feeling a shit, guilty I guess on several levels. I don't any more. I feel great.'

'So do I.'

'No hang-ups, no regrets?'

'No hang-ups, no regrets.'

'What about my extending for an extra week?'

'It sounds good.'

They made their way slowly back along the coast, stopping at Cagnes and Le Saint-Paul and on the night before her flight from Nice stayed at the Hermitage in Monte Carlo and gambled in the high stakes room in the casino, where Alyce won £1,200 to his £2,000.

As they left the caisse, Jordan carefully pocketing the French certificate recording his winnings, Alyce said, 'What's the benefit of that?'

'In England gambling winnings aren't taxable. This is proof of where the money came from.'

'It makes you sound very rich.'

'It's the law. I always try to obey the law,' said Jordan.

At the airport the following morning Alyce said, 'It's been great. You've been great. Everything's great.'

'There's been a lot of times we've thought and spoken in echoes, like now.'

'Best I don't offer my New York address?'

'No,' he agreed. 'Nor mine in London to you.' He hadn't intended to anyway. 'Keep safe and stay happy.'

'And you.'

They didn't kiss goodbye. He stood watching her go through the departure gates. Alyce didn't turn as she did so. Jordan stayed that night at the Negresco and the following day brought forward his return flight to London, deciding as the plane climbed out over the sea that it had been his best vacation yet. But that it was time to get back to work and briefly – although profitably – be someone other than Harvey Jordan.

Someone like the targeted Peter Wightman.

# Four

Identity stealing, Harvey Jordan's dedicated profession, is an overcrowded activity, for a variety of reasons, all of them to the thief's benefit and favour. It is a crime almost childishly – and mostly legally – easy to commit and therefore so prevalent that law enforcement agencies are overwhelmed, reducing the risk of detection and even less of arrest virtually to zero. People – supposedly clever, financially savvy people – appear to ignore every piece of advice and warning given by every financial organization or adviser. And those same financial organizations and advisers, despite that advice and those warnings, keep showering the head-in-the-sand birdbrains with ever more credit facilities and cash-gaining opportunities to be milked like a milch cow by ever ready suckling predators. Of whom Harvey Jordan judged himself the most adept, if not the most financially successful single operator.

Jordan could have doubled, maybe trebled, his income; even gained the ultimate position of being *the* most financially successful. But that would have required his masterminding and controlling a gang as so many others in the business did, multiplying their ID stealing – and profits – tenfold or more. Which did not attract or tempt Harvey Jordan in the slightest. If he ran a gang, its profit would obviously have to be divided by its number, which, while increasing his personal income by as much as another tax-free £2 million a year, correspondingly increased among one or more of that number the likelihood of error, incompetence or idiotic mistake, resulting in his being caught, despite the odds against that occurring remaining in his and their favour. Harvey Jordan knew he was good. What he didn't know – and wasn't interested in finding out – was how consistently good others were. Nor did he imagine others, for their part, would have the patience to operate with the care and attention to detail that he did and upon which he would have insisted in any extended partnership.

It had taken him three months to prepare himself fully to impersonate Peter Thomas Wightman, a 42-year-old newly elevated senior partner in the legal firm of Jackson, Pendlebury, Richardson and Wright in Chancery Lane, in the Holborn district of London. He'd learned the man's name and that of the firm within which he'd been promoted from the legal notices of the *Daily Telegraph* and further researched it from the publicly available Bar directory issued by the General Council of the Bar and *Waterlow's Solicitors and Barristers Directory*, in which the names of all solicitors and barristers in England are listed. *Who's Who* gave Jordan the prep school – Downside – and Balliol College, Oxford, at which Wightman had read law. From the main office of the Company House register at

Crown Way, Maindy, Cardiff, he legally obtained details of the after tax profit of Jackson, Pendlebury, Richardson and Wright and the individual income and dividends to all its partners, including Wightman.

Jordan discovered Wightman's age – but far more importantly for his eventual purposes the maiden name of the man's mother – by paying a series of ten-pound search fees for details of births, deaths and marriages from the Family Records Centre, EC1, London. The maiden name of Wightman's mother had been Norma Snook. On the marriage certificate to John Wightman, an accountant, she was described as a solicitor. Peter Wightman had married Jean Maidment eighteen years earlier, at St Thomas's Church, Maidstone. There were three children, and from the voters' register records at the British Library he'd found the family lived in Kitchener Road, Richmond, Middlesex, and by memorizing the number plate as he drove past the detached property – and then checking at the national car registration office in Gwent, Wales, purporting to have been involved in a slight traffic accident with someone who had not stopped – confirmed that Wightman's car was a dark green, two-year-old Jaguar.

The detail of Jordan's research was continued in the form of the final precaution he always took just prior to embarking upon a new operation; this was never to work from the address of the flat in Marylebone, which he owned under his own, genuine name, but always from another apartment rented in the name of his intended victim. That, for his assault upon Peter Wight-man, was in Sydney Street, in Chelsea, from which he worked countrywide and with his usual untroubled and undetected success for a month, which ended with a somewhat disappointing profit of £154,000.

His final role for Sydney Street was to use it as the base for his next rental in Hans Crescent, Knightsbridge, under the name of Paul Macul-loch, a Harley Street cosmetic plastic surgeon whose A1 credit rating Jordan intended to use to its full and hopefully increased advantage.

He'd telephoned ahead to warn the Maryle-bone concierge of his return and when he arrived, the man, John Blake, already had his accumulated mail bundled and waiting for him.

'A good trip, Mr Jordan?' enquired the man.

'I've known better,' admitted Jordan, picking up his letters.

# Five

Attorneys-at-law was stridently displayed in red, beneath the identifying letterhead of Brinkmeyer, Hartley and Bernstein recorded in black typescript. The Madison Avenue, New York, NY 10022 address of the firm was in black, too. So, running down the right-hand side of the covering letter, were the names of the fifteen lawyer partners, headed by those of the three company founders. The man who had in legibly, rounded letters signed Jordan's letter – David Bartle – was the fifth in the list, presumably indicating his seniority. The letter, dated three weeks earlier, announced itself to be a summary of the official documents that were enclosed, couched in stiffly formal legalese.

Harvey William Jordan was cited under N.C.G.S Section 1-52(5) as defendant in the forthcoming preliminary hearing, date still to be negotiated and agreed between all involved parties, in the cross-petitioned divorce action between Alfred Jerome Appleton and Alyce Louise Appleton, nee Bellamy. Alfred Jerome Appleton was bringing suit against Harvey William Jordan claiming substantial damages for alienation of affection and criminal conversations, resulting in the initiation of divorce proceedings. Coupled and enjoined in those proceedings were further, but separately itemised, claims brought by Alfred Jerome Appleton for stress, loss of earnings resulting from that stress, public humiliation and derision resulting from that stress, damages and loss of commercial earnings and public confidence in the firm of Appleton and Drake from the forthcoming divorce proceedings, and medical and counselling expenses resulting from each and every aspect and condition arising from each, several or all of those allegations against Harvey William Jordan.

David Bartle sought immediate written acknowledgement of receipt of his letter and its accompanying formal claims, together with the name, street and city address, email and telex contacts with Harvey William Jordan's attorney with whom all further and future correspondence leading up to the indeterminate hearing date could be conducted.

It was difficult for Jordan to think, as cold as he was, shivering as he was, which had nothing to do with how cold he felt. There was too much to co-ordinate, to put into the order in which he had to deal with it, get out of it. How to get out of it? The wrong question, he corrected himself, the shaking subsiding. How had he *got* into it? Been found? Discovered? And by whom? A private enquiry agent – a private detective – obviously. Jordan felt a fresh sweep of unreality, snatching out for the discarded papers, shuffling through until he found the itemised statements of claim. It was all there, his suite number at the

Carlton hotel in Cannes, registered as a solitary occupancy but pointedly separated by only a short distance along the same corridor from that of Alyce. And then their odyssey. Their room number, as Mr and Mrs Jordan, at the Residence de la Pinade at St Tropez and the hotels at Cagnes and at Le Saint-Paul and the Hermitage in Monaco. As well as all the restaurants in which they'd eaten, the name of the catamaran as well as that of the chartering company, in which they'd sailed to the prison of the man in the iron mask, and to Porqerolles – even, astonishingly, their individual winnings that last night at the Monaco casino. Not *a* private detective, acknowledged Jordan. An expert himself in the gathering of facts and information, Jordan knew it would have needed a squad to have assembled all this. And it wouldn't be confined to just specific times against specific dates in individually identified hotels and places. There would be photographs, possibly dozens of photographs, an engulfing mud slide of identifying collages.

The coldness melted under a burn of personal anger. How, to someone supposedly so professional at always being – and remaining – Mr Invisible, could it have happened to him? How could he have remained so blissfully, blindly, stupidly unaware of his every move being tracked and recorded as intimately by not one but perhaps several! Several so obvious they not only kept him and Alyce under constant, twenty-four-hour surveillance but doubtless took albums of supporting, claim-incriminating photographs!

Everything – his carefully hidden and absolutely protected offshore fortune, his Mr Invisible anonymity, his very existence – was threatened. He had to find a way out. An escape. He finished the first glass of wine and immediately poured himself a second. But then stared at it, untouched. Not again, not this time, he warned himself. He'd never been a true alcoholic; not able to function without it. He'd just needed the escape from reality that booze provided.

What – where – was his escape now?

Was he subject to the jurisdiction of American divorce and civil courts? He didn't think he was or could be but he'd need legal advice. The word legal echoed in his mind, like a cracked bell. Harvey Jordan's absolute and essential necessity, the watchword by which he drew breath to survive, was always to avoid the very thought of contact with any legal authority. Now, today, his name and his address – God only knew how much else from all the legally and publicly accessible sources Jordan himself so assiduously pursued – was now legally, traceably, recorded! Displaying him to everyone and everything. It was right for him to feel so cold. He was, figuratively at least, naked, exposed for all to see and know and to dissect as and how they chose.

Not quite, came the faintly – too faintly – welcoming contradiction. They'd restricted themselves to France, to Alyce Appleton's carefully noted and recorded departure from Nice airport on the official legal documents before him. American not English private detectives then, hired to follow Alyce from New York and watch her and anyone with whom she came into contact. If they'd continued to keep him under observation – stayed with him all the way back to England – they would have followed him to Sydney Street and after that all over England, not here, to Marylebone, where the papers had been delivered. Jordan snatched out again, not for the documents but for the envelope in which they'd been delivered, the recorded delivery sticker belatedly registering, now as brightly as if it were in multi-coloured neon. Attorney-at-law David Bartle, from Brinkmeyer, Hartley and Bernstein, had documentary proof of his having received the accusations made against him. He couldn't deny the claims had been delivered. How had the law firm got this correct address? His mind momentarily blocked again, then cleared. It had to be the Carlton hotel. Not just an hotel: a *grand* hotel, in every definition of the accolade, one of whose services was permanently holding in its files the names, personal details and preferences of its regular clients from their first and succeeding visits, a source of information Harvey Jordan had himself utilized in the past. If he'd been followed on the return flight from Nice – instead of being abandoned there – and to Chelsea his assumed name of Peter Wightman would have been discovered, against comparison with the inevitable French photographs, and British police possibly brought in to resolve the mystery of conflicting identities. So he'd been lucky with a partial escape, Jordan decided, trying to rationalize his problems. But partial escape wasn't enough. It had to be complete.

Jordan was waiting in the apartment lobby for the arrival the following morning of the attentive doorman, John Blake, who at once confirmed his signing for the recorded delivery of the American letter.

'I guessed it was important: that's why I put it on the top of your pile, as I told you,' reminded the doorman. 'They took a note of my name and home address, too. It was all right my signing for it, wasn't it?'

The man had told him, remembered Jordan, and he'd tossed the letter, along with everything else, in a jumbled mess on top of the bureau without bothering to look at it. 'They? There was more than one man?'

The balding man shook his head. 'I'm sorry, Mr Jordan. I meant the Post Office. It was the normal postman but I'd never before seen the receipt form he asked me to sign. He said it was important – that I had to – because it was a legal document.'

Shit, thought Jordan. 'When was that: when was it delivered?'

'Five days ago. I did do the right thing, didn't I?'

'Of course you did,' assured Jordan, with difficulty. Where had the package been – to whom had it gone for onward delivery – in the intervening days from the letterhead date? Why hadn't the French surveillance carried on to England? So much he didn't know, couldn't protect himself against!

'I'm very sorry if—'

'I told you nothing's wrong,' stopped Jordan. Could he risk going on, hinting at the apprehension? He didn't have any alternative, so much and so quickly did he have to catch up. 'Has anyone, more than one person maybe, been asking about me?'

John Blake frowned, uncertainly. 'No.'

'You're sure?'

'I'd have remembered, Mr Jordan. You know I would.'

'Yes, I do know you would.'

'What shall I do – say – if anyone does come asking questions?'

He had to close the conversation, end it. 'Tell them that you're not sure about anything: that you need to think. But get some method of contact, like a visiting card. And let me have it.'

'Of course, Mr Jordan. You know you can trust me.'

'I know that, John,' insisted the man who didn't trust anybody and wasn't sure he could any longer trust himself. 'We're not talking anything world shattering. I just don't want to miss out on a business deal that's looking good. I'm caught up in a competition I want to win, just as they do.'

'I understand,' said the man, nodding sagely at the imagined confidence.

Back in his apartment Jordan made coffee he didn't want, merely occupying the time until offices woke up and became occupied, looking down at the bureau and its sleeping, so far unused computer, tempted to access the Appleton and Drake website. Not without more preparation and planning, he cautioned himself. He'd already made too many mistakes, allowed too much carelessness: every step he took, every move he made, from now on had to be the correct one, thought out and evaluated. The thin ice was already creaking underfoot.

Jordan stifled his impatience until nine thirty before telephoning the American embassy in Grosvenor Square, ignoring the recorded, single digit invitations to self-select what he wanted until a human voice came on the line. His impatience flared again at the pedantic questioning for his reason to be put through to the legal department, but he curbed it again, eventually getting a connection without disclosing his name, already having a false one ready if he was repeatedly pressed, which he wasn't. It was a softly spoken, southern-accented woman who picked up the receiver. Frowning at his own realization of the threadbare cover-up, Jordan said he was calling on behalf of an English friend whom it appeared likely was about to become involved in maybe more than one, although definitely linked, court cases in North Carolina. He was seeking the name of a London legal firm with experience of American law to which his friend could approach for guidance.

'I'm afraid we are not allowed to provide that sort of recommendation, for the obvious reasons,' said the woman. 'If the advice of such a recommendation were flawed or in error, the American government could lay itself open to separate legal action for damages.'

'All I'm seeking is the name of a legal firm

which could provide guidance in a divorce situation,' pressed Jordan.

'Sir, I've already told you we cannot provide recommendations for any legal opinion of any kind. And for that reason we don't hold the names of any English firms qualified to help you...' The pause was timed. 'Or your friend. I'm sorry.'

'Wait!' pleaded Jordan, fearing that the woman was about to ring off. 'Do you know any other agency or organization that could help?'

'The same caveat applies, I'm afraid. You'll have to proceed through English legal or government sources.'

'There must surely be American law firms with English affiliates!'

'Like you, I'm sure there must be,' agreed the woman. 'I'm afraid we don't have a list of them.' Before replacing the telephone, she said, 'Have a nice day.'

Jordan didn't imagine he would and it was not yet ten in the morning.

Her name was Lesley Corbin. She wore a severe black business suit, black framed glasses, but no wedding ring, which in the circumstances of the meeting didn't interest Harvey Jordan any more than her suppressed attractiveness. The appointment had been arranged by a secretary who hadn't indicated a gender: he'd wrongly assumed Lesley Corbin to be a man, not a woman, yet another mistake to add to his increasing, self-criticising list. After further refusals to recommend a suitable law firm, for the same reason as the American embassy, from the Law Society and the Anglo-American Society, Jordan had chosen the woman's firm from *Waterlows' Solicitor and Barristers Directory* from which he'd chosen his most recent identity theft victim.

He would have felt more comfortable if Lesley Corbin had been a man. After the briefest of preliminary introductions it took her a full ten minutes, which he timed from the sonorously ticking clock on the mantle above an unlit fire, to go through the contents of the American letter, frequently referring back and forth between the different statements of claim. It seemed much longer.

'I expect you to be completely honest, answering all my questions,' she began, when she finally looked up.

'Of course I will be,' lied Jordan.

'And understand that I am not legally qualified to offer advice on American divorce law.'

'That was made clear when I made the appointment. What I'm really seeking is a reference to a firm or a lawyer who can help me. In *Waterlow's* this firm is described as being international. When I called, I was told you were their foremost divorce specialist.'

'It is and I am. But not in divorce matters in the United States with the added complications of linked damages claims; in America divorce legislation varies from state to state, with state by state Bar examinations. I know what alienation of affections is but I've no idea what criminal conversation means.' There was just the slightest of lisps.

51

'All I'm seeking is guidance – a reference – to someone who can help me.'

The woman looked down at the papers strewn around her desk. 'Are you married?'

'No.'

'Are you in a relationship that could be construed as a common law marriage?'

'No.'

'Did you seduce Alyce Appleton?'

'No.'

'Did you sleep with Alyce Appleton?'

'Yes. We had a brief affair, a holiday romance.'

'So you seduced her?'

'No,' again refused Jordan. 'That makes it sound as if I pursued her: persuaded her against her will. I didn't force myself upon her. She was quite willing. Eager, in fact.'

'As you were?'

'As I was,' agreed Jordan. He hadn't so far had to lie.

'Did you know she was married?'

Jordan hesitated. 'Yes. She wore a wedding ring as well as an engagement ring. But she told me she was getting a divorce from her husband.'

'Did she tell you before or after you slept together?'

Jordan had to think. 'After. She made it sound as if she initiated proceedings against him, for his adultery—'

'And was getting her own back,' interrupted the lawyer.

'Exactly that.' He gestured to the papers lying between them on the desk. 'That claim makes it look as if she's the guilty party and I'm the cause.'

'That's precisely what it looks like: as it's supposed to appear. The husband's lawyers are making him out the innocent party.'

'It's not true. Before we even got together she spent one morning reading stuff she later told me were divorce papers. Everything had already been started.'

'Did she show the divorce papers to you? Did you read them?'

'Of course not.'

'So she could have been lying?'

The question brought Jordan up short. 'No...! She wouldn't...'

'We're not talking love here, are we? We're talking a holiday romance of what ... one, two weeks?'

'Three,' said Jordan, with difficulty. 'Just over three.'

'You plan to keep in touch? Exchange addresses?'

'No.'

'So she could have been lying?' the woman repeated. 'Setting you up?'

He didn't get set up! thought Jordan. He had been once but never again. He was the person who set other people up. 'I don't think she'd do that.'

'You got to know her – trust her – that well in just over three weeks, at the end of which you didn't exchange addresses?'

'I thought so.' He was sounding like a complete and utter idiot; had *been* a complete and utter idiot.

'Whose idea was it not to exchange addresses, hers or yours?'

'Hers. But it couldn't have been a set-up, could it?' demanded Jordan, gesturing again to the papers. 'We were being watched, every minute of every day. People had to be there already in place, ready and waiting.'

'Which is exactly what they would have been doing if she and her husband planned the whole thing in advance. All they needed was the willing victim. And you were it.'

No! mentally refused Jordan. He was always the cheater, not the cheated! It couldn't have happened the other way round. 'Why! What's the gain?'

Lesley shrugged. 'Make your own list. Alyce getting her divorce, if she set it up on her own. Both of them bleeding you dry, as well as Alyce getting her divorce, if they were working together.'

'She didn't know if I had any money or not.'

'When you met you were staying in a suite at one of the best and most expensive hotels in the South of France. And went on staying in them and eating in the best restaurants as Mr and Mrs Jordan, with you paying for everything. It's a reasonable supposition that you've got money.'

'I can't believe that's how it is.'

'I'm not saying that it is. I'm just putting it forward as one of several possibilities.'

'You're a divorce lawyer, an expert?' challenged Jordan.

'Yes?' questioned the woman.

'How many times have you come across the

sort of situation you've just suggested?'

'Three,' the woman answered, at once. 'And I'm not saying it's what's happened to you. Maybe Alfred Appleton is vindictive to the point of paranoia. I've known that, too.'

'OK!' said Jordan, forcing himself on. 'I accept you can't give me specific advice about American divorce law, from state to state. But what about jurisdiction? What if I ignore that letter and those claims? What could a North Carolina court do to me – against me?'

'If you ignore it all, you mean?' queried the woman.

'That's exactly what I mean.' Why did lawyers need the same things said three different ways!

'You got any assets in America – property, bank accounts, anything upon which a lien could be imposed?'

'None,' declared Jordan.

Lesley Corbin began shuffling the documentation back into order. 'You certainly couldn't, in my opinion, be forced to respond, as if it was something extradictable. You'll need an American lawyer – one who's passed the North Carolina Bar exams qualifying him to practise in a court there – to tell you what happens to the actual divorce application, if you don't turn up. What worries me is what in this country would be considered contempt of court, which gets judges very angry. By not turning up, the inference is guilt. With the detail contained in all these papers we've got to assume that they've not only got a lot of photographs of you two together but copies of hotel bills, affidavits from hotel staff and statements from the yacht charterers. Further proof of guilt if you don't contest the allegation. Sufficient, maybe, for the financial compensation claims to be pursued in your absence, whatever happens or doesn't happen to the actual divorce. I don't think any judgement against you could be pursued in an English court. I need to check. But it would certainly be registered in every enforcement authority throughout the entire United States. Which would mean your never again being able to visit America: be on a plane that just touches down on American soil, in transit. There could be countries, Canada is the most obvious, where there might be civil action reciprocity that would mean you couldn't go to any of those countries, either, whoever and wherever they are...'

'What about publicity ... public identification,' broke in Jordan, impatient again and anxious to resolve his most pressing concern.

Lesley Corbin smiled, as well as nodding her head. 'Precisely what I was leading up to. Publicity is their – his, if it's not a conspiracy and Alfred Appleton is acting alone – hydrogen bomb. You don't go to enter a defence, a total refutation, they don't just blow you to smithereens: they evaporate you. Again, we need American law guidance. But I've seen – you've seen, I'm sure – enough publicity exposures on television and in newspapers here in England to know you could face the equivalent of being hanged, drawn and quartered by publicity.'

The physical reaction had long gone beyond shivering coldness. Harvey Jordan now felt empty, disembowelled, as if just such medieval justice had been exacted upon him. Without sufficient consideration, he blurted out, and too late realized this was another mistake, 'I'm trapped – no way out.'

'There's always a way out,' said the more controlled woman. 'We're talking now about maximum damage limitation: avoiding, if we can, the sackcloth and ashes exposure that's going to make you a public, humiliated figure in England and America.'

'That's got to be a gross exaggeration!' Jordan protested.

'You want to expose yourself to as little as a fifth of it?'

'Not a tenth of it.'

'What do you want me to do?'

'Stop it happening. Stop any of it happening,' insisted Jordan.

'God does miracles. I just do the best I can.'

'Do the *very* best you can.' In his worst nightmare Jordan had never imagined – come close to contemplating – that he could be trapped like this again. But he'd recovered before. He'd recover again. And not just recover. Punish again, too.

57

# Six

The following day continued to be unreal, Jordan remaining aware of – watching – everything around him but having no contributory part or involvement in any of it, as if he were part of a ghost movie in which the character can see and hear and participate but can't be seen or heard by anyone else. Which was, in fact, how he wished his life could revert, to how it was before. But couldn't any longer. By the day after he was a long way towards recovery: Harvey Jordan reborn, the all thinking, all calculating, ahead-of-the-game operator. But not *totally* recovered. To have believed that, and tried to convince himself of it, would have been ridiculous: absurd to have even begun to think that. He'd become complacent, careless, not thinking clearly or properly enough just because he'd had it too easy for too long. Not any more. This was his wake-up call, at klaxon-decibel level. He'd get out of it, even if he didn't at this precise moment know how; he'd minimize it to the point of no longer being dangerously exposed, and he'd never again relax as he had relaxed. Maybe, even, cut himself away from places he knew so well – where too many people knew him so well – to find a new and different vacation spot. Not just one. Several. Move around the Caribbean and the Far East and the Pacific, not bother any more just briefly being known and favoured. And wherever it was, enjoy the readily and always available Ghilanes of the world.

This was all reassuring – necessary thinking – for the future. But there were more immediately pressing and essential practicalities. His antennae tuned to its maximum sensitivity, despite every indication that the surveillance had stopped in France, Jordan set out to once more become – and remain – Mr Invisible. It was instinct to set his intrusion traps but he did not emerge on to the pavement from his apartment block until he could see the yellow flag of an empty taxi to take him to the rail terminal at Waterloo, alert to everyone in the queue behind him, to buy a ticket to Basingstoke. He disembarked just two stops down the line at Clapham, remaining on the platform until it cleared of the four others who got off there as well, recognizing no one from the earlier queue. He took a waiting taxi to Sloane Square, a long enough journey upon which to isolate any following cab, which he didn't, and went underground there but only took one station west, changing from the District to the Piccadilly line at Victoria to loop east as far as Green Park for lunch at The Wolseley at a table specifically reserved for its uninterrupted view of the only public entrance into the restaurant. He did not suspect anyone of showing any specific interest in him throughout the meal. Conscious of how many observers must have been involved in the surveillance of himself and Alyce in France, Jordan didn't detect any brief signals between people entering or leaving the restaurant during what might be a change of possible observation shifts. He had the bell captain order a taxi that was waiting for him at the kerbside when he left, altering the given destination of Euston as the taxi was travelling north up Regent Street, and reached the newly rented service apartment in Hans Crescent just before 4 p.m.

Waiting there for him were all the credit and store cards – one from Harrods, which he could see from the apartment window – credit reference file replies and pin and ATM withdrawal numbers, everything he'd applied for in the name of plastic surgeon Paul Maculloch. Jordan put it all in his combination-locked briefcase, pausing at the moment of leaving to look around the flat he was never going to use, thinking how comfortable his brief stay there might have been.

John Blake hurried from behind his reception desk the moment Jordan entered the Marylebone apartment block. 'No one's enquired after you all day,' the man reported at once. 'There haven't been any telephone calls, either.'

'I'm hoping to hear something soon,' said Jordan, caught by how honest he was continuing to be.

All the intrusion traps inside the apartment were undisturbed. Jordan was on the verge of shredding everything in Paul Maculloch's name when a sudden need to keep the rental overtook him, a warming and satisfying confirmation that he had definitely recovered from the understandable shock of the recent news. It still took the increasingly confident Jordan an hour to minutely shred most of what he'd accumulated to pass himself off as Paul Maculloch and which now had a very important although quite different purpose. At the end of that hour he was left with a copy of the man's birth certificate, parental marriage certificates, passport, proof of rental occupancy of the Hans Crescent apartment and a single A1 credit reference file. With difficulty he managed to get it all into the already over-crammed concealed safe in the bedroom closet, containing, in varying denominations, the £154,000 profit from his countrywide tour as Peter Wightman.

There would be substantial inroads into that, Jordan accepted, his mind now fully concentrated upon the financial cost with which he was confronted. The short let and now very necessary rental of Hans Crescent would amount to £21,000, which objectively he didn't begrudge as a complete loss. The further £200 he'd spent getting all the Maculloch credit information wasn't totally wasted, either. The big uncertainty – although objectively again perhaps not the biggest – was how much all the legal advice was going to cost him. This was why he had to bury the tax-free profit from fifteen years of identity stealing as deeply and as untraceably as possible.

Harvey Jordan had left Lesley Corbin with the understanding that she would find an American attorney fully licensed and qualified to protect –

and if necessary represent – him at every degree and level of every linked North Carolina claim. And as he insisted on the best he would have to wait for her to come back to him after a careful selection. Jordan hadn't waited upon the convenience of others for more years than he could remember and had already decided not to allow Lesley Corbin more than one more full day before calling her back, irrespective of any agreement. But, now he needed the time, maybe even more than one day, to keep things in the satisfactorily protective sequence he had to establish.

While he was still at school Jordan had mentally tested himself – and invariably won – against chip-speeded computers to work out complicated arithmetical percentages and currency fluctuations and aggregates, and from his early programming career, concentrating on internet gambling games, he knew to the last penny the amount of his carefully hoarded and, hopefully, totally hidden fortune. The majority of it was beyond investigative reach in the tax-avoiding and secret haven of Jersey, the largest of the Channel Islands, to which he could literally carry cases of cash on the short sea crossing from England without any danger from putting hand baggage through X-ray airport security checks. The current, untraceable amount in safe deposit boxes in the island's capital, St Helier, was £2,805,000. In addition, in separate boxes, was the Chagall painting, an assortment of seventeen uncut and unset, but officially provenanced, diamonds and three diamond-set antique bracelets which conservatively, building in the fluctuations of jewellery prices, brought the stash up to £3,600,000. Jordan intended this stash, short of physical imprisonment which Lesley Corbin insisted impossible, to remain untouched and officially unplundered, whatever the outcome of his current predicament.

The risk, despite Leslie Corbin's assurances, was closer to home. In London, at Coutts, Lloyds TSB and NatWest, there were bank accounts, none of which exceeded £5,000, maintained for the access to safe deposit facilities at all three and in which was spread close to £1,800,000, which he'd looked forward to increasing to more than £2,000,000 by distributing among them the £154,000 profit from the most recent sting. But Jordan didn't think he could do this any longer because all three accounts – and safe deposit facilities – were in his genuine name against his genuine Marylebone address, which was known to the litigious Alfred Jerome Appleton and his bulldozing legal team of Brinkmeyer, Hartley and Bernstein. All this had to be kept from Appleton and his lawyers, despite whatever financial recovery opinion was offered by Lesley Corbin, who had already freely admitted being unqualified in American–English exchange agreement law.

Jordan quit his booby-trapped apartment even earlier the following morning, using the rush-hour congestion to ensure he was not followed; he spent an entire cab-and-tube dodging hour before finally arranging from a public street telephone a meeting, in the name of Paul Maculloch, with Royston and Jones, a private bank in Leadenhall Street in the financial square mile of the City of London. It was the sort of interview with which Jordan was thoroughly familiar, every document supporting his Maculloch identity ready when it was demanded. He opened the Maculloch account with £4,500 – below the amount legally required to be officially reported under drug trafficking legislation – from his most recent expedition and was promised that the safe deposit facilities would be available as early as the following day because of the advantages of it being a private bank, which was precisely why Jordan had chosen it. His personally appointed manager hoped it was the beginning of a long association and Jordan said he hoped so, too.

There was still no waiting message from Lesley Corbin when he returned to Marylebone, for which Jordan was grateful, and from which he left the following morning again before recognized office hours. By ten Jordan was sure once more that he remained unaccompanied and unwatched and by eleven opened the first of his deposit boxes at Royston and Jones with the contents of all but £3,000 each from what had been in safe deposit in Lloyds TSB and NatWest. He left £4,500 in Coutts in the second exchange that afternoon.

He was back in Marylebone in time to return Lesley Corbin's waiting message, telling her he had an early appointment the following day and couldn't get to her until the afternoon, which she said would be perfect because she'd set up a conference call exchange with a lawyer in New York, where it would still only be morning.

'I finally managed to get the names of two lawyers qualified to appear in North Carolina courts: oddly, both now have firms working in New York. The first was Daniel Beckwith. The other is David Bartle, who Dan knows has been engaged to represent Appleton.'

'So we don't have a choice?'

'No.'

'How good is Beckwith?'

'The recommendation said he was very good. That's all I've got to go by. If he wasn't, I guess he'd still be practising in North Carolina.'

'I hope you're right,' accepted Jordan. 'Will you run the best check you can on him?'

'Of course.'

Unsure how much ready cash he might need in the immediate future, the next morning Jordan broke an – until now – unbreakable rule and left £40,000 in his apartment safe, putting the rest, as well as all the Paul Maculloch identity documents and passport, in the Royston and Jones vaults before noon. It left him enough time for lunch at the conveniently close Joe Allens in Covent Garden, where he drank one gin martini and ordered a hamburger, wondering if it would be a diet to which he would become accustomed in the coming weeks. He hoped not.

But it easily could have been if Jordan chose.

Jordan arrived early to be told that Daniel Beckwith, to whom he was going to talk by telephone link-up, was the senior partner in the firm of Beckwith, Pryke and Samuelson, whose offices on Lexington Avenue were two block across and two down from those of David Bartle on Madison Avenue. Lesley Corbin insisted that Beckwith was one of the best attorneys in Manhattan – 'and therefore one of the most expensive, $500 an hour with additional daily courtroom refreshers I didn't ask about' – with a ninety percent success rate for his clients.

'I'm looking for a 100 percent in my case.'

'I've already emailed him a full account of our discussion,' said the woman, who was again dressed in black, which Jordan decided had to be her working uniform.

'I'm grateful for what you're doing,' thanked Jordan, sincerely, an unusual emotion for him.

'It's what you engaged me to do,' she reminded.

'What did he say? Think, I mean?'

'He knows the other lawyer, which is hardly surprising as they both qualified in Raleigh, North Carolina. When Dan and I spoke he said he and Bartle liked to play hardball.'

'I'd already worked that out for myself. Did he think that Appleton had a case?'

'All he's got is what I told him, which obviously isn't enough to give an opinion. It won't be until you hire him – *if* you hire him – and he gets all the papers from the other side. We haven't really begun yet.'

Maybe even £40,000 wasn't going to be enough, Jordan thought. 'Did he say...' he started but was stopped by the jar of the telephone.

Lesley Corbin cupped the receiver with a hand

and said, 'It's the New York call. The switch-board are holding it. The speaker phones are in the boardroom.'

Jordan followed her into the adjoining room and took the seat she indicated. The red light on the speaker in front of him clicked on when she fitted her telephone receiver into its master holder, set up in front of where she sat. She said, 'Morning, Dan. Harvey's here with me.'

'Afternoon, Lesley. Afternoon, Harv,' came a relaxed American voice.

'Good morning,' said Jordan. It was the first time he had ever used such equipment and he felt self-conscious on it. He hated the abbreviation of his name.

'I've read what Lesley mailed me. Might need to expand upon it a little today. This'll be pro bono. The timer starts if you decide to engage me.' Beckwith's voice was very measured, every word carefully enunciated.

Seeing the frown on the face of the man who had always avoided any contact with the law, Lesley Corbin mouthed, 'No charge.'

Jordan said, 'That's very good of you. I'm very anxious to sort it all out. It reads like they're driving an express train at me.'

'That's exactly what it's meant to read like,' said the American. 'Don't let it frighten you, which is also what it's meant to do. Let's go through a few things.'

'Alienation of affection I understand, although I don't think I am guilty of it,' said Jordan. 'What the hell is criminal conversations!'

'Potentially the most expensive lay you ever

had,' said Beckwith. 'It used to be on every statute in every state and made the female spouse a chattel of the husband. Which was why it's been struck off in most states now. Your bad luck is that it still exists in North Carolina – the state in which Appleton and Alyce were married – and therefore the state in which Appleton is bringing suit.'

'Because it still exists there?'

'Obviously,' said Beckwith.

'How much is potentially very expensive, thousands or millions?'

'Millions.'

'You're joking!'

'There's nothing amusing about being accused of alienation of affections *and* criminal conversation in North Carolina.'

'What can I do?'

'Talk some more,' said the American. 'Lesley's notes told me these divorce proceedings had already been initiated before you began this affair with Alyce?'

'That's what Alyce told me.'

'But you had slept together *before* she told you?'

Jordan felt hot with embarrassment, aware of the woman studying him from across the table, and wondered if he was actually colouring. 'Yes. But before it started I'd seen her writing upon – signing, I suppose – a lot of documents she later told me were divorce papers.'

'But you didn't actually see them: know for yourself that they were divorce papers?'

'No.'

'Lesley told me you thought of it as a vacation romance, that you didn't even exchange addresses when she flew back here to New York?'

'That's what I did – still do – regard it as. And no, we didn't exchange addresses.'

'You often have vacation romances, Harv?'

Jordan hesitated. 'I've had them before, yes.'

'Often?'

Jordan shifted uncomfortably in his seat. Lesley Corbin was expressionless on the other side of the table. 'Two or three times. It's not a crime, is it?'

'According to section 1-52(5) of North Carolina law that's exactly what it is,' reminded the American lawyer. 'You never kept in touch with any of the others?'

'No.'

'Let's hope Alfred Appleton's detective agency hasn't found any of them,' remarked Beckwith.

'Why?' demanded Jordan. 'I don't see how they could have found anyone with whom I had an affair in the past. But I don't see the point of your saying what you just have!'

'You're probably not going to see the point of a hell of a lot you're going to be asked before all this is over, Harv. You've read the claims; you know where they're coming from. You're accused of being a home wrecker, a womanizing rich guy. It would help Appleton's case a whole lot if he could produce another wronged, abandoned woman.'

'I didn't abandon Alyce Appleton or anyone else I met in the circumstances we're discussing!

It was a passing thing, for both of us! That's why we didn't swop numbers or addresses. It's not the way it happens.'

'You're sounding angry, Harv. Indignant.'

'I *am* indignant!'

'And angry?'

'OK. And angry. Something that happens all the time, not hurting anyone, is being blown up out of all proportion into my being responsible for the crime of this or any other century.'

'OK, Harv. I think we've taken it far enough. Maybe it was a little unfair.'

'What the...?'

'I've been testing you out, in case you do engage me. And if you do, we've got a whole bunch of work to do getting you ready. It took me about thirty seconds, sixty tops, to make you lose your temper and start trying to justify yourself. You lose your temper in a court in which you're accused of wrecking another guy's marriage – try to justify what you did and say it's no big deal because no one got hurt – you're a dead man. You understand what I'm telling you?'

'Yes,' said Jordan, meek voiced but still angry. 'I still think it was a shitty trick.'

Beckwith laughed, sounding genuinely amused. 'Us lawyers got bagfuls of shitty tricks. If we go forwards you're going to have to learn every one of them, so you don't get caught out again. And what I've just done wasn't entirely a trick. You sounded just right to convince me that you believe yourself the fall guy. Lesley set out some questions you'd raised, about jurisdiction?'

'Can you answer them?' asked Jordan, eagerly.

'In a nutshell, I hope. Any decision or verdict reached in a North Carolina divorce court couldn't be exacted against you, personally, in England if you chose to ignore the claims and didn't turn up. The inference, however, would be that everything alleged against you has a basis of truth. And I know Lesley has warned you how judges feel if they consider they are being treated with contempt?'

'Yes.'

'And Lesley's right, about the possible use of publicity. You duck and run you stand the very real – almost inevitable – chance of having your skin nailed to the barn door, for everyone to see. You fight it and we knock away the foundations of every claim and allegation, one by one, you're a guy who's done what thousands of married guys and married gals are doing right now, even as we speak. And Appleton loses, not you. But here's a very necessary warning. This particular divorce legislation in this particular state is an absolute bastard, everything in favour of the plaintiff.'

'If I contest it I have to come to New York?'

'And North Carolina, to face everything down like the wrongly accused man that you are.'

'I'd like you to represent me and defend me against this action,' decided Jordan, formally.

'And I'd like to do it,' accepted Beckwith. 'I want all the original correspondence from Bartle couriered to me, today if possible, so that I can issue an official response. I'll courier my con-tractual terms and conditions back, to be completed with you by Lesley, who can also take a preliminary personal statement, telling me all about you, and when we've got the wheels turning we can meet here, in New York. Everything will obviously be decided in Raleigh, the capital of North Carolina.'

'I'll handle everything from this end,' promised the woman. 'I think it's been a good meeting.'

'So do I,' said the American.

'Don't you, Harvey?' she encouraged.

'Very good indeed,' said Jordan, recognizing his first lie but knowing there were going to be a lot more.

'I really did think it went well,' said Lesley Corbin, as she disconnected the telephone link.

'I wasn't very comfortable,' admitted Jordan.

'Men never are when they're caught in public with their trousers down; women, neither,' she said and smiled. 'You'd better get used to it, Harvey. It's going to get a hell of a lot more embarrassing. What you've got to hope is that it's contained within the four walls of a closed divorce court.'

# Seven

After the constant bustle of the week's beginning, particularly the dodging and weaving that started off each day, Harvey Jordan welcomed his first opportunity to remain the following morning in his flat, his next appointment with Lesley Corbin not until the afternoon. But it wasn't a chance to relax; the opposite, in fact. The forthcoming meeting was to provide the personal information the American lawyer had asked for during their transatlantic telephone conversation and Jordan recognized how well and how carefully he had to evaluate – but most importantly of all, not to forget – anything and everything he told the woman. Jordan worked hard to convince himself that after going through most of his life successfully being somebody else it shouldn't be overwhelmingly difficult for him to keep his story straight. But it had been a bad mistake not to realize how he was being ensnared in France. And he was determined against any further disasters, most definitely in any courtroom setting where any information he provided today could be publicly challenged and shown to be a lie.

Overnight, questions that he should have asked – were *essential* he ask – Daniel Beckwith or at least obtain guidance from Lesley Corbin crowded in upon him and Jordan spent the morning listing them, prompted as he did so to add others. The biggest imponderable factor was what exactly the American enquiries in France had discovered and which could be put to him. It was also vital that he remember everything he had told Alyce Appleton, whom it was logical to assume would have told her legal team and with which he could be confronted, either by her or her husband's lawyers. There'd been his lie that he was independently wealthy, from a family inheritance which he successfully utilized as a venture capitalist investor. And the sympathy-seeking improvization built around his divorce. Beckwith hadn't minimized the financial im-plications of the damages claims, which made his income and its source directly relevant. None of which Jordan could substantiate beyond the returns accepted by the British Inland Revenue as a professional gambler. Jordan couldn't im-agine the lost love of his life nonsense being introduced in any court examination or record, except for its connection with his supposed occupation and income, but it was something not to ignore but rather to be explained away if it were raised. He couldn't think of any awkward personal information in the South of France, apart from his address lodged at the Carlton Hotel in Cannes which Appleton's side appeared already to have obtained, by which he could be confronted. Neither did he imagine any of his previous conquests about whom Beckwith had questioned him being traced: he couldn't himself remember all of their names and he'd determinedly avoided being photographed with or by any of them. Alyce hadn't carried a camera and shunned the approaches from any of the restaurant photographers as forcefully as he had, although there were those that he'd already anticipated having been snatched of them together. And he'd paid every bill in cash, the deposit for the car rental going against his hotel bill.

Jordan was at Lesley Corbin's Chancery Lane office fifteen minutes before the appointed time, his query list memorized but in his inside pocket if he needed any reminders, together with all the official personal documents she'd asked him the previous day to bring, which he had although reluctantly, professionally aware of their illegal usefulness.

The package Daniel Beckwith had couriered from New York appeared the same size as he remembered Alyce Appleton completing at the hotel, although substantially thicker, topped by a copy of the lawyer's terms and conditions of engagement.

'I've never heard of agreeing contracts with lawyers?' said Jordan. It was one of the questions on his list.

The woman shrugged. 'It's sometimes done here between solicitors and barristers, on behalf of clients. Maybe it's to do with the particular circumstances of this situation, different jurisdictions and regulations in different countries, in addition to different American states being involved. I've gone through it. I didn't find any reason why you shouldn't sign: it's as much for your protection in an American court as it is for his being paid his fees.'

'You think they're reasonable?' seized Jordan, wanting to concentrate on finance as quickly as possible.

'I warned you about costs,' reminded the woman. 'The court refreshers are $2,000 a day. What can't be quantified at the moment from what Beckwith provided – or what he hasn't yet been provided *with*, from the other sides – is exactly how many days the case might take. It's obviously a contested case – you contesting the claims against you, presumably as Alyce will be doing even if they are conniving – so it definitely won't be a short hearing.'

'Give me a ballpark figure,' demanded Jordan.

'Impossible,' refused the lawyer. 'You want to do some sums on the back of an envelope, allow a month...' She paused. 'A minimum of a month.'

'Presuming the court won't sit on a Saturday or Sunday, that will be something like $40,000 in court refreshers alone?'

'And there's the hourly $500 for all the pre-liminary consultations,' added Lesley. 'There'll also be search fees, impossible at this stage to estimate. And if you're going to have to go back and forth, possibly several times, and pay hotel bills while you're in New York and Raleigh, you've got to calculate travel and living ex-penses. Also impossible to estimate. And my fees and expenses, which I haven't got around to thinking about yet. That's why I can't give you a ballpark guess. But I did warn you that it wasn't going to be cheap.'

'What if all the claims are dismissed, that I've been forced to defend myself against marriage destroying allegations that aren't justified?'

'In this country a judge would have the discretion to apportion costs, according to culpability. I'll raise it with Dan when I respond to all the stuff he's sent over for us to complete today. But you've got to bear in mind that you *did* sleep with her. And that you knew she was a married woman.'

'That was surely her decision?'

'I said I'll raise it with Dan. You ready to start on his stuff?'

'That's what I'm here for.'

The woman isolated a document several pages thick and said, 'OK, let's learn all we can about Harvey William Jordan.' She smiled up. 'You brought your birth certificate, as I asked you?'

His hesitation at handing it across the desk to her was instinctive at parting with such an essential tool of his trade.

'What is it?' She frowned.

'I don't particularly like surrendering personal documents.'

The frown remained. 'It'll be copied, here today, like all the other stuff he wants. And couriered, in the possession of a messenger from the time it leaves here until it's handed over to Dan's firm in New York.'

Another silly lapse, Jordan thought, self-critically. 'Sure. Stupid of me. I've not been involved in anything like this before.'

'We have to know, with supporting details, what you do for a living,' she went on.

'I need to understand something,' said Jordan, coming to the most highlighted note on his reminder list. 'There'll be lawyers acting separately for Alyce as well as those acting for Appleton? And Dan acting for me, right?'

'Yes,' the woman agreed, curiously.

'I read somewhere that statements are exchanged between lawyers, in advance of cases beginning?' Jordan was inwardly churning at having a lie to explain away.

'That's the system.'

'Are facts checked, before cases begin? So that they can be contested in court, if they're doubted?'

The frown came back. 'Sometimes. What's your problem?'

'I told Alyce I was a venture capitalist, from a family inheritance.'

'And you're not?'

'I'm a gambler,' announced Jordan, the vocation long accepted by the British tax authorities.

'You mean you don't have a job, an occupation or a business? That that's all you do, gamble professionally?'

'Yes. But it's not as easy as you seem to imagine. To succeed as a professional gambler you've got to win more than you lose, as I do.'

'Why didn't you tell her what you really did?'

'I thought venture capitalist sounded better, I guess,' Jordan said as he shrugged, wishing what he was telling Lesley Corbin sounded better. The agreement with the British tax authorities had

78

taken almost three years, but always through correspondence, never personal encounters like this. Verbally it didn't sound very convincing. Jordan had perfected a method of providing what the British Inland Revenue finally recognized as legal proof of income but needed to know if it would be accepted by an American court and American lawyers. Even if it was it was going to require a great deal more physical effort. And a lot more dodging and weaving to avoid it being discovered that he was duplicating to satisfy two, not just one, demand. He wished he could better gauge Lesley Corbin's thoughts from the quizzical expression on her face.

'You make enough from gambling to live at the best hotels for months at a time, as you did in France?' she pressed.

'It fluctuates. I haven't starved so far.' Because I very rarely wager any actual money, he thought. She was never going to accept it! She'd see through it as a lie, and a bad one at that, as if through polished glass.

'Dan wants some financial information,' she said, flatly.

'I guessed he might,' said Jordan, constantly bemused by his unusual honesty. Heavily he went on: 'I can't produce audited books, if you know what I mean.'

The woman smiled, as Jordan hoped she would. 'Or income tax returns?'

'I could produce copies of those,' Jordan promised, glad he'd taken duplicates to remind himself from year to year.

'So there are accepted tax records, if they're

demanded?'

'I'd prefer them not to be,' admitted Jordan, edging forward.

'Let's leave official interest for the moment,' she said. 'I could accept a cash deposit, to be held in a client account.'

She wasn't going to challenge him! It was going to work! 'Information of which will be made available only to America?'

'It's only applicable and required by America,' she pointed out. 'I will accept your cash deposit, as I am verbally accepting your instructions. I am not required to know anything more about a source of that cash; that's Dan's responsibility. I will talk personally, by telephone, to Dan – not set out the question by letter – and when you get to New York you'll need to talk in more detail to him. We've got to keep in mind how important it is to minimize any publicity. Do you understand?'

'Very clearly,' assured Jordan. 'As I'm sure you understood my concern. How much will you want that deposit to be?'

'That's what I'll talk to Dan about.'

'I'm glad we're having this conversation.'

'To cover as many eventualities as possible is *why* we're having this conversation.'

'I'm feeling more comfortable about it now.' How easily those who practised law were prepared to bend it. Maybe becoming a lawyer would be his next career change.

'When I speak to Dan he'll want to know if you can adequately defend the action? Financially, I mean.'

'I can.' Because ultimately I won't be paying the money, thought Jordan, the decision hardening in his mind. He had a lot to set up as soon as he got to America – *if* he got to America.

'We'll need to meet – meet, not even talk on the phone – after I've spoken to him.'

'I understand.' He'd been lucky, finding Lesley Corbin. Jordan hoped it was another omen.

Lesley flicked the edge of the document from which she was working. 'This is very much a pro forma. Dan will need more in these new circumstances. How do you gamble? On what, I mean?'

'Professional gamblers don't gamble,' lectured Jordan. 'They only ever put their money on certainties.'

'Don't go polemic on me. What do you gamble on? Where do you gamble?'

'High stake rooms at casinos: poker, blackjack, roulette, backgammon,' he said, reciting the games he'd been one of the first to programme for Internet use. 'Horses, too. I've got the maximum £30,000 Premium Bond block, which in the four years I've held it has produced a return of an additional £20,000. I consider that a gamble. But definitely *not* the lottery: the odds aren't good for anyone.'

'I think it would be wise for us to be careful,' said Lesley, lecturing in return. 'The law is that receipted proof of casino profits can be issued for tax purposes. I presume you provide those, with your tax returns?'

Jordan only just stopped himself laughing outright at being told of the system he'd bled dry for so long. 'Some.'

81

The woman smiled again. 'We'll maybe need some; as many as you can produce,' insisted Lesley. 'Supported by dates, places and amounts. For horse race winnings we'll need courses, the actual names of horses, winning slips if they can be kept.'

The duplication of which Jordan had anticipated. 'I'm sure I can manage that.'

'Start collecting them from now on. I don't want you unable to face a challenge about income source.'

'I will. See if I've got anything hanging around, as well,' promised the man who never left anything financial hanging around.

'What we've talked about so far makes a lot of Dan's other questions irrelevant at this time,' decided the woman, going back to her list. 'I'm going to leave the occupation question blank, until I've talked to Dan.'

'You're the lawyer.' And am I glad, he thought.

'You are not married?' Lesley started again, briskly.

'No.'

'Have you ever been?'

'Divorced, a long time ago.'

'You've got the papers to prove that?'

'Yes,' said Jordan, uneasily.

'Children?'

'No.'

'Are you in a relationship that makes you responsible for any dependants?'

'No.'

'Do you suffer any permanent illness or disease?'

'What?' questioned Jordan, surprised.

'You had sexual relations with a married woman. According to what Dan has set out here, if you are suffering from AIDS or any sexually transmittable disease you didn't tell Alyce about before you entered into a relationship you could be criminally charged with assault, as well as giving Alfred Appleton grounds for several additional claims. Murder or manslaughter even, if Alyce becomes infected with AIDS from which she subsequently died.'

'I am not suffering from AIDS or any other sexually transmitted disease.'

'That will have to be attested by a sworn medical statement.'

'You're joking!'

'I thought we'd agreed there is nothing amusing about the circumstances in which you find yourself.'

'I'll arrange the tests.'

'I've already made your appointment for eleven o'clock tomorrow, in Harley Street. A Dr Preston.'

'Thank you.' How close, Jordan wondered, would Dr Preston's consulting rooms be to those of plastic surgeon Paul Maculloch, whose stolen identity was proving to be so useful, although not in the way originally intended.

'Did you give – or exchange – gifts with Alyce Appleton?'

'No.'

'Exchange addresses?'

'You know we didn't!'

'For the record.'

'No.'

'Did she provide any details of her husband's business?'

'She told me he was a commodity dealer.' The rest was for him to find out, Jordan promised himself.

'That's a generalization.'

'She didn't specify. Just told me the name of the firm, Appleton and Drake.'

'Did you independently enquire into what they specifically traded?'

'I had no reason. I wasn't interested.' But now I am, mentally added Jordan. How long would it take him to find out all that he needed about Appleton and Drake?

'Did you have any prior knowledge of or about Alyce Appleton?'

'I don't understand that question,' protested Jordan.

'It's not difficult,' retorted Lesley Corbin. 'The common thread through every claim Appleton is making is that you've intentionally stolen his wife.'

Jordan was momentarily halted by the irony. 'I do not steal other men's wives. Neither am I a gigolo.'

'That wasn't part of the question but I'll include it in your answer. It might be apposite. Did you know before you began the affair that Alyce Appleton was rich?'

Harvey Jordan's hesitation now was to keep his reply as honest as possible, following the golden precept that the fewer the lies the fewer there were to remember and by which to be trapped. Cautiously he replied, 'Her jewellery was obviously expensive. And she was staying in a suite in an expensive hotel. But then so was I. I didn't pick her out for either of those reasons. I didn't pick her out at all! We got into conversation. Things developed.'

'As things developed with other women before, according to what you've already told me, already told Dan?'

'You're making me *sound* like a gigolo!'

'Remember what Dan said about training you to respond properly to questions! Look upon this as an early lesson. Questions can be phrased to make you lose your temper, which you came close to doing there.'

'I did not get into conversation with Alyce Appleton because I thought she was rich, nor to take advantage if she were rich,' said Jordan, pedantically. 'I paid for every hotel room, meal and yacht trip we shared.'

'You got receipted bills, in your name?'

'For Christ's sake!'

'That's not an answer.'

'No, I do not have receipted bills in my name.'

'Credit card counterfoils?'

'I paid for everything in cash. I thought I'd already told you that.'

The woman looked up from her documents. *'Everything* in cash! That surprises me, in this day and age of convenient plastic.'

'I'm not part of "this day and age of convenient plastic".' Only other people's plastic, came the thought.

She grinned briefly at the continuing pedantry.

'Which brings me to a financial question I forgot. What debts, outstanding or unpaid credit or store card liabilities or financial court orders do you have against you?'

'None.'

Lesley came up to him again. *'None?'*

'That's what I said.'

'What about a mortgage? Or car finance? Or overdrafts?'

'I own my apartment in Marylebone outright. I do not have a car. Or any overdrafts.'

She shook her head. 'That's amazing!'

'That's how it is. How I choose to live.'

'Professional gamblers *really* don't gamble, do they?'

'Not this one.'

Lesley Corbin moved on to another document in the American pack. 'As well as the birth certificate we've already talked about, Dan wants at least three photographs of you, a copy of your parents' marriage certificate and a copy of your passport. And now we've got to add your divorce papers.' She looked up again. 'Have you brought it all, as I asked?'

'I've brought them but I want to know why he wants it all?'

'I'm just relaying the request,' Lesley said. 'Dan wouldn't have asked if it wasn't necessary. Like I said, it's all going to be couriered so it will all be safe.'

As he handed each item over Jordan said, 'The exchange of statements from the other sides? Will I be shown them, before the case?'

'Inevitably Dan will take you through them;

that's the whole purpose of an exchange, to isolate factual errors or outright lies.'

'So we'll be able to gauge whether they're working together, to set me up?'

'I only mentioned that as a possibility and I'm beginning to wish I hadn't because that's all it is and quite an unlikely one at that,' said the lawyer. 'If it is and Dan can prove it, that's you off any divorce or alienation of affection hook and all the other damages claims. Which is the good news. The bad news could be that it would establish a case for attempted deception, which would make it a crime to be heard in a criminal court with you as the major prosecution witness. And would almost inevitably attract the publicity back here you want to avoid.'

Jordan walked directly down Chancery Lane, crossed Fleet Street into El Vino and huddled himself into the furthest corner of the back bar with a large glass of Chablis, not so much to drink as to justify his occupation of the secluded table. His feelings during the conference with Lesley Cordin had gone up and down like an elevator, finishing at ground or even basement level. He realistically supposed that it didn't even come close to the exchanges that were to follow – his first lesson, the woman had called it – but it had been far worse than he'd expected. His high point had been Lesley's acceptance of where his income came from, but as their conversation – and her demands for evidence – progressed, he'd objectively realized that lawyers representing someone as determined as Alfred Appleton appeared to be wouldn't believe it so readily as she had, whether or not there was any connivance between the commodity trader and his wife. Despite Lesley's repeated insistence that she had been offering the most outside of all outside possibilities, which she now regretted, Jordan had clung to the hope of it being dramatically proven in court to provide his absolute, guilt-free salvation. Which now it couldn't be. His lowest point was Lesley Corbin's easy but unarguable illustration of how a finding of collusion could result in a criminal prosecution with an even greater risk of the publicity he was so desperate to avoid. The worst feeling of all was of being incarcerated in an ever-tightening, constricting straightjacket from which he couldn't and wouldn't be able to escape suffocation.

Harvey Jordan immediately recognized the self-pity that had brought him down before and didn't want – wouldn't allow – again. He hoped Lesley Corbin had been right about there always being a way out and that the way he had in mind would materialize. He really did have a lot to do to make it work.

# Eight

Since the legal tightening up of the money-laundering legislation demanding proof of cash receipts and profits – most directly targeted against the proceeds from drug trafficking – it had become much more difficult for Harvey Jordan to operate his well established, and so far foolproof, scheme to obtain tax evidence of his supposed income. When he had first embarked upon his career, casinos had been far more casual than they were now monitoring the big chip purchases against money paid out when those same chips were cashed in. In the much mourned early days Jordan had been able to buy £50,000 worth of chips with the stolen identity money, then move from the most crowded tables too frequently for any one croupier or pit boss to remember the minimal stakes he placed against what he won or lost. He would then return to the caisse to get a tax receipt for all but a little of what he'd changed in the first place. Jordan estimated he actually did win on fifty percent of his casino outings – always betting evens – and every time he did it represented a bonus.

Since the legislation Jordan believed he had isolated the casinos that noted the chip-pur-chasing amounts against the money reclaimed, which had greatly reduced his choice and made getting the necessary paperwork that much harder. And now he was confronted with a demand to at least double – possibly even treble – his receipt collecting to satisfy not just his well organized and regulated return to the English Inland Revenue but an American court and its assembled lawyers if a source were demanded for the cash he was to deposit with Lesley Corbin's firm for the forthcoming divorce hearing.

Jordan reassurred himself that he could overcome the casino difficulties from horse racing. By visiting some courses without making any effort to evade the still feared surveillance he could also actually prove to the opposing American legal teams that he genuinely was a professional gambler. By buying betting slips from on-course bookmakers in full public – and hopefully photographed – view and milling around them again at the end of a race, he would appear to be collecting his winnings, whether there were any or not and which was immaterial. All he needed was the date, place, race title and name of the winning horse. And to insist, if he were challenged, that he hadn't been able to retain the slip. He would, though, keep those with which he did coincidentally win.

It was going to involve a lot of late nights and a considerable amount of travelling, even if he restricted himself to race meetings conveniently around London, which he couldn't do all the time because, as he'd told Lesley, a professional gambler only followed certainties. And until the

American ordeal was over his role had to be that of a very visible and successful professional punter, not that of someone whose identity he had stolen. That reflection physically stopped Jordan, half dressed in preparation for another unwelcome and unwanted day.

Realistically nothing was more important than what was happening – or about to happen – in America and his doing everything possible to reduce whatever damage might come from it. But he had no idea how long it was going to be before it was resolved: however, whenever, it might be resolved to his benefit. But until it was, he couldn't begin to think about any further identity thefts. It could, he supposed, be as long as a year. Which made it the most frightening uncertainty of all and it hadn't even been on his list of questions to ask Lesley Corbin or Daniel Beckwith.

Again, unsettlingly, Harvey Jordan felt the tightness of the slowly crushing straitjacket he now found himself in.

Dr James Preston was a small, electric-haired man who fussed nervously around his disordered office, his unbuttoned white coat flapping about him like startled wings, head jerking constantly about him in an apparent search for something mislaid or forever lost. Not looking at Jordan he said, 'You've got some notes? Samples?'

'Neither,' said Jordan. 'The appointment was made by my solicitor, Lesley Corbin. It's for a legal case.'

'Legal case?' demanded the venerealogist,

frowning directly at Jordan for the first time.

'In America,' offered Jordan.

The man flustered through a hamster's den of papers on his desk, finally coming up with a confirming official letter from Lesley Corbin. Looking up again he said, 'HIV, negative or positive? Any venereal infection?'

'To prove I am not suffering from anything.' Jordan supposed he should be amused by the shambling, mad doctor imagery, but he wasn't. As Lesley had reminded him the previous day there was nothing amusing in the situation in which he found himself.

Preston stared from beneath his upright shock of pure white hair. 'You think you have caught something?'

'It's to guarantee that I haven't infected some-one. Anyone.'

'Ah!' exclaimed the man, in final under-standing. He went back to the appointment slip. 'It doesn't say,' he said, as if offering an ex-planation of his own.

'That's what it's for.'

'You suffered from anything in the past?'

'No.'

'It's possible for me to find a trace, if you have.'

'I haven't,' insisted Jordan.

'You're sure?'

'Positive.'

'Have you got any discharge? Irritation? Rashes? Need to pass water frequently?'

'No. No symptoms, if those are the symp-toms.'

'You sure?'

'Positive,' sighed Jordan, again. Why the hell had Lesley Corbin picked this man?

'When's the last time you had a full medical examination?'

'I've never had a full medical examination.'

'Who's your regular doctor, from whom I can obtain your records and case notes. I'll need you to sign the authority for me to ask for them, of course.'

'I don't have a regular doctor.'

The white-haired head came up again. 'What do you do if you are ill?'

'I'm never ill. If I were I'd go to a hospital.' To have a regular doctor meant records being created and invisible men didn't have records.

'This is for court purposes?'

'Yes.'

'I'll need to give you a full medical, as well as giving you the specific examination that's been asked for. I can't do one without the other.'

'Why don't you do that and get it over with?' demanded Jordan, impatiently.

Jordan later decided he wouldn't have agreed so readily if he'd known it was going to take almost three hours. He had to supply five phials for all the necessary blood tests and two for urine examination, as well as a faeces sample. There were two sets of chest and lower body X-rays and his blood pressure and rate was tested not just by an arm cuff but on a treadmill meter. His lung capacity was measured by his blowing into an asthma tube and his vision to the very bottom line of the alphabet chart. Although a prostrate assessment was ticked on one of the blood test cards the doctor also insisted upon a rubber gloved anal examination, which was a great deal more uncomfortable than with the later, narrower colostomy probe. The final forty-five minutes was a verbal exchange to discover any illnesses or complaints Jordan could have conceivably suffered during his remembered childhood up to that day, whether or not it had required doctor or hospital consultation, follow-ed by a determined effort by Preston to complete a medical history of Jordan's parents.

At the end the doctor said, 'I think you're the only person I've ever examined who never suf-fered a single childhood illness, nor has needed any medical advice since.'

'I guess I've been lucky.'

'And you're sure you can't remember a single illness from which your parents suffered?'

'Seems I've inherited their healthy genes.'

'What were the causes of their deaths?'

'They died together in a car crash,' said Jordan, which was a lie. His father had died first, of cancer, and his Alzheimer's-afflicted mother of pneumonia but Jordan was bored and impatient to end the pointless encounter.

'You're responsible for payment, I assume?'

'Wrongly,' said Jordan, who'd anticipated the approach. 'Your secretary will have the name and address of the lawyer who booked this if it's not on the note you've got there. Send your account to her, along with the results.'

Preston was on the internal phone before Jordan finished speaking, his face clouding at the confirmation of what Jordan had told him. The doctor said, 'Solicitors are very dilatory in settling their accounts. Will you please tell Ms Corbin that I expect payment within the period stipulated upon my invoice?'

'Of course,' said Jordan, without any intention of doing so. 'You didn't tell me how my examination went?'

'I have obviously to wait for all the tests results but there's every indication of your being remarkably fit: nothing obviously wrong at all.'

Apart from you knowing – and a record now existing – of every physical detail about me, thought Jordan.

The irritating medical examination, for which he'd allowed only an hour, completely disrupted Jordan's schedule, leaving him with only thirty minutes to keep the afternoon appointment with the photographer. In the taxi taking him there Jordan decided to abandon until the following morning the intended visit to Hans Crescent to check for any further correspondence in his Paul Maculloch name; he was anxious to begin at once his money-manipulating casino tour.

Jordan had booked for passport photographs, waiting until he got to the studio to add three larger prints and agreed at once to the obviously increase fee, interested only in getting the picture session over as quickly as possible. He was back in the Marylebone apartment by six and out, showered, changed and with £20,000 from the bedroom closet safe to begin the chips-for-cash receipt switch by eight. For an hour he played poker at the high stakes table of one of his favourite gambling clubs in Brook Street, Mayfair, before quitting £2,300 ahead to move to the roulette room. There he moved between three tables, increasing his winnings by another £7,000 before dropping £6,000 in an unstoppable consistent slide. By the time it did stop he was down to his poker profit. It took him another hour playing blackjack to take his winnings up a further £1,500. He cashed in and got his tax receipt for winnings of £24,500. Throughout Jordan remained constantly alert but failed to isolate anyone paying any particular attention or interest in him.

Jordan hesitated for a moment as he left the club, turning to the doorman for a taxi, but abruptly deciding, without any reason, to walk into Park Lane. When he reached Park Street the darkened interior of the last car in the parking line at the corner was briefly illuminated in the headlight beam of an approaching taxi, perfectly enabling Jordan to see a man he remembered at every table at which he'd played that night.

# Nine

'Being followed!' Lesley Corbin frowned but smiled very slightly as well. The combination made her nose wrinkle.

'I believe so,' said Jordan, discomfited by her doubting expression.

'When, how, did you come to believe that?'

'Three nights ago. I'd been gambling, in Mayfair. When I came out of the club I saw a man, waiting in his car. He'd been in every room in which I'd played, during the evening.'

'Watching you?'

'I hadn't been aware inside. I only recognized him outside, in the car.'

'What else?'

'That's it,' said Jordan, further discomfited by the emptiness of what he was saying. He had abandoned the intention to go to Hans Crescent and that night returned to the same Mayfair club, where he'd lost almost £5,000. He didn't see the man in the club or isolate anyone waiting in a car when he'd left to take the same route to Park Lane for a taxi.

The woman wasn't frowning any more but the smile was hovering. 'You haven't thought you've been followed since?'

'I haven't been aware of it,' qualified Jordan.

'They watched me pretty effectively in France without my suspecting it, don't forget. Do you think they've begun some sort of surveillance here?'

Lesley humped her shoulders. 'They could have, although I would have thought they've already got all they need for their case as far as the adultery is concerned.'

'So I'm becoming paranoid?'

The smile widened. 'I didn't say that. Or think it. They might have decided it's necessary, now that Dan's got involved and confirmed you're going to contest the accusations.'

'Could you ask him what he thinks? I don't like the idea of my every move being watched.'

She hunched her shoulders again. 'There's nothing we can really do about it, if they are.'

'It's an unsettling feeling.' He'd have to check Hans Crescent tomorrow, Jordan realized. By now there'd probably be something from his new City bank if nothing else in the name of Paul Maculloch.

'It's not actually against the law, although if you could prove it we could apply for a harass-ment order. Proving it would be a problem. And attract publicity to the case in America, which we don't really want, do we?'

'We'll leave it,' decided Jordan.

'That's probably best,' agreed the lawyer. 'I've got more from Dan. And I've got the medical report and the photographs.'

'And I very definitely want to talk about Preston!' declared Jordan.

'I want to talk about Preston, too,' said Lesley.

'You'd better listen to me first.'

'You first, about everything,' agreed Jordan. He saw that Lesley Corbin had several, separated sets of paper arranged in front of her on her desk.

She selected the smallest of the files. 'Dan's emails. There'll definitely need to be what he calls a financial lodgement, in view of what you do for a living. He's talking of an initial tranche of $100,000, which I've roughly converted to around £55,000.' She looked up. 'Is that all right?'

'If you mean can I provide that much in cash, the answer's yes, but on the understanding we reached earlier.' Not just a trip to Hans Crescent, Jordan thought: he'd need to get more out of the safe deposits at the Royston and Jones bank. What was set aside in Marylebone was gambling stake money. And at the moment it amounted to less than he'd started out with. His resentment against Alfred Appleton was building by the day.

'I talked personally with Dan,' said the woman. 'Our understanding is acceptable as far as he's concerned. But he stressed it's only an initial tranche.'

'What if I'm not found to be responsible for the marriage collapse?'

'Again, roughly as we thought. An American judge would have discretion but we're not denying that you slept with Alyce Appleton. It comes down to whether or not you – or rather Dan – can satisfy the judge you're not a marriage wrecker. Dan thinks he can, on our exchanges so far.'

'So £55,000 might be sufficient?'

'Initial was the word Dan used,' insisted Lesley. 'How long the hearing lasts – as far as you are concerned – will again depend upon the judge's view of your personal responsibility and culpability. I think at this stage Dan's going to try to argue you out of the case at the beginning, in chambers if possible. But if the judge, who hasn't been selected yet, won't agree that schedule and wants to hear the actual divorce evidence first, you'll go to the back of the queue. In that event, it could last the month, maybe longer.'

'If I made the initial deposit £75,000 I would have some living and travelling money too, wouldn't I?'

'I'm not sure that would come within the acceptible provisions of the arrangement.'

'Can you ask?'

'Of course.'

'What about publicity?' asked Jordan, inevitably coming to his overriding concern.

Lesley Corbin extended her hands, palm upwards, in a 'who knows?' gesture. 'If you're dismissed from the case before it starts, in a chambers hearing, Dan doubts there'll be any: you're no more than a name. Dan hasn't got as far as any detailed exchange papers, to discover if any other men are being cited, as well as you. Or, if there are, whether they're contesting the allegations as well. Whether or not there is any publicity is really dependent upon Appleton and the sort of case his side intends. And what the judge permits.'

'So we're not much further forward?'

'The main purpose of this meeting is to fix when you can go out for your first meeting in New York,' announced Lesley.

'As soon as possible, to get it all over as quickly as I can,' said Jordan at once. 'I thought I'd made that clear!'

'I needed to check with you first,' she said, detecting the irritation in Jordan's voice. 'Give me a day.'

'I'll fly out on Saturday, give myself Sunday to get over the jet lag and see Dan on Monday.' That gave him the rest of the week to check Hans Crescent, get at least £75,000 from the new Leadenhall Street bank and hand it over to Lesley Corbin.

'That sounds good. I'll check with Dan. Fix a time for Monday.'

'Tell me about Preston,' demanded Jordan.

Lesley went to the pile on her left. 'Your blood pressure's 160 over 90, which he says is too high. And your cholesterol level is 7: it should be well under 4. You should get treatment for both, according to him. On the plus side, you're not HIV positive. Nor are you suffering any sexual disease.' She looked up expectantly. 'And he's invoked medico/legal consultation rates and put in a bill for £1,550.'

'*What*!'

'That's in line with what's charged by medical experts for legal cases. He's claiming he should have been told by me: got a price agreed.'

'He's a robbing, conning bastard!' said Jordan, the hypocrisy never occurring to him. 'He wasn't asked and didn't need to carry out such an examination!'

'It does appear you've got some medical problems you should get treated, however. I'll argue with him about the fee, of course: get it reduced.'

'Reduced a hell of a lot,' insisted Jordan.

'And here's the photographs,' she said, offering an envelope across the desk.

Jordan had always kept any type of identifying document to an absolute minimum and in his judgement these photos approached a dangerous level of identification. His immediate decision was very definitely to stick with the pictures in his current passport, of which he still had a substantial supply, which were already three years old and would hopefully misrepresent him further when it needed renewal in another seven years. If he were dismissed from the American case he'd do whatever he could to get Beckwith to recover these current images for him to destroy. The short, schoolboy-cut, sandy blond hair, normally so easy to gel into a different style for various identities, here was too recognizable, and the contact lenses he'd uncomfortably used to accentuate the blueness of his eyes were *too* blue, making him starrey-eyed, He didn't, either, consider he'd sufficiently distorted his mouth by sucking back his top and bottom lip, as he had in his previous photographs.

'I think they could have been better,' criticised the lawyer.

So do I, better at disguising my features, thought Jordan. 'Did you ask Dan why photographs were necessary?'

'We left it for you to ask him yourself,' she reminded. 'As I said, it's got to be for comparison against photographs of you and Alyce in France.'

'I would have thought my being in court was a good enough comparison.'

'Prior exchange of documents,' Lesley said.

'I need to hand over the £75,000 deposit.'

'Yes, you do,' she agreed.

'I'll have it ready by Friday.'

Lesley Corbin looked at her open diary, on the far left of the desk. 'Three thirty?'

'Three thirty's fine.'

'What are you going to do about the blood pressure and the cholesterol?'

'Nothing.'

'You sure that's wise?'

'Believing anything that that bastard says isn't wise.'

'Anything else – any uncertainty – still on your mind?'

'If I think of anything I'll mention it on Friday.'

There were, in fact, more uncertainties on Jordan's mind, more than he could count and most of which he couldn't talk about to Lesley Corbin. Or anybody else. He *was* straitjacketed: by frustration and impotence and ... and by no longer being in charge of himself and whatever was happening to him. He wanted immediately – now – to hit back. Fight back. Cause Alfred Jerome fucking Appleton as much and as many

problems as Alfred Jerome Appleton was causing him. No, Jordan contradicted himself at
once. More problems. Far more. He wanted to
fuck Appleton in every way but physically, far
worse and far more painfully than he'd ever
been screwed before. Worse, even, than the
retribution he exacted against the man who'd
stolen his own company and in effect destroyed
his marriage. Abruptly – anxiously – Jordan
wanted to see a photograph of the man: ingrain
every line and feature of his face, of everything
about the man, as he ingrained every detail about
his victims before embarking upon another
identity-stealing operation.

For the first time since being overwhelmed by
so much he didn't understand and couldn't
control, Harvey Jordan smiled, decisions clearing in his otherwise cluttered mind. He didn't
understand everything and couldn't anticipate
how anything could or would turn out. Not yet.
But he would eventually, as he always did. And
when he did – as soon as he did – Alfred Jerome
Appleton would learn what an implacable, unrelenting enemy he'd made.

What about Alyce Louise Appleton? came the
abrupt, prodding question. Jordan couldn't
believe – didn't want to believe – that Alyce was
the promiscuous part of some conspiracy. Jordan, a professional himself, was sure he would
have recognized it: picked up the alarm-sound-
ing clue, which he hadn't. But he couldn't be
sure, he accepted, objectively. He had to keep
an open – but not a vindictive, revengeful –
mind until he got to New York and learned a

great deal more.

Which he would. He'd search and probe and discover everything, and when he had he'd reach his own verdict and exact his own punishment upon everyone who'd decided Harvey Jordan was a ripe, easy-to-pluck victim.

It had taken a long time – too long – for him to flesh out the decision. Now that he had he felt encouraged, confident, sure he could win, whatever it took. That night Harvey Jordan won slightly over £11,000 and finished the evening feeling even more confident. Alert as he permanently was, he didn't pick out anyone, either inside or outside the casino, whom he suspected of watching him, either. Maybe he had been paranoid after all.

# Ten

There'd been the familiar quickening of his hearbeat upon landing at JFK, going through the airport formalities and choosing the Triboro bridge route in preference to the tunnel to get into Manhattan; there was never an alternative to entering New York above ground to see the snaggle-toothed skyline sketched out before him as he crossed the East River. But today Harvey Jordan felt different from how he had felt before. On this trip – hopefully – he was going to regain some control of and over his life, his anonymity, instead of being jerked constantly around at the end of someone else's demanding, manipulating strings. Dear God, how much he wanted that! He guessed he was wishing too much too soon, but he couldn't prevent himself hoping.

Jordan believed he'd finished the week ahead, which was where he always had to be: ahead, choosing the moves and the routes instead of following those where others tried to lead him. He'd ducked and dived for more than two hours after his last meeting with Lesley to reach Hans Crescent, where he found two bank documents from Royston and Jones that needed his immediate signature and, believing he remained unwatched after so much evasion, carried them at once to Leadenhall Street to hand-deliver them and to have any further correspondence held until his return from America. Then he'd crossed from the administration to the securities division to collect, in full, the £75,000 advance to which the American lawyer had agreed. He hadn't been able to fit all of it into the Marylebone safe so he'd taken the overflow with him to gamble that night in a much more downmarket, but conveniently myopic, casino in Tottenham Court Road and added £3,200 to what he was increasingly regarding as a war chest. When he'd delivered the £75,000 to Lesley Corbin she said she wished she was coming to New York with him and fleetingly Jordan wished she were, too, although his current entrapment had driven even the remotest thought of personal relationships out of his mind, more so than he usually felt when he was working. He considered himself to be working now, as hard – harder even – as he had had to before in order to rebuild his first destroyed life. He'd asked Lesley why she didn't come some other time, because this looked like the first of several trips and she'd said maybe, if she could gain access to the court when the actual hearings began to experience an American court in action and Jordan regretted his glib responses, not having initially believed she was serious. He regretted, too, talking to her about the man in the car outside the Mayfair club because he hadn't had the slightest suspicion in the Tottenham Court Road casino or anywhere else – certainly not on the outward flight to America – that he was being watched and feared now he'd made himself look stupid. Having restored his pride, Harvey Jordan hated making himself look stupid.

Jordan's triple-glazed suite at the Carlyle was further distanced from the donkey-bray wail of emergency sirens by being back from East 76th Street and, although he didn't then feel tired, having fitfully dozed in his first-class sleeper-bed during the last BA flight of the day out of London, Jordan went directly to bed after an omelette from room service, not having eaten on the plane. He was determined against any over-hanging jet lag during his Monday meeting with Daniel Beckwith. Despite his noise precautions Jordan slept badly, subconsciously always aware of where he was. And why.

Since the stomach-lurching letter from Brink-meyer, Hartley and Bernstein he'd actually thought little of Alyce Appleton, beyond her ever present name. But in a dream-cluttered half sleep his mind perfectly pictured her hunched over the official-looking papers in the Carlton lounge in Cannes and again, in the bikini wisp that had made it necessary for him to briefly remain in the sea, off the Ile St Marguerite, and most vividly of all of her lounged naked, languorously offering herself, on the bed of their tower suite at the St Tropez hotel. She'd said something to him then, something he couldn't now remember but wanted to because he thought it was important and therefore something that he should recall. Jordan finally awoke, completely, still trying to recollect the remark she'd made. But couldn't.

Daniel Beckwith was a towering, hard-bodied man well over six feet tall whose blond hair Jordan guessed to be longer than Lesley Corbin's. A thrown-aside tie lay on top of a carelessly discarded jacket puddled in a side chair to expose on the lawyer a check shirt more at home on the ranch than a lawyer's office; the large, three-pinned oval buckle of the man's embossed leather belt was actually centred with the head of an animal, a bison maybe, and Jordan wondered if there were stables somewhere in the building for the lawyer's horse. The man was halfway across the office as Jordan entered, hand already outstretched in greeting. Jordan tensed expectantly and just managed to avoid a wince at the knuckle-cracking shake.

'Good of you to come, Harv: very good. Got a lot talk about.'

'After speaking to Lesley and you I didn't

think I had much of a choice,' said Jordan, taking the chair to which the lawyer gestured. Jordan thought there was a tinge of an unidentifiable accent in the laid-back, measured voice. Jordan's right hand actually ached.

'There was a choice and you made the right one,' assured Beckwith. 'You want to toss your coat, make yourself comfortable, go right ahead.' He jabbed an intercom key, declared, 'When you're ready, Suzie.' And clicked off before there was any response from the other end. He smiled a perfectly sculpted, white-toothed smile and said, 'Coffee, to help you stay awake after your trip over. Drink it all the time myself.'

'I'm OK with my jacket. Coffee would be good, though.' Jordan had begun work immediately after the bad night at the Carlyle, walking the length of Wall Street to identify conveniently grouped banks for what he intended in the immediate future – and avoided any alcohol – and isolating three possible short-lease apartments. His favourite was on West 72nd Street. Despite the exertion he'd slept badly again and been awake since five so he welcomed the coffee, which arrived on a tray with two mugs and a pot holding at least two pints. The titian haired girl whom Jordan guessed to be Suzie wore a clinging red sweater and a tight cream skirt to display pert breasts and rounded slim hips to their best and obvious advantages. She said 'Hi' to Jordan as she passed on her way out.

Beckwith said, 'We keep Suzie on the payroll as a warning to clients what they're allowed to think but not do.'

Jordan heard the girl laugh behind him at what he guessed to be a well rehearsed joke, wondering if it didn't constitute sexual harassment. He smiled because he knew he was expected to and accepted the coffee the lawyer poured, mildly impatient at the irrelevance. Or was it irrelevant? he asked himself, remembering the American's warning against losing his temper.

Beckwith patted the dossier on his desk with a heavy hand and said, 'Got all your stuff. And Lesley tells me she's set up an escrow account with the deposit.'

'I don't understand how you can move that much cash without fulfilling some financial regulations.' Jordan hadn't expected to talk about money so soon but was glad the lawyer had introduced it early on. As always it remained one of the foremost questions in his mind, the more so after his bank identification the previous afternoon.

'There are regulations and they will be fulfilled,' guaranteed Beckwith. 'And we're not transferring it all at once. I draw upon it, as and when it's necessary, supported by a federal bank agreement to prove to your English authorities that it's a bone fide, government agreed exchange for legal purposes upon the sworn oath of Lesley's firm and my own. All expenditure and receipts have to be exchanged between the Fed and your Bank of England. But it's between firms, not individuals. So your name never appears. It's covered by multinational trade legislation but we qualify under it. And there's nothing in the legislation requiring duplication with your Inland Revenue and our IRS. I guess there will be one day, when the loophole's discovered, but at the moment you're lucky we can utilize it.'

'I'm glad it exists for the moment. And that I can draw on it. I'd like an initial cash advance of $25,000.

The lawyer frowned. 'That much?'

'I'm thinking of some working trips to Atlantic City. Maybe Las Vegas even.'

He'd carried just short of $10,000 into the country and wished it could have been more, although the immediate intention didn't include casinos.

'OK,' agreed Beckwith reluctantly.

'Let's hope my luck holds.' Jordan was sure that in addition to it preventing any discrepancy between his income tax submission and the money he was making available here was Beckwith's need to ensure he could afford to pay for his defence. Jordan made a mental note to check the scheme when his current problems were finally over. There might be an advantage he could use, although he couldn't at that moment imagine what it might be.

'You've got to depend more upon me than upon luck,' warned the lawyer.

'I know that,' accepted Jordan. 'I can't believe how I've come to be caught up in all this.'

'People can't – or don't – until it happens to them.'

'Can we cut to the chase, right now?' urged Jordan, finally giving way to his impatience.

'You know from Lesley how it happened: my side of the story. What are my chances of the action being dismissed?'

Beckwith laughed at the question, pouring more coffee. 'There are too many things I still have to hear and learn and question before I could even begin to answer that. And even after I do hear and learn and question, I don't think I'd like to try an answer, even then. At this point I haven't had the individual statements of claim from Alfred Appleton's side, specifying the grounds for those claims against you. Or what I need from Alyce Appleton's lawyers. This meeting is for us to get to know each other, maybe exchange a few thoughts. We've got a long way to go.'

The same warning that Lesley had given him, Jordan remembered. 'How can we get any thoughts together until we know their case ... cases?'

'I said exchanging a few thoughts, not finalizing our side.' Beckwith reached to his right, turning on a tape recorder. 'So let's start doing that right now. Who made the first move down there in sunny France, you or Alyce?'

'You mean who spoke first?'

'You tell it your way.'

Jordan hesitated for a moment. 'She spoke first. I'd been reading in the hotel lounge. Remembered a phone call I had to make. She stopped me as I was crossing the room and told me I'd left my book behind. I said I was coming back...'

'Did you make the call?'

'Up in my room.'

'I thought you were in a suite?'

'I was. Up in my suite. Do we really need to be as pedantic as this?'

'Harv, I need to be so pedantic I know the colour of your underwear ... maybe Alyce's, too if I'm going to be able to undermine what might be put against you. I ask the questions, any question, you answer them, OK?'

'OK.'

'So you made the call?'

'Yes.'

'Who to?'

Shit, thought Jordan, anticipating the follow-up question. 'A restaurant overlooking Cannes harbour. I wanted to eat there that night.'

'So there'll be a record of the reservation in your name, the restaurant will be able to confirm the call?'

'No,' said Jordan, seeing his way out. 'The line was engaged. I tried twice but then gave up. I walked down that night and managed to get a table without a reservation.'

'With Alyce.'

'No,' refused Jordan again, the relief moving through him at the unchallengable escape.

'Having given up trying to make a connection you went back downstairs?'

'Yes.'

'What happened then?'

'I stopped on my way back to where I'd been sitting, thanked her for trying to stop me losing my book. On the way out I think I'd asked her to watch that it stayed safe.'

'And?'

'She'd been writing, earlier. It looked like a lot of documents, in a large envelope. She'd stopped by the time I got back. The envelope was beside her in a chair, along with a lot of her other stuff. It was the only chair at her table so I invited her across to where I was sitting, for a drink.'

'So she spoke to you first but you hit on her?'

Jordan sighed, heavily. 'I didn't *hit* on her! She'd tried to do me a favour, I thought I'd buy her a drink to say thank you.'

'I don't care how long you stand in the box in court or how much you're exasperated, I don't want to hear a sigh like that again.'

Fuck you, thought Jordan. Aloud he said, 'I'm sorry.'

'You will be, if you get caught out by another lawyer to make you lose your temper and it shows. I warned you already.'

'I won't forget again.'

'I'm not going to let you forget. What happened next with you and Alyce?'

'We'd talked about books, the first day we began speaking. I knew *The Man in the Iron Mask* was based on a true story of a prisoner once being imprisoned on one of the islands off Cannes and invited her on a trip the following day, without telling her what it was or where it would be. I rented a catamaran and took her there. We —'

'Stop!' demanded the lawyer. 'Where are we now, first or second day?'

Jordan had to think. 'Second. We spent all day

together.'

'What about the night?'

'And the night.'

'This has got to be exactly how it happened. So tell me – *exactly* – how it happened. Let's go back to the first day you began talking.'

'There's nothing much to tell about that first day. After lunch I went into town, had dinner, alone, at the harbour restaurant and then went back to the hotel.'

'Was she there?'

'I didn't see her.'

'Why didn't you invite her to dinner with you overlooking the harbour?'

Jordan shrugged 'I don't know. I just didn't.'

'Did you think something might develop between you?'

'Not particularly. I was alone, she was alone. Everything was relaxed and easy.'

'The second day you went on the catamaran trip to the island?'

'Yes,' confirmed Jordan.

'What time?'

'I don't...' stumbled Jordan. 'In the morning. We had lunch on the boat, after looking at the jail.'

'How did you manage that?'

'Manage it?' questioned Jordan, confused.

'When did you rent the catamaran?'

'The first afternoon. After lunch I went into the town, found some yacht charterers and booked the catamaran and had it provisioned for the trip.'

'So you set up a pretty big expedition?'

'I chartered a yacht for a one-day cruise. To take Alyce somewhere I thought she'd be interested in seeing.'

'You went out on the catamaran, you saw the jail where the man in the iron mask was held? Then what?'

'We swam.'

'Naked?' Beckwith asked.

'In costumes. The catamaran had a crew.'

'And a cabin?'

'Of course it had a cabin.'

'Did you change together?'

'Separately.'

'Who changed first?'

Jordan had to think again. 'I did.'

'What sort of costume did you wear?'

'What?' queried Jordan, not understanding.

'Trunks? Boxers? What?'

'Boxer shorts.'

'What about Alyce?'

'A bikini.'

'A brief bikini? Or a two piece?'

'A brief bikini.'

'How brief?'

'Very brief,' said Jordan, remembering his delay in getting back on to the catamaran.

'So *she* was coming on to *you*?'

'I guess you could say that.'

'Harv, we're not guessing here! We're trying to keep your ass as far away from the burner as we can. You're being accused of stealing Al Appleton's wife literally from under him, causing him physical and mental damage and making his business – and income – suffer from what

116

you did. There have been jury awards well over the $1 million mark on just one such criminal conversation claim and you're looking at a damned sight more than just one. And the courts – and the judges – have the power to add on punitive damages, too. You understand what I'm telling you? How much it could cost you?'

'I understand.' Jordan didn't welcome being treated like an idiot any more than he liked consistently being called Harv. But it certainly seemed that he needed training. And much more help than he'd imagined up to now.

'Go on,' ordered Beckwith.

'We got back to the harbour around six. I'd taken the hotel car to get there but Alyce said she wanted to walk back: it's not far. I asked if she wanted dinner but she said she wasn't hungry after the lunch we'd had on the boat, that she was tired and wanted to go straight to bed.'

Beckwith came forward across his desk. 'Go to bed around six in the evening?'

'Yes.'

'What did you do? Say?'

'I didn't finish telling you what she said. She said she wanted to go to bed but not alone.'

Daniel Beckwith began to smile. 'Tell me the actual words.'

'"I want to go to bed. But not alone",' quoted Jordan. Why, he wondered, was he feeling un-comfortable, embarrassed?

The smile widened. 'Alyce Appleton spoke to you first, in the hotel lounge? Alyce Appleton wore the very briefest of bikinis, to show you what was on offer? And Alyce Appleton told you

117

that she didn't want go to bed alone?'

'It didn't...' started Jordan but stopped. Then he said, 'Yes. That's how it was.'

'She chased you,' insisted Beckwith. 'You didn't chase her: seduce her.'

'We both knew what was happening.'

'Harv! For fuck's sake when are you going to start listening to me! What you've just told me, was that how it was? How it happened that you came to be in bed with Alyce Appleton?'

'Yes.'

'She made it easy for you? Invited you?'

'If you—'

'Harv!' halted the lawyer, warningly.

'Yes.'

'We're getting there, Harv. At the moment you're not making it easy for either of us but we're getting there.'

'I'm not trying to make it difficult, for either of us! Me most of all. I didn't understand the direction you were coming from.' Why hadn't he? Jordan demanded of himself. It surely wasn't that obscure?

'Trying to stop you getting skinned alive is the direction I'm coming from, Harv.'

'Lesley said she thought I might have been set up, by Alyce and her husband together,' said Jordan. 'You think I could have been?' Jordan felt humiliated even by asking the question.

'It's a way I might be tempted to go. Depends on the papers when I get to see them. Even as it is, you've got the beginnings of a defence if we can get the court to accept what you're telling me.'

'It was a holiday affair, for Christ's sake!'

'This is a divorce, with more damages accusations than I've ever encountered before,' said Beckwith. 'Two very different things that so far you haven't got your head around.'

Jordan was suddenly swept away by a disorientating tiredness, for the briefest of moments his actual awareness ebbing and flowing. 'Is there any more coffee in that pot?'

'You OK?' enquired Beckwith, pouring the dregs.

'I'm fine,' exaggerated Jordan. 'We haven't talked about the actual hearing. Will the court be closed or open?'

'Depends upon a request from the plaintiff or defendant. There needs to be an application for a closed court from one or the other.'

'I'm a defendant, aren't I? Can't I make the application?'

'*Primary* defendant,' qualified Beckwith. 'Which you're not. And I don't see it coming from Appleton.'

'So we're dependent upon Alyce for the hearing to be private?'

'If she wants it to be. How serious is your problem with an open court, public hearing?'

'As serious as it damned well can be! I don't want to be publicly identified as a wife stealer. Because I'm not.' The coffee was cold and too bitter and Jordan put it aside.

'I may get some indication from pre-trial hearings.'

'What about those pre-trial hearings?' seized Jordan. 'Surely we can argue for my dismissal

119

from the proceedings, before it even gets to court?'

'I'm going to file for dismissal, of course. But I'm not going to hold out hopes that I don't have.'

'This is a fucking travesty,' exploded Jordan, despite all the warnings against losing his temper.

'Travesty is a word invented for the law,' said Beckwith. 'My job is ensuring you're not a victim of it.'

More my job that yours, thought Jordan.

Jordan was glad when almost at once Beckwith closed the meeting by announcing that the first of the exchanges from the other lawyers had been promised by the middle of the week and suggested a second session on the Thursday. Relieved, too. Jordan didn't believe he'd hand-led himself well – maybe not even convincingly – during this first encounter with the American: the remaining, disorientating jet lag might have contributed a little to how ineffectual he con-sidered himself to have been, but he couldn't find a reason or excuse for the rest. He should, Jordan supposed, be encouraged by Beckwith's argument that Alyce had been the instigator of the affair, but he wasn't. He hadn't had to exaggerate or lie answering the lawyer on how it had begun but there was no way of proving it to be the truth, so it came down to his word against hers. He wished he could remember what Alyce had said lying naked on the hotel bed in St Tropez. And that the questions crowding in upon him at this moment had come to mind when he'd been with Beckwith instead of now, when it was too late.

Finally, objectively, Jordan confronted a hovering feeling he could identify. He hadn't regained control of or over his life today and he was scared. Shit-scared.

# Eleven

The lawyer skimmed the photographs across the desk and said, 'Here's the guy who hates your guts and wants all your money.'

If Appleton ever found out what more was going to happen to him – which he never would – he was going to hate his guts a whole lot more, thought Jordan, picking up the prints. Alfred Jerome Appleton was a fleshy, heavy-featured, prominent-nosed man who combed his receding hair straight back, giving himself a high forehead, just above the left temple of which was a deep red strawberry mark. They were portraits but showed enough of the man's shoulders to indicate a build to match his features. Jordan was sure, even before meeting him in the flesh, that Appleton would tower over him, although only ever physically.

'And here's his reason,' said Beckwith, following with the photographs of Alyce. They reminded Jordan of the sort of pictures police released of someone after they had been arrested, charged with a crime and pictured for a criminal record file. Alyce was staring expressionlessly at the camera, her hair brushed – although not very well – straight down. Jordan didn't think she'd bothered with any make-up, either, apart maybe for a lip liner, and she had worn her dark-rimmed spectacles, which she hadn't when they had been together except when she'd needed to read. Her eyes were partially closed behind them. She was wearing black – Jordan couldn't decide whether it was a dress or a sweater – without any visible jewellery. He was caught by the impression that, while not as determinedly as he'd tried, Alyce had posed to make herself as different as possible from how she normally looked.

'That is Alyce, right?' asked Beckwith, form-ally.

'Doing her bag lady act on a bad day,' confirmed Jordan. 'Appleton looks years older.'

The lawyer went to the papers before him. 'Eleven years older, to be precise. Appleton's forty-one to Alyce's thirty-one: there's a couple of months between the birthdays that makes it eleven months at the moment.'

'You got all the papers now?' demanded Jordan.

'The first of the formal exchanges, yes.' It was a tossed aside blazer in a heap today, the shirt less strident than before, although the bison belt was the same. 'Alyce's lawyer is a guy named Bob Reid: don't remember him from when I practised down there.'

'How's it look, as far as I am concerned?'

'On first reading I think there's enough for me to apply for a pre-hearing dismissal of some if not all of the damages claims,' said Beckwith. 'The dates are in your favour. Alyce is citing two gals by name – a Sharon Borowski and a Leanne Jefferies – and others unnamed, all the adultery before you and Alyce met in France. And she's claiming the same sort of criminal conversation damages against one of them, Leanne Jefferies.'

'Why not Sharon Borowski?' broke in Jordan.

'I don't know at this stage.'

'Tit for tat,' declared Jordan, suddenly. 'I've been trying to remember something Alyce said, when we were together. I asked outright about her marriage, used a silly expression like "what's the status of your marriage?". She said there wasn't one, that it was over. I suggested she was playing tit for tat, she said "something like that" and asked if I was offended, at being used by her. I told her I wasn't.'

Beckwith concentrated on one of the document bundles on his desk, before leaning eagerly forward over it as he had at their first meeting. 'Her exchange doesn't say anything like that! But then I wouldn't expect it to. It's certainly something I can put to her if we ever get into a full divorce court hearing.'

'Would it help?'

'Like hell it would help,' insisted Beckwith. 'It fits with what you already told me of her coming on to you ... the woman scorned syndrome.'

'What *does* she say, about her and me? About what happened in France?'

'She doesn't contradict your account at all, that it was a holiday thing with some revenge on her part. That her marriage was over and that what happened between you was a no-strings situation, certainly – most importantly – that nothing was pre-arranged. The covering letter from her attorney wants a meeting, ASAP.'

'What for?'

'Undefined,' said Beckwith with a shrug. 'I'm guessing a co-operating defence.'

'I'd like to think that, too,' said Jordan, meaning it. 'My more immediate thought, though, is that it doesn't look as if this is a conspiracy between her and her husband.'

'Mine too,' agreed Beckwith. 'But let's not get to feel too comfortable too soon.'

'I also don't think Appleton's case makes sense. If there's chapter and verse in Alyce's divorce application, with proof of Appleton screwing two named women as well as various others *before* Alyce and I even met, where the hell's his case against me? It's ridiculous.'

'I told you already that I know David Bartle and his firm, by reputation. And that they play hardball. At the moment I don't think it makes any more sense than you. But Bartle wouldn't be going this route if the judge might repeat your word – ridiculous – when he comes to make his judgement on the claims.'

'Lesley told me in London the point of ex-changing intended evidence is to prevent surprises in court?' questioned Jordan.

'It is,' agreed Beckwith. 'They're making me work from the first gun.'

'So you think they might be holding something back?'

'They'll be doing so at their peril. Dramatic, last presentation of evidence is OK for movie or television. You try it in reality and you're likely to get it struck from the record. Which loses – defeats, in fact – the whole nonsense of trying it in the first place.'

'You going to meet Alyce's lawyer...?' He stopped, not able to remember the name.

'Reid, Bob Reid,' supplied the other lawyer. 'Talk, certainly. Hear what he wants to discuss. That's where the indication might come from, of Appleton's game.'

'I want to know everything there is to know about Alfred Appleton himself,' announced Jordan.

Beckwith shuffled through his papers. 'Got the profile here,' he said, not looking up. 'We'll flesh it out further through our own people, of course: try to find the things he doesn't want us to know. Here's what there is so far. He's a graduate from the Harvard Business School, actually born in Boston. Old family, old money. Father was a banker. Set up his own commodity business shortly after his marriage to Alyce when they settled in Manhattan, according to what his side have supplied. Predominantly trades in metals although there's a spread – cereals, pork belly on the Chicago market, some currency – through others in the firm. Company turnover of $75,000,000 in the last pre-tax year...' The lawyer looked up at the same time as making a note to himself on a yellow legal pad.

'I'll need to get in much more detail Appleton's personal trading history in view of the itemised claims he's filed.' Beckwith made another note. 'Full medical history, as well, for the mental and physical suffering he's alleging you caused.' Beckwith returned to the file supplied by Appleton's lawyer. 'Married Alyce Bellamy – that's another old family, old money North Carolina name – ten years ago. No children. A yachtsman, sails out of East Hampton. Manhattan address on West 94th.' He smiled and looked back up. 'That's about it.'

That didn't amount to even half of it, judged Jordan. But Beckwith had been encapsulating. 'You think I could have my own copy of Appleton's personal details? Alyce's too?'

Beckwith frowned, although lightly. 'You going to do the research or am I?'

'I want to know everything – and more – about a man you say hates my guts. And who you describe as the reason for that hatred. I read it all, I might come up with something else, something that fits, like I did today remembering her tit for tat response.'

'I was trying to lighten things up a tad,' said Beckwith. 'Of course you get your own copies. I *want* you to have your own copies. There are reasons.'

Now it was Jordan who frowned, not understanding. 'What reasons?'

'Read everything for yourself first. Take your time.'

'What about my being there at the meeting with Alyce's lawyer?'

Beckwith shook his head, his uncertainty genuine now. 'I'm not sure about that: if I want it or if Bob Reid would want it. Let me speak to him first, see what he's got in mind. Might be something I hadn't thought of.'

'I hope not!' said Jordan, too quickly, although at the same time admiring the unexpected humility.

'So do I,' replied the lawyer with a grin, 'but you're still doing it, speaking before you properly think.'

Jordan ignored the rebuke. Instead, mocking, he said, 'I also think – after full and proper consideration – I should stay on until you see Alyce's guy, don't you?'

'A day or two maybe,' allowed Beckwith.

'Can I have my copies: something to read through while I'm waiting? And the advance I asked for?'

Suzie's outfit today was an aquamarine tube dress with the same effect as the previous tight sweater and skirt. She said, 'Hi!' as before, after collecting what needed to be duplicated, but this time there wasn't any flirtatious repartee.

Beckwith said, 'You got over the flight now?'

'Totally,' assured Jordan. 'Spent the last couple of days in Atlantic City.' He had considered Las Vegas, which he knew well, against Atlantic City, which he didn't, but decided upon somewhere to which he could conveniently commute from Manhattan.

'How'd you make out?'

'Dropped a little. Nothing disastrous but it's why I'd like a cash infusion. Need to get the feel of the place.' Jordan preferred European to American casinos, believing that the electronic surveillance of the individual tables in the American ones – in addition to the alertness of the croupier, dealer and pit boss – was far more likely to catch his minimal stake technique. His two long nights on the Atlantic coast had cost him close to $2,000, which he philosophically accepted was about right for the all important pieces of paper.

'Losing's an occupational hazard, I guess?' suggested the lawyer.

'It happens,' agreed Jordan, reluctantly. But was soon to stop, he thought, as Suzie re-entered the room.

Jordan objectively acknowledged that there'd already been false starts and dents to his confidence, but for the first time he decided that with the statements of Alfred and Alyce Appleton tightly in his possession this really *was* the beginning of him regaining his lost control; of actually setting his own agenda, not conforming to that of others. Just as objectively he recognized that he would have to be more careful than he'd ever been in, or with, anything he'd ever tried to plan before.

If Alfred Appleton's lawyers got the faintest hint of what he had in mind – Reid or Beckwith as well, Jordan supposed – the sky would come crashing down upon him. But he'd lived as an identity thief without once being caught out for the last fifteen years by his own hidden and extremely profitable agendas. And could – most

128

definitely *would* – do it again now, just as successfully undetected as he'd always been. Being ensnared as he had in France didn't come into any equation or conflict: everything about France was totally different. Just as this new agenda would be completely different.

Jordan accepted that he had far more to do – and very differently – than was usual in one of his identity frauds. But then he was starting with a lot more, he consoled himself, gazing down at the copied divorce application statements of Alfred and Alyce Appleton set out on the bureau of his locked Carlyle suite, the Do Not Disturb sign displayed on the outside of his door, the hotel telephone exchange under orders not to put through any calls, no matter how persistent or convincingly argumentative the caller.

Opening the thicker of the two files before him Jordan decided that Daniel Beckwith had most definitely encapsulated the information, although not in any obstructive way; the personal material in the Alfred Jerome Appleton dossier would not have appeared relevant to the lawyer. To Jordan it was an Aladdin's cave of treasure that would normally have taken him weeks to compile. And still would not have been as comprehensive. There was Alfred Jerome Appleton's copied birth certificate from which Jordan learned that the maiden name of the man's mother had been Channing. There were the reproduced, personally identifying pages from the man's passport, still with three years to go before renewal. The actual apartment number – 593 – at West 94th Street was accompanied by the unlisted, personal telephone number. The East Hampton address was on Atlantic Avenue. The man's Internet address was also given. The most unexpected bonus of all was the man's New York commodities trading licence. Appleton's private bank details not only provided the account number but also the man's Social Security and private health care insurance numbers. Also listed were the clubs and organizations to which Appleton belonged, the most predictable of which was the Commodity Floor Brokers and Traders' Association. He belonged, predictable again, to two Long Island yacht clubs. And there were photographs, not the posed formal ones that Beckwith had produced in his office, but a selection of amateur pictures: several of Appleton at the helm of a spinaker-bloomed twelve-metre racing yacht, its name obscured; and others of the man receiving awards, twice in sailing clothes at open-air ceremonies, yachts in the background, three at dinner-jacketed banquets. Alyce, smiling in admiration, was close at hand in three of them. In each the bull-shouldered, thick-bodied man dwarfed her, as Jordan had already decided Appleton would physically dominate him.

Jordan eased back in his chair for what was to become the first of several reflections, intentionally allowing the pages – and his initial savouring of them – to mist before his eyes. So much detail, he mused. With more to follow, once he read on, because there would doubtless be spelled out, perhaps literally, the allegedly damaged marriage, social, health and financial loss to support the individual claims. All to establish the severity of each and every loss. He wasn't scared, Jordan recognized, pleased with the awareness. Apprehensive perhaps, because there was still so much more that he had to learn and there was still the hovering risk of public exposure which had to be prevented. But not as scared as he had been, those few short days ago. Nor when he realized he had been robbed of everything. Now he was thinking for himself, letting the ideas germinate in his mind, sufficiently independent of others, necessary though legal representation was.

Appleton's personal statement was preceded by a legally phrased caveat that it was preliminary and therefore subject to revision or amendment. There was an immediate reference annotation to the formal beginning, which recorded the marriage having taken place on April 12th, 1996, at the Sacred Heart cathedral at Raleigh, North Carolina. Jordan at once turned to it, to find a copy of a full, two-page cutting from the *Raleigh News and Observer* describing the marriage as the bringing together of two historically established families: there was a Jeremiah Bellamy among the early settlers colonizing the east coast and a Jeremiah Appleton was one of the Boston rebels against the taxation demands of Georgian England. The wedding photographs showed a little changed Alyce but a much slimmer Appleton.

Appleton's statement recorded their setting up home on West 94th Street after a honeymoon in Hawaii. He described his marriage to Alyce as happy for the first four years, with both he and Alyce dismayed by a series of miscarriages. That dismay increased with Alyce's failure to become pregnant despite a year's IVF treatment. Neither considered adoption an acceptable alternative option. The marriage came under increasing strain because of the amount of time and commitment Appleton had to devote to his business in the early years of its establishment. There were frequent, sometimes violent disagreements between them. Appleton did not consider Alyce sufficiently supportive. She preferred East Hampton, where there was an inherited Appleton family house, and a pattern developed for Alyce to spend the majority of her time there, with his living most of the week alone in Manhattan, returning to Long Island at weekends.

In 1999, for the first time, they discussed divorce, which he neither wanted nor sought. In an effort to avoid it, Appleton, for varying periods of time, commuted daily by seaplane service from Sag Harbour to the 23rd Street facility on Manhattan's East river, despite the strain involved – he was a nervous, reluctant flyer – and it meant his not being able to devote as much time as he considered necessary to his business. Here there was another indexed reference, in which, when he turned to it, Jordan found a selection of financial statements starred to illustrate trading losses. Jordan made a quick mental calculation and estimated the across-the-board deficit from the submitted statements totalled close to two million. Appleton claimed that to stem those losses and get his personal trading back to the profit level he'd achieved when he worked the necessary weekly hours in Manhattan, he would have to reduce his Long Island commuting to three days a week.

In January, 2005, Appleton claimed Appleton and Drake had suffered its largest three-monthly trading loss of $950,000. He and Alyce mutually agreed in that month to a trial separation, Appleton living in the Manhattan apartment, Alyce remaining in East Hampton. During that period of separation he became involved in two brief affairs, one of three weeks with Sharon Borowski and one of a month with Leanne Jefferies. He terminated both and sought a reconciliation with Alyce, to which she agreed. There was a short conjugal reunion of less than two months, Appleton once again commuting by seaplane. In September Alyce insisted on their sleeping separately and he began to suspect she was having an affair. She denied it when he confronted her. She initiated divorce proceedings, citing the two women with whom he insisted he had ceased any contact with before returning to live as much as possible in East Hampton. It was during that reunion that he'd admitted the affairs to her 'to wipe the slate clean'. He asked her to consult a marriage guidance counsellor with him, to which she agreed but refused to continue after three joint sessions. When she announced her intention of spending the summer in Europe, he became even more convinced that Alyce was involved with another man and engaged the private detective agency that discovered her relationship with Harvey William Jordan. The index reference here contained what was described as sample proof of a premeditated liaison, further evidence of which would be produced at the divorce hearing. From the samples Jordan recognized three photographs, one of them aboard the catamaran, the second of their lunching together on the sea-fronting terrace at the Residence de la Pinade and the third at the Cagnes hotel. There were copies of Mr and Mrs Jordan's room registrations from the St Tropez and Cagnes hotels.

Appleton claimed to have become depressed from the moment of Alyce's refusal to share the same bedroom. The combination of psychiatric consultations, loss of confidence, mental distraction, prescribed tranquillisers and medication to treat the mental and physical effects of his wife's behaviour had made it virtually impossible for him to run or control his business for the past several months: there had been long periods when he had been unable to work at all. He was still undergoing psychiatric and medical treatment. There was no prognosis to indicate how long it would be necessary for him to continue either. Because the costs were therefore ongoing, invoices up to the date of the hearing would be presented at the time of that hearing, together with an estimate of likely expenditure in the future.

While openly admitting his now deeply regretted adultery, Appleton insisted he had done everything in his power to sustain and preserve his marriage to Alyce. His wife had never been subjected to physical violence. She had enjoyed a personal allowance of $10,000 a month – unaffected by the financial upheavals of his business, for which he considered her a contributory cause – with Appleton paying all the household bills and expenditures. He provided Alyce with a new, personal Mercedes every two years. He also contributed towards the upkeep and staff costs of the Bellamy family mansion at Raleigh, North Carolina, in which Alyce's widowed mother still lived.

Appleton further insisted he was devastated by the collapse of his marriage and even as late as her return from France had been prepared to re-engage in a marriage guidance programme and attempt a further reconciliation. Alyce had refused to discuss either with him, having formally instigated the proceedings from France, where she had been adulterously involved with Harvey Jordan. From whom, the statement concluded, Appleton sought exemplary and punitive recompense for each and every claimed damage.

Jordan stretched back from the bureau for the second time, surprised that it had grown dark outside without his noticing, trying as objectively as possible to decide where he fitted into the mosaic. And very quickly concluding that he wasn't part of it at all. He wasn't denying the adultery in France but there was no proof or evidence – because none existed – of there having been a premeditated assignation. Which made it impossible for him to be held responsible in any way whatsoever for the collapse of an already collapsed marriage. And if that accusation didn't stand – which it couldn't – he was sure he was not responsible for any damage, commercial, mental or physical, for which Appleton was demanding financial compensation.

He still had Alyce's initial submission to read, Jordan remembered.

Her personal documentation matched that of Appleton and included two addresses, the North Carolina colonial mansion on Raleigh's King George Street and a Manhattan apartment at 341 West 84th Street. Jordan's immediate impression was that Alyce's account of her marriage was going to be remarkably similar to that of her husband, until he reached the second page of her statement. In it were named a long list of trusts and charitable organizations – and a hospital and clinic in Raleigh – all financed and run by a Bellamy Foundation, of which, until a year after her marriage, Alyce had been executive director. Alyce's marriage activated a two-million-dollar family trust in her favour. When Appleton announced his intention of setting up his own commodity trading business she loaned him $500,000 on the clear understanding that it was a loan, although no formal papers were legally drawn up or sworn. Over the following five years she loaned the company a further $500,000, again with no formal papers being signed to establish it as such or of her being named as a director. She received no repayments or dividends reflecting the total loan of one million dollars, but upon Appleton's insistence that it minimized any tax liability she accepted

Mercedes cars in lieu. Under this word-of-mouth arrangement she was given a total of four cars during the period of their marriage.

Alyce used the same word as Appleton – dismay – to describe her failure to become pregnant but attested that before entering the year long IVF treatment she underwent gynaecological examination to establish if she were capable of becoming pregnant and bearing a child. The results were positive; there were no problems. Appleton refused similar medical examination, which caused arguments between them. After the unsuccessful IVF treatment Alyce suggested adoption but Appleton was adamantly opposed, which resulted in further arguments.

Almost from the establishment of his commodity trading business Appleton insisted it was necessary for him to work late into the evening; frequently – as often as twice a week – she would be in bed before he returned. Despite the apparent dedication to work and some indications of success – there was an indexed reproduction from the *Wall Street Journal* describing Appleton and Drake as emerging stars in metal market dealings – Appleton repeatedly told her he was personally suffering substantial losses in his own tradings, although he never showed her books or financial statements. Because of the amount of time she remained alone in the Manhattan apartment Alyce developed a preference for East Hampton. There she worked actively for local cystic fibrosis and breast cancer charities – having by then resigned her position on the Bellamy Foundation – and enjoyed sailing, a mutual interest through which she and Appleton met.

Alyce asserted that it was she who suggested they divorce, so little time did they spend together. During that discussion she made it clear she wanted the return of her one million dollars. Appleton argued against divorce but suggested a trial separation of six months, to which she agreed. Towards the end of that six months Appleton further suggested that he return to live in East Hampton and commute during the week. She agreed but regarded it as a continuation of a trial, particularly after his confession of affairs with Sharon Borowski and Leanne Jefferies. Appleton was adamant that both had been totally unimportant and that he was making the confession to restore their marriage. His confession supported her belief that there had been many other sexual liaisons. There was renewed discussion about their having children and they resumed conjugal relations. He once more refused any fertility tests but Alyce decided to undergo a second series of fertility examinations, prior to taking gynaecological advice about further IVF.

The bombshell came when Jordan turned to page five of Alyce's account. On the second of her resumed examinations Alyce received the results of tests taken at the first. There was incontestable evidence that she was suffering from chlamydia, a venereal infection that can render a woman sufferer infertile or result in severe eye conditions in any child she bears. Alyce declared that she had been a virgin at the time of her marriage to Alfred Appleton and had been involved with no other sexual partner during her marriage, not even during their period of separation. It was the discovery of her venereal infection that brought about her refusal to sleep with Appleton and the reason for her beginning the divorce proceedings which she finally instituted on her vacation in France, which she described as 'getting away from the awfulness of the deceit with which I have lived for so long'.

During that vacation she had an affair with an Englishman, Harvey Jordan. It was a casual, entirely consensual relationship that was not premeditated and ended upon her return to the United States with neither of them intending any future contact or association. She deeply regretted the affair, to which she had succumbed from loneliness and self-satisfying spite at the total betrayal of which she believed herself the victim.

Jordan's sank back into his seat as the fury churned through him, his mind dominated by only one question. How good a venerealogist was the money-grabbing Dr James Preston?

# Twelve

'Why the hell didn't you tell me yesterday about Alyce's infection?' demanded Jordan, still as angry as he had been when he'd finished reading her statement the previous night. He'd been on the phone as nine o'clock struck, insisting upon an immediate meeting, but had to wait until noon.

'Because I wanted you to read everything through for yourself,' responded Beckwith, calmly. 'This way we can take it forward, not spend hours talking back and forth because you didn't have everything in context.'

'What context! She's got a venereal disease and I slept with her!'

'Your choice not to ask. Her choice not to tell you,' reminded the lawyer, still calm. 'And you've got a medical report that says you haven't *got* an infection.'

'Is that why you had me undergo that examination in England: that you already knew she had it?'

'No,' denied Beckwith. 'It's regular practice with such damages claims in North Carolina. I didn't know about Alyce until I got her exchange yesterday. It surprised me as much as I guess it surprised you.'

'Surprise doesn't cover it! And I don't think you can feel the same way about it as I do,' refused Jordan. 'What about her medical report?'

'Not part of the first exchange. And if it helps I understand chlamydia responds to antibiotics. The effect is worse in women and their babies than it is in a man.'

'That assurance doesn't help a damn, either,' refused Jordan, again. 'She says she didn't have any other sexual partner except Appleton, before me.'

'I've read what she says.'

'And she knew she had it before we slept together?'

'Yes?'

'So if he gave it to her and she knowingly passed it on to me I've got a claim against both of them, haven't I?'

'Your report says you're clear.'

'I think the doctor who examined me was a robbing asshole. Maybe incompetent, too. I want another test ... a second opinion.'

'I do, too,' said the man, offering a paper across the desk just as Lesley Corbin had done in England. 'Dr Abrahams is the venerealogist we use regularly. Suzie's got you an appointment for this afternoon – I guessed you'd want it as soon as possible. We've copied the English medical report. Abrahams wants to see it.'

People making decisions for him again, thought Jordan. 'What about me counterclaiming?'

'Sure, if you are infected. You slept with anyone else since Alyce?'

141

'No,' denied Jordan. 'What about what Alyce says, that Appleton slept around – admits himself to have done so with two different women – but refused to have any examinations? Could a court *order* him to have one?'

Beckwith pursed his lips, making an uncertain expression. 'There could be a technical argument against it, claiming assault.'

'That's what Lesley told me you wanted my medical examination for: that if a sexual infection is knowingly transmitted there's a criminal case to be made. It's been established in law with AIDS, hasn't it?'

'We're sure as hell getting an interesting case here.'

With more and more potential for publicity, thought Jordan, worriedly. 'You had any contact yet with Alyce's lawyer?'

'Speaking with him later today.'

'I want to be at any meeting,' insisted Jordan.

'I hadn't forgotten.'

'I think I've got more right now than before.'

'Not if you're going to issue suit against her, you haven't! We sue her you don't get within a million miles of her lawyer until we go into court.'

Jordan was getting that straitjacketed feeling again. 'How long'll it take Abrahams to make his reports?'

Beckwith shrugged, not knowing. 'Tell him you're in a hurry.'

'Which I am.'

'Why don't I talk things through generally with Bob, down there in Raleigh?' suggested

142

Beckwith. 'Get a feel of where he's coming from; he's seeking a meeting with us, after all. We're in the driving seat.'

'Do whatever you've got to do to push things along: to get me off this fucking great hook from which I don't believe I should be hanging in the first place,' said Jordan, impatiently.

'You're losing your temper,' accused Beckwith.

'You're damned right I'm losing my fucking temper! And we're in Lexington Avenue, Manhattan, not in some half-assed court in Raleigh, North Carolina.'

'That half-assed court in Raleigh, North Carolina, has the legal power, upon each and every one of Appleton's claims, to award against you a maximum of fifteen million dollars.'

'You didn't tell me that, either!' accused Jordan.

'It didn't arise in the conversation until now. And now it has.'

'I couldn't come anywhere near a figure like that!' protested Jordan.

'I'd increase my fees if I thought you could,' said Beckwith. 'For the moment you've got to remember the difference between where you are, when you have to.'

'I will.' This was a juvenile, who-punches-whom first argument, Jordan acknowledged. 'Let's stop this shit, shall we?'

'Probably a good idea,' said the already smiling Beckwith. 'If I were you, I'd be pissed, too.'

'Is this the way these things go? Upon so little?'

'This case is getting features all of its own,' admitted the lawyer.

'Can I call you again, after you've talked to Alyce's lawyer? And I've seen the venerealogist?'

'I think you should. Some things might be clearer then.'

'I hope so,' said Jordan, meaning it.

The difference was dramatic, in each and every way. George Abrahams' surgery on West 58th street was a space-age comparison of chrome-gleaming, germ-forbidden sterility against the sagged-cushioned, frayed-carpeted Harley Street townhouse conversion of James Preston. George Abrahams was a close-cropped, rarely smiling man in a white jacket-and-trouser clinical uniform so starched that Jordan expected it audibly to crack when the man moved. Abrahams looked too young to have gained all the qualifications, the framed testimonials, which lined the walls, and Jordan was confident even before the man looked up from the English venerealogist's report that if he'd contracted something from a three-thousand-year-old Egyptian burial pyramid, Abrahams could have diagnosed and cured it.

'Why do you want these findings confirmed?' asked the American, when he did finally look up. Abrahams' tone was as sterile as his surroundings.

'We didn't know when that examination was carried out that the woman in whose divorce I am being cited had a sexual infection.'

Abrahams went back to the first report. 'Which sexual infection, precisely? The report here refers to HIV.'

'Chlamydia.'

Abrahams said, 'That's not signed off.'

'Which is why I am here.'

'How long was your relationship with her?'

Jordan sighed, without intending to, at the familiarity of the questioning. 'Just short of a month. We met on holiday, in France.'

'She tell you she had an infection?'

'Of course not! I wouldn't have slept with her if she had, would I?'

'Probably not,' agreed the other man, as flat-voiced as Beckwith had been earlier. 'What symptoms have you got?'

Jordan felt hot with a mixture of embarrassment and frustration at the conversation: it was as if his penis was under permanent microscopic examination. 'I don't have any symptoms! The examination I had in London was because my lawyer asked for it; apparently it's a recognized need in the sort of case in which I am involved. Since I had the examination we've learned what she was suffering from.'

Now it was the American who sighed. 'This doctor in London? When you talked did he say he was examining you for non-specific urethritis, caused by something other than gonorrhoea?'

'No. He did not mention that.'

'Have you had any penile discharge?'

'He asked me that.'

'Now I'm carrying out the examination,'

reminded the specialist, the irritation sounding in his voice. 'What's the answer?'

'No.'

'Lower abdominal pain or discomfort?'

'No.'

'Irritation?'

'No.'

'Genital inflammation? Rash?'

'No.'

Abrahams smiled up from the notes he was making. 'So far, so good. Now I want blood, urine and sperm samples.'

'Sperm?' queried Jordan.

'Try to remember when we were kids and we all did it, like a lot still do. I've got photographs and movies if it will help.'

It took Jordan almost an hour to fulfil every test, after Abrahams' physical pubic examination; at one stage Jordan even considered Abrahams' pornographic offer. Back in the venerealogist's office Jordan said, 'I'd like the results as soon as possible, sent direct to my lawyer.'

'That's what they will be, returned as soon as possible.'

'No,' said Jordan. 'I really mean like tomorrow, whatever it costs. Couriered direct from wherever they're being analysed. Can you arrange that?'

'Chlamydia is not a difficult disease to treat and cure. There's no cause to panic.'

The exasperated burn came again. Jordan said, 'Tomorrow, OK? Whatever it costs.'

'Tomorrow,' agreed the doctor. 'If you're positive we'll arrange more appointments, get it cleared up. If you do need treatment you'll either have to use a condom or abstain during any treatment.'

'At this precise moment I feel like staying celibate for the rest of my life!' said Jordan.

'Friday,' Beckwith told Jordan, on the telephone.

'What's he want to talk about?'

'A combined strategy, as I thought. We didn't go into detail on the phone.'

'Did you talk to him about my being with you?'

'No.'

'Why not?'

'You know why not. We don't know yet whether we're going to sue Alyce. If we do then Friday's meeting between Bob and me will obviously be cancelled.'

'Abrahams has promised to have his results by tomorrow. They're going to be couriered direct to you.'

'What did Abrahams say?'

'That if I've contracted anything he'll treat it. That chlamydia responds well to treatment. Did you talk to Reid about it?'

'I told you we didn't go into the details of anything on the telephone. He did say Alyce is sorry you've got dragged into this.'

'Not as sorry as I am!'

'If Abrahams keeps his promised schedule, we'll know by tomorrow if we are going to sue her,' Beckwith pointed out.

'I've already worked that out. If the results are

OK I could come down to Raleigh with you.'

'We'll see.'

'What's to see? If I'm with you we can decide on the spot whether it's going to be a joint strategy or not. Get things moving.'

'Harv! Let's see what tomorrow's report says. We're not in a race here.'

'I am! I'm in a hurry – in a race – to get this whole bloody nonsense over and done with. And if you can't help me I'll find someone who can!' As well as being in a hurry to start the retribution I intend, Jordan thought. There wasn't any time limit on his returning to England. The only essential consideration was continuing the rental of Hans Crescent and there was still weeks to go before he needed to do that.

'I'll call you the moment I hear from Abrahams,' promised the lawyer. Stiffly he added, 'You get any thoughts about changing your legal representation in the meantime, I'll do all I can to find you the best lawyer with North Carolina Bar exam qualifications to take your case over. It'll probably mean your going down to Raleigh for consultation, of course.'

'I'll think about it,' said Jordan, refusing to be bullied.

Frustration remained Jordan's most persistent feeling. That and having his penis and his bodily fluids so persistently and literally under a microscope, like a rare specimen of humanity displayed on a slab. Should he call Beckwith's bluff and change lawyers? He was strongly tempted; after the first few minutes from putting down the

148

telephone on the lawyer he'd reached out to call Beckwith back to tell him he did want to change. He had literally held back, his hand hovering over the receiver, fighting the anger which he now realized, belatedly and with a fresh blip of frustration, was what Beckwith was constantly urging him to do. He really didn't want to change. Despite Beckwith's Wild West affectation – strangely incongruous for a man born and raised on the eastern seaboard state – and the irritating Christian name abbreviation, Jordan liked the man. And believed he was a good lawyer, despite there being no criteria upon which to judge. He had to be, surely, swimming among the legal sharks of Manhattan in preference to the calmer waters of North Carolina? He'd let it go this time, Jordan decided, and at once contradicted himself. He'd let it *ride*, see how things developed. If he were subsequently dissatisfied, Beckwith's offer to withdraw remained on the table between them.

Jordan's telephone rang just before ten the following morning. Beckwith said, 'You haven't got a problem. There's not a trace of any venereal infection. And I've spoken to Bob. He's happy for you to come along. Suzie's already bought the tickets.'

The furnished service apartment Jordan had isolated on West 72nd on his second day in Manhattan was still available and by just after 1 p.m. Jordan had secured a three-month lease in the name of Alfred Jerome Appleton with a full cash deposit covering both rental and charges. He also paid cash for a telephone connection, with an unlisted number. He gave the name and address of the First National Bank on Wall Street for a reference. He was at that bank, the first of those he had chosen, an hour later. He opened the account in Appleton's name with an initial cash deposit of $3,500 and Appleton's genuine Social Security number so conveniently available from the exchanged court documents. The bank official made a particular note that Jordan would predominantly use electronic banking, although he did need bank, credit card and chequebook facilities and gave Appleton's mother's maiden name for the security reference. Jordan authorized all charges to be directly debited from his account and warned the man to expect a realtor's bank reference request for West 72nd Street. The bank official hoped they'd have a mutually satisfactory relationship and Jordan said he was sure they would.

# Thirteen

Jordan wasn't at all surprised that Daniel Beckwith's vehicle was a personalized number-plated 4x4 with extra-wide wheels and special trim, along with dark-tinted windows. And coloured red. When he got inside Jordan saw it was equipped with satellite navigation, which didn't surprise him either. He hadn't expected to be able to see so clearly beyond the smoked glass, though.

'You all set?' greeted Beckwith. Today's outfit was faded denim workshirt and jeans, with tooled cowboy boots and the regulation big buckle belt. The bison motif reminded Jordan of the shoulder-hunched photograph of Alfred Appleton.

'You're in charge: you tell me.' And then I'll tell you, Jordan thought, a decision already formulating.

Beckwith snatched a glance across the car as he began the manoeuvre to get to the Triboro bridge and the Van Wyke expressway for the airport. 'What's the matter?'

'I'm where I don't want to be, facing – by your calculations – a potential financial judgement against me of millions, is what's the matter.'

'You got your head up your own ass, Harv,'

declared Beckwith, taking the macho car up the ramp towards the bridge, the traffic easier going out of Manhattan than it appeared to be getting in from the unmoving, traffic-congealed contra flow. 'That cost estimate was before we got yesterday's squeaky clean medical report. Which turned your problems a hundred and eight degrees in your favour: you're now back on the sunny side of the street. Sit back, smile and enjoy the warmth.'

'No!' refused Jordan. 'There are things we need to get straight between us, Daniel! And listen. I use your full, complete Christian name, don't try to abbreviate it. You want to play out some macho fantasy with the way you dress and the car you drive, that's fine. That's your fantasy: get your rocks off. But I don't like being called Harv, when my name is Harvey. And I don't like having appointments made for me before I even know they're being made, what those appointments are for or why, even, they're necessary. I've wiped my own ass since I was about five, without any help from anyone, and hope I can go on doing it without leaving stains on my underwear for a long time in the future. As I intend doing a lot more – everything – for myself in the future.'

Beckwith snatched another glance as they turned into the La Guardia slip road. 'Sounds to me like you've made your decision about your legal representation. So why you bothering to come down to Raleigh with me today?'

'I *have* made my decision,' confirmed Jordan. 'My decision is that I want to be called Harvey when we talk and that I want to be consulted in advance before arrangements are made on my behalf and that I don't want to be lectured about losing my temper – because I've got that completely on board and totally under control. But I want to continue with your representing me because we're a long way down the track now and I really don't want to go back – or down to Raleigh to find somebody else – to start all over again.'

'Which isn't exactly an overwhelming vote of confidence.'

'Which it wasn't intended to be. It was intended to tell you how I felt and how I'd like things to be between us from now on.'

'Otherwise...?'

'Otherwise we'll have another conversation, very similar to this. And I will go down to Raleigh. Which brings us back to your choice.'

Beckwith took the car into the short stay parking lot, ignoring three available spaces until he found one that he wanted, close to a side wall. He hesitated after they got out to walk side by side with Jordan, still unspeaking, into the terminal. When they reached the departure pier he handed Jordan his ticket, deferring to him to check in first. The flight was already being called and they continued on into the aircraft. On the plane Beckwith stood back for Jordan to choose his seat and as always Jordan took the aisle.

Finally, when they'd settled in their seats, Beckwith said, 'You travelled around America a lot, Harvey?'

'Not a lot. Las Vegas, of course. The west coast a few times. New Orleans, before the hurricane disaster.' It would have been a mistake to acknowledge the name correction.

'Pity we couldn't have driven to Raleigh and back in one day. Great country.'

'I've changed my mind about returning to England too quickly,' announced Jordan. 'I'll have to go back sometime, of course. But I want first to make sure everything is on track here: get a much clearer idea how it's going to work out.'

'Maybe a good idea. It's your decision.'

'Based upon your guidance.'

'That's what you're paying me for.'

'How are we going to do this meeting with Bob Reid?'

'Officially it's between attorneys. But there's no reason for you not joining in if you think you've got a point to make that we've missed.'

'I'll keep that in mind.' He'd corrected the situation to where it should have been from the beginning, Jordan decided. It was a good feeling, the best he'd had for several days.

Raleigh, the first American state capital Jordan had visited, was hung with direction signs to the sites and events of its early settler history like flags at a victory celebration and Jordan got a tourist's commentary to each and every one of them from Daniel Beckwith as the lawyer drove their hire car in from the airport, culminating in a brief detour to Capitol Square to see the horse-mounted statues of the three North Carolina-born statesmen who'd risen to become United States presidents.

They were only five minutes late getting to Reid's offices, just two streets away from the square, and were ushered directly in. The first person Jordan saw, before the waiting lawyer, was Alyce Appleton.

She wore a dark grey trouser suit, brightened by a pink sweater, but it still reminded Jordan of Lesley Corbin's official business uniform. Alyce had on the dark framed spectacles, too, but the thin wedding band was no longer next to the diamond engagement ring. She wore little make-up but Jordan remembered she hadn't in the South of France.

Jordan's initial thought was how difficult it was to imagine the antipathy he now felt towards someone with whom he had so recently – no more than three months, he guessed – made such uninhibited love.

Looking more towards the two lawyers than the woman, Jordan said, 'I didn't understand this was how it was going to be?'

'Neither did I,' frowned Beckwith, turning accusingly towards the other lawyer.

'It was obviously necessary for me to inform my client what was happening—' began Reid.

'And I insisted on being here as well,' broke in Alyce, a hint of uncertainty in her voice.

'I saw no legal bar,' finished the Raleigh lawyer. He was a plump, red-faced, jowly man who needed the tightness of the waistcoat as well as the fastened jacket of his black pinstriped suit to hold in his stomach to prevent himself looking fatter than he was. The owl-round glasses looked precarious on his button nose.

'It might have been better if we'd discussed it earlier between the two of us,' said Beckwith, cautiously.

'I thought we already had. If your client can be present, so can mine,' said Reid, an asthmatic catch in his voice. 'We're both present to guard against conflicting problems ... which I don't anticipate there being.' He looked at Jordan. 'Do you have any objection to Alyce being here?'

Daniel Beckwith outmanoeuvred before they'd crossed the threshold of a court, thought Jordan, feeling wrong-footed himself. 'Not if it will achieve more quickly what I want to be achieved. You're the lawyers, to judge it legally.'

'I want a written, without prejudice, understanding between us,' insisted Beckwith.

'As I do,' said Reid. 'With the attachment of a memorandum of agreement from your client. Alyce has already signed hers. I've taken the liberty of having the documentation prepared.'

Something else done for him without his knowledge or agreement, Jordan recognized, looking at Beckwith, who nodded. Jordan said, 'OK by me.' He signed first and while the two lawyers were completing the formality he said to Alyce, 'Hello, belatedly.'

'Hello.'

Neither smiled.

Jordan said, 'So much for not exchanging addresses.'

'I'm sorry ... about all of it ... about everything. I really didn't know ... suspect ... it's awful and I really am very sorry ... embarrassed, too. Extremely embarrassed.'

'I thought I was going to be sorrier than I already am until late yesterday afternoon.'

Alyce frowned, shaking her head. 'I don't understand...?'

'It wasn't until late yesterday afternoon that I got the all-clear from the venerealogist.'

Alyce flushed, visibly. 'You surely didn't think?'

'Of course I surely thought,' Jordan cut her off, mocking her words, close to letting the anger erupt. 'You really surprised that I surely thought?'

'This wasn't set up as a fight,' broke in Reid.

Jordan switched his attention, his anger locked down, pleased the way the reactions were coming. 'What, exactly, was it set up for? I don't believe I should be involved in this situation at all and want to be out of it ... don't want to go anywhere near a courthouse. That's how it is – all of how it is – as far as I am concerned. Now tell me how I feature as far as you are concerned.' He'd listened intently to himself, not just to the words but to his tone, and was sure Beckwith wouldn't be able to accuse him of either losing his temper or his control.

It was Alyce who responded, ahead of her lawyer. 'I don't believe you should be involved or need to go anywhere near a courthouse, either. That's why I wanted to be here. Just – and only – to tell you that. And to say sorry. Which I already have. Now I've said both – and hope you believe me – there's no need for me to stay any longer if it's a problem for you.' She stirred in her seat, as if to get up.

There was an abrupt silence in the room, each man looking to the other. To his client Reid said, 'You're here now. Agreed to the confidentiality. You might as well stay; get some idea, beyond what's briefly already been said, what's going to come from Harvey's side.'

Talking directly to Jordan, not to her lawyer, Alyce said, 'What do *you* want me to do? Get out and stop embarrassing you more than I've already embarrassed both of us? Or stay?'

The embarrassment *did* surge through Jordan at the awareness of how he'd behaved. 'Why not stay?'

Alyce flushed again. 'What about my apology! Do you believe and accept I didn't imagine you'd become involved? Or are you determined to stay tight-assed?'

Jordan stared at her for a long time before saying, 'Thank you for your apology at my becoming involved. Which I accept.'

'Now what about you?' Alyce pushed on, positively red faced now. 'How about an apology from you, for actually believing – contemplating – for a moment that I'd put you at risk from what my bastard of a husband exposed me to! You know what that makes me, your thinking that: it makes me sick to my stomach!'

'Maybe our coming down wasn't such a good idea after all,' intruded Beckwith. 'We're not achieving anything here.'

'Let's all calm down. Drink some coffee or something,' urged Reid. 'We break up like this the winner's going to be Alfred Appleton, with us the losers. We're on the same side, aren't we?'

'I'd hoped we would be,' said Alyce. 'Now I'm not so sure.'

'Coffee or what?' bustled Reid. 'Let's cool down. Compose ourselves.'

Alyce had tea. The three men chose coffee. Reid led them all away from any formal setting, to an annex to his office. It was fitted with easy chairs and sofas and polished long-leafed plants that seemed to survive in pots filled with wood chippings, not earth.

There was another brief although less awkward silence. Then, looking between Jordan and Alyce, Beckwith said, 'OK, you've each read the other's initial statement and we've got the medical problem out of the way. So let's move on from there, shall we?'

Jordan seized the moment, a lot of questions already formulated. 'What about the court? Whether it'll be an open or closed hearing?'

'We want it closed,' replied Reid, at once. 'I've already intimated that to Appleton's people. And to the court.'

'To what response?'

'None, positively, not yet,' said Reid. 'But Bartle inferred they'd oppose it.'

'Scare tactics,' judged Beckwith.

'That's what I think,' agreed Read.

'We can support your applications, even though we can't initiate it,' Beckwith promised. 'Which we will if I don't succeed in a pre-trial submission to get Harvey dismissed from the case.'

'Which we'll support you in,' said Reid. He looked directly at Jordan. 'That's at Alyce's

159

insistence, before she and I talked about anything else. That's one of the main reasons for my
asking her to be here today.'

'Thank you,' said Jordan, uncomfortably,
looking between the woman and her lawyer.

'You're closer to the ground here than I am,'
said Beckwith, talking to Reid. 'You any
indication yet who our judge might be?'

'Not officially,' said Reid. 'I'm guessing at
Pullinger.'

'Ah!' said Beckwith.

'That doesn't sound as if you're pleased?'
questioned Jordan, gauging the tone in both
lawyers' voices.

'Judge Hubert Pullinger prides himself on
having the strongest and loudest moral voice not
just in the county but in the entire state of North
Carolina; far beyond that, even,' explained Reid.

'Whom I remember from when I practised
here makes early, preconceived judgements
from which he can rarely be persuaded by
contrary evidence or argument.'

'Can't you apply for an alternative judge?'
asked Alyce.

'He's also the *senior* judge on the circuit,' said
her lawyer. 'It would be about the worst move,
politically or tactically, to try to make. If he gets
the case, we have to live with it.'

'Why are you guessing he'll get it?' asked
Jordan.

'He has first pick. And this is his sort of case,'
said Reid.

'I want to know something: something very
important,' demanded Jordan, coming to another
160

query on his long list. 'We've gone past – never touched upon, even – what the hell criminal conversations are. Will someone set it – or them – out for me, beyond saying that they're expensive!'

Before deferring to Reid, Beckwith briefly, but with a hard-faced stare, looked at Jordan and Reid intercepted the look. The local lawyer coughed a hollow cough and said, 'I guess that's a question for me?'

'It's a question to anyone who can answer it,' said Jordan.

Reid coughed again. 'In layman's language, criminal conversation is judged as an injury to the person. Appleton's in this case, committed by you. It's what's technically known as a short liability tort, whereby it is only necessary to prove and establish that sexual intercourse took place, which both of you admit. It's also necessary to establish that a valid marriage existed. Which it did. And that the suit is brought within statutory limitations. Which – once more – it is...'

'It is not a defence that the defendant – you – did not know that Alyce was married, that Alyce consented to the act of sex, that Alyce was separated from Appleton, that Alyce seduced you or that the marriage was an unhappy one. Or that the spouse – Appleton – had been unfaithful,' completed Beckwith in a breathless rush, anxious to prove he knew the legislation as well as the other lawyer.

It took several moments for Jordan to absorb it all and when he spoke he was still not sure that he had, not completely. Shaking his head in disbelief he said, 'This should have been spelled out at the very beginning! While I was still in England. From what you've just told me, the two of you, I've got absolutely no defence whatso-ever against the claims that are being brought against me!'

'You asked for the law, which you got,' said Beckwith. 'My job – Bob's job, in Alyce's case – is to advance arguments that fit your specific circumstances and persuade the judge that my interpretation of that law is in your favour. Which I think I can.'

'As I think I can,' came in Reid.

'I sure as hell hope you can,' said Alyce. 'You haven't set out the law as specifically as that to me, either, until now.'

'I think I have,' said Reid.

'I don't,' refused Alyce.

'Appleton's surely the guiltier party!' said Jordan. He looked hesitantly at Alyce. 'I'm sorry about this, talking as if you're not here, but he has to be the person who gave Alyce chlamydia. And admits to two affairs.'

'There were more, I'm sure,' said Alyce. 'All that time he spent by himself in Manhattan! He wasn't by himself in bed.'

'My first pre-trial submission is going to be a court order for Appleton to undergo a venereal examination,' said Reid. 'And our enquiry people are trying to find other women. The more we get the more Pullinger will come towards us.'

'I've now undergone two medical examinations,' said Jordan. 'And I've been told by both specialists that it's a curable infection. What if he's had treatment: that there's no trace of his ever having had it?'

'I'm also going to apply for an order that his side produce his complete medical records, if they won't do it voluntarily,' said Reid. 'And I've already asked Bartle for them to be volunteered.'

'What about Sharon Borowski and Leanne Jefferies?' demanded Beckwith.

Reid shifted in his seat at the insistence. 'Sharon Borowski's dead: killed in an auto smash eleven months ago; she no longer features. Leanne Jefferies is another commodity dealer, although not with Appleton's firm. Works for Sears Rutlidge. Thirty, single. As far as our enquiry people can discover it really was a short relationship, as Appleton says it was. No indication of their still being together. But we're issuing criminal conversation claims against her, of course, as soon as I get the name of her lawyer. That's going to be another court application, as soon as I get a judge.'

'The bank records are selective,' Beckwith pointed out.

'Already noted,' said Reid, at once. 'I've filed for consecutive statements.'

'What about the money you gave him?' Beckwith queried, looking at Alyce. 'There must be a paper trail, from your statements?'

'Withdrawn in cash, handed over to him in cash, in tranches of varying amounts, not a lump sum,' said Alyce. 'Like being repaid in

Mercedes cars, he told me it was better taxably for it all to be done in cash.'

'Didn't it ever occur to you that you were being conned?' asked Jordan, the expert.

'Let me tell you about my husband,' said Alyce, quiet-voiced, analytical. 'When I married him I thought he loved me, which I don't think he ever did, not at any time. It's difficult now for me to believe that I loved him, but I think I did. He's got a good act. I certainly trusted him, another mistake. It took me a while to recognize him as a manipulating bully. Realizing that he was a cheat – a cheat in every way – took even longer: long after he persuaded me to relinguish my position as chief executive of the parent Bellamy Foundation. You want the analogy, it's easy if you'll allow the cliché. Alfred Jerome Appleton is a Jekyll and Hyde, everybody's friend, everybody's helper, the first with the biggest charity cheque, all for the big reputation and the big benefit it'll bring him. Cross him and he'll run right over you – squash you into the ground and enjoy doing it. But no one knows that, suspects it, even. And won't believe that it's possible for him ever to be like that, if we don't get a closed court. It'll be all my fault, all my lies. That's why he'll be happy with an open court. It'll be a stage for him to perform on. That's what he does, every day: performs, puts on an act to appear someone other than who he really is.'

Jordan stirred, in self-recognition. And had another thought, even more self-indulgent, as he heard Beckwith say, 'No chance that Pullinger might know Appleton? Have had some social contact?'

'What the hell...?' demanded Jordan.

'Prior knowledge or awareness would be grounds for disbarment,' explained his lawyer.

'Absolutely not,' said Alyce. 'In Boston – the entire state of Massachusetts – he probably knows every judge there is to know: every important person there is to know. But not down here.'

'That's something to bear in mind,' insisted Beckwith. 'What about you? Any chance your family's come into contact with Pullinger? Same exclusion would apply.'

'Not that I'm aware,' said Alyce. 'Today's the first time I've heard the name. I could ask my mother: I'm living with her at the moment.'

'What about Appleton's claim, in his statement, that he provided financial support for your mother?' asked Reid.

'Total nonsense,' rejected Alyce. 'The Bellamy Foundation dwarfs the Appleton wealth ten times over. I think it was around that time, just after we got back from Hawaii, that I told him of my trust inheritance.'

'He didn't know you were an heiress before you got married?' asked Beckwith, seemingly surprised.

'I don't think so,' said Alyce. 'It was something that never came up.'

'And when it did he asked you to lend him $500,000 to help start his commodity business?' pressed Reid.

'It wasn't like that, a flat demand for a half

165

million,' qualified Alyce. 'He said it would help if he had some cash infusions, from time to time. Which, of course, I gave him; was happy to give him. And then he asked for more, which grew into another half a million.'

'Which you were still happy to give him?'

'*Lend* him,' insisted Alyce. 'Things weren't going well by then; beginning to break down, although I don't think I properly recognized what was happening at the time.'

Jordan wasn't having any difficulty recognizing anything. His concentration – and retention – was absolute but it didn't preclude his thinking in parallel. The feeling of dismissive antipathy towards Alyce had gone, replaced by the un-diminished earlier embarrassment. Alyce Appleton was someone he'd briefly known, become briefly but pleasurably involved with but never imagined encountering again. Now he was reunited by unsought circumstances. What about *right* now, at this precise moment? Jordan couldn't decide. It all sounded as he supposed it should sound, the necessary first meeting of lawyers, the initial strategy discussion that Beckwith had described it as being, but Jordan couldn't actually discern any strategy evolving. Objectively Jordan acknowledged his attitude was driven by his overwhelming impatience – matched by his overwhelming need – to be rid of it all. But he couldn't recognize any forward planning being formulated: it was all backward looking, not forwards. A closing remark of Alyce's – 'I came genuinely to think of him being seriously paranoid' – brought Jordan conveniently back into the conversation.

'Why should he have had you followed, as he obviously did, all the way to France? For the information he gathered about us there he must have engaged an army of private detectives!'

'That was my final confirmation, about his being paranoid,' stressed the woman, colouring again as she spoke. 'I suppose he must have engaged them when I announced I was going ahead with the divorce...' She hesitated. 'I was not involved with anyone here. I'm still not, so there was nothing for him to find here, in America.' She gave an uncertain movement. 'France happened –' she looked at Jordan – 'I wish it hadn't: wish you hadn't got caught.'

Before Jordan could speak Reid said, 'That's a point to pursue...'

'And I will, as you should,' picked up Beckwith. 'He'll have to call the people he put on to you. We can take them back before France.' He looked to the other lawyer. 'You can establish on oath what Alyce has just said, that she wasn't cheating before France. And from that I can establish that there was no prior contact between Alyce and Harvey, *until* France.'

'But France still happened,' said Alyce.

'But not until after you'd sent me, in a letter with a date on it, in an envelope with a French postal date on it – both of which I'll submit as evidence – instructions to file for your divorce. As far as you were concerned, your marriage was over. It wasn't when your husband had his two admitted mistresses?'

167

'Isn't that covered – excused – by all the caveats you explained earlier in the criminal conversation statute?' cut in Jordan.

'Depends how I argue it,' insisted Reid.

Maybe there was a benefit to the meeting after all, thought Jordan. He said, 'What about after France? Do you think Appleton would have had the surveillance maintained?'

'It might be something to pursue when we get to court,' said Reid.

'I don't see the point or purpose of continuing the expense,' said Beckwith. 'He had his evidence by then, didn't he?'

It wasn't the reassurance he'd wanted but realistically there was no way either lawyer could say any more, accepted Jordan. 'If he has he'll know Alyce and I have met again, here today.'

'In the presence of your lawyers, both of whom have legally attested the meeting in the without prejudice documentation,' Beckwith pointed out. 'It can't be used in any court hearing to any benefit to Appleton, which is why it was drawn up.'

'In the presence of your lawyers,' echoed Reid, to emphasize his following point. 'Just in case there is continuing surveillance, I don't think it would be a good idea for you and Alyce to get together in anything other than in our presence.'

'With which I fully concur, ' said Beckwith.

Alyce snorted a derisive laugh. 'One of the few things that we can be assured of at this stage is that the likelihood of that being on either of our minds just doesn't exist.'

'I agree. To everything,' said Jordan.

'I'm still waiting, though,' said Alyce, openly challenging Jordan.

'I really am sorry for the way I behaved earlier,' said Jordan.

'I wish I believed you,' said Alyce.


It was just after nine that night when Reid's home telephone jarred in his den but he was still there, waiting. He said, 'I was beginning to get worried wondering what had happened to you.'

'There were delays at your end and then we got stacked at La Guardia,' said Beckwith. 'It was a goddamned awful trip back.'

'How'd you think it went?'

'Better than I thought it would, after the rocky start. I certainly don't think they knew each other, before France.'

'Neither do I,' agreed Reid.

'I hope we don't get Pullinger.'

'I'll keep on the case until we find out for sure.'

'I think they'll do well in court.'

'I was worried about Jordan, as you know. I thought he did OK.'

'I thought Alyce did, too. Can't have been easy for her, as Jordan said, talking about her as if she wasn't there.'

'Cute little gal. I envy him France.'

'We need Appleton's medical report,' insisted Beckwith. 'If he's infected we can both blow Appleton out the water.'

'I'm worried about that,' admitted Alyce's lawyer. 'It's too obvious a weakness in his case.

I wrote to Bartle after you left, demanding the production of a specific report, as well as the medical history. And to Leanne Jefferies. I don't imagine she's going to be so fond of Appleton now that she's going to be sued for criminal conversation.'

'You think Appleton could have an actual mental condition, as Alyce intimated? It could help as much as the proof of chlamydia. And should show on his medical history.'

'If I don't get what I want from Bartle I'm definitely going to file for a pre-court hearing,' assured Reid. 'Jordan really make that good a living from gambling?'

'Seems like it,' said Beckwith.

'I thought your guy made a good point about surveillance,' said Reid. 'I wish my people had produced as much on Appleton as his people did on Jordan and Alyce in France.'

'There's still time. We don't have a court date yet.'

'I'm glad we're working together.'

'So am I.'

'Let's keep in touch.'

'Let's do that.'

# Fourteen

Harvey Jordan decided there was no reason for him to have considered as wasted time the frustrating day he'd spent in the Carlyle suite waiting for the results of the American venerealogist's examination. He would have been distracted then, not devoting his absolute concentration upon what he wanted to do and the preparations necessary to do it. And the trip to Raleigh had been a useful interval to think things through as well as the opportunity to put things right between himself and Daniel Beckwith.

Today was the moment to start putting into practice the several decisions he'd reached and become pro-active: to start to work, in fact, with just the slightest variation from normal. Not wanting to risk being followed to all the places of public record and reference that he might need to visit – despite having so much useful information already available from the legal exchanges between the lawyers – Jordan's first priority was to resolve the surveillance uncertainty. How to do that had come to him during the Raleigh meeting.

The most compelling reason for staying in grand hotels was the comprehensiveness of their services, which he utilized by having someone from the Carlyle's guest assistance go out to buy the laptop he needed, which had the double benefit of him not being seen to make the purchase if he were still being watched and further distancing him from it by having its purchase price registered against the hotel and not charged by name against him, personally. It took Jordan the entire morning to configure the machine and put it on-line, not through an American provider but through the British Telecom Yahoo broadband server. He set up his payments through England, too, from the Paul Maculloch account at the Royston and Jones private bank.

From his previous lawful career Harvey Jordan had brought an unrivalled computer expertise to his new illegal career, in which phishing was essential. The first requirement for successful hacking was never to initiate a direct intrusion into another system, but to work through an intervening, unwitting 'cut out' server. The reason for such caution was twofold: computer protection had become extremely sophisticated since its inception, with many preventative systems utilizing tracing facilities to identify the source of a detected illegal entry attempt. It was this unknowing 'cut out' buffer computer system that showed up if Jordan's cyber burglary got ensnared in a firewall, not Jordan's laptop. The second advantage was that Jordan only got charged for the cost of accessing his cut out. Everything he did through it was billed against the unsuspecting host. Having penetrated the host system, like an intrusive cuckoo, Jordan then installed what in the self-explanatory vernacular of the trade is known as a Trojan Horse.

Over his years as an identity borrower Jordan had successfully stabled his Trojan Horses in a number of illegal sites throughout the world unknown to the genuine owner and while he religiously destroyed the individual computers he only ever used for one identity stealing operation, he'd left his secret entry doors open to all the host sites, creating a bank upon which he could draw without having to hack in to a new system. That day he chose to return to a long term cuckoo's nest in the mainframe of a beer-distributing company in Darwin, Australia, that he hadn't used for five years. He still worked as carefully as he always did, with every new job, alert for the first indication that his previous presence might have been discovered during a virus or illegal entry sweep during his absence, but there was no tell-tale hindrance or unexpected 'entry denied' flash on his screen and the 12,000 mile connection was made in seconds.

Continuing on was easier than normal, because he already had not just the publicly available website address of Appleton and Drake, a few blocks away from where he sat in Manhattan, but Alfred Appleton's personal registration entry code supplied in the exchanged legal documents by Appleton himself. Jordan was, effectively and electronically, looking over Appleton's shoulder in three minutes, and by another five had tied up a new, untraceable Trojan Horse within Appleton's computer through which he could monitor every incoming and outgoing email the man had stored in the past and was likely to save in the future.

Which was only the beginning of what turned out to be a very successful and productive day. Like the gambler he was supposed to be – but wasn't – Jordan had hoped Appleton would have conducted his correspondence with David Bartle at Brinkmeyer, Hartley and Bernstein through his office facilities and so it turned out to be. It took Jordan a further thirty minutes to get into the law firm's main computer system from which he moved on to embed a separate monitor in the lawyer's personal machine. He scrolled patiently through the inbox and sent box of Bartle's email service to discover the name of the ultra-efficient private enquiry agency, called unoriginally, Watchdog, whose offices were downtown, on Elizabeth Street in Little Italy. Jordan had been surprised by how easy it had been penetrating the computer systems of both Appleton and Bartle, despite the advantages he'd had from the legal documents, but expected more difficulty entering that of Watchdog. He was surprised once more than it only took him another thirty minutes to get through the company's firewall and a further fifteen to get his Trojan Horse and his own password in place in the personal computer station of Patrick O'Neill, the director with whom Bartle had conducted all his email correspondence.

Jordan was cramped, physically aching, from the concentration with which he'd worked, without a break, into the middle of the afternoon. He still only allowed himself the briefest pause,

174

just long enough to walk through the suite to the bathroom to wash his face and make himself a tall vodka and tonic from the well equipped, ice-maker and glass-backed permanent bar in the suite's living room, excited at the possibility of being able to answer the most persistently nagging question since the entire episode began.

It took him much longer than the previous hacking, because he had constantly to switch back and forth between in and out emails between Bartle and O'Neill to maintain a comprehensive continuity between the exchanges and even then there were gaps which Jordan assumed to be caused by the two men on occasions preferring the telephone to their computers.

As Jordan's understanding grew he learned that O'Neill had acted as an on-the-spot supervisor in France, with a staff that at its height grew to ten – with the addition of two photographers – once they'd established the affair between him and Alyce. Two of the Watchdog staff had actually flown on the same plane as Alyce from New York, and dated before that flight to Europe was a lengthy memorandum from O'Neill explaining that despite an intense, two months' surveillance in Manhattan and East Hampton, they had failed to uncover any evidence whatsoever of Alyce being involved with another man. There were several references to him in France as being 'someone of obvious wealth' and as 'someone who is very familiar with this area of France'.

And finally Jordan found what he was

specifically looking for. He guessed it was an email response from Bartle to a telephone call, which would have had to have taken place on the day Alyce flew back to New York from Nice, maybe even from the airport itself. The lawyer had written that O'Neill was to maintain the surveillance on Jordan while he remained in France but that it shouldn't be continued back to England. In that email Bartle had written: 'There is incontrovertible evidence of adultery sufficient for proceedings to be initiated and the expense in obtaining it has already been substantial.'

Satisfied that he was no longer under Watchdog surveillance Jordan quit the hotel and spent the rest of the afternoon opening four separate accounts at the four other already chosen Wall Street banks in the name of Alfred Jerome Appleton. As with the First National he specified that he would be predominantly using electronic banking and provided the West 72nd street apartment as the mailing address to which bank and credit cards and cheque books should be delivered. He used cash – ranging from between $2,000 to $3,000 – to establish the accounts, anxious now that they were set up to get back to the Carlyle for the first of the many intended phishing expeditions.

He got back into Appleton's personal computer by five thirty and through it, using Appleton's unopposed, never rejected password, had the key electronically to pass through every door to wander wherever he chose within the firm of Appleton and Drake. A tour, Jordan both professionally and logically accepted, was too much to attempt in one visit: too much, possibly, to complete over a number of visits. But there was no hurry. The initial priority was to establish the value of the company, which again at this first visit was impossible to calculate. What wasn't impossible, though, was to confirm that it ran into millions of contracts bought short or long, all set out like prizes in a raffle to which he held all the winning tickets. Apart from Appleton and his partner, Peter Drake, there were five additional traders and between them, after the briefest journey through the combined buy and sell portfolios, Jordan conservatively estimated there were more than 6,000 already logged trades, going through the entire gamut of the company's range, from metals, its major activity, through its currency, cereal and Chicago meat subsidiaries.

Jordan had only twice before stolen the identity of a commodity trader, but from that experience he knew the basic trading operations, the most important of which was that any buy-or-sell contracts agreed by traders were double-checked and confirmed by the 'back office', a secondary, double-checking filter to prevent any contract being overlooked beyond its regulated, three month completion date. But once it was checked and registered – and most important of all dated – it remained on the trader's book until it was moved on. Which meant, after the back office confirmation, the lid to every cookie jar was open to him, to plunder at will. That night he limited his targeting stings, concentrating upon currency contracts, because of all the commodities they fluctuated the most, sometimes by the hour, and therefore were the most difficult to track. He further limited himself on this first visit to a transfer to the First National bank account, and even more strictly limited the amounts – all of them less than five hundred dollars – he electronically transferred from four, two-day-old currency trades, each in excess of one million dollars from which five hundred dollars would not be detectable, nor swell the initial fake Appleton account beyond what the bank were legally required to automatically report to the financial regulating authorities. The following day, Jordan determined, the taps would be opened more fully to fill all five accounts.

At last, closer to exhaustion that he could remember for a long time, Jordan closed down the laptop and pushed himself back from the bureau to go to the bar to make himself another celebratory drink, putting on room lights as he did so. He carried his glass to an easy chair, needing its relaxing softness. Gazing out unseeingly over the jewellery-box glitter of the Manhattan night, he shook his head at the memories of all the unnecessary, time-wasting scurrying around London he did in order to avoid any potential surveillance when there had been nothing or no one to avoid or from whom to hide. And then he laughed, recognizing how frenetic he would have seemed if people *had* been watching him. It might have all been unnecessary and time-wasting, and he didn't like being made to scurry like a frightened rabbit, but he was glad he'd taken the precautions. There was even a positive benefit: his own money was now far better hidden than it had been and, pointless though most of it had proved to be, it *had* been a useful, if exhausting, lesson. As he'd reflected before, he had definitely become complacent, dangerously believing things could never go wrong to upset his perfect life, which he certainly didn't believe any longer. But he was correcting the situation now, Jordan told himself, looking across the room at the blank-eyed computer: pro-active at last, thinking for himself, in charge, in control of himself. Before this was all over there were going to be people – Appleton in particular – who'd fervently wish that he weren't so in control.

Jordan started work again early the following day, first re-entering the available golden goose of Appleton and Drake and again, from the already dated currency trades, spreading $10,500 in transfers between his five Appleton bank accounts. Next he got into his own law firm's computer to leapfrog into Daniel Beckwith's personal station, staying there long enough to read the exchanges about himself between Beckwith and Lesley Corbin in London, and then between Beckwith and Reid in Raleigh. He was intrigued to read Lesley's early opinion of him as 'arrogant although knocked off his feet being caught with his pants around his ankles, a position in which it is always difficult to remain upright', and the correspondence between her and the American lawyer questioning the income possible from professional gambling. It was Lesley, too, who had first suggested he would need repeated instructions on how to conduct himself in court to avoid antagonizing a judge or jury. She'd again used the word 'arrogant'.

Jordan's need for court training was referred to once more in the correspondence between Beckwith and Reid. Of more interest to Jordan was the email discussion between the two American lawyers about potential damage awards, with one suggestion from Reid that if there were individual judgements against Jordan on each listed claim, the total adjudication could go as high as twelve million dollars. Reid's qualification – 'in reality I can't see it reaching half that figure if all awards go against him' – didn't do anything to reassure Jordan.

Neither did Beckwith's response. 'A sum in either of those amounts would inevitably attract national if not international publicity,' Beckwith had written. 'And from what we already know from our preliminary enquiries, both the Appleton and Bellamy families have a recognized social and financial standing on the east coast, which is an added publicity attraction. My client is anxious to avoid publicity, as you tell me your client is, which makes it imperative we establish as soon as possible who the judge is going to be. If it is someone who enjoys notoriety – as I remember several did from the time of my practising in Raleigh – there might be a difficulty in you successfully arguing for a closed hearing. We need to liaise closely on this point.'

Jordan was curious that there had been no exchange between the two men following the Raleigh conference, quickly correcting his impatience with the self-reminder of how recent it had been. Whenever it came – and for as long as he required it in the future – he had this permanently open window into their every thought: into every thought of anyone with whom he found himself entangled.

Except Alyce, he corrected himself sharply. Her lawyer would have been the obvious pathway but nowhere in the man's computer address book could Jordan locate any email exchanges between Reid and Alyce, and so successful and unobstructed had his entry been into all the other computer systems that there was a blip of positive disappointment at his not being able to worm his way into the last of his targets.

He'd been wrong about all his suspicions of Alyce, Jordan acknowledged not even having to force the unfamiliar honesty. He'd been wrong about believing she might in some way be complicit with her husband in trying to get money from him, wrong in imagining that she would have exposed him to the sexual complaint with which she'd been infected, and wrong to have made his hostility so blatantly obvious towards her during the Raleigh encounter. Objectively, continuing the honesty, Jordan accepted that he had been as much the cause of Alyce's misfortune as she was guilty of being his. Judging from what he had just read of Appleton's efforts to uncover Alyce's infidelity to compensate for his own, if he had not so deliberately set out to

181

seduce her, Appleton would have wasted even more money having her pursued by the inappropriately named Watchdog.

Fully aware of the contradictions and inconsistencies there were in the vocation he followed, Jordan would have been the last to claim that he suffered a conscience from his actions and certainly didn't consider that conscience was part of what he was feeling now. But there was at least a genuine regret at behaving as he had towards her in Raleigh. Maybe, he thought, there would be other opportunities to apologize.

There had been several times in the past, working as successfully in America as he had in England, when Jordan had actually considered relocating permanently to the United States. Everything he needed to adopt and take advantage of a new identity was so much more easily and publicly accessible in the States, if a person knew how and where to look – which Jordan did. Upon application the essential and identity-proving Social Security number was readily available; so essential that it was more often than not printed as a guaranteed payee authenticity, along with full addresses, upon personal cheques, which was why he had included Appleton's on all five accounts he'd opened in the trader's name. As he knew from the legal exchanges, it was on Appleton's bank record. Determined upon avoiding any conceivable error on this very particular occasion he confirmed it as he accessed all the social register entries in Boston through the public library reference books and the archives of the *Boston Globe*. Through this he learned the Appleton family history from the Boston tax rebellion, that was the incendiary to the War of Independence, to the marriage of Alfred Appleton's parents, from the records of which he double-checked the family name of the commodity dealer's mother. From the same sources he got the names of the man's prep schools prior to Harvard, into which he phished to learn that pre-college as well as at Harvard Appleton had been considered dilatory and disinterested in anything other than sailing. Through the Harvard records Jordan discovered three police references to drunken driving offences, none with conclusions, all presumably minimized into cautions due to his family money and influence.

It was while he was scrolling through the final Harvard records, cross-referencing dates wherever possible, that Jordan began to be troubled by an inconsistency that he could not immediately isolate, but which remained in his mind as he forced himself on. It was not until he had downloaded everything on to hard copy and was cross-referencing from all his various sources that it became obvious to him, although the basic mystery remained even more tantalizing.

Jordan realized that he had assembled virtually enough information about Alfred Jerome Appleton to write the man's biography. But, missing from any publicly available source Jordan had so far accessed was what Appleton had done in the three years after his Harvard graduation.

How, where and doing what had Appleton spent that time? Jordan wondered.

And wondered further how much it would benefit him to find out. Which he would, Jordan thought, adding this to his list of determinations. And then he thought that Alyce would probably know.

# Fifteen

But there again, she might not, Jordan accepted. He would still have liked to ask her in the hope she could provide a short cut to the information, but didn't think he could – or should – so soon after the lawyers' warning in Raleigh against he and Alyce meeting alone, to which she might not have agreed anyway. And there was the problem of providing a reason for asking the question, although that was not insurmountable.

Instead – after his early morning and now regularly timed raid upon Appleton and Drake's easily available gold mine – Jordan escaped the entombment of the previous two days in his hotel room to take up the search in his preferred way of working by walking the corridors of the reference section of the New York public library, beginning in its Milstein genealogical division. At first it appeared to be a good route. Because the library is the largest sourced library in the world the history of the Appleton family of Boston was far more extensive than any he had been able to access from his laptop, particularly the details of Appleton's sailing prowess, which was recorded with several indexed newspaper and yachting magazine reports. Jordan logged each and, when he had completed primary source searches, worked his way steadily through the microfiched copies of thirty-five different publications.

From them Alfred Appleton began to emerge a world class yachtsman, predicted, not just as a potential US Olympic team choice, but also as an obvious selection for the American team that competed in the America's Cup in 1992. The date rang an immediate bell in Jordan's mind: 1992 was the second of the missing three years. The final reference to Alfred Appleton was in *The Yacht*, in its February edition of that year. The two-line item recorded Appleton's withdrawal – for 'personal reasons' – from among those on the selection list. Jordan switched from where he was working to access the records of the New York Yacht Club, the America's Cup's governing body. Appleton was named four times in the selection procedures in late 1991. Without explanation the man's name dropped out of the list in November of that year. The only other mention was the same as that in *The Yacht*, of Appleton's withdrawal. Again, there was no offered explanation other than the amorphous 'personal reasons'.

Was he trying too hard, Jordan asked himself, so outraged at his entrapment that he was too eager to attach importance where none existed? It was years – although not too many – before Appleton's marriage to Alyce, so those 'personal reasons' were too far in the past to have any possible relevance now. Or did they still have relevance, if the characteristics of honesty or integrity or moral rectitude or whatever other words covered personal behaviour – Appleton's, not his – still applied? Jordan still wanted to know: he still wanted a fully supplied and primed arsenal of every available weapon at his disposal for the battles – wars even – with which he might conceivably be confronted. Or have others declare against him.

But who to fire these supposed weapons? He couldn't, not yet. He was the unwilling conscript press-ganged on to a battlefield upon which he didn't want to be and upon which he couldn't officially shoot back at those who were shooting at him. Others – Beckwith or Reid or both – had to press the triggers, which meant they had to be led to where the ammunition was. He'd come in at the end, to fight his own, already decided and increasingly well-planned guerilla campaign, not needing anyone else's help or company.

Guerilla campaigns relied upon intelligence, the sort of intelligence he was assembling. He was sure there was still some – maybe a lot – that Alyce could provide. How really difficult would it be to seduce her a second time, the difference being that they both kept their clothes on?

Calling upon a sailing analogy, Jordan decided

186

that he was stuck in the doldrums, becalmed by circumstances with no forward movement after such an initial fair wind. This was surely *because* it had been such a good beginning, he acknowledged, pleased at the quickness of the balancing awareness. He'd achieved so much because so much had been literally handed to him on a plate in days instead of his having to probe and scour for weeks or months. So, he consoled himself, thoughts of doldrums and becalming were nothing more than stupid impatience.

He continued to access his strategic computer monitors, disappointed – but no longer impatient – at the absence of any further traffic involving the impending divorce action. It was an afterthought – which surprised him for it not having occurred before – to occupy some of the time towards the end of the week expanding what he already knew of the Bellamy family, which took him back to the New York library's reference section.

What it lacked in terms of noted and recorded American history, it compensated for in longevity with forefathers predating the Appleton arrival in the New World by a good seventy years. A Nathaniel Bellamy was recorded as having fought in the Battle of Yorktown in 1781 and a William Bellamy briefly served on the personal staff of George Washington, although there was no cited, historical event accredited to either man. There were, however, substantial and continuing listings of over three hundred years of Bellamys who'd served in the North

Carolina legislature and five – Alyce's grandfather being the most recent – who had been elected senators to Congress in Washington. It was the grandfather who had founded the Bellamy Foundation which was described as one of the largest charitable groupings in the country. The printed records contained no reference, apart from her birth, to Alyce until her marriage to Appleton. The concentration then had inevitably been on the bonding between the two American founding families, all the details of which Jordan already knew. The one relevant – and contradictory – fact that did stand out to Jordan was the substantial land holdings throughout the state, predominantly in Forsyth, Rowan, Macon, Allamance and Durham counties, of the Bellamy family, which made nonsense of Appleton's claimed offer of financially supporting Alyce's widowed mother. Jordan wondered if Reid had picked up on that – or had it properly pointed out by Alyce – to refute the need, impudence even, for such a suggestion when the case finally reached court.

On the Friday morning, with an empty weekend before him and no contact from Daniel Beckwith, Jordan decided to go again to Atlantic City, and during the drive there made up his mind to call the lawyer on his Monday return. If there was no likelihood of any active court movement, he could use the following week to go back to England and ensure no problems had arisen with the Paul Maculloch identity and the rental of the Hans Crescent flat. With the uncertainty of everything here in America it would be a sensible precaution to extend that lease for a further six months.

'Pullinger,' announced Reid.

'Shit!' said Beckwith.

'It's scarcely a surprise,' said the North Carolina lawyer. 'Hope you don't mind my calling at a weekend, instead of waiting until Monday?'

'I'm glad you did. No point in holding back,' said Beckwith. 'You got the official notification?'

'A friendly call from the circuit office. I'm getting the formal notification in Monday's mail.'

'I guess I'll get one too.'

'You should do.'

'What about a hearing date?'

'Still to be fixed.'

'I guess this puts me first out of the gate?' said Beckwith.

'I had Pullinger's record checked. He's heard three alienation of affection and criminal conversation cases. Each time he's refused pre-trial submissions for dismissal.'

'I ran the same checks,' said Beckwith. 'I've still got to try it.'

'Of course you have,' agreed the other lawyer. 'I'll file for an attendance of interest, obviously.'

'You heard any more from Bartle?'

'I'd have passed it on if I had. I might also apply to Pullinger for a compliance of exchange order, particularly over the medical records.'

'The more we can get Pullinger irritated by the behaviour of the other side the better,' agreed

Beckwith.

'What about Leanne Jefferies?'

'As soon as I get an attorney's response I'm issuing Alyce's claim for alienation of affections and criminal conversation,' said Reid.

'And a medical report for her,' prompted Beckwith.

'The demand will go with the other claims.'

'Anything more from your enquiry people?'

'I'd have passed it on if there had been.'

'We should meet again sometime next week.'

'I guess it's my turn to come up to you,' offered Reid. 'You going to include Harvey?'

'He's very hands-on. And the more he's included in things the better I think he'll perform in court if the dismissal submission fails.'

'I might talk to the circuit office about availability for a closed hearing,' said Reid. 'It's not dependent upon whether you succeed or not.'

'The sooner the better,' said Beckwith. 'The moment there's a public listing the media are going to be alerted. You warned Alyce against any public comment?'

'I have, although it wasn't really necessary. She wants to dig a hole and go hide in it. How about your boy?'

Beckwith's snigger became a laugh. 'He's a tetchy son-of-a-bitch about what and how he's called: to be referred to as "my boy" would send him ape. He certainly doesn't need any warning about talking to the press. He'd like to go hide in the same hole as Alyce.'

'Which was the start of both their troubles,' reminded Reid, coarsely. 'You got your diary with you to talk about next week?'

'Your convenience,' offered Beckwith.

'Wednesday,' chose the other lawyer. 'I might stay over.'

'I'll leave the evening free, in case. Harvey's at the Carlyle, incidentally.'

'High roller,' commented Reid.

'That's what he tells me he is.'

'Let's hope he stays lucky.'

'Let's hope we all stay lucky.'

'Getting Pullinger wasn't lucky,' reminded Reid.

'Luckier,' Beckwith corrected himself.

Jordan picked up the waiting message slips as he checked back in to the Carlyle and returned Beckwith's call the moment he entered his suite.

Beckwith said, 'I tried to get you a couple of times?'

'I went to Atlantic City.'

'How'd you do?'

'Finished $4,500 up over the two days.' And got accredited receipts for a total of $23,000 representing the money he'd taken in to the casinos and switched back and forth between dollars and chips, he reminded himself, more than satisfied with the trip. As he was more than satisfied with the accumulation in the five Appleton accounts in the Wall Street banks, which now stood at $56,000. The following morning he intended withdrawing most of it to put into the waiting safe-deposit boxes.

'We've got Pullinger, the judge we didn't want,' declared Beckwith.

'I was going to call you today to tell you I was thinking of briefly going back to England; see how things are there.'

'You still can. Nothing's going to happen except Bob coming up on Wednesday, to talk a few things through. Bring ourselves up to date.'

'I'll put it back,' decided Jordan at once. 'I'd like to be with you.'

'I thought you would. There's no real reason, though.'

'I'll be there,' insisted Jordan. And lay out as many leads as I can for you to pick up, he thought.

'Your choice.'

'Will Alyce be there?'

'I don't know. Why?'

'Just wondered,' dismissed Jordan. 'Where on Wednesday? What time?'

'I'll let you know.'

He had a day and a half to get all his ideas together for the meeting, thought Jordan: more than enough time.

# Sixteen

The surprise wasn't that the New York meeting was in Beckwith's office but that Alyce was again ahead of him. And that Jordan was pleased to see her. He said, 'Hello, yet again,' and she smiled, very briefly, but didn't speak. To the two lawyers Jordan said, 'I'm sorry to be late. I allowed myself forty-five minutes! I don't know how you manage to work at all in Manhattan.'

'It's an art form,' said Beckwith.

'So how bad is it that we got Pullinger?' asked Jordan, as he sat.

Beckwith sighed. 'You want coffee?'

'I'd rather catch up on what I've missed.'

'You haven't missed anything,' said Reid, as irritated at Jordan's impatience as the other lawyer. 'We small-talked, waiting for you.'

Jordan was aware of Alyce smiling again and this time wished she hadn't. 'Thank you. Coffee would be good.' As well as his not appearing so anxious would have been good, he realized. He'd been thoroughly pissed off by the gridlock and the time it had taken him to stash his bank account money into the safe-deposit boxes, neither of which were causes for him flustering in as he had. He smiled his thanks to Suzie when she came in with his coffee, which he didn't really want, wondering how she managed to breathe in her second-skin virginal white trousers and top.

'So let's pick up on your question,' began Beckwith. 'We're stuck with Pullinger, which is bad luck but something we have to live with. What we really have to do is use the cantankerous old son of a bitch more to our advantage than to Appleton's –' he turned to Alyce – 'I guess we've already covered the ground but we're going to have to talk about your husband as if he's the enemy, OK?'

'As far as I am concerned he *is* the fucking enemy. So let's stop apologizing for something that doesn't need or deserve apology,' responded Alyce.

There was a brief, although not actually shocked, silence and Jordan was glad that her impatience had risen to match his, hoping she took his smile as appreciation, not condescension. As in Raleigh they were away from an official working area. There were more polished plants than in Reid's annex and a skyscraper view uptown towards the unseen park. All the sepia photographs on the wall were of early American settlers and Native Americans, most in full tribal regalia, which Jordan supposed was fitting for someone of Alyce's ancestry and Beckwith's dress code.

'Let's do just that,' said Beckwith, recovering. 'I got the formal notification on Monday and the same day filed for a pre-trial dismissal hearing on our part. I haven't yet got an acknowledgement, obviously...' He paused, gesturing to Reid.

'And I've filed for court acceptance, to be party to each and every pre-hearing application. As well as making our own applications. The first is for court enforcement of our being supplied with Appleton's medical records. The second, again against Appleton – which is the only legal way open to me – is to enforce Leanne Jefferies, upon risk of contempt, to comply with the demands of Alyce's damages claim by providing an attorney reference. Once I have her lawyer through whom to work I can apply for her medical records, to establish if she was a sufferer from chlamydia—'

'What about the other admitted mistress, Sharon Borowski?' broke in Jordan, his script – as well, he hoped, as its presentation – well prepared during the preceding day and a half.

Reid frowned, appearing irritated at having been interrupted. 'I already told you, she's dead—'

'The result of a car accident, not a sexual disease,' broke in Jordan again, looking directly at the North Carolina lawyer. 'Bad luck, Sharon, rest in peace. But if Appleton caught it off her, not Leanne, got himself fixed, and Leanne is provably clean, who gave it to Alyce? I didn't, which we can prove. Which leaves your case that Alyce didn't have any lovers previous to me shot to bits before you even begin, don't you think, Bob?'

From the reaction from both lawyers Jordan thought it was turning into a conference without words: clearly it was a possibility neither had considered.

Eventually Beckwith said, 'That's a damned good point.'

'I suppose Pullinger could order the production of Sharon Borowski's medical records,' said Reid, although doubtfully. There was an asthmatic catch in his voice.

'Do doctors keep medical records of people who've died?' asked Alyce, quietly. 'I wouldn't have thought so.'

'What I do think is that it could be one great big problem for us,' finally admitted Reid.

'Doctors might not keep medical records,' Jordan pointed out. 'Police or coroners might. If she died in a traffic accident there would have been an autopsy, wouldn't there? With a pathology report?'

'Let's hope there was and that the medical examination went beyond finding the immediate cause of death,' said Reid. He was talking now with a discernible wheeze.

The lawyer was embarrassed by his oversight, Jordan knew. As the man deserved to be. Jordan didn't expect any more criticism from his own attorney for playing amateur advocate. 'Could Pullinger refuse to hear a dismissal submission?'

'If he did we could appeal over his head. So he won't,' said Beckwith. He looked towards Alyce. 'I'm going to need to call you, of course.'

'Of course,' she accepted.

'It'll be an opportunity to bring out things that Appleton's attorney might object to being introduced during your full hearing,' picked up Reid, talking to his client. 'That's why I want participation access.'

'Like the missing three years?' questioned Jordan, seizing the obvious opening. They'd judge him a total smart-ass after today. But Jordan didn't give a damn because it was his own ass he was trying to save and that was his only consideration.

There was none of the earlier initial irritation at Jordan's intervention from the two lawyers, although Beckwith said, 'Why do I think we're going to be found wanting again?'

'I've got little else to do here but read the statement exchanges and think about what's there and what's not there,' said Jordan, weighing each word before he spoke, determined against being caught out himself. 'I've spent some time in the library, reading reference books: there's a lot about the Appleton and Bellamy families and their lineage. Appleton left Harvard a golden boy, no suggestion of a job apart from representing his country in the Olympics and being part of the 1992 America's Cup team. It wasn't a question of "if" he'd be selected. It was a done deal. Except it didn't become that. Appleton withdrew, for "personal reasons", from any consideration of selection, for either the Olympics or the America's Cup.' Jordan was talking to Alyce now. 'You any idea what those personal reasons were? Here's a guy, always in the papers, society superstar and then abruptly, nothing for about three years until he joins his first Wall Street brokerage firm before breaking away to set up his own commodity businesses about six months before marrying you.'

For several moments Alyce remained looking

197

contemplatively into her lap. 'I didn't know him in the early nineties, although I knew *of* him, of course. And you're right, he was the golden boy and there was the expectation of him sailing in the Olympics and for the Cup. No one ever really knew why he pulled out of either.'

'*He* pulled out?' pressed Jordan. 'Weren't there any rumours. Didn't you ever ask him, after you got married?'

'I can't remember them all but there were a lot of rumours,' said Alyce. 'There was something about a girl, but that was an obvious speculation: he had the pick of the crop. And I did ask him, after we got married. He said he didn't want to talk about it but that he'd had a nervous breakdown that had to be kept under wraps, that no one would trust a nut who'd needed psychiatric treatment to handle their money...'

'What's the point you're getting to, Harvey?' queried Beckwith. 'As Alyce says, it was before she knew him. Where's the relevance with what we're dealing with now?'

'Maybe there isn't any,' conceded Jordan at once. 'But doesn't character and morality and integrity feature a lot in what we're dealing with now? Why would a man guaranteed to feature – to represent his country – in the two most outstanding events of his chosen sport abruptly back off?'

'Because he got sick, like Alyce just said,' suggested Reid.

Jordan stared at the lawyer, letting the seconds build into minutes. 'Don't you think it's worth having your enquiry guys poke around a little,

198

ask questions? Find out if it's true? I do.'

'So do I, for whatever's discovered,' said Alyce. 'You've forgotten the conversation we had in Raleigh, about my believing he had a mental problem? It could account for a lot of his behaviour. Still could.'

'Like suggesting Alyce's family might need his financial support when from what Alyce tells us was the reverse, when he set up on his own,' said Jordan, snatching for another point. 'Didn't he have family money of his own? You establish he's a fantasist, you establish he fantasized about Alyce having affairs, to excuse his own.'

'You seem to have been working hard on this,' accused Reid, irritation returning. 'Harder than me or the people I employ to find out things for me.'

'I'm not in any sort of contest with you or any-one you employ,' rejected Jordan. 'And I'm not trying to prove anything. I've got every good reason to work harder than anyone else and you can count them all in dollars. Your enquiry people letting you down? Fire them and get better ones.'

Reid flushed, his face hardening further. 'I'm not trying to get into an argument with you here.'

'I just told you, neither am I,' insisted Jordan. 'I thought this was a conference to exchange ideas to help all of us.'

'Which it is,' Beckwith hurried in. 'You got any other specific thoughts or ideas?'

'Nothing specific,' said Jordan. There might even be a benefit from upsetting Reid; assessed from the preceding hour the lawyer certainly needed to try harder than he appeared to have done so far.

'We've started to get the media approaches,' disclosed Reid, anxious to move on. 'I've had calls from the *News and Observer* and from NBC17.'

'They've tried to reach me, too, at the house in Raleigh,' said Alyce. 'I haven't returned the calls, obviously.'

'I told them it was a closed matter,' continued Reid. 'Nothing's appeared so far. The uncertainty is what Appleton's side will say publicly. I've told Bartle I'm going to file for a closed court. Confirmed it in writing, too, in the hope that will restrict whatever Appleton's people might say. If they make a statement ahead of my application, knowing that I'm going to make it, Pullinger might consider it contempt, which would be in our favour.'

'You spoke to Bartle by phone first?' asked Beckwith.

'Yes,' nodded Reid.

'Didn't he give any indication if they'd oppose it?'

'He said he hadn't been called by the media but didn't know if Appleton had, that he hadn't heard from him. And that they're having a meeting today, as we are. They've received notification of Pullinger's appointment, as we have.'

'How'd he sound?' asked Jordan.

Reid humped his shoulders, frowning. 'We're on opposing sides. He didn't sound like anything. If you mean did we talk in any detail, we didn't. I made it sound like I was offering a favour, warning him about Pullinger's possible reaction.'

'Which I might reinforce,' said Beckwith, contemplatively. 'I haven't informed Bartle I'm filing for dismissal. Pullinger could consider it contempt if either Bartle or Appleton spoke in advance of that hearing, too...' He smiled around the room. 'In fact that's what I *will* do! Telephone him today and follow it up with a couriered letter he'll get before today ends.'

'He's meeting Appleton today,' reminded Jordan, unnecessarily. 'You do it right now you give him the opportunity to warn Appleton off from saying anything.'

Now it was Beckwith who let the seconds build before saying, 'Thanks for the prompt, Harvey. We're all of us anxious to button down on publicity. *Right now* was exactly when I was going to break off to make the call: leave Alyce and you and Bob to maybe have some more coffee, talk among yourselves.'

Fuck you, thought Jordan, refusing the intended intimidation. 'It's good to hear we're all moving in the same direction, Daniel. I'll pass on more coffee, though.'

As Beckwith left the conference annexe Alyce said to her lawyer, 'How long before we actually get to court? Get to the end of it all?'

'We get to the end when we get to the end,' said Reid, clumsily. 'I'm not going to agree an actual hearing date – I don't mind how many postponements I get because of Appleton's awkwardness – because every difficulty he creates is to our advantage with a judge like Pullinger. I let one thing go, because we're in too much of a hurry –' he was talking not to his client but directly to Jordan – 'through impatience and the wish to get everything out of the way as quickly as possible, the more you're at risk, both of you, of coming out the guilty parties. And like you've already told me, Harvey, you're counting that risk in dollar signs.'

He had to allow the other man some recovery, Jordan decided. 'Take as much time as is necessary to get it absolutely right.'

'That's precisely what I'm going to do,' insisted Reid. 'What Dan and I are going to do between us, get everything absolutely right.'

Reid had recovered enough, thought Jordan. To Alyce he said, 'You living permanently back in Raleigh now?'

'Mostly. I might stay over a few days here, having come up for this. Check the apartment out. There's got to be a lot of mail.'

'I postponed going back to London because of today. I'll probably go back in a day or two. And I'm sorry about before, that day in Raleigh. I was out of order.'

Her obvious surprise matched that of her lawyer. Alyce said, 'You already apologized for Raleigh.'

'Today it's my idea to do so.'

Alyce smiled, uncertainly. 'Thank you.'

Daniel Beckwith returned noisily from his outer office, his jacket discarded elsewhere, yellow legal pad notes bunched in either hand.

'Bartle isn't seeing Appleton until later this afternoon, so the timing was perfect. He took the point of the call. Several points, in fact. Told me he'd obviously be at the dismissal application, anticipating that he'd be instructed to oppose it.'

'He mention my call?' asked Reid.

'Not a word about it,' said Beckwith.

'What impression did you get?' asked Jordan, inferring that this latest legal exchange had been more productive than that with Reid.

'That neither he – nor Appleton – had expected you to defend the action,' replied Beckwith, smiling. 'I played it for him to come to me. Which he did. He seemed surprised that you were here in New York, that I wasn't representing you *in absentia*.'

So surveillance still hadn't been re-established, Jordan immediately deduced. 'Is that good or bad?'

'Good, for us. Opens the door for me to challenge everything that's claimed against you as well as against Alyce, if my dismissal is rejected and the main hearing proceeds with Leanne Jefferies additionally brought into the action. We don't actually have an outright defence: you've both admitted the adultery. But it strengthens the point – provides the strong mitigation – that Bob hit on in Raleigh, that as far as you were both concerned Alyce's marriage to Appleton was over.'

Jordan hesitated, his mind on what he'd illegally read in Patrick O'Neill's report of the Watchdog agency's failure to find any evidence of Alyce having lovers in Manhattan or Long

Island. 'You know who Appleton's enquiry agency is?'

'Still waiting to be told,' said Reid.

Jordan held out a calming hand towards the North Carolina lawyer. 'We're not in competition, remember? But whoever they are they must have been watching Alyce here, in America. And found nothing. Which they would have done, if there was anything *to* find, judging from the completeness of their observations in France. That's surely in Alyce's favour: part of the mitigation even?'

'I'm not sure it goes as far as the mitigation, but it's a point I thought we'd already touched on,' said Reid. 'Nothing's going to go unchallenged but there's a danger in the very word you used – completeness – in what they achieved in France. It'll be a narrow path to walk. But I'm obviously going to walk it...' The man paused, looking at the other lawyer. 'I'm not sure whether it does more harm than good to your case.'

'Neither am I,' agreed Beckwith, philosophically. 'But the rules are the rules. Your primary responsibility is to your client, my primary responsibility is to mine. We both do what we have to do.'

That hadn't ended up as he'd intended, acknowledged Jordan. There was still more than enough time to improve upon it. He was encouraged at Appleton's lawyer being wrong-footed by him personally contesting the claims, if indeed Bartle had been wrong-footed; he only had Beckwith's impressions from one end of a telephone conversation.

The two lawyers had continued talking during Jordan's reflections, but to all practical purposes they were technically establishing between themselves – although always consulting Alyce and Jordan on their availability – the precedence of pre-hearing submissions and unfulfilled exchange demands to Bartle to be made individually between the two of them. Twice, when they weren't part of any discussion, Alyce smiled at Jordan, on the first occasion mouthing 'thank you', which Jordan didn't understand.

It had gone six before they finally broke off, Jordan holding back for Alyce and Reid to leave the building separately and ahead of him. Still in the annexe, Beckwith said, 'I thought everything went very well.'

'I want everything to go better than very well,' said Jordan. 'I want everything to go *completely* in our favour.'

'He's an arrogant son of a bitch,' accused Reid. 'Suddenly he's a trial lawyer!'

'I told you he was arrogant before you met,' reminded Beckwith. 'The points he made were valid, though.'

They were eating in a restaurant in Little Italy, a cavern filled with noise making it difficult for them to hear each other and impossible to be overheard by others.

'We'd have got it covered,' insisted Reid.

'He covered it first,' said Beckwith. 'I prefer clients who think for themselves instead of expecting me to do everything for them.'

'You really think Bartle was surprised at your third-party involvement?'

'I even thought at one stage he was going to suggest a pre-trial consultation between us.'

'To slim down the claims to an agreed settlement?' guessed Reid.

'There's an argument for doing so. As you said at the meeting, the adultery is admitted.'

'Do you think Jordan would go for it?'

'He's made the point a few times that gamblers don't gamble. If he got the possibility of millions pared down to a few thousand – but with the guilt legally established – it might appeal to him.' He gestured towards the other lawyer. 'You just dropped spaghetti sauce down your tie.'

Reid scrubbed at himself with his napkin. His head still bent he said, 'That would kind of divide us, wouldn't it?'

'And be a clever legal move for Bartle to make.'

'What are you going to do?'

'Nothing. Wait for him to come to me. Like I told you, it's only my guess.'

'When are you going to file your dismissal submission?'

'Tomorrow. Everything's ready.'

'So we could get a submission date set as early as next week?'

'Not if Bartle hasn't complied with all the exchanges. And we're still waiting on Leanne Jefferies. I really can't see why he's holding back on Appleton's medical stuff.'

'Unless it proves Appleton was or is infected.'

206

'If it does, Appleton's case is holed below the waterline,' insisted Beckwith. 'It can't be that simple.'

'Then why?' demanded Reid.

'I don't know,' admitted Beckwith. 'When I file for dismissal I'm going to make the point that if I lose the submission I can't proceed to full hearing until I've received everything that's legally got to be exchanged.'

'Did you tell Bartle that?'

'It was when I told him exactly that I thought he was going to offer negotiation.'

'Maybe you've put a fox into the hen coop?'

'Rather me doing it to him than the reverse, his doing it to us.'

'You going to mention it to Harvey?'

'Not unless I get the approach from Bartle. There's no point until I do.'

'I'd like to hear, the moment you do. It could affect everything as far as I am concerned.'

'Of course you'll know. If it happens...' Beckwith pointed across the table. 'You've dropped some more sauce.'


Jordan recognized Alyce's voice the moment he picked up the telephone in his Carlyle suite. 'Hello,' he said, in reply to her opening, pleased the curiosity didn't sound in his voice.

'I want to say thank you again, for what you did today, said today. A lot of things wouldn't have been brought out if you hadn't been there.'

'Change your lawyer if you're not happy,' offered Jordan.

'He's the best there is in Raleigh.'

'Which doesn't say much for Raleigh.'

'From being with you in France I wouldn't have thought you were this ruthless.'

'This isn't France and we're not having an adventure. This is reality with blood on the floor.'

'I wish it wasn't,' Alyce countered.

'You and me both. How did you know I was here, at the Carlyle?'

'Bob told me. He showed me your statement, too. Why did you tell me you were an investment banker when you're not?'

'I thought it sounded better: more respectable.'

'We weren't being respectable.'

Jordan hesitated, considering his reply. 'And now look where we are.'

'If you don't get dismissed from the case I want to take full responsibility in court.'

'You discussed that with Bob?'

'No.'

'Don't you think you should? It might screw up the way he's going to argue your case.'

'I did use you, to get my own back on Alfred.'

'And told me as much in France. You didn't know all this was going to happen.' He'd have to tell Beckwith what she was saying: offering. It might do more to harm than help his defence, although he couldn't think how.

'We'll see. You going to make the trip back to England?'

'I think so. You going to stay on here in Manhattan?'

'I think so. When will you be back?'

'I don't know. I shouldn't need more than a

day in London. I can fly back here on the last flight the second night.'

'I want it all to be over soon.'

'You said.'

'You don't mind my calling?'

'Of course I don't.'

'I'm sorry you got caught up in everything like this,' Alyce apologized.

'You said that, too. More than once.'

'Take care.'

'And you. Try to think more about the three years immediately after your husband left Harvard.'

There was a pause from Alyce's end of the line before she said, 'You have this number?'

'No.'

'You have a pen?'

'Yes.'

She dictated it and added, 'Call me when you get back?'

'I will,' promised Jordan. He knew from accessing the computers of Appleton and his enquiry agency that they weren't under surveillance any more, so they didn't have to bother about their lawyers' warnings about being together.

# Seventeen

Harvey Jordan extended his intended absence from New York by twelve hours, getting back into Manhattan by the middle of the third day. There were three messages waiting for him at his Carlyle suite, which he'd maintained to provide just such a contact point. One was from Daniel Beckwith. The other two were from Alyce. Before responding to any of them Jordan checked his intrusion traps, which were undisturbed, and after that settled before his laptop at the bureau and steadily worked his way through his illegal Trojan Horses, none of which he'd accessed from London, adhering strictly to the unbreakable operational rule never to cast his phishing nets from more than one dedicated computer. He was particularly careful going into the system of Appleton and Drake, alert for any indication that his entry had been picked up on, which there wasn't. Still preying on the currency trades, he spread almost $22,000 between his five accounts.

From Beckwith's system Jordan was easily able to infer contact from legal representation of both Alfred Appleton and Leanne Jefferies through the exchanges between his lawyer and Alyce's, even though they were disjointed and incomplete because the two attorneys were obviously communicating, irritatingly, sometimes by email and on other occasions by telephone. Jordan's further, even more irritating discovery was that Leanne Jefferies was being represented by Brinkmeyer, Hartley and Bernstein, the same firm engaged by Appleton but by a different partner. Leanne's lawyer was Peter Wolfson, whose name was listed directly below that of Appleton's attorney, David Bartle, on the company letterhead. Jordan ignored the immediate disappointment, quickly switching to his Trojan Horse stabled in the Brinkmeyer system in his search for electronic correspondence between Wolfson and Bartle. As he'd feared, there wasn't any.

Jordan finally allowed the frustration to burst over him, physically hot. If Bartle and Wolfson were going to discuss everything between themselves within their own Madison Avenue building, which was clearly and most naturally what they would do, apart from occasional, but so far uninitiated, email contact with either Beckwith or Reid, there was no possibility of him eavesdropping on their thoughts or strategies. Objectively acknowledging his over-expectation, Jordan had still imagined he could sit upon the highest pinnacle overlooking everyone's manoeuvrings and scrabblings, always to be ahead of every opposing move. What he had – *precisely* with all his computer entries – was the best spot in the foothills. Still sufficient. Still enough. But only just: not, by any assessment, as complete as he wanted his monitoring to be. But then he hadn't yet accessed every site open to him. Still hopeful, Jordan followed his well-marked trail into every other hidden observation point in every other invaded computer. But found no further revelations, finally slumping back in the over-padded chair.

He'd hoped for so much more, some closely guarded confidence – confessions or admissions even – between the lawyers and their clients that he could have turned to his advantage. He at least knew things were moving forwards. For the moment, but not much more than a moment, he had to be satisfied.

Jordan was connected at once to Daniel Beckwith, who said, 'Welcome back! I hear there's more money in the pot?'

More for my benefit than yours, thought Jordan. He supposed he shouldn't be surprised by the quickness with which Lesley Corbin had alerted Beckwith to his visit to Chancery Lane to deposit a further fifty thousand dollars – she was the essential conduit, after all – but he was. 'I thought it was a good idea. What's happened here while I was away?'

'We've got our pre-trial submission hearing next Wednesday,' said the American. 'We need to meet before then, obviously. And travel down on the Tuesday...' There was a pause. 'You want Suzie to make your hotel reservation along with mine? Or do you want to do it yourself? The hotel choice isn't great.'

Beckwith had been curbed, Jordan recognized. 'We'll need to be together in the same hotel. I'd be grateful for Suzie doing it at the same time as

212

she books yours. What other developments have there been?'

'Leanne is being represented by the same people who are looking after Appleton, although obviously not by the same attorney. She's contesting Bob's claim of criminal conversation.'

Why hadn't he found that on Reid's computer? wondered Jordan. An official, legal and lengthily argued rebuttal on original court-submitting papers, he guessed; he still thought there would have been some email reference he could have picked up upon. Jordan was discomfited at the possibility of more windows being shut against him. 'How's that affect us?'

'It doesn't, directly. Her lawyer is a guy named Wolfson, Pete Wolfson. Bob hasn't yet got their official response, just a phone call telling him they're opposing it.'

'What about medical records?'

'Promised by the week's end. I've already filed for a court order, demanding production in case it doesn't arrive by then. Even if it does it'll form part of the record for Pullinger to realize their reluctance.'

'There doesn't seem to be any point in our meeting until Friday at the earliest then?' suggested Jordan.

'The medical stuff doesn't directly impact upon our application,' Beckwith pointed out. 'We're not reliant upon it, one way or the other, at this stage.'

'I want to be as up to date as possible,' insisted Jordan.

'You will be,' assured Beckwith.

He was appearing too anxious again, accepted Jordan. 'What about media interest?'

'Increasing,' replied Beckwith. 'I got a call from the London *Times* the day before yesterday. Bob's hoping to get his closed court hearing next week too, depending upon the length of ours, which technically has to precede what Bob does. I don't see why we should need more than one day, although Pullinger could reserve judgement. Which shouldn't stand in Bob's way, even if Pullinger refuses my submission.'

'Did *The Times* have my name?' demanded Jordan, alarmed.

'That's all that's listed, nothing else that could identify you,' said Beckwith. 'I refused to talk about anything: answer any questions.'

'They must know I'm English to have called in the first place.'

'Your being English wasn't the direction of their approach. It was all about the break-up of two of the oldest American colonial families.'

'They could get the lead from Appleton's side,' said Jordan, more to himself than to the other man. He should have warned the London concierge, John Blake. He still could, although not today. It was 8.30 p.m. in England. Blake would have left the building by now. It had to be his first telephone call tomorrow.

'I warned Bartle about contempt,' reminded Beckwith.

'They wouldn't be risking that, guiding people to me. And I can't imagine the threat of it restraining British newspapers for a moment.'

'I can't do any more than I've already done to

prevent your identity coming out,' said the lawyer, the impatience obvious.

Too anxious again, accepted Jordan. 'Let's wait until Friday to meet.'

'You going to be at the Carlyle all the time until then?'

'All the time,' promised Jordan.

'I'll call you if anything comes up in between. Let's say eleven on Friday. I'll have Suzie make plane reservations to Raleigh as well. This time next week we should know where we are.'

'That's what I want to know,' said Jordan. 'Exactly where we are.' The light on his telephone console began to flicker, indicating a waiting call.

'You're back!'

'Just walked through the door.' Jordan instantly knew the voice. 'I was just going to return your calls.'

'How was London?' asked Alyce.

'I got done what I went there to do.' Jordan hadn't expected it to take most of one day to extend the Hans Crescent lease, sort out the query letters held for him at Royston and Jones bank and – a spur of the moment decision, despite what he was now accumulating in the accounts in New York – to withdraw additional funds to deposit with Lesley Corbin, all of which had delayed his return by those twelve hours.

'You spoken to Dan yet?'

'A minute or two ago.' This could so easily have been a casual, how-was-your-trip conversation.

'So you know Leanne entering a defence?'

215

He had to ignore the lawyers' warnings against contact with Alyce, Jordan decided: without being able to intercept any computer correspondence between her and her lawyer she was his only access to her side of the case. Testingly he said, 'Only that. Dan didn't go into any detail.'

'We're matching every claim Alfred is making against you,' responded Alyce, without hesitation. 'And intend inviting the jury to award punitive damages against Leanne Jefferies, as well. Bob sent our detailed claim to her lawyer yesterday; he's from the same firm representing Alfred, incidentally. Bob thinks that's a bad move on their part. Could be interpreted that Alfred and Leanne are still involved.'

As this conversation could be interpreted against him and Alyce, Jordan thought. The idea came with that reflection, as well as the awareness that the prompt to Reid had to come from Alyce. He said, 'The way to bring it out in court would be for Bob to cross-examine her on who was paying for her defence.'

'Yes it would, wouldn't it?' agreed the woman, just as quickly.

From the tone in which she talked Jordan imagined the woman to be smiling. 'Maybe you should mention it to Bob?'

'Already decided,' said Alyce, the smile still in her voice.

'You back in Raleigh?'

'Still in Manhattan. I had more to do here than I thought.'

'The application for my dismissal from the case is being heard next week.'

'I know. I'm on standby to be a witness in your favour, if necessary.'

'Why didn't you tell me?' He had to lead her thinking into telling him everything.

'I thought I did at the conference in Raleigh; that I would support the application in any way I could?'

'I hadn't appreciated it to be as positive as that. I can't imagine how I could help as far as you are concerned, but you know I'll be there for you in whatever way I can.'

'I think you did tell me. But thank you for telling me again.'

'Let's do that,' urged Jordan. 'Tell each other things at the risk of repetition.' He had to know *everything*.

'I...' started Alyce but abruptly stopped.

'What?' demanded Jordan.

'Nothing,' refused Alyce. 'Newspapers – the media in general – are chasing me. That's another reason – the main reason, I suppose – for my not going back to Raleigh. They're watching the estate: virtually camped outside.'

'But not here in Manhattan?'

'This is a new address, since I got back from France. What about...?' Alyce trailed to a halt again.

'What?'

'My arm's getting tired, holding the phone up for so long.'

He needed the continuing conduit, Jordan reminded himself again. 'Your guy – and mine – insisted we shouldn't meet unchaperoned.'

'Which I think is bullshit.'

217

'That's what we're employing them for – advice.'

'I still think it's bullshit. We're adults, for Christ's sake!'

'Looking at a lot of potential problems we don't want to make any worse.'

'I shouldn't have started this.' The smile had gone from her voice.

'Nothing's started.' He needed her, Jordan recognized. Needed her as a source of information and needed her support if she had to be a witness at the dismissal hearing. And he knew from accessing the Watchdog computer less than an hour ago that neither he nor Alyce remained under any surveillance.

'Let's forget it,' she said, tightly.

'What were you thinking of?'

'I don't know what I was thinking of. It's not important.'

'We're each of us too dependent upon the other to fall out.'

'Who's falling out?'

'It sounds to me like we could be. The first time I made the mistake and I apologized, twice.'

'It just seems so ... I don't know ... childish I guess, that we can't talk to each other properly.' Now the impatience had gone.

'It would be better if you came here, somewhere public, and we had dinner very publicly in the restaurant, rather than me coming to your apartment.'

'I wasn't inviting you to my apartment.'

'Then my suggestion works. I'll make a reservation and be waiting for you in the lobby ... say seven, seven thirty.'

There was a brief silence from the other end of the line before Alyce said, 'I'll be there at seven.'

There'd be a minimal insurance in telling Daniel Beckwith, Jordan supposed. But not tonight. Afterwards.

Alyce Appleton came into the hotel lobby precisely at seven with the self-assurance of someone who knew her rightful place in such moneyed surroundings; an impression that had come to Jordan in France but which he had forgotten until now. She saw him at once – which he'd intended, unlike the initial subterfuge at the Carlton – and continued on without pause, her face opening into a smile as she reached him. The blonde hair was loose and he saw at once that the diamond ring had been discarded, as well as the wedding ring. The shawl over one shoulder matched the blue of her skirt and made the perfect contrast against the paler sweater and Jordan was conscious of the looks that followed her, from women as well as men.

She said, 'Hi. Quite like old times, meeting in hotels again!'

'Not quite the same, though,' qualified Jordan, surprised by the lightness.

'Perhaps not,' she agreed, falling into step as he led towards the bar. She chose mineral water to his martini. As they touched glasses she said, 'You want to know a secret?'

'As many as there are to know,' Jordan said,

meaning it.

'I almost chickened out at the last minute, about coming tonight. I actually went back from the corridor into my apartment, to think.'

'Why didn't you?'

Alyce shrugged. 'This is my call, isn't it, us meeting like grown-ups? I thought about what we discussed on the phone, about Alfred and Leanne still being together.'

'Are they?' pounced Jordan, at once. 'Have Bob's enquiry people come up with something?'

She shrugged again. 'I mean about what you said, about their both being represented by the same firm. Bob hasn't told me anything of what his detectives have discovered. That's what they are, aren't they? Detectives?'

'I guess,' dismissed Jordan, disinterested in an immaterial definition; he knew from his earlier exploration of Reid's computer that there had been no email contact from any enquiry agency. 'But you changed your mind again and now you're here.'

'And I'm glad. What happened in France was wonderful and what's happened since is total, awful shit and I like the idea of our being able to behave for a couple of hours as normal people – as friends, most definitely not lovers – and now we've got it out of the way I want to stop talking about it. There!'

'Very positive,' judged Jordan.

'I used to be once, before I married Alfred. He took me over. Mr Svengali.'

'I didn't get the impression of you being beaten into submission in France.'

'In France I'd escaped. I was free. It was a good feeling. One I hadn't known for far too long. Not since...'

Jordan waited and when she didn't continue said, 'Not since when?'

Alyce shook her head. 'France really was wonderful. Immediately before that, back here, I'd actually tried therapy, imagining it was my fault everything had gone wrong with the marriage. This is beginning to sound just like one of those therapy sessions, without the couch and with more noise. I don't want to talk about it any more, OK?'

No it's not OK, thought Jordan, disappointed. He said, 'OK. Why don't we eat?'

He'd personally chosen a corner banquette table at which they could sit side by side but separated at its apex, looking out over the dining room. She deferred to him choosing the wine, as he had in France, and restricted herself to two glasses, again as she had in France. He accepted her suggestion of the Chesapeake soft shelled crabs and they shared a chateaubriand. Jordan cut short Alyce's renewed apology for him becoming involved in the divorce action and they agreed that neither was looking forward to the following week's court hearings.

'Who's ever heard of an affair being described as a criminal conversation, for Christ's sake!' exclaimed Alyce. 'It must date from the time we burned witches.'

'Everyone in North Carolina has heard of it, apparently,' replied Jordan, ignoring the rhetoric. 'And I agree it's unbelievable that laws like it still exist in the United States of America ... exist anywhere that imagines itself to be halfway civilized. Our problem is that there's nothing we can do about it except go with the system, as half-assed as it is.'

'Does Dan really think he can get you dismissed from the case?'

'I guess he wouldn't be trying if he thought it would be a total waste of time.'

'When are you going down to Raleigh?'

'Somewhen over the weekend, I suppose. I've agreed to Dan making the arrangements. You?'

'The same, I guess. You know where you're staying?'

Jordan shook his head. 'Dan says there isn't a wide choice.'

'There isn't. I'm glad I changed my mind tonight and came after all. It reminds me a lot of France.'

'But for the differences we've already agreed.'

'But for the differences we've already agreed,' she echoed, smiling. 'That reminds me of France, too. Saying the same things to each other.'


'No doubt whatsoever?' queried Jordan, although he accepted there couldn't be from what Daniel Beckwith had just told him.

'Read it for yourself,' suggested Beckwith, pushing the venerealogist's report across the desk.

Jordan did, twice. Looking back up to the lawyer he said, 'So how did Alyce, who says I was her only other sexual partner apart from her husband, contract chlamydia?'

'That's what I asked Bob, before you got here this morning. And what he's going to ask her.'

'What else did he say?'

'That Alyce is thirty-one years old and if she's only ever had two lovers so far she's the next in line to the Virgin Mary.'

'That's not funny.'

'Bob wasn't trying to be funny. He's one big pissed off attorney.'

'Alyce lied: is lying,' decided Jordan, the awareness spreading through him. He hadn't learned anything from the Carlyle dinner, making it a waste of time, but he'd had that time to waste and he'd enjoyed being with her – and talking to her again the following day when she'd telephoned to thank him – and now he knew she'd been treating him like a fool – treating all of them like fools.

'She's got to be lying, hasn't she?' said Beckwith. 'It's knocked Bob's case to hell and back. He'd just read Leanne Jefferies' medical report when I spoke to him this morning. She's clean, too.'

'I met her this week,' suddenly declared Jordan, knowing that it was essential that he did. 'The same day that I got back from London. We had dinner together.'

'You met Leanne Jefferies?' frowned Beckwith, confused.

'Alyce,' corrected Jordan. 'She called me after I spoke to you that morning. Called it childish that we shouldn't meet. You should know.'

'You're damned right I should know!' erupted

223

the lawyer, his face colouring. 'We told you, Bob *and* I, that you shouldn't be together without one of us being there as well. Why the fuck...?'

'It did seem childish that we couldn't meet, like two normal people,' said Jordan, defensively. 'We had dinner, talked...'

'Stop right there, right now!' ordered Beckwith, his face redder with anger, holding up a hand. 'Did you sleep with her?'

'No, I didn't sleep with her!'

'You sure?'

'What the fuck do you mean, am I sure! Of course I'm sure! How could I not be sure?'

'I want it all ... what you ate, what you drank, who you saw or who might have seen you, every single thing you said and talked about to each other ... every fucking thing you did!'

'Let's work your questioning backwards,' insisted Jordan, refusing the returning intimidation. 'We didn't fuck. The conversation came down to reminiscences, of France, apart from Alyce telling me that during their marriage Appleton psychologically controlled her. We would have been seen, by the hotel CCTV, always in public places. We had one drink, in the bar – she drank water, I had one martini – we ate soft shelled crabs and steak, with a vintage Chateau Margaux. I got the concierge to call her a cab and personally put her into it, all of which should be shown on the CCTV and confirmed by the hotel staff. We weren't alone or out of sight for a minute and we can prove it. OK?'

'No, not OK,' rejected Beckwith, stridently. 'You were told, both of you, not to get together

224

in any way or circumstance that could be construed that your relationship was ongoing. Whether you considered that advice childish or stupid doesn't come into any calculation or thinking. It doesn't matter a damn what you think or whether or not you agree with that advice. That's what you're paying a whole bunch of money for me to provide and why you're stupid, if you choose to ignore it. We know now – and the court is going to know – that Alyce has lied. And the court is also going to know – because I've got to tell them to avoid being made to look a jerk if I don't tell them and there's even more photos of you and Alyce in a hugger-mugger hotel setting – that you're still seeing each other. Which totally fucks my plan of insisting next week that there is no continuing relationship, that you're not trying to alienate Alyce's affections and that you're not engaging in every definition of criminal conversation, according to the relevant North Carolina statute...' The man paused, breathless.

Recovering, he said, 'I don't think I've missed any of the important points of how well you've done blowing your defence to a multi-million-dollar damages claim right out of the water, do you, Harv? You think I've overlooked something, why don't you tell me?'

'It's Harvey. My name is Harvey, not Harv.'

'At this precise moment your name is cunt-of-the-month. Alyce Appleton has a string through your nose ring and you could end up a very poor man.'

'Leanne Jefferies' attorney is from the same
225

firm representing Appleton,' argued Jordan, weakly. 'Doesn't that indicate they're still together?'

Beckwith sat staring across the table at Jordan, unspeaking, until finally Jordan said, exasperated, 'What?'

'Let me ask you what. What the fuck has that got to do with anything? It's nothing whatsoever to do with you, with us, with our case. If Appleton is still fucking Leanne's brains out that's for Bob to prove and get Leanne to pay for, for her criminal conversations. I'm trying to get you off the hook and you've stuffed it right up your own ass. You know what I'd like to do right now? I'd like to withdraw from this case and from representing you. I think you've put me into a no-win situation and I'm a *win* person, not the other way round.'

'So why don't you withdraw?'

'Because if I did I'd render you unrepresentable by any other attorney, which would leave you swinging in the wind, and I've got more integrity than that. I'll go on doing my absolute and very best and you'll pay through the nose for every second that I'm doing it. Until today trying to help you was damage minimization. Now it's damage limitation, with whatever minimization I can work in as a bonus.'

'I suppose I should thank you.'

'I've had more than a gutful of what you suppose and I couldn't give a bag of rotting shit for your gratitude. I'll have to tell Bob about your tryst, obviously. Now we'll have to go down to Raleigh tomorrow, give ourselves as

226

much time as possible to see what he's going to do and re-assemble my submission...' The lawyer hesitated, halted by an afterthought. 'You got any more hand-holding assignations planned with Alyce, the forgetful virgin?'

'No. And we didn't hold hands. Or anything else.'

'Good,' said Beckwith. 'And don't, not ever again.'

# Eighteen

There was a palpable tension between the three of them in Reid's office annex on that deserted Saturday. Dividing them, on Reid's desk, were the finally supplied medical reports on Alfred Appleton and Leanne Jefferies, as well as covering letters and copies of the woman's rebuttals to Alyce's criminal conversation damages claim. There were, also for the first time, photographs of Appleton's supposedly brief mistress. Jordan was not surprised that, although older by six years, Leanne closely resembled Alyce in appearance and physique, confirming the adage that men always chose lovers that reminded them of their wives.

Reid gestured towards the documentation and said, 'So there it all is, as far as my cases are concerned. A heap of shit.'

'Not helped by continuing cosy hotel meetings between you and Alyce,' came in Beckwith, whose criticism of Jordan's Carlyle dinner with Alyce had concluded the review meeting in advance of the forthcoming court hearings. They'd flown down on the first available flight and this time there hadn't been any tourist detours, just a fifteen-minute delay booking into the Hilton hotel. Reid had alerted them that Appleton intended to stay at the Sheraton during the hearing.

'Let's right now get some of that unnecessary shit out of the way to concentrate on what's really important,' demanded Jordan. 'I don't see and won't concede that Alyce and I having had an innocent dinner, before or after which nothing occurred to resume our affair, could be any great big deal. Neither do I see the necessity to volunteer it to the court. I volunteered it to you so you wouldn't be caught out. Neither of you will be under oath to tell the whole truth and nothing but the truth if this goes the whole way. I will be. Alyce will be. If it gets brought out, it gets brought out. Let's deal with it then. I didn't see any reason why I shouldn't meet her as I did and I still don't. And I don't – and won't – believe either of you haven't sat on your hands in the past about something you knew but didn't want to come out in court and therefore didn't say anything about. You both still with me?'

'And wish I wasn't,' said Reid.

'I'm not your immediate problem,' insisted Jordan, waving his hand towards the separating desk and what was on it. 'Those medical reports are your immediate problem. What does Alyce say about them?'

Both lawyers had fixed expressions on their faces, but only Beckwith was visibly flushed.

'What she's said from the beginning,' replied the heavily breathing Reid. 'That she's only had sexual relationships with her husband and with you. Which has—'

'OK,' stopped Jordan. 'So what do your enquiry people say? I know you're employing them, because you've told me. What you haven't told me is anything that they've so far discovered to help, in any way whatsoever. Appleton's people failed to find any proof of Alyce's cheating, until France. At the moment your opposition snoops are doing more for you than your own people are doing for you, don't you agree?'

'I've no reason nor cause to defend those I'm employing,' rejected Reid, awkwardly. 'But as you've raised it again I certainly intend bringing out Appleton's failure to discover any lover other than you.' The man looked sideways, to the other lawyer. 'But I don't intend mentioning the Carlyle dinner. Alyce hasn't told me about it; you have. We're co-operating for mutual benefit, not disadvantage, and at this precise moment I don't need any more disadvantages than I've already got.'

'I'm listening to what everyone's saying,' assured Beckwith, dully. 'Maybe I won't volunteer the Carlyle episode either. But can we establish here and now –' he turned to include Reid – 'and you get the specific undertaking from

229

Alyce, that there's no more social meeting, not even if the Pope is in the same room with you. I don't care if you think it's a childish insistence, or whether Alyce thinks it's a childish insistence, or what the fuck either of you think about the divorce statutes of North Carolina. Like it or not, they *are* the statutes, the rules, by which you're being judged.'

'I think we went through this yesterday, in New York,' dismissed Jordan.

'And before yesterday in New York we very specifically went through it down here in Raleigh. And you – and she – ignored the advice,' persisted Beckwith. 'It happens again, I'm definitely withdrawing.'

This time Jordan didn't respond with the direct challenge of the previous day.

Instead, he said, 'So what about the most immediate problem?'

Turning again to the other lawyer, Beckwith said, 'To get Harvey dismissed I'm obviously going to have to call Alyce on Wednesday. And hit her as hard as is necessary to prove she's both promiscuous as well as being prepared to lie.'

'I've already told her that – told her the impossible position these medical reports put her in,' said Reid. 'I thought it was the way to get an admission about who else she slept with and who gave her the infection.'

'What did she say?' asked Jordan, disregarding any professional protocol. There was an incongruity – yet another nagging inconsistency – hovering in Jordan's mind but it wouldn't harden into a positive thought.

230

'I already told you,' snapped Reid. 'She insists there's only ever been two men, her husband and you.'

'She can't maintain that in court, confronted with this medical evidence,' said Beckwith.

'I told her that, too. And late last night I heard from Wolfson. He's filed for Leanne's dismissal; he told me he's subpoenaing Alyce. He's obviously going to use Leanne's medical report.'

'I think your client's going to be massacred,' said Beckwith, unsympathetically.

'I think so, too,' agreed Reid.

'Isn't it your job to prevent that happening?' demanded Jordan.

'The moment she tells me the truth I'll start trying,' said Reid, just as belligerently.

'You've got two days to persuade her,' Beckwith told the other lawyer. 'Until you do convince her your case isn't worth a bucket of piss.'

'It still won't be, even if she does change her story,' said Reid.

'You've got *three* days,' corrected Jordan. 'She told me at the hotel she was coming down this weekend, which gives you tomorrow, Sunday, to talk to her if she's already arrived.'

Reid looked casually at his watch. 'Maybe I'll give her a call when we're through.'

The man was giving up before any fight began, looking for a mitigating escape, just as he was, Jordan decided. 'What about the Carlyle meeting? If you both decide not to mention it in court, unless she or I are directly challenged, you'd better tell her not to say anything about it either, hadn't you?'

231

'I'm definitely not going to mention it now,' confirmed Beckwith, talking not to Jordan but to Reid. 'You'd better do what Harvey suggests.'

'Of course I'll warn her!' said Reid, irascibly.

'What about those missing three years after Appleton's graduation?' pressed Jordan, already knowing there was no computer correspondence between the lawyer and any enquiry agency, although accepting that it all could have been done by written letters, formal reports and telephone calls. He began concentrating upon what lay on the separating table. As nothing there was directly linked to him he didn't have the automatic legal right to copies of his own. Reid had only paraphrased everything, not offering facts he could study and memorize in detail. All he could make out were the different names of the supplying venerealogists and their different addresses, both of which were in Boston.

'What the hell good is anything that long ago going to provide?' demanded Reid, repeating his earlier objection.

'You won't know until you find out, and from where I'm sitting you don't seem particularly anxious to find out.'

'I don't need to share these conferences with you!' retorted Reid. 'Get out!'

'You sure you don't?' said Jordan, not moving from his chair. 'The way I recall it I've so far thrown most of the positive ideas into the pot.'

'You know fuck all!' erupted Reid.

'Which is what you're complaining about, knowing fuck all,' said Jordan. 'Maybe you need to change the direction of your enquiries as well as changing the people you appoint to make them for you.'

'And maybe you need to do what I've just told you and get the hell out of my office and my building!' said Reid. 'We're through, all three of us!'

That night the local television station finally broke the story of the divorce between the thirty-one-year-old member of one of North Carolina's earliest settler dynasties and that of the scion of one of the founding New England families. As well as still photographs of both Alyce and Appleton – two from their wedding – there was archival TV footage of Appleton competing in yacht races off Long Island and at the Cowes Week regatta in England's Isle of Wight. The story was based upon a court submission to be made in the coming week on behalf of a cited co-respondent in Alfred Appleton's case against his wife, alleging criminal conversations. Harvey Jordan was mentioned by name but there were no photographs.

Jordan waited until after seven in the expectation that Daniel Beckwith might make contact but decided against calling the lawyer's room in the floor above, wanting an uninterrupted evening. He ordered dinner from room service, glad his photograph hadn't appeared on television, reminding himself to call John Blake again at the Marylebone apartment block the following day, to check once more about media approaches. Glad, too, that he'd brought with him the laptop and all the copied correspondence to which he was entitled, in addition to the names and

Boston addresses he'd memorized that afternoon in Reid's office. He didn't know, but he guessed he was going to need it all to satisfy whatever it was that was nagging in his mind.

Reid had promised it was the best seafood restaurant in Raleigh, one that he didn't know from when he'd practised there, but Beckwith had been disappointed. He was uncomfortable, too, that the local lawyer was already on his third gin martini, very dry and straight up, without any diluting ice. Beckwith was still on his first.

'You should dump the motherfucker now,' insisted Reid. 'He's so fucking smart, what's he need a qualified lawyer for!' The man had pushed his lobster aside, scarcely touched.

'You fully up to speed to argue against Leanne's dismissal?'

'I will be by the time it gets before Pullinger.'

'Jordan's a pain in the ass and I suppose I should apologize for today as he's my client, but nothing much – nothing that seriously contradicts or undermines anything Appleton's filed against Alyce – seems to have been turned up.'

'Tell me anything better that your guys have found!' demanded the other man, with drunken truculence.

'The cases are different,' Beckwith pointed out. 'All I've got to argue with is North Carolina law ... and unfortunately the morals of your client, now that we've got all the test reports. We're admitting the adultery. We didn't have any alternative.'

'I'm going to speak with the enquiry agents on

Monday. Put a burr up their ass. And seeing Alyce tomorrow. How the hell can I prepare any sort of a defence – a case – until she starts being straight with me! She's the plaintiff who initiated the divorce proceedings, for Christ's sake!'

Reid gestured with his empty martini glass for a refill. When the waiter responded the man looked enquiringly at Beckwith who ordered Chardonnay, a glass, not a bottle.

Beckwith said, 'You don't have enough time, if Wolfson gets his hearing at the end of the coming week. Even if she comes straight tomorrow there's still whatever might come out under my cross-examination on Wednesday which you'll have to go through with her all over again. You need to apply for a delay; it was a sharp move for Wolfson to file for dismissal right on the back of my application.'

'You think you'll get judgement in your favour?'

Beckwith accepted his wine from the returning waiter, reflectively cupping the glass between both hands to consider the question. 'Depends what I can bring out from Alyce. Now we've got the medical proof that Appleton and Leanne can't have been the cause of Alyce's infection, my strategy has got to be that Alyce entrapped Harvey as the fall guy, intending to name him herself to cover up for her unknown lover, whoever the hell he is. Or *they* are. But didn't have to, because of the entrapment Appleton already had in place for her. Before the medical clearances, I reckoned my chances of dismissal were less than fifty percent, thirty tops. Now I'm still only giving myself fifty percent, with a son of a bitch like Judge Herbert D Pullinger.'

'Everything depends on what Alyce says. Or doesn't say,' said Reid, more maudlin than reflective.

'What time are you seeing her?'

'We fixed ten.'

'Tomorrow's Sunday. We could brunch somewhere after you've met with her?'

'I'll call.'


Harvey Jordan continued to be troubled by the uncertainty that came to him during the acrimonious – and therefore distracting – meeting with the two lawyers, and still hadn't resolved it by the time he finished the uninteresting room service meal, which he abandoned half-eaten and pushed on its delivery trolley out into the corridor to give himself as much space as possible for what he intended to do, regretting, along with a lot of other things, not having asked Suzie to book a suite. Changing to one was his first priority on an already long list for the following day.

Daniel Beckwith's courtroom ability remained worringly untested, although Jordan was hopeful. He wasn't at all hopeful about Robert Reid, whom he suspected to have taken Alyce Appleton's case more for its inherent benefit to his reputation for representing such a prestigious North Carolina family than trying too hard contesting an incontestable case in an American state governed by archaic divorce statutes. And Jordan's concern for Alyce wasn't at all altruistic. It was, as always, to save himself. Which was why he needed – as Harvey Jordan always needed – to know everything with which he might be challenged before any challenge occurred.

Whatever was nagging him from that afternoon's encounter had to have some connection with something that had preceded it. But what? He had first to examine the official, printed-out and accusing material, Jordan decided. After that, he'd go through all the illegally accrued correspondence from each and every carefully collated source from all his invaded computers. After that Jordan wasn't sure where else he would look or explore, apart, as always, his burgeoning Appleton bank accounts. And by then he didn't expect to still be as unsure as he was, because by then he would have found the elusive inconsistency. If he didn't find it the first time he'd have to go back – and back again – until he did.

Harvey Jordan was a necessarily methodical, analytical man and decided to begin his search in reverse, setting out in sections upon his bed all that he'd memorized from what had been haphazardly strewn over Reid's desk, and continued moving backwards through all the court papers with which he had been formally supplied, right back to the original stultifying, stomach-wrenching opening letter from David Bartle at Brinkmeyer, Hartley and Bernstein informing him of his being cited as co-respondent in a financial damages-seeking divorce action. There was far more material than he'd anticipated and, aware that repeated reading of already familiar material could result in self-hypnotic oversights, Jordan further sub-divided his already separated divisions. He then settled unhurriedly to read. He did so, totally concentrated and without pause for an hour, at the end of which he'd failed to isolate any incongruity or anomaly.

Irritated, because he was sure the key to what he wanted had to be somewhere in there, Jordan started all over again, creating further sub-divisions until virtually all of the bed space was occupied. And still he found nothing, this time after searching for another full two hours.

Jordan allowed himself a contemplative break, moving from the uncleared bed to his laptop, scrolling through every downloaded exchange from every invaded computer. He was well into the initial correspondence between Daniel Beckwith in Manhattan and Lesley Corbin in London, insisting upon the first venereal examinations by the avaricious Dr James Preston when the long-sought answer began to formulate in Jordan's mind. He forced his cramped body up from his chair to walk stiffly to the bed display, still not able to be completely sure because all he'd been able to memorize that afternoon were the names and addresses of the Boston examiners, not their specific findings or conclusions.

But they were very definitely set out in the results of his own, second examination in New York by George Abrahams. This convinced Jordan that he was taking the right path. Just as he remembered now – and didn't have the slightest doubt whatsoever – that despite their detailed discussion about the medical findings, there had been no reference to anything Reid had done – or rather hadn't done – to get any medical or autopsy result analysis on Sharon Borowski to ascertain if she might have been a chlamydia sufferer.

Jordan only realized the time had gone midnight when he saw it on his own watch as he reached out for the telephone, halting the move to pick it up to ring Beckwith on the floor above. The fact that the following day – or this day, to be precise – was Sunday didn't preclude his hacking into the computers of the two Boston venerealogists to counteract the still hovering uncertainty. His challenge would be far more effective – unchallengable in return – if he could prove what he could only so far suspect.

Jordan guessed the following day was going to be even more fractious than the one that had just passed. And didn't give a fuck. Reid probably would, though. And Beckwith. He'd funded his five New York banks from the accounts of Appleton and Drake that morning and didn't expect there to be anything he hadn't already read to have been added over the weekend, so he decided the long postponed revisit could wait until the following day.

# Nineteen

He was glad he did, because what Harvey Jordan found when he logged on soon after 6 a.m. on the Sunday morning he regarded as another auspcious beginning to the day. In the correspondence attached to his five accounts he found three separate loan offers, the largest – from the Bank of America – up to a maximum of $10,000. In total, the loan offers, each of which he intended accepting, came to $24,000, which, added to what he'd accumulated from his daily withdrawals from Appleton and Drake's account, came just short of $72,000. Keeping that day's transfers to each of the five below $4,000 – and sub-dividing those to avoid them appearing even as large as that – Jordan increased the pot to $83,000, realizing that he had to return as soon as possible to New York to withdraw cash for his safe deposits again to avoid him exceeding the money-reporting limit. By the time he did, he expected loan offers from the two outstanding banks.

By 7.30 a.m. Jordan had obtained the computer addresses of the two Boston clinics. The specialist who had attested that Alfred Appleton was free of any venereal infection was Mark Chapman, whose clinic was on Boylston Street.

Leanne Jefferies' consultant, Jane Lewell, practised on Haymarket Square, on the opposite side of the common. Both had personally dedicated laptops. Jordan set out to embed his Trojan Horses again through his undetected Australian cut-out, ensuring any recorded trace of his entry would be wiped out by leaving an erasing virus activated the moment the main frames of both clinics were booted up on the Monday morning. It took Jordan almost three full hours to hack past the protective firewalls – a second immediately confronted him after he picked his way through the first – into Chapman's personal and dedicated desk top. Jordan presumed the double barrier was to ensure patient confidentiality, which he was determined it wouldn't, but it still surprised – and mildly irritated – him that it was more difficult to get into the doctors' records than it had been to penetrate the other systems.

Jordan's patience was rewarded just after ten with the opening up on his screen of the detailed procedures and examinations Appleton had undergone for the preparation of Chapman's report. It coincided to the minute by the jarring ring of Jordan's phone. Jordan hesitated, momentarily tempted to ignore it, before picking it up.

'I had dinner with Bob last night,' announced Beckwith.

'And?' prompted Jordan.

'I wish it had been more productive,' Beckwith allowed.

'I think he's ineffective and inefficient,' judged Jordan.

'I told you the medical stuff knocked his case from under him.'

'What's he doing about it?'

'Seeing Alyce...' The lawyer paused, 'Just about now, in fact.'

'Not with you?'

'She's his client, not mine. We're co-operating, that's all.'

'You must be thrilled with all the stuff you're getting from him,' mocked Jordan.

'We might be meeting later, brunch maybe, depending on what he gets from her.'

'"We" meaning you and I or "we" meaning you and Reid?'

'Bob and me. He's still pretty sore about the way you spoke to him.'

'I would have thought he'd be used to being spoken to like that by now,' dismissed Jordan. 'I might need to speak to you later.'

'What about?'

'I'm still sorting through stuff,' avoided Jordan. 'Did you actually see – read – those medical reports on Appleton and the woman?'

'Yes. Why?'

'I'm curious about something.'

'You off playing amateur lawyer again?' demanded Beckwith, although without any irritation.

'Just curious,' repeated Jordan. Hurrying on to avoid any further questioning he said, 'And I'm changing rooms. This one is too small. I'll leave a message with the new number when I get it, if you're not around.'

'And I'll call you, when I get back from seeing

Bob. *If* I see Bob. If I don't maybe we could lunch?'

'Let's keep in touch,' agreed Jordan. Now he was actually in to Appleton's records he could well be through by lunchtime.

Jordan used his own written report from George Abrahams as a rough template to check against the findings from Appleton's consultation, his disappointment growing as the two appeared – according to his layman's understanding – to match, with the exception of their haematology groupings, Jordan's being O, Appleton's A. Patiently Jordan went through Chapman's examination a second time, alert for anything he might have missed on his first reading, and again finished with the same understanding. It did not take Jordan as long to break into Dr Lewell's computer at her Haymarket Square clinic. At first reading her examination of Leanne Jefferies appeared the same as Appleton's, with the exception of her blood group being AB. Jordan went through it a second time, once more using Abraham's report for a comparison and once more achieved what appeared to be a match. As an afterthought he went through both comparing them to what Dr Preston had supplied in England, with the same result.

There *was* a disparity. Jordan was sure of it: sure that he just wasn't seeing it. But what? He'd only been able to get the briefest look at both reports on Reid's desk, too fleeting – and too distant – to absorb beyond the more prominently printed names and addresses of the two venerealogists. But with Abrahams' document spread out directly in front of him Jordan's impression was that his own report was actually longer than those of either Dr Chapman or Dr Lewell.

There was an obvious reason for the apparent differences, Jordan realized. His own completed and signed findings weren't comparable precisely *because* those for Appleton and Jefferies weren't completed and signed: what he'd read on his phishing visit into the computers of Appleton and Leanne's doctors were still in note form, not assembled into dictated documents. He'd wasted his time, Jordan acknowledged. All three sets of information seemed factually comparable but he needed the presentations of the opposing venerealogists to decide the diagnoses reached from them, not just the results of various tests.

Despite it being well past noon and therefore obvious that Beckwith and Reid had met, Jordan still called his lawyer's room, but got no reply. He was given the choice of three suites and chose the largest, transferring everything and resetting his entry traps. He left a message with the suite number, as well as the fact that he was lunching in the hotel coffee shop, which turned out to be unnecessary because the table he was allocated had a perfect view of the entrance through which a returning Daniel Beckwith would come.

The scrod, with a side salad, was hugely better than his previous night's dinner, which proved the undeniable hotel lore that a hotel restaurant was always better than room service. He still had something far more important to prove and hoped Beckwith wouldn't be too long getting back.

Something else he couldn't understand had just occurred to him.

'The bitch wouldn't budge,' declared Reid. 'I had her read both medical reports and explained every which way that it made her denials of any other affairs completely untenable, but she wouldn't change her story by as much as this!' He held up his hand with his forefinger and thumb too close together to show any intervening daylight. The Bloody Mary he had in his other hand was his first, and still only half-drunk, and Beckwith was glad.

'Did you tell her I'd cross-examine her as hard as I could?'

'Of course I did.'

'Didn't that worry her?'

Reid shook his head. 'She said she didn't care how tough you were. That she was telling the truth and that was that. And that the judge and jury could make up their minds whether to believe her or not.'

'Which they won't.'

'Of course they won't! They'll decide she's promiscuous and that Harvey was one of many—'

'Which I might capitalize on,' broke in Beckwith, as the opportunity opened up to him. 'If Alyce is a serial adulteress Harvey was just that, one of many who shouldn't be made to pay for all the others.' He sipped his own Bloody Mary, enjoying the drink and the abruptly occurring possibility.

'It's a dangerous argument,' warned the other lawyer. 'It'll still cost him.'

'But not as much as it might fighting every damned claim head on. This way I get to show that Harvey didn't alienate any affection: that a lot of other unknowns did before him. OK, Harvey screwed her but he isn't the marriage wrecker.'

'If Pullinger finds in your favour that takes Leanne off the financial hook. And gives Appleton the petition, too.'

'What are you going to do?' asked Beckwith.

'What little I can, which is very little indeed,' said Reid. 'Argue mitigation, in view of Appleton's admitted adultery. That's all I've got.'

'What about Wolfson's submission for Leanne's dismissal?'

'You're right that I should seek a postponement,' conceded Reid. 'It'll be too close behind yours and there's no way of anticipating how much blood there's going to be on the carpet when you're through. I'll enter the postponement application tomorrow.'

'On what grounds?'

'More time for preparation, in view of the lateness of their medical production.'

'What if Pullinger demands details?'

'The medical stuff *was* late.'

'And left you with nothing.'

'And left me with practically nothing,' agreed Reid. 'You ever regret becoming a lawyer?'

'Every time I lose,' said Beckwith. 'It doesn't last.'

'This time it will,' said Reid. 'This was my big one.'

'It still will be.'

'But for all the wrong reasons.'

'You want another drink?' invited Beckwith, his own glass empty.

'It didn't help yesterday and it won't help today,' refused Reid. 'I already feel like shit without any outside help.'

'She's sticking to her story,' Beckwith told Jordan. 'It loses the case for her but gives us a hell of a good mitigation argument that'll reduce any damages if Pullinger won't dismiss you from the case altogether.'

It was 4 p.m., Jordan saw, glad of the extra time he'd had to prepare his explanation to his lawyer without disclosing his computer hacking. 'Is Bob still with you?'

There was a momentary silence from the other end of the line. 'No. Why? Didn't you hear what I just said?'

'I heard what you just said,' assured Jordan, impatiently. 'Did you actually *read* the results of Appleton and Leanne's chlamydia consultations? Remember enough for a word for word comparison with what Abrahams supplied about me?'

'What the fuck are we talking about now, Harvey?'

'Did you?'

'You're not making a whole lot of sense,'

247

protested the lawyer.

'Please answer what I'm asking you.'

'Bob offered them to me, as I already told you. And I glanced at them. But no, I couldn't quote either of them, word for word.'

'I wasn't given them to read: Bob para-phrased,' Jordan pointed out.

'They're nothing to do with your part of the case.'

'They were lying on Bob's desk. And they were much shorter than what Dr Abrahams supplied in my case.'

'Because I told him I wanted every detail that could possibly arise or be challenged. That's what I'm trying to do: prevent you stumbling into a bear trap ... which I think I now can, because of Alyce's denials. Leave it, for Christ's sake!'

'According to the depositions, Appleton ended his relationship with Leanne Jefferies when, seven, eight, nine months ago?' persisted Jordan, coming to his prepared reason for talking about the chlamydia reports.

'I don't have the papers before me. Eight, I guess. I can check, from the stuff I've brought down with me.'

'And Leanne lives in Manhattan, right?'

'I told you, I don't have the papers before me: everything's in my briefcases. You want me to look it up?'

'I already have, from what's been made avail-able to me. Her apartment's on East 106 Street.'

'We soon going to get to wherever it is you're heading, Harvey?'

248

'Why does Leanne Jefferies, who lives in apartment 38b, 3200 East 106 Street, Manhattan, and who hasn't had any relationship for eight months with Alfred Appleton, go all the way up to Haymarket Square, Boston – where the Appletons are one of the most respected of founding families – to undergo a medical examination to establish her sexual cleanliness?'

The silence this time from Beckwith's end of the telephone was much longer than before. Finally the lawyer conceded: 'I don't know.'

'Wouldn't it be a good idea for someone to ask her, preferably in court? And for us to compare everything Abrahams said about me with what their specialists wrote about Appleton and Leanne?'

'I'll call Bob at home, now. Arrange a meeting for tomorrow.'

# Twenty

Harvey Jordan isolated the discrepancy within fifteen minutes, which was hardly surprising as he was the only one among the three of them to have studied the entire and detailed computer notes of Dr Mark Chapman and Dr Jane Lewell and knew his own venerealogist's assessment practically verbatim.

'Antigens!' declared Jordan, straightening up

from his comparison of the court-presenting dossiers of the three American doctors. The fourth, prepared by the English specialist, James Preston, was also on the table, although to one side and not part of the main comparison.

'What?' demanded Beckwith.

'Antigens,' repeated Jordan, isolating the reference in George Abrahams' deposition, copies of which were before both lawyers to compare against those on Appleton and Leanne Jefferies, which were also in front of them. 'And doesn't that turn everything on its head!'

'It might if we understood what in God's name you were talking about,' complained Reid.

Beckwith had warned Jordan of Reid's over-night resentment – initially rejecting outright the suggestion of another meeting between them – at the possibility of Jordan's further criticism, and there'd been a discernible hostility during the half an hour they'd already spent together. Uncaring, Jordan insisted, 'See the mention, in what Abrahams wrote...?' His finger traced the passage.

'I'm there,' confirmed Beckwith.

Reid nodded, without speaking.

'Now, go on,' urged Jordan, quoting, '"The patient's blood, which is group O, was subjected to further, microbiological haematological examination to establish the presence, if any, of chlamydia antigens, which would have remained present if the patient had suffered the venereal infection but undergone successful antibiotic curative treatment. There was a complete absence of chlamydia antigens, which confirms

250

the patient, Harvey Jordan, had never been a sufferer..." ' He looked up, inviting a reaction.

None came from either lawyer, both of whom were moving between the three separate papers. He had to be careful not to give any indication of having seen the case notes, Jordan reminded himself. He said, 'There's no reference in the reports, from either Appleton or Leanne's specialists, of antigens. Or of an examination of their blood to look for them. Appleton's says: "haematological examination found no evidence of the chlamydia bacteria in the patient's A blood grouping." Leanne's specialist says: "The patient's blood, which is of the AB type, was completely clear of any chlamydia infection." But there's no indication of any microbiological tests to prove that neither Appleton nor Leanne didn't have antigens in their blood, which would be the medical proof that they *never* suffered from it.'

Beckwith came up from his frowned com-parison, his face clearing. 'You're right! Their depositions only prove that Appleton and Leanne are clear *now*!'

'And it does turn everything on its head,' agreed the finally smiling Reid. 'The most im-portant being that Alyce could be telling the truth after all.'

Beckwith wasn't smiling, though. To Jordan he said, 'You did well, picking up on the omis-sion. Well for Alyce. But not so well for your-self. If Alyce hasn't been sleeping around, the defence I intended against your criminal con-versation claims goes out the window.'

'Does it?' demanded Jordan. 'What about what else we've already talked about this morning comparing the depositions, which were so late being delivered that you, Bob, think they're grounds for a postponement? Aren't you a tad curious that Leanne's medical report was prepared by a Boston venerealogist, not one far more conveniently located in Manhattan? I am.'

The two lawyers looked at each other before Reid picked up the English deposition. 'Your guy Preston didn't list antigens clearance, either.'

'Preston was anything but *my* guy: he was little more than a medical fraudster whose professional opinion – inadmissible in an American court anyway – was so inadequate that I had the second tests here, by Abrahams,' refuted Jordan.

'I think you're right,' said Beckwith, talking to Jordan. 'If Pullinger thinks, has the vaguest suspicion even, that something is being withheld from him – which isn't taking it as far as him thinking that he's being lied to – we're throwing the party.'

'How we going to do this?' demanded Reid, the resentment – and resistance – finally going. 'These –' he lifted and let drop the Boston depositions – 'are part of my case, not yours. A stickler to the rules like Pullinger won't let you introduce them into your submissions.'

'Not a problem,' assured Beckwith. 'There's no North Carolina rule against our co-operating, is there?'

Reid considered the question. 'None, as far as I'm aware. I need to check.'

'You've got a day and a half to do that: and for us to work out a way around it if what I want to do is barred. A day and a half as well to chase up all the other outstanding queries to be answered by your enquiry people,' said Beckwith, pointedly not looking at Jordan. 'I want to hit Appleton as hard as I can, first time. It could determine the outcome of everything, your case as well as mine. We'd all of us be home free.'

Reid did look towards Jordan, but still without any animosity. 'Thank you. You've put in a lot of work: more than any client should do; be required to do.'

'I want to keep my hands on my money,' said Jordan, meaning it.

'And I want to say I appreciate it,' said Reid. 'Alyce should, too.'

'You got a side office here that I could use?' Beckwith cut across the apologies, talking to the other lawyer. 'I need to call a lot of people. And go through a lot of law books I don't have down here with me.'

'You can take your pick of whatever you want,' offered Reid.

'Who's going to talk to Alyce, tell her she's no longer facing an inquisition?' asked Jordan.

'I am,' said Reid. 'I was pretty tough on her yesterday.'

'Let's not get too confident,' cautioned Beckwith. 'I still need to call her as my witness on Wednesday. And I won't have her holding back on me.'

'I'm not going to tell her that all her problems are over,' assured Reid.

'That's good, because they're not, for any of us. Not yet.' said Beckwith.

Beckwith seemed passingly bemused by Jordan's announcement that he was returning to New York during the intervening thirty-six hours but didn't ask why, instead warning Jordan to be back in Raleigh in more than good enough time to be in court for the opening of the submission application. Jordan caught the first flight that morning, which got him into Manhattan before ten. He didn't go directly to the Carlyle but detoured instead to West 72nd Street, where the three expected loan applications were waiting, as well as another from the Chase Manhattan, also with an initial $10,000 maximum. Finally at the hotel Jordan completed all four and hand delivered each along Wall Street, at each stop completing forms for the monthly repayments to be directly debited against the account. At each he also withdrew money from every account to spread between his various safe-deposit boxes. At all five banks he was greeted effusively but without any curiosity or suspicion by the managers with whom he'd opened the accounts. Back once more at the hotel Jordan spent a long time painstakingly going through every outlet at Appleton and Drake – concentrating upon the accountancy and financial control divisions – for any indication of his embezzlement having been discovered. And found nothing. He completed the visit by distributing a further $15,000, for the first time moving from the company's currency division section to metals.

His most essential tasks completed, Jordan settled down to bring himself up to date from each of his other illegal entries, going first to his own lawyer, still in Raleigh, and found no additional material. He did better with Reid. There was contact, timed three hours earlier, with an enquiry agency named DDK Investigations. In it Reid complained at the lack of progress to a man identified as Jack Doyle in any of the enquiries they had previously discussed by telephone. In the email Reid repeated everything to which he wanted an urgent response. The reason for Appleton's withdrawal from the America's Cup selection and the three-year gap after Appleton's graduation from Harvard topped the list.

Beckwith was not at the Raleigh hotel when Jordan first telephoned, but picked up the phone on Jordan's second attempt, just before nine. It had been a hell of a day, apologized the lawyer. He wouldn't know until tomorrow if George Abrahams could get to Raleigh for the Wednesday hearing to appear as an expert witness; if the venerealogist couldn't re-arrange his diary Beckwith might ask for a postponement. He'd warned the court he didn't expect to conclude his dismissal submission in one day and that there was a possibility of it even extending to three. He'd advised the lawyers appearing for Alfred Appleton and Leanne Jefferies that sections of their depositions were likely to be questioned, suggesting that Drs Chapman and Lewell be put on standby to be called as witnesses. Beckwith had then been cautioned by

255

Pullinger's court clerk that the judge was extremely intolerant of his sittings being disrupted by what he considered time-wasting and inappropriate presentations.

'Which there's every likelihood of Pullinger deciding from my calling so many witnesses,' concluded Beckwith.

'What about Alyce?' questioned Jordan, intentionally switching the discussion.

'Bob told me she can hardly wait to confront Appleton in court.'

'Let's hope she's not disappointed.'

'Let's hope none of us is disappointed,' said the lawyer, heavily. 'When are you getting back?'

'The plane's scheduled for three tomorrow afternoon.'

'Let's meet in the bar at six.'


The plane was on time, which gave Jordan more than an hour to move that day's tranche of money into his banks, as well as again checking through the financial control and monitoring division to ensure he remained undetected.

Jordan was in the bar, waiting, when Beckwith arrived, in jeans, workshirt and cowboy boots. The lawyer ordered a martini – 'because I think we've got cause for a celebration' – and led Jordan to a table out of the hearing of anyone else in the room.

George Abrahams had re-arranged his diary and was arriving on the first Wednesday morning flight, the lawyer reported; a room had been reserved for Abrahams at their hotel for the

Wednesday night as a precaution against the submission not being completed in one day. There had also been further telephone calls from the lawyers representing Appleton and Leanne confirming their attendance but without any indication whether their venerealogists would accompany them. If they didn't, Beckwith said, he might apply for an adjournment, depending upon how his application went, primarily – although it was essential he cross-examine both specialists – to irritate Judge Pullinger at the other side's prevarication. He'd arranged with court officials – as Reid had for Alyce – for them both to enter the court precincts through back access points, hopefully to prevent them being pictured by the expected TV cameramen and media photographers: there'd been several telephone approaches during the day from New York and local journalists, even though, as Beckwith's application was pre-trial, it was automatically to be heard in camera. That would give him the opportunity to pressure the other side with unspecified challenges and potential revelations into applying for the eventual full hearing to be private. Reid was attending, as was his legal right, as an observing attorney because Alyce was listed as a witness, and in any case intended applying for a closed court if the submission wasn't made on behalf of either Appleton or Leanne.

'I think we've got them running scared,' said Beckwith. 'I can't remember a lot of times when I could have dropped everything to confront an unspecified, out-of-town court challenge like the other side's lawyers have done here. Neither can Bob.'

'You're talking lawyers appearing,' said Jordan. 'What about Appleton and Leanne being here personally?'

'We won't know that until tomorrow, when the court convenes. If either were my clients I'd keep them away.'

'Could you call them, as witnesses, if they do turn up?'

'I haven't officially listed them. If they do show I could apply for Pullinger's discretion. Which I might well do, even on a minor point. There'd obviously and very definitely be a legal argument which I'm sure I could use to move Pullinger into our favour.'

'What are our chances of a complete dismissal?' demanded Jordan, bluntly.

'I've been through this with Bob,' said Beckwith.

'I want you to go through it with me!'

'Slightly less than fifty percent. Which, as a gambler, you've got to accept as pretty good odds.'

For the briefest of seconds Jordan was disorientated by the reminder of how he was supposed to make his living. 'I try for better.'

'I can't offer you anything better.'

It was a desultory dinner between two people brought together beneath the same roof who had already talked out all there was to discuss, each striving for conversation until the very end, when Beckwith suddenly said, 'To use an expression that you're more familiar with than me, we could be on the home straight here. I don't want any surprises, OK?'

'What's that mean?' demanded Jordan, genuinely bewildered.

'You haven't had any contact with Alyce, not since that night in New York?'

'You know I haven't.'

'I don't know you haven't. That's why I'm asking you.'

'I haven't.'

'Not even by telephone.'

'No.'

'You'll be on a witness stand tomorrow, on oath. I don't want any outbursts.'

'If there was going to be an outburst – if I didn't have the anger locked away – I'd have already shouted you down for what you've just asked me about Alyce.'

'Bob thinks you're carrying a torch for her.'

'After the mess she's got me into! You've got to be joking! Bob Reid's talking through his ass.'

'There's too much in what you've just said for me to handle all at one time,' ended Beckwith, getting up from the table. 'Breakfast tomorrow at eight, OK?'

# Twenty-One

Having steadfastly and successfully avoided any criminal proceedings so far in his life, Harvey Jordan had prepared himself for an understandable uncertainty at actually entering a court for the first time and was pleased – as well as relieved – that none came. On their way from the hotel Beckwith had talked expansively of courts being theatres in which people – lawyers particularly – performed but that wasn't Jordan's most positive impression, although he conceded that there could be some comparisons. There was certainly a formidable cast being assembled, their fixed expressions befitting impending drama.

As the appellants on that initial day, Jordan and his lawyer had the first table to the left of the court, just inside the separating rail. Directly behind that rail, in the public section, was George Abrahams, with whom Beckwith was at that moment hunched in head-bent, muttered conversation. The width of the entry gate through the rail separated Jordan from the position of Alfred Appleton and his lawyer, David Bartle. Beyond them, at another table, were Leanne Jefferies and Peter Wolfson. Behind the rail, on the right of the court, were a group of motionless, silent people among whom Jordan presumed to be the Boston venerealogists. Half turned in their direction as he was Jordan was instantly aware of the entry into the court of Alyce, Reid attentively at her arm. Alyce wore a neutral coloured, tailored suit and very little make-up and came through the court and the final gate looking directly ahead, to take her place at the separate table beside Jordan's, on the far left of the court. As she finally sat Alyce looked at Jordan. But not as far as the opposite side of the court to her husband and his lover. Jordan smiled. Alyce didn't, turning away.

Reid leaned towards Jordan and said, 'You get in OK, avoiding the photographers?'

'I think so. You?'

'I'm sure we did.'

'Alyce OK?'

'It's the first time she's been near Appleton since it all began. She's a mess.'

'Tell her it's OK.' What on earth did that mean? Jordan wondered, as he said it. Alyce looked very pale.

'I have already. She thought she'd be all right. She's not.'

Beckwith returned through the gate and asked Jordan, 'What was that about?'

'Alyce is nervous.'

'So am I,' said Beckwith, jerking his head back towards the public area. 'We've got a hell of a point to make. Choosing the moment to make it is the problem.'

'What the...?' started Jordan, to be overridden by the loudly demanded, 'All rise!'

If this were theatre then Judge Hubert Pullinger was already wearing his costume for the role, thought Jordan, as the man upon whom so much depended entered the court. Pullinger's raven-black gown hung shapelessly around a stick-thin, desiccated frame, an appearance denied by the scurrying quickness of his movements. The head came forward, though, when he sat, reminding Jordan of a carnivorous hunting bird, complete with the disease-whitened face Jordan remembered from a television documentary on vultures, ripped off flesh hanging from its beak. Halfway through the court clerk's official litany identifying the hearing there was an impatient, head twitch towards Beckwith, an appropriately bird-like pecking gesture.

Beckwith hesitated until the clerk's recitation ended before rising, with matching, head-nodding deference, to name himself, his client, and his purpose in making his application under the provisions of statute Section 1-52(5) of the North Carolina civil code.

'Which I do, your honour, with some difficulty and trepidation,' Beckwith added.

The pause was perfectly timed to allow Pullinger's interception. 'Both of which problems I can understand from having read the advanced case papers,' said the man. The voice was not bird-like, but surprisingly strong from such a dried-out body.

'Papers in which, in my submission, some of the facts are incomplete and because of which I am seeking the leniency of the court properly to provide,' picked up Beckwith, no satisfaction at his timing in his voice.

'This is a procedural hearing, on behalf of your client, for dismissal as I understand it of both the claims for alienation of affections and for criminal conversations,' interrupted the judge, yet again. 'Should I not hear and consider your applications before being asked to show leniency?'

Jordan's concentration was more towards the right of the court than to the judge, at once alert to the half smiled, head-together exchange between Appleton and his lawyer to the judge's persistent intercessions. Jordan acknowledged that despite the impression he'd earlier formed from photographs of the man, he had totally misjudged Appleton's size and appearance. Appleton seemed much taller than the stated six foot three inches, the fleshy stature heightened by his over-all, clothes-stretching heaviness. There was no longer anything of the sportsman Appleton had once been. The weight, oddly, appeared to bunch at his shoulders and neck, pushing his head forward, actually bison-like, over a belly bulged beneath a double-breasted jacket opened to release its constraint and enable the man to sit, legs splayed, again for comfort. His face was red, mottled by what Jordan guessed to be blood pressure, the fading hair receded far more than it had seemed in the photographs. The marked difference in their appearance dictated that he restrict to the absolute minimum his personal visits to the banks in which he had opened accounts in Appleton's name, Jordan reminded himself.

The smiling, head-nodding David Bartle was a large man, too, although physically overwhelmed by his client. Bartle had the sun-weathered face indicating that he, too, might have been a yachtsman, the colour emphasized by an unruly mop of prematurely white, unrestrained hair. It was not as long as Beckwith's but it appeared to be because Beckwith had his held at the nape of his neck by a securing band. Apart from the restrained hair there was nothing of the Wild West imagery, either. Beckwith wore a conservatively striped suit, shoes and a striped club tie beneath the collar of a crisp white shirt.

There was a similar, although more subdued, reaction to the judge's pressure from the furthermost table to the right of the court, at which Leanne Jefferies and her lawyer sat heads also tightly together. As close as she now was to him Jordan decided that the apparent similarity between Leanne and Alyce was misleading to the point of there being no resemblance at all, limited to the blondness of their hair colouring and the style in which both wore it. Leanne was much sharper featured and could not have risked the minimal make-up with which Alyce succeeded. Leanne wore a powdered base and darkly shadowed eye mascara and the redness of the lipstick was close to being too harsh: the woman looked every day of her five years seniority over Alyce, the age Jordan knew the woman to be from his sessions with Reid.

'I fear I am inadequately expressing myself, your honour, for which I apologize most profusely,' said Beckwith, without the slightest

264

indication of apology in his voice. 'The leniency I seek is not out of the expected sequence that would normally govern a dismissal submission.'

'Why should I be expected to agree to any such course?' Pullinger broke in once more and Jordan decided that his mental analogy of a constantly pecking, flesh ripping vulture was an apposite one.

'To prevent yourself and this court, even at this early stage, progressing further with such preliminary evidence which is, in my contention, inadequate, and risks being misleading unless now addressed and which, if not addressed, seriously endangers the arguments I intend making on behalf of my client...' Beckwith's pause was clearly timed as an invitation for another interruption, which this time didn't come, creating the silence that hung in the court like the belated rebuke that Jordan was sure Beckwith intended. There were no longer any satisfied expressions from the tables on the other side of the court, either.

'Mr Beckwith?' prompted Pullinger, finally.

'Your honour, I seek your guidance,' said Beckwith, refusing to expand, and Jordan felt a frisson of alarm that his lawyer was pushing his false humility too far, a concern that was almost immediately confirmed by Pullinger's further silence.

Breaking it, as he had to do, Pullinger said, 'Are you moving towards inviting this court to find impropriety, Mr Beckwith?'

'I am asking this court to allow me to proceed

in a way different from a normal submission of its type,' avoided Beckwith, adeptly.

Pullinger went to the opposite side of his court. 'Mr Bartle? Can you help me with this set of circumstances?'

The now serious-faced Bartle was on his feet before Pullinger finished the question. 'Your honour, I am at as much a loss as I fear you are. I have not the slightest idea to what counsel is referring or alluding. Because of which I formally ask for the court's protection.'

'Mr Wolfson?' switched the judge.

'I am equally at as much of a loss as my colleague, your honour, and ask as anxiously as he for the protection of the court,' responded Wolfson. He was a small man compared to those immediately adjacent to him, with a moustache and Vandyke beard so immaculately trimmed that both looked artificially stuck to his lip and chin, furthering Beckwith's earlier theatrical comparison.

Looking between the two lawyers, the judge said, 'I give both of you the guarantee of such protection –' coming around to Beckwith as he spoke – 'and warn you, Mr Beckwith, of the irritation of this same court if the allowance you request emerges in any way whatsoever to be a frivolous manoeuvre.'

'I am grateful for such an allowance, your honour,' responded Beckwith, who had remained standing throughout the exchanges.

'Remain extremely careful, Mr Beckwith,' repeated the emaciated man. 'Extremely careful indeed.'

'Which is precisely what I hope you will find I am being at the end of this consideration,' said Beckwith.

Jordan thought, Shut the fuck up! Don't gloat at having got what you wanted.

Dr Abrahams was at the rail gate before Beckwith completed the summons, not needing the prompt from the usher to complete the oath. The man was equally well prepared listing his qualifications, but Beckwith stopped him halfway through the recital, taking him back to identify in full every acronym, particularly Abrahams' qualification as a veneralogist. That established, Beckwith went with the man's impatience to record the length of his experience and the extent of his microbiological specialization.

'Qualified as you are as a microbiologist also means that you are equally qualified and practised as a serologist?'

'It does,' replied Abrahams, in his clipped, formal manner.

'For the benefit of the laymen among us in the court, what is serology?'

There was the vaguest sigh from the man. 'Technically the study of serum. In practise the study of the blood to identify bacteria and viruses, in effect, identifying antibodies and antigens prevalent in communicable diseases and infections.'

'Continuing in laymen's terms, infections caused by bacteria?'

'Not always, but predominantly.'

'Virally created infections?'

'Yes.'

'What are antibodies? And antigens?'

'Bodies that form in the blood to resist a toxin.'

'Formed how? By what?'

'I am sure the court is fascinated by this expedition into the mysteries of microbiology and serology,' broke in Bartle, noisily grating back his chair as he stood. 'But is there to be a practical point to emerge from this dissertation?'

'A question that was beginning to exercise my mind,' said the judge. 'Mr Beckwith?'

'A very practical and relevant point indeed, your honour,' responded Beckwith, at once. 'It is to establish the importance of the...' the pause was intentional, a verbal marker as all the man's other theatrical hesitations had been '...omissions to which I wish to draw the court's attention.'

'My patience is limited, Mr Beckwith,' reminded the judge.

'And will not be stretched much further, ' promised Beckwith. Going back to Abrahams the lawyer said, 'You were about to help the court with an explanation of antibodies and antigens.'

'Both are traceably formed – created – within the blood by a patient's natural immunity or resistance to a disease or infection, as well as by the induced resistance of antibiotics,' said Abrahams.

There was a lot of movement now – sufficient to attract the judge's frowned attention – between the two lawyers to the right of the court and the people directly behind them, Bartle finally getting up from where he sat to lean over the rail for closer consultation.

As aware of the activity as Jordan, Beckwith stopped his examination, looking between the animated groups and the judge and said, 'Your honour, does the court require a recess here?'

'I do not intend a recess but I might very well require an explanation,' said the judge.

Bartle turned, startled, back into the court, standing fully. 'I apologize if I have caused the court inconvenience, your honour.'

'You have and it will not be tolerated again,' snapped Pullinger, the redness of his irritation pricking out on his bloodless cheeks. 'Any more than I will tolerate ill-prepared cases being prematurely brought before me or much more deviation from expected presentations. You will proceed, Mr Beckwith, with the limitations of my patience in the forefront of your mind.'

'Dr Abrahams,' resumed Beckwith. 'If an infection is resisted – defeated – by natural immunity or medication, do such antibodies or antigens remain traceable within a patient's blood?'

'For a time,' replied the doctor. 'That length of time depends, understandably, upon the type of infection or disease and the treatment to defeat it.'

'Let us come to sexually transmitted diseases and infections,' invited Beckwith.

For the first time the lawyer's pause was for breath, not to tempt the judge's impatience but Pullinger seized it. 'Not a moment too soon, Mr Beckwith.'

'Observing, as always, your honour's guidance,' responded Beckwith, just as swiftly. To the doctor the lawyer continued, 'You have extensive experience of the identification and treatment of sexually transmitted disease, do you not, Dr Abrahams?'

'I do.'

'Is the manifestation of antibodies and antigens that you have described applicable in sexually transmitted diseases?'

'Yes.'

'In syphilis?'

'Yes.'

'In gonorrhoea?'

'Yes.'

'What about chlamydia or to use its more accurate clinical name, Chlamydia trachomatis?'

'Yes.'

'Within the last month you examined the man I represent in court today, Harvey William Jordan, for venereal infection, specifically Chlamydia trachomatis, did you not?'

'I did. I also extended that examination to include syphilis and gonorrhoea.'

'Can you describe, as simply as possible for the court's benefit, how you conducted those examinations?'

'I took invasive urogenital swabs, as well as those from the throat and rectum. I also took blood and urine samples.'

'What were your findings?'

'Negative, to every test for every possible infection.'

'Specifically in the case of chlamydia, the tests

are clinically referred to as polymerase chain reaction, PCP, or ligase chain reaction, LCR, a sensitive detection method for chlamydia DNA?'

'Yes.'

'Which were negative?'

'Your expert witness has already attested to that,' came in Pullinger.

'I am anxious that there should be no doubt whatsoever of the findings, your honour,' said Beckwith.

'You have established that to my satisfaction, Mr Beckwith. I am still waiting to discover the other point you have promised me.'

'Dr Abrahams,' returned Beckwith, 'had my client, Harvey Jordan, suffered any venereal infection that required medical treatment would the antibodies or antigens resulting from that treatment have been evident in his blood, even though he had been successfully cured by treatment from a doctor or specialist other than yourself of which you had been unaware?'

'Yes, in the case of syphilis and HIV, possibly in the case of chlamydia.'

'Were there any such antibodies or antigens?'

'No.'

'What is the irrefutable medical conclusions from the absence of any antibodies or antigens from the blood of Harvey Jordan?'

'That he has never suffered or contracted a venereal infection.'

'Which is very specifically spelled out and made clear in Dr Abrahams' medical report already supplied to this court!' exploded the now

271

very visibly flushed Mr Justice Pullinger.

'But not in any other medical report laid before this court, those of Alfred Appleton and Leanne Jefferies, both of which were delayed until the very last possible moment for presentation before your honour,' Beckwith pointed out, finally sitting beside Jordan.

Pullinger did recess the court, from which Bartle and Wolfson hurried out, trailed by their respective clients and the two venerealogists. Beckwith went through the rail for another, although brief, consultation with Abrahams.

Reid crossed from his table when Beckwith returned and said, 'That was brilliant.'

'I was flying by the seat of my pants from the conversation I had with Dr Abrahams,' admitted Beckwith.

'Even more brilliant,' insisted Reid.

'I'd only heard of Pullinger by reputation,' said Beckwith. 'I didn't imagine he'd really be such a son of a bitch.'

'You think there's something to be found in the medical reports of the other side?' prodded Jordan.

'That's the way Abrahams told me to go,' said Beckwith. 'I'm going to press as hard as I can to find out.'

'And I'm going to risk trying an application about Sharon Borowski: as many applications as I can, while I think Pullinger will be favouring us,' disclosed Reid. 'If he slaps me down, he slaps me down.'

Jordan saw that Alyce was still staring straight

ahead, ignoring everybody. When he pushed his chair back Beckwith said, 'Where are you going?'

'Stretch my legs. Say hello to Alyce. No reason why I shouldn't, now that we're in court, is there?'

Beckwith shrugged.

Reid said, 'Keep it brief.'

Alyce didn't look in his direction as Jordan approached and there was a hesitation even when he reached her table and said, 'Hi!'

'Hello.'

'How are you?'

'Hating every moment of it! I was looking forward to it – facing him down – but now I'm here I feel ... ashamed, I suppose. We had to sneak in ... There were television cameras ... It was awful.'

'Did they get photographs of you?'

'Bob doesn't think so.' She looked across at the two remaining lawyers. 'What's going on ... I don't understand what Dan is doing?'

'The medical reports on your husband and the woman are incomplete.'

'Does it matter?'

'It could, quiet a lot,' said Jordan, carefully.

'Is it to do with what Bob said about you?'

'What did Bob say about me?' said Jordan, only just keeping the demand out of his voice.

'That you were clever and that you'd found something that helped me ... about what I was telling him.'

'It could be. Let's see how the rest of the day goes.'

'I don't want to see how the rest of the day goes. I want to run away and hide and not come out for a long time.'

'That's...' started Jordan but stopped.

'That's what?'

Jordan's first thought had been to describe it as childish. Instead he said, 'Giving up, with no reason to give up.' His mind butterflying beyond his conversation with Alyce, Jordan thought it was difficult to conceive how someone like her could have gone to bed – had grunting on top of her – someone as heavy and animal-like as the man he'd just seen for the first time in court. Beckwith and Reid were properly listening to what he said now – despising him as well for being a smart-ass and he didn't give a damn about that – and he'd go on pushing if he had to until what he'd read, but obviously not expertly understood, from the venereal case notes of Alfred Appleton and Leanne Jefferies was explained. But what if the case notes didn't mean anything? Everything would rebound back upon them. Like Beckwith, Jordan hadn't believed that the judge could be such a cantankerous old bastard.

'What's she like?'

'Who?' said Jordan, momentarily lost in his own thoughts.

'The woman he fucked, Leanne?'

'I don't believe you haven't looked at her!'

'I haven't looked ... don't want to look.'

Jordan still didn't believe her. 'Much older than she really is, compared to you. Doesn't compare at all – as well – with you...'

'Perhaps she does things I wouldn't.'

'After France I can't imagine what that might have been.'

Alyce shook her head, dismissing the memory. 'I'm going to ask Bob if it's absolutely necessary for me to be in court.'

'Would that be a good idea?'

'That's what I want. Why shouldn't it be all right?'

'It could look to the judge – and the jury, when it's eventually convened – as if you're the guiltier party. Which you aren't.'

'I don't care what it looks like.'

'Don't you care who's proved to be guilty: if you're branded as the slut that he's trying to make you out to be?'

'Not really.'

'I don't believe that.'

'I don't care what you...'

'Believe?' Jordan finished for her.

'I don't want us to fight.'

'Neither do I.'

'Then let's not.'

Jordan turned at the sound of Reid's returning approach and saw that two of the men who had remained beyond the rail behind Appleton's table were staring at him and Alyce. When Reid reached his table the lawyer said, 'I told you to keep it brief.'

'Why don't you worry more about the strain on Alyce than our simply talking together?' said Jordan, aware as he spoke of the opposition entourage re-entering the court.

\* \* \*

275

'I fear there has been created the possibility of a severe misunderstanding which I wish –' Bartle turned to indicate the next table – 'as well as my colleague, Mr Wolfson wishes, to make clear I am most anxious to correct—'

'And which I am even more anxious to have explained to me,' predictably broke in Pullinger.

'It is fortunate, your honour, that present in this court today are the two medical experts who conducted the required examinations upon my client and that of Ms Leanne Jefferies, who is enjoined in this matter.'

'How did that come about, that they should be present?' persisted the judge.

Bartle lowered his head, not immediately replying, which Jordan decided to be in frustration at the constant intrusion. Beside him he saw Beckwith was scribbling a soldiers' battalion of exclamation marks on his yellow legal pad.

'I was obliged, as was my fellow attorney, Mr Wolfson, to have been alerted prior to today's hearing by Mr Beckwith that there was some disparity between the required medical assessments.'

'You had the evidence of Mr Beckwith's expert witness in your required pre-hearing presentations,' reminded Pullinger. 'Why weren't the omissions from your side corrected before today, so that this whole matter could have been resolved without the time-wasting disruption to which it has been subjected?'

Bartle turned pointedly to where Beckwith sat. 'I regret, your honour, that neither myself nor Mr Wolfson were specifically advised what the challenge was going to be. Had we been, then this court would not have been caused the delay to which you are quiet rightly drawing attention. My request, sir – with which my colleague, Mr Wolfson, is in full agreement, to prevent any further delay in the proceedings – is that this session be adjourned until tomorrow to enable the apparent discrepancies to be rectified, with our deep and respectful apologies.'

Pullinger kept the lawyer standing for what seemed to be an age in the completely hushed court, irritably waving the man back into his seat when the uncertain Wolfson made as if to get to his feet, imagining that the judged wanted a supporting request.

Instead Pullinger turned to where Jordan sat with his lawyer and said, 'Mr Beckwith?'

'I am, as always, at your honour's disposal and would not seek any further to delay the progress of my submission or anything else that might be brought before the court,' said Beckwith. 'But I would draw your honour's attention to the fact that had the omission not been brought to your honour's early attention this entire case might have proceeded with insufficient evidence at the court's disposal, which I am sure you would deplore. A re-presentation of the medical reports will, I hope, rectify that problem, but I would respectfully request that your honour gives me the opportunity, upon such re-presentation, to explore the matter further if those re-presentations are applicable to the submission that I have not yet had the opportunity to pursue.'

'I certainly will wish to examine most carefully what is provided to this court tomorrow,' said Pullinger. 'And give you now the under-taking that you will be allowed to do the same, as all three expert witnesses are present in court and as it is my wish that they so remain until the court decides otherwise.' The vulture's head swivelled. 'I expect to be provided by 9 a.m. tomorrow with the redrafted medical report upon your client, Mr Bartle, and yours, Mr Wolfson. And I will say, at this point, that I will not tolerate another single instance of expected court protocol being inadequately complied with.'

'It wouldn't have been right for me to have interceded,' declared Reid. 'You'd won the point, hands down. If I had tried to add on more applications it would have defused everything.'

'I know. Thank you,' said Beckwith.

They'd gathered in Reid's Raleigh office, after the local lawyer had smuggled Alyce out of the court and into a waiting car.

'I will do, tomorrow, if it all goes well,' per-sisted Reid, defensively.

'You did the right thing,' assured Beckwith. 'I said I'm grateful.'

'Any trouble getting Alyce away?' asked Jordan.

'I don't think so. I didn't see any cameras.' Reid nodded to his telephone console. 'There've been four or five media enquiries, asking me to call back. I'm not sure that I will.'

'Alyce told me she doesn't want to be in court,' said Jordan.

Reid's face tightened, irritably, at Jordan's
278

awareness. 'She told me the same thing. She wants the judge to excuse her.'

'You going to go to Pullinger with that?' asked Beckwith.

'Certainly not before the case has even properly started,' said Reid.

'I don't think it would be a wise application to make at any stage,' said Beckwith.

'You think she's up to it: sitting through everything that's going to be said, all the details likely to come out?' asked Jordan.

Reid shrugged, uncertainly. 'Apparently there's a lot of family pressure building up, disgrace and shame to the established dynasty, that sort of shit.'

'Being excused court, to which I can't imagine Pullinger agreeing in the first place, isn't going to help, is it?' said Beckwith. 'Alyce is involved in a divorce action, simple as that. She's got to hope you get Pullinger's agreement to a closed hearing. That'll give her the best protection she can hope for.'

'And each day she's got to scuttle about like a cornered animal to avoid being photographed,' said Jordan.

'Harvey! The media have got enough stock photographs of Alyce to open a picture gallery. If Bob gets a closed hearing the media pressure will relax after a couple of days and she'll settle down to the reality of what she's in and that'll be that.'

'Medical reports are the focus of the moment,' said Jordan, looking between the two lawyers but stopping at Reid. 'You've still got to get

Pullinger's order to try to get those of Sharon Borowski. Why can't you get a doctor's request for Alyce to be excused on the grounds of mental and physical stress?'

'Hey! Hey! Hey!' protested Beckwith, loudly. 'Where the fuck are we going here? You appointing yourself Alyce's champion, defending her against all the woes of a collapsed marriage in which you are very much the exposed defendant? You're still in the shit right up to your chin and if what we started today doesn't work out in our favour, sinking down even further. Let's you and I worry about you and me and let Bob worry about Alyce and the reputation of her famous family, OK?'

'She doesn't deserve to have to go through all this!' insisted Jordan. 'Did you look at Appleton today? See what he looked like?'

'We haven't sat through all the evidence yet: don't know what Alyce deserves or doesn't deserve to go through,' refused Beckwith. 'You've got to come back on course – on board – to why and how you're here, what it could cost you and has already cost you and worry about your own ass, nobody else's. Not even an ass as cute as Alyce's. You hearing what I'm telling you, Harvey? Or are you going soft on me?'

Jesus Harry Christ! thought Jordan. Did he really need to hear what his lawyer was telling him! It was as if ... He didn't want or need to know what it was. What he needed – as Beckwith had just told him – was to remember where he was, why he was there and how much in the end it was likely to cost him. 'I was just trying to

280

be fair,' he said, lamely.

'Fairness has got nothing to do with anything,' said Beckwith. 'Start getting your priorities in order, OK?'

# Twenty-Two

Harvey Jordan was too experienced at performing, at *being*, someone else for there to be any outward indication of his shocked realization that he was showing the slightest concern for anyone other than himself, certainly somebody, however inadvertently, who had turned his life on its head as Alyce Appleton had done. He continued the review of the day's events with the two lawyers in Reid's office and responded sufficiently in the car returning him and Beckwith to the hotel, but the moment he got there was relieved to escape into the seclusion of his locked suite uninterrupted to examine and analyze what he started out regarding as an inexplicable lapse.

As such it was unthinkable, virtually beyond comprehension. And there'd actually been previous warnings from Beckwith, before that day's very necessary and positive rebuke. But it didn't demand sackcloth-and-ashes penitence, Jordan reassured himself. There was even a partial, acceptable, self-explanation. The situation into which he'd been pitch-forked wasn't one to which he was accustomed and professionally skilled, unlike the environment – the bank account fraud being the most obvious – in which he knew practically by instinct every move and trick, was able to recognize every manoeuvre. It was *because* he knew every trick and manoeuvre that he'd adjusted and now had all his electronic spyholes already drilled: and because of them had that very day knocked Appleton's lawyer flat on his fat ass to end up, so far at least, hopefully with the judge tilting in Beckwith's – and therefore his – favour.

But it was still different from what he normally did and how he did it. Apart from his dealings with the New York banks he wasn't playing a part, pretending to be someone else whose identity he would shuck off like an unwanted skin when he'd achieved all that he wanted. In court he really was Harvey William Jordan, doing everything and more to escape an entrapment and its potential cost under an incredible medieval law comparable to the rack or being hanged, drawn and quartered, financially if not physically. So it made good and very practical sense to show consideration to Alyce, to protect her even, because from today's behaviour she was doing very little to protect herself, with the wheezing Bob Reid scarcely doing much more. Jordan had meant what he'd told her today. He didn't want to fight her: didn't feel any animosity towards her for what had happened. He didn't yet know – and couldn't anticipate – how he

282

might need her but whatever and however that turned out to be, it was essential that at all times she remained on his side. Essential, too, that she confirmed that France had been nothing more than a holiday dalliance, ending with no commitments and no regrets but most importantly of all, with no alienation of any affections. He most certainly couldn't risk Alyce turning against him and changing her story – the true and genuinely honest story – if things started to go wrong with her case and her defence.

And Daniel Beckkwith should recognize that. Jordan determined that Beckwith definitely would if the lawyer started lecturing again at any time in the future about how he was treating Alyce. Because he'd spell out to the man the obvious reasons for doing so: let Beckwith know that what he was doing needed to be done solely for his own self-protection. Maybe remind the thwarted cowboy, even, of everything he'd done and suggested already to bring them out ahead in today's confrontations. For Reid or Beckwith or both of them to imagine that he actually had some lingering interest in Alyce beyond getting as far away from her and everything in which she had involved him was a load of crap. He'd tell Beckwith that, too, if it ever came up between them again.

It had been good to think things through, analyze everything in his mind. And he had analyzed it, subjectively as well as objectively. The two lawyers had got it wrong, perhaps understandably, and he had acknowledged how easily it had been for them to make the mistake.

Now it was over, resolved in his mind which was the only consideration because his escape from each and every problem with which he was confronted was all that mattered.

Jordan was first in the bar after his nightly laptop session, freshly showered and changed ahead of either Beckwith or George Abrahams, with whom they'd fixed dinner before quitting the court. Abrahams, the next to arrive, hadn't changed his clothes but he appeared more relaxed outside both the court and his consulting rooms. Beckwith arrived again in jeans and the bison-figured belt and tooled cowboy boots, hair flowing unrestrained.

The conversation was awkwardly stilted in the beginning, Jordan initially happy to leave the obvious effort to Beckwith and the venerealogist, waiting for something of relevance before intruding himself, alert to an inviting opportunity. It came as he was completing the second drinks order, from a remark from Abrahams. There was an echo of something that had passed between the two lawyers during their earlier, after-court conference but Jordan seized it ahead of his own attorney.

'Isn't there an agreed format, a template, in which these types of medical reports are prepared, for presentation to a court?' Jordan asked.

'I don't believe so,' said Abrahams. 'It's not particularly common: this is the first time in over a year, fourteen months to be exact, that I've been asked to prepare the sort of assessment I did upon you.'

Jordan looked between the doctor and his

lawyer. To Beckwith he said, 'I understood when I first arrived from England that it was far more frequent than that: that Dr Abrahams was your regular consultant?'

'Dr Abrahams is the specialist I've called upon since I began practising in Manhattan. Twice, I think.'

'Twice,' agreed the doctor.

'So each specialist presents his assessments and findings on a case-by-case basis, in the form of his own choice?' persisted Jordan.

'I suppose so,' said Abrahams.

'In other situations – I'm not asking you to betray any other lawyer or case confidentiality – have you ever before encountered the sort of omission about antibodies or antigens that was thrown up today?' asked Jordan, who was unsure if the doctor's pause following the question was for recall or the man's reflection upon confidentiality.

Eventually Abrahams said, 'I've come across it once before. It was the first time the venerealogist for the other side had prepared such a court assessment. It was lack of experience, not an intentional withholding.'

'What are you suggesting the fault is in this case?' seized Beckwith.

'I'm not *suggesting* anything,' bristled the man.

'It sounded to me as if you were surprised in this particular case,' said Beckwith.

'Dr Chapman is a recognized microbiologist in the field of sexually communicable infections,' said Abrahams. 'He's published, to some professional acclaim, two specific papers, one even more specifically upon chlamydia. I would not have expected him to have ignored antibody reference or evidence, either positive or negative.'

'Surely a positive finding would be of the utmost significance!' pressed the lawyer.

'Of course it would,' finally confirmed Abrahams, his familiar testiness returning.

Beckwith did not respond to Jordan's look, although Jordan was sure the other man was conscious of his attention. As he was sure of several other things. One was that Abrahams had been reluctant, without pressure, to appear to criticize a colleague whose publicly acknowledged work the man admired. Another was that Chapman's reputation beyond Boston hadn't been established by either lawyer, which yet again was more a failing of Reid, to whose case it was of more direct importance than Beckwith's, although after that morning's hearing that was now arguable. And the third was that if he hadn't persevered – although Jordan accepted he hadn't started out with any targeted intention – another potentially important discovery would not have been made. Quickly he said, 'What about Dr Lewell?'

'I know nothing of Dr Lewell's work,' replied the man. 'I did not know of her until this case.'

'The English examination that I underwent before coming here?' Jordan asked Abrahams. 'What did you think of it, professionally?'

Again Abrahams hesitated, before saying, 'Muddled. Completely inadequate.'

'Which was why I arranged the second examination by Dr Abrahams,' stressed Beckwith.

'Had you already exchanged that initial, inadequate English report with the lawyers representing Appleton and Leanne Jefferies?'

Now it was Beckwith who hesitated, recognizing the possible inference from the question. At last he said, 'Yes. That's why I had it carried out in England, as part of the accepted, pre-court exchanges. Then I changed my mind and decided we needed something from an American specialist.'

'Without telling the other side?'

Beckwith nodded but did not speak.

Jordan said, 'So, until you officially exchanged the second report they would have thought you were proceeding upon the first, English findings, findings which Dr Abrahams has just told us were muddled and completely inadequate?'

'You've made your point, Harvey.'

'Good,' said Jordan. 'Why don't we go and eat?'


Jordan breakfasted in his room, more interested in accessing his computer sites than eating. He was disappointed that there was no email traffic but remembered that neither the opposing lawyers nor the Boston venerealogists had local facilities and that any communication would have been restricted to telephone or possibly hotel faxes. The overnight arrangement had been for Jordan and the microbiologist to link up with the two lawyers at Reid's office, although Beckwith was alone when they reached it. Jordan hadn't bothered with television in his suite, so the local newspaper coverage he'd read in the taxi, relegated to an inside page, was the first he'd seen of the previous day's court opening. The legal restrictions limited the account to the basic facts of the pre-hearing application being postponed on a procedural technicality, to be reconvened that day. The stock photograph of Alfred Appleton was from his yachting days, which made the image virtually unrecognizable as the man whom Jordan had seen in court the previous day and because of the way she had dressed herself down, with practically no make-up, the library picture of Alyce wasn't a good representation, either.

'Bob has had to go to persuade Alyce to show up,' announced Beckwith. 'She called him last night, saying her doctor was prepared to appear today and say the strain would be too much for her to be in court.'

'I don't want to be kept here another day,' protested Abrahams, at once. 'I should have been back in New York today; my diary's shot to hell!'

'You will be back tonight,' promised Beckwith. 'We can go on in her absence, with the judge's agreement; she's not part of my application. But Bob thinks Pullinger would consider it a spoilt girl's cop-out and I agree. I don't want to lose whatever we might have gained yesterday.' He looked at Abrahams. 'We've managed to get print-outs of Chapman's medical journal papers you talked about last night, back at the hotel.

They could turn out to be very useful.'

'When will we know if Alyce is going to show up?' asked Jordan.

'Bob's going to call from his cellphone.' The lawyer looked very directly at Jordan, as if expecting him to say more, but Jordan didn't.

'You think I could safely make a late afternoon reservation back to New York?' asked the doctor.

'Maybe wait a while: give ourselves an hour in court to see how things go.'

They rode unspeaking to the Raleigh court-house, using the same entry route as the previous day through connected city buildings. Jordan looked intently through the windows as they walked, but failed to detect any photographic ambush.

Beckwith's cellphone went as they were ascending the inner steps leading up to their assigned court. The lawyer hunched briefly over it, his back to the flow of people up and down the stairs. Turning back to Jordan, he said, 'Alyce is coming. So's her doctor.'

Alyce looked visibly ill, walking falteringly but unaided and in total contrast to the striding confidence that Jordan remembered from her entry into the Carlyle hotel just a few days earlier. There was no make-up at all and the plain black dress, devoid of any jewellery, accentuated the pallor of her face. Again she ignored everyone, including Jordan, but when she reached her adjacent table she turned back for the reassurance of her doctor's presence. The man was about the same age as Alyce, be-spectacled and blond haired. He'd taken a seat

289

directly behind her, nodding in reassurance at her look. Reid did not go directly to sit beside Alyce but continued on to the court clerk, gesturing as he talked to the blond newcomer. The clerk, in turn, had a whispered conversation with Pullinger after the judge's arrival and Pullinger said at once, 'Mr Reid?'

'I should explain, your honour, that with your honour's agreement the man sitting directly behind my client is Dr Walter Harding, the medical director of the Bellamy Foundation hospital here in Raleigh,' introduced the lawyer. 'Mrs Appleton is in court today with great difficulty, brought on by the strain of this matter. Dr Harding is prepared to testify before you, should your honour require it, as to Mrs Appleton's physical condition. He is also prepared to remain in court, with your agreement, to ensure Mrs Appleton's condition does not deteriorate further.'

The frowning judge looked invitingly to where Bartle and Wolfson sat. Bartle came at once to his feet and said, 'It is regrettable that Mrs Appleton is feeling such strain but I would remind the court that distress and strain are inevitable consequences of proceedings such as these which have not, in this case, actually begun yet. And that we hope Mrs Appleton recovers sufficiently to avoid any serious disruption or delay.'

'Sentiments with which I fully concur,' said Wolfson, rising as Bartle sat.

'As do I,' said Pullinger. 'And with which I am sure you also agree, Mr Reid?'

'Absolutely, your honour. And thank you for the court's understanding.'

Jordan was close enough to his own lawyer to hear Beckwith whisper, 'Shit!'

'Still on the subject of delay, I trust we are ready to proceed on the matter of medical submissions?' asked the judge, going back to the two opposing lawyers.

This time they both rose together, each holding a bundle of papers separated by various tags. 'These are redrawn medical reports prepared overnight by Drs Chapman and Lewell, upon which my fellow attorney, Mr Wolfson, would also like to address the court,' announced Bartle.

Jordan was conscious of a movement from Beckwith, close beside him, but there was no whispered conversation.

Pullinger allowed some silence to build up in the court before saying, 'Mr Beckwith?'

'My expert witness, Dr Abrahams – at some professional and personal inconvenience – has remained here in Raleigh to assist your court, your honour,' opened Beckwith, as he stood. 'I very sincerely hope that he will not be detained beyond today. I equally hope that we will be able, expertly and professionally, to examine these new submissions, by recalling Dr Abrahams to the stand to give this court the benefit of his expertise. I would also respectfully ask, pending whatsoever is to emerge from the statements this court has yet to hear from the attorneys representing Alfred Appleton and Leanne Jefferies, that their respective expert medical witnesses can be called to the stand to

291

be examined on oath upon their resubmitted findings.'

There was immediate and obvious movement between the two now identified venerealogists, culminating with Chapman groping forward to attract Bartle's attention. The attorney half turned towards the gesture but shrugged it off. Instead he rose to say, 'Your honour, I hope already to have indicated an apology to your court, for a totally inadvertent misunderstanding which I am quite satisfied I can explain to your honour without any further need to protract what is, after all, a subsidiary matter to the main purpose of this court.'

'Your honour!' erupted Beckwith, before Pullinger could respond and by so doing coming close to being over-theatrical. 'I am going to refrain from making the most obvious comments upon what has just been said to your court. Mr Bartle and Mr Wolfson have their expert witnesses behind them in this court! What earthly reason is there for those expert witnesses *not* being called to be questioned about their original findings, which could have substantial import upon my application before you today and which I in no way consider subsidiary?'

'A question I would be interested in having answered for me,' commented Pullinger. 'Can you help me, Mr Bartle?'

It was not Appleton's attorney who responded but that of Leanne Jefferies. To fresh movement behind both opposing lawyers, the bewhiskered Wolfson said, 'Your honour, I wish to assure this court that my expert witness, Dr Jane Lewell, is at your court's disposal.'

'As is mine,' tightly conceded Bartle.

The skeletal Pullinger let the court subside into foot-shuffling, throat-clearing near silence, his vulture-eyed concentration unbroken upon the right of his court. Eventually he said, 'Mr Bartle?'

'Your honour?' responded Appleton's attorney, forced to his feet again.

'I do not consider that you satisfactorily responded to my invitation. I no longer offer that invitation, but it will remain on record and most certainly in my mind and I would like you, Mr Bartle, and you, Mr Wolfson, both to bear that very much in mind as this matter proceeds, to whatever its end. Do you, Mr Bartle, fully understand what I am saying?'

'I do, your honour,' said Bartle. 'And in the light of your honour's comments I withdraw my request to make a statement to the court.'

'Mr Wolfson?'

'I do, your honour. And I also withdraw the suggestion of my making a preliminary statement.'

'Distribute to the relevant parties the newly provided material,' the judge ordered his clerk. 'There will be a recess of fifteen minutes to provide an opportunity to study that material.'

'Dr Abrahams,' opened Beckwith. 'Will you tell this court what is indicated in the medical reports upon Alfred Appleton and Ms Leanne Jefferies that have only this day, less than an hour ago, been submitted?'

The venerealogist shifted on the witness stand. 'Both Alfred Appleton and Ms Leanne Jefferies have been successfully treated for Chlamydia trachomatis.'

'What is a chlamydia microimmunofluorescence test?'

'That which is carried out to establish the presence of chlamydia antibodies following the infection of cervicitis in woman and urethritis in men.'

'Cervicitis in women and urethritis in men are conditions caused by a chlamydia infection, are they not?'

'Yes.'

'Do the medical reports of Drs Chapman and Lewell show that Alfred Appleton suffered urethritis and Ms Lleanne Jefferies suffered cervicitis?'

'Yes.'

'What is antichlamydia IgG?'

'The antibody found in the blood of sexually active adults in response to the infection and which may be detected after successful treatment.'

'Do the reports of Drs Chapman and Lewell show that Alfred Appleton and Ms Leanne Jefferies had antichlamydia IgG in their blood at the time of their examination by Drs Chapman and Lewell?'

'Yes.'

'Could there be the slightest doubt about that?'

'Not according to what I have been shown today.'

'Could it have been produced by another

complaint or infection?'

'The microimmunifluoscence test is remarkably sensitive and specific. It is medically recognized to be accurate in ninety-nine percent of woman and between eighty to ninety percent of men.'

'Your honour!' protested Bartle, rising. 'The fact that my client suffered chlamydia is not contested.'

'Nor is it on behalf of my client,' said Wolfson, in support.

'But it was not admitted to this court until an hour ago!' insisted Beckwith, who had not sat during the interjection. 'I would ask you to find, your honour, that this court be allowed the fullest opportunity to explore this matter, including how and why it was withheld from this court until this later hour.'

'It was not withheld!' refused Bartle.

'It was most certainly not supplied, which is a requirement of such pre-hearing exchanges,' came back Beckwith.

'You will proceed, Mr Beckwith, hopefully without any further interruptions, in the hope of this court discovering the truth of the matter,' ruled Pullinger.

'The court has already learned of your outstanding qualifications in your particular profession field, Dr Abrahams,' picked up Beckwith. 'As I understand it, there is no formularized presentation for reports such as these we are discussing. Is that right?'

'That is so.'

'Did you subject the appropriate samples you

took from my client to a microimmunofluorescence test?'

'Of course.'

'Which was negative?'

'As I said in evidence yesterday.'

'Had that microimmunofluorescene test proved positive and produced antichlamydia IgG antibodies, would you have omitted that finding from the report you submitted to this court?'

There was shuffling from the lawyers' tables on the right of the court but before either Bartle or Wolfson could rise, Pullinger impatiently made a waving down motion with his hand.

The venerealogist still did not answer and Beckwith said, 'Dr Abrahams?'

'As we have already established, there is no formularized style of presentation.'

'That wasn't my question, doctor. Please answer it.'

'No. Of course I would have included it in my report.'

'Why?'

Abrahams' irritation at the question came out in a snort, which he tried to turn into a cough, looking directly from the witness stand at Dr Chapman. 'Because the whole purpose of such reports is to establish whether or not there is – or has been – an infection!'

'Thank you,' said Beckwith, abruptly sitting.

And said it again to the judge's invitation to continue his submission when the court reconvened after the luncheon adjournment that Pullinger ordered at the conclusion of Abrahams' evidence, with the agreement that the venerealogist should be released to return to New York.

'Your honour!' interrupted Bartle, jerking to his feet. 'I would once more respectfully invite your honour to accept, with the apologies I have already expressed and would reiterate, my explanation for this most unfortunate misunderstanding, this oversight, and not further delay the progress of this case by calling Dr Chapman.'

'An application that I also most earnestly request with Dr Lewell,' said Wolfson, bobbing up as Bartle sat, as if both lawyers were performing vaudeville, if not theatre.

'Why "most earnestly", Mr Wolfson?' demanded Pullinger.

Leanne's lawyer looked blankly to the raised bench, initially appearing not to understand the question. The confusion increased when he did understand. 'I meant ... maybe a mistake on my part, your honour. I meant my client and I are anxious not to impede the progress of the court now that this medical difficulty has been resolved.'

'I do not for a moment find that what you refer to as "this medical difficulty" has been resolved to my satisfaction,' refused Pullinger. 'Having been found – exposed – to be so lamentably wanting, are you, Mr Wolfson, or you, Mr Bartle, seeking to bulldoze this court to bury those failings?'

Both Bartle and Wolfson were standing now and their replies – 'under no circumstance whatsoever, your honour' – came practically in unison. Beside him Beckwith created another

297

battalion of exclamation marks on his yellow legal pad, taking Jordan's mind back to their adjournment lunch in the court cafeteria, at which Alyce, her doctor and Reid had not appeared. To Jordan's insistence there, a euphoric Beckwith had gauged the chances of getting his dismissal at seventy-five percent. So surprised had Jordan been by the estimate that his initial, unconsidered thought had been that if he were discharged he could, within days, be back in England, the nightmare relegated to the place of bad dreams. Until a question hurried him back to reality. What, he asked himself, about Alfred Jerome Appleton and the personal promise he'd made to himself: what Alyce had in France called tit for tat? The fact that if he were discharged he wouldn't be penalized for hundreds of thousands – millions even – didn't come into any calculation. The bill would still be huge, here in America and in England. And he didn't intend spending as little as a single bent penny of his own money in payment or settlement for anything. Appleton would, though. Jordan was more implacably determined than ever to recover everything and more – far more – for the upheaval the man had caused. So he wouldn't be returning to London whatever the outcome of today's hearing. Only when Alyce abruptly turned towards him did Jordan realize that throughout his reflection he had been looking at her. She frowned, questioningly. Jordan looked hurriedly away.

'I hope I can be convinced of that,' Pullinger was saying, nodding again to Beckwith to resume.

Dr Mark Chapman came reluctantly to the stand and took the oath looking fixedly at Appleton and his lawyer, not averting his gaze until Pullinger stated, for the record, that the doctor had been called to give evidence upon the application of a defendant lawyer.

'Dr Chapman,' began Beckwith, at Pullinger's indication, 'will you give, again for the benefit of the record and in full, not by acronym, your medical qualifications?'

Chapman's hesitation lasted so long that Jordan briefly thought the man was going to refuse, but finally Chapman responded, with clipped, stilted formality, the faintest trace of an Irish accent in his voice.

'In addition to those qualifications, you also contribute to medical journals upon subjects within your chosen expertise, do you not?'

'Yes.'

'Regularly?'

'No.'

From the way Beckwith was standing Jordan could see the faint smile on his lawyer's face and guessed Beckwith had reached the same conclusion that he had, that the venerealogist intended to remain monosyllabic.

'How many articles have you been responsible for in, say, the last five years?'

Chapman thought before replying. 'Six.'

'To the admiration of your peers? Dr Abrahams, for example?'

From Bartle's table there was movement that ceased at Pullinger's quick look.

'I do not know.'

'You have not received letters of appreciation, congratulation, from other specialists in your field?'

'Not from Dr Abrahams.'

'But from others?'

'Occasionally.'

'As I made clear, I asked you to give your qualifications in full for the benefit of the court record. In assembling them for myself I discovered the possibility of you taking up a position as lecturing microbiologist at Boston's leading teaching hospital, which would accord you the title of professor, would it not?'

'The appointment has not yet been made.'

'Were it to be made in your favour, Dr Chapman, would you include the diagnostic importance of antibodies and antigens in your lectures?'

The man's second hesitation was as long as the first. Eventually Chapman said, 'Of course I would!'

'Of course you would,' echoed Beckwith. 'Because as we have heard in very informative detail from Dr Abrahams, the discovery or otherwise of antibodies and/or antigens is a very necessary part of the investigation into infections and disease, either bacterial or viral, are they not?'

'Yes.'

'Why then, doctor, didn't you include your discovery of antichlamydia IgG in your examination of Alfred Appleton, the purpose of which was to establish whether Alfred Appleton had suffered, or was suffering, a chlamydia infection?'

'I was responding to the instructions with which I had been served,' said Chapman, with the quickness that hinted at prior preparation.

Now it was Beckwith who let the silence build into a mocking echo. 'You were responding to the instructions with which you had been served?'

'Yes.' Chapman's concentration was again on Bartle.

'Which were?' persisted Beckwith.

Chapman had both hands gripping the side of the witness stand, as if he physically needed its support and his face was markedly flushed compared to his complexion when he'd first entered it. Formally, his voice fluctuating, he recited, 'To examine Alfred Appleton and carry out various recognized tests to establish whether Alfred Appleton was suffering a venereal infection, specifically chlamydia. At the time of my examination, he was not. That is what I said in my report.'

'Your *original* report,' qualified Beckwith.

'My original report,' agreed the venerealogist.

'At the time of that original report – during your investigative examination – you found antichlamydia IgG in Alfred Appleton's blood, did you not?'

'Yes.'

'Which proved that he had suffered such an infection and been treated for it?'

'Yes.'

'But you chose not to include that finding?'

'I was following the remit that I had been given. At the time of my examination, Alfred Appleton did not have a venereal infection.' The man continued staring fixedly at the table at which Appleton and his lawyer sat.

'Your honour!' broke in Bartle, groping to his feet. 'Can I help by confirming what Dr Chapman is telling the court? The remit to which Dr Chapman is referring was mine.'

'Knowing of its relevance in the case before us, you did not ask Dr Chapman to provide evidence of your client having an infection in the past, only if he suffered it at the *time* of examination?' demanded the judge, making no effort to keep the incredulity from his voice.

'That is so, your honour,' confirmed Bartle. 'The fault, the oversight, is mine, not that of Dr Chapman. And I humbly apologize.'

'I think, Mr Bartle, that this is something about which I have to reflect further.' Turning to the other side of the court Pullinger said, 'I think you have established your point, Mr Beckwith.'

'With respect, your honour, I have a few more questions.'

A frown flickered across the judge's face. 'Let's move along, Mr Beckwith.'

'Dr Chapman,' resumed the lawyer. 'Studying as I have your professional qualifications, I noticed also that you attended Harvard, as did Alfred Appleton? You were contemporaries, in fact?'

'Yes.' There was a fresh tightening to Chapman's face.

'Did you know Mr Appleton at Harvard?'

302

'We were acquainted.'

'How were you acquainted?'

'We shared a mutual interest.'

'In sailing?' queried Beckwith.

'Which I'm sure you already knew,' flared the other man, giving way at last to anger.

'I did indeed, Dr Chapman. But the court didn't until now. Have you continued to sail with Mr Appleton?'

'Yes.'

'So how would you describe yourself? As an acquaintance or as a friend?'

There was yet another pause before the man said, 'As a friend, I suppose.' The voice was quieter, controlled again.

'Did you attend your friend's marriage, to Alyce Bellamy?'

'Yes.'

'How would you describe Alyce Appleton, nee Bellamy, as an acquaintance or as a friend?'

'Your honour!' protested Bartle.

'I agree,' said Pullinger. 'I think you have extended this examination sufficiently, Mr Beckwith. Is it your intention to call Dr Lewell?'

'It most definitely is, your honour.'

'I shall permit it, on the grounds of fairness, but not with the same latitude as I have with this witness. Is that clear?'

'Very clear,' said Beckwith.

'Then I don't expect the need to remind you.'

Dr Jane Lewell's qualifications were not as extensive as those of either George Abrahams or Mark Chapman, but did include those of microbiology and gynaecology. She was a tall, thin

303

woman, her face dominated by heavy, thick-rimmed spectacles. There appeared little attempt at make-up, nor to colour the greyness in her hair which she wore very short, cropped to the nape of her neck. Jordan's immediate impression, when she began responding to his lawyer's questions in a flat although confident voice, was that she was setting out to be as monosyllabic as the specialist doctor who had preceded her. It was quickly confirmed in a series of staccato, yes or no answers, despite Beckwith adjusting his questions to achieve fuller responses. Pullinger's mounting impatience came to its head after she agreed that Leanne Jefferies had suffered a chlamydia infection with Peter Wolfson's interrupting admission that her first, inadequate report had been a strictly accurate diagnosis according to his limited remit.

'So there we have it!' insisted Pullinger. 'Both expert witnesses adhered to the very strictest letter of their legally permissible instructions – instructions that remain very much in the forefront of my mind – that had their evidence been presented in its original form could have seriously misled myself and a subsequent jury, but for the intervention of Mr Beckwith. It is now established for the benefit of subsequent proceedings that both Alfred Appleton and Leanne Jefferies suffered a venereal infection. Is this matter now concluded to your satisfaction, Mr Beckwith? It most certainty is to mine.'

'With respect, your honour, I have questions to this witness that will occupy no more than five further minutes.'

'Which I will time to the precise second,' said the judge.

'The domicile of Ms Leanne Jefferies is 3200, East 106th Street, apartment 38b, Manhattan, is it not?'

'Yes.'

'Are you Ms Leanne Jefferies' gynaecologist?'

'No.'

'Had she been a patient of yours prior to her coming to you for the examination we are discussing today?'

'No.'

'According to what has been indicated here today, it was Peter Wolfson, her attorney, who made the appointment, with its very specific remit, for Leanne Jefferies to be examined by you?'

'Yes.'

'Until this occasion, has Peter Wolfson had clients examined by you?'

'No.'

'Did you not think it strange that a woman domiciled in Manhattan should be asked to travel all the way to Boston for an examination for which there are...' Reverting to theatrics, Beckwith consulted papers on the table in front of him. 'There are to my rough calculation twenty consultants with qualifications matching yours within thirty minutes, even allowing for the worst traffic?'

For the first time the woman lapsed into the previously familiar hesitations. Finally she said, 'Yes.'

'Did you ask her?'

'Your time is rapidly running out, Mr Beck-with,' warned the judge.

'Dr Lewell?' hurried Beckwith.

'No, I did not ask her.'

'How friendly, professionally or otherwise, are you with Dr Chapman?'

'You will answer that question and that will be the end of your examination,' ordered Pullinger.

'We are friends, professionally and socially,' said the woman.

# Twenty-Three

The chambers of Judge Hubert Pullinger were as frigidly austere as the man himself, wallpapered practically from floor to ceiling with legal books, each precisely in its regulated, indexed place, scribbled notes in the centre of an other-wise unmarked blotter, pens in a regimented holder beside a telephone console. The chester-field, with matching chairs, was in red oxhide and unoccupied because Pullinger kept the four lawyers standing before him, his attention totally concentrated upon David Bartle and Peter Wolfson. The only physical indication of Pullin-ger's fury was the involuntary tap of an index finger, as if he were keeping occasional time with the sticky tick of the mahogany-cased grandfather clock creating the sole sound in the room, apart from the asthmatic rasp of Reid's breathing.

The judge still wore his robes and when he finally spoke, eyes now lowered over his prepared notes, the tightly controlled voice was so quiet that at first, until they adjusted, both Bartle and Reid strained forward to hear properly.

'Throughout the course of this outrageous day I have almost lost count of the offences that you, Mr Bartle, and you, Mr Wolfson, have caused and inflicted upon my court. The most obvious is contempt, the worst to which I believe I have ever been subjected in twenty-five years upon this bench. There is no mitigation or explanation that I will accept from either of you. I have been minded to abandon the full case before it officially opens – which is why I have interrupted the current application before its completion – to report you both to your respective state regulatory and licensing authorities, with the recommendation that you both be subject to official enquiry into your total lack of professionalism. That is still a course open to me and one I might choose to pursue. In deciding to postpone that decision I am mindful of the inconvenience and costs that would be caused your clients, as well as those of Mr Beckwith and Mr Reid. I find no reason why any of them should suffer because of your conduct. When the court resumes, however, I intend advising both doctors who appeared as your expert witnesses that I shall complain to their licensing authorities, dissatisfied as I am with the explanations both have offered. It is I who decide the interpretation and application of the law, not either of you with the sleight of hand of snake-oil salesmen...'

Pullinger paused, clearing his throat after such an uninterrupted diatribe. 'As both of you would appear to need guidance in law, I will remind you that the course I have chosen today, to address you as I am now doing, is highly unusual and might even be construed as undue and premature bias, although I give you my absolute assurance that this is not nor ever will be the case. It does, however, open the way for both or either of you to object to my continuing to hear any more of this current application or the divorce itself and apply for a new judge. That would, of course, require me to justify this meeting, which I am fully prepared to do. I will continue this recess to enable you both to consider your course of action and discuss it with whomever you choose – and to advise Drs Chapman and Lewell of what I have told you – but warn you that if you decide to continue I will not tolerate any more of the behaviour to which I and my court have been subjected. This meeting is concluded.'

'Your honour—' tried Wolfson, immediately to be faced by Pullinger's halting hand.

'I have already told you, Mr Wolfson, that I will not accept any mitigation or explanation attempts,' rejected Pullinger. 'Leave my chambers and comply with every request I have made of you. Yours are now the decisions to be made.'

Once more neither Alyce, her lawyer nor her accompanying doctor were in the court cafeteria, but it was mid-afternoon, not a recognized break time and Beckwith, without pause, had swept Jordan up on his way from the chambers confrontation, ahead of everyone else who endured it.

With difficulty Jordan held himself back until they'd collected their unwanted coffee and chosen a table beyond the hearing of any surrounding table. And then he demanded, 'Is it all over: am I out of it?'

'That wasn't why we were summoned to chambers,' calmed Beckwith. 'I haven't even made my dismissal submission yet; you know I haven't.'

'Then what *was* it for?'

Jordan sat without movement or question throughout his lawyer's recounting of the in-chambers meeting. At its end Jordan declared, 'We're there, surely!'

'We're nowhere,' dashed the lawyer. 'If they go for a new judge, we've lost everything we thought we'd achieved. No new judge could be told how we'd exposed the shit they tried to dump on us!'

'You can't be serious!'

'Pullinger's hog-tied them, whichever way they try to run. Which I guess he had to do, being the judge he is. Better than any other judge would have worked out how to do it, in the circumstances.'

'What would you do, in their position?'

'Suicide is the first thing that comes to mind.'

'I'm being serious, for fuck's sake!'

'I was, to an extent. Seriously I think I'd go for

309

a rehearing.'

'What sort of delay would that involve?'

'Fuck knows! Months, I guess. Appleton and Leanne would have to start over again, from scratch. I don't know of any case – any set of circumstances – like this on record.'

'So it would attract more attention than it already has?' queried Jordan, posing the most prominent of his several concerns.

'Inevitably.'

A lot of his carefully stabled Trojan Horses would be useless too, Jordan accepted. He'd virtually have to start over to put himself as far ahead as he had this first time. 'Can Pullinger stop like this, right in the middle of your application? Couldn't he carry on and decide on my dismissal?'

'I just told you, I don't know of any other legal situation like this that's ever arisen in North Carolina or anywhere else in North America with the criminal conversation statute still in existence. We might have a way out. If today collapses, I'm going to have a lot of time to go through the records, to see if there is a precedent we can use.'

'What about the cost of the sort of delay you're talking about?'

'I'll certainly apply for costs of everything so far. I don't see how Pullinger could refuse or Appleton's side resist...' Beckwith broke off at the sight of the court usher entering the cafeteria and rose in anticipation, saying, 'Decision time,' as he did so.

They were the last to return to court, although

310

Reid was settling Alyce in her seat ahead of them. She sat docilely and Jordan's impression as he followed to the adjoining table was that Alyce appeared practically catatonic. It was very different on the other side of the court. Everyone was flushed, the two doctors shifting constantly in their seats: Appleton was gesturing with Bartle but Leanne was pulled away from her lawyer, as if she wanted physical separation. Beckwith didn't sit but continued on to Reid's table for a huddled discussion until the shouted announcement of Pullinger's re-entry. The judge didn't hurry this time, pointedly re-arranging his robes around him. Having done so, he said, 'Counsel will approach the bench.'

The four lawyers arranged themselves in front of the judge in the order in which they sat. Pullinger said, 'Well?'

'My client wishes the hearing – and the case in full – to continue before your honour,' said Bartle. 'But my expert witness, Dr Chapman, wishes to address the court.'

'My client also wishes to continue before your honour,' echoed Wolfson. 'Dr Lewell also seeks to address you, your honour.'

Pullinger nodded in dismissal and as he retook his seat Beckwith hissed, 'We're going on! Christ knows why, but we are.' Looking towards his lawyer as he was, Jordan saw Reid hunched towards Alyce, who showed no response – no awareness even – of what she was being told.

'Dr Chapman and Dr Lewell will stand,' ordered Pullinger. When both did the judge continued, 'For the record I will repeat what I know, upon

311

my instructions, has already been communicated to you by your respective lawyers, for whose clients you appeared before me, as well as providing written medical opinion. It is that I intend reporting to your governing, licensing body my displeasure at the manner and lack of professionalism of both your evidence and your written opinions. I am, in turn, advised that you both wish to make representations before me. I am refusing to hear those representations: this is not the court to hear or adjudicate upon your professional conduct. For me to hear whatever it is you wish to say could prejudice any future enquiries in which you might be involved. You will both be provided with a full transcript of all the proceedings in which you have featured thus far, as well as a copy of what I write to your licensing authority.'

'That isn't fair!' protested Chapman.

'This will not be argued and neither of you will make outbursts in my court, which I order you to leave, immediately. Usher, escort the two doctors from the premises!' Switching his attention to the other side of the court, Pullinger said, 'Let's get on, shall we, Mr Beckwith?'

Jordan was aware of a flicker of interest from Alyce as his lawyer stood, reminder notes in his hand. He was aware, too, of Beckwith's pause: the actor preparing himself for his opening speech.

Beckwith said, 'As your honour has already had cause to remind us, this is a court of law. It is not, despite the evidence that might be brought before it, a court of morals. It is the law, its interpretation and its administration, upon which I seek to address this court...' Alyce had definitely emerged from her private world, Jordan decided. He was encouraged, too, by what he inferred to be several nods of approval from the judge.

'I submit for your honour's ruling that the North Carolina statute Section 1-52(5) is an inextricably connected hybrid of two parts,' continued Beckwith, using his reminder notes more as a gesturing prop than a memory prompt. 'From the first comes the accusation, if proven to your honour's satisfaction, of alienation of affection, which surely requires the intercession between spouses of a third, destructive party, with the result that the marriage irretrievably breaks down. The second support to Section 1-52(5) is the offence of criminal conversation, which I further invite your honour to interpret as the intentional, alienating seduction by a destructive third party. I seek to prove, to your honour's satisfaction and agreement, that my client, Harvey Jordan, is not liable to the accusation of criminal conversation because at the moment and time of the admitted affair with Mrs Alyce Appleton there no longer existed in Mrs Appleton any affection whatsoever to be alienated. Therefore there can be no case for criminal conversation. In the submitted papers before you Alfred Jerome Appleton admits adultery with at least two different women. At no time during their marriage, in which considerable difficulties arose, did Mrs Appleton betray her marriage

313

vows. Indeed, there will be evidence produced before you that Mrs Appleton did everything in her power to save her marriage from irretrievable collapse, even attempting a reconciliation and resuming conjugal relations with her husband. It was during this attempted reconciliation that Mrs Appleton contracted chlamydia that has become the subject of so much discussion already and upon which I will not dwell further at this point, although there are points I intend to raise in my closing arguments. Any lingering affection – the remotest possibility of a lasting reconciliation – vanished when Mrs Appleton discovered she had contracted a venereal infection from her husband, who could have been the only source or cause of that infection. She initiated divorce proceedings, the intention of which was communicated to her husband before her departure for a lengthy vacation in the South of France. At the time of that departure Mrs Appleton considered herself married to her husband in name only, a name she sought to divest herself of as quickly as possible. In France she was a lonely woman, a betrayed and humiliated woman only recently cleansed of a sexual disease uncaringly passed on to her by her promiscuous husband...'

Alyce was listening intently now to every word, Jordan saw, actually with a pen in her hand although she did not appear to be taking notes. Both opposing lawyers were, as well as Pullinger. Appleton and Leanne Jefferies were gazing directly ahead, as if oblivious of each other.

314

'And in France this lonely, betrayed and humiliated woman met my client, Harvey Jordan—'

'A gambler!' broke in Pullinger. The inference was of accusation.

Beckwith managed to pick up practically without pause. 'That is indeed how Mr Jordan makes his living, which some might regard as an unusual career: certainly out of the ordinary to those of us who follow a more mundane profession. But I would suggest that at this very moment those working on the trading floors of Wall Street – Mr Appleton himself, as a commodity trader – could be described as gamblers. The very men who made America the world leader it is today, the Astors and the Vanderbilts and the J.P. Morgans, were chance-taking entrepreneurs, which is an interchangeable word for a gambler...'

'Quite so,' nodded Pullinger.

'Harvey Jordan was an entirely innocent party in a long ago divorce, the papers of which are before you,' resumed Beckwith. 'He was on vacation in the South of France, a region he knows well and in which he vacations most years. He always stays, when he is in Cannes, at the Carlton Hotel. Where, by total and absolute coincidence, Alyce Appleton was also staying. Their meeting was not pre-arranged. It was a chance encounter, like so much is in life. Harvey Jordan took Alyce Appleton on the shortest of excursions along the coast. They had an affair, the briefest of episodes which ended with her return to her country, his return to his country.

They did not exchange addresses or telephone numbers. Neither considered it as anything more than what it was: a holiday liaison. Harvey Jordan was not engaged in criminal conversations, intent upon alienating the affection of Alyce Appleton from a husband in name only, for whom her only attitude of mind was contempt for what he had inflicted upon her. To be judged guilty – liable – for an offence, your honour, there surely needs to be evidence produced that a law has been contravened. Here I respectfully submit that there is nothing in law that supports the accusation against my client.'

For several minutes after Beckwith sat – which seemed to catch the opposing tables by surprise – there was the necessary silence for everyone to digest what Beckwith had said. Pullinger broke it. He said, 'That was an address too eloquent to have been kept from a jury, which must, I suppose, forever remain their loss. What you have told me is, of course, based upon the pre-hearing statements of Mr Jordan and Mrs Appleton. Do you not intend calling them, to support what you just said?'

Jordan's impression was that for the first time Beckwith was disconcerted, although he concealed it well. Quickly rising again the lawyer said, 'My address was upon the admitted and uncontested facts, your honour. They require, of course, to be subjected to the examination of the other side.'

For someone who had always until now existed as Mr Invisible, never to be seen and even more importantly never to be recognized, Harvey Jordan's feeling at being the sole object of everyone's unrelenting attention lurched into the surreal. He was confident that he had his hand upon the Bible and was correctly reciting the oath, but his mind suddenly blanked of everything he had so carefully memorized to word-rehearsed perfection. The bewildering out-of-body experience remained throughout the early, officially required formalities and only began – and then very slowly – to ease when, straining for concentration, Jordan forced himself to respond to Beckwith's gentle, yes or no confirmation, of his already provided statement.

Beckwith's abrupt departure from that statement: 'Did you consciously, predatorily, set out to seduce Alyce Appleton?' – finally brought Jordan back to the reality of his surroundings.

Every answer had to be thought through, although without any obvious hesitation, Jordan warned himself: he couldn't risk once being caught out in a lie. 'No, I did not.'

'How, then, did you look upon Alyce Appleton?'

Jordan gave an uncertain gesture, to give himself time. 'As a fellow guest at the hotel, someone with whom I got into casual, passing conversation.'

'Yet you lunched together the first day of your meeting?'

Jordan gave another delaying shoulder movement. 'She'd prevented me losing the book I was reading. It was a snack rather than lunch. It was

317

entirely inconsequential.'

'What gave it consequence?'

'Nothing happened specifically to give it any consequence. We talked about books and writers. I knew from my knowledge of the area that Alexander Dumas' novel, *The Man in the Iron Mask*, was based on fact and that the victim was at one time imprisoned on an island just off the coast of Cannes. I invited her on a surprise trip to see it.' Beckwith was building up to how he and Alyce went to bed that first time, Jordan accepted. It hadn't been ugly, as it would sound here now, in a cold court. It would make Alyce appear a whore, which she wasn't. Abruptly Jordan remembered Beckwith's ballpark estimate of the potential damages if Pullinger found against him and Beckwith's angry insistence that Alyce's words made her out to be the pursuer, not the pursued.

'You chartered a yacht, sailed to the Ile St Marguerite and saw the prison in which the man in the iron mask was incarcerated?'

'Yes.' He'd limit his answers as much and as best he could, Jordan decided.

'Then what did you do?'

'We had lunch.'

'On the yacht?'

Beckwith was looking very directly at him, Jordan saw, with what he gauged the beginning of a warning frown. 'It was a catamaran. And yes, that's where we lunched.'

'What happened after that?'

'We swam.'

'To do which you had to change. Did you

318

change together, in the same cabin? Or separately?'

'Separately.'

'You didn't suggest that you should undress together?'

'No.'

'Did it not enter your mind that you might suggest it, Mr Jordan?'

'No.'

'Did you not find Mrs Appleton attractive?'

'Yes.'

'Sexually attractive?'

Jordan hesitated, looking at the woman, who looked directly and expressionlessly back at him. 'Yes.'

'Yet it did not occur to you, in the circumstances in which you found yourself, to suggest you undress together: make a sexual approach to her?'

'No.'

'Why not?'

'It did not seem ... I don't know ... I didn't.'

'Did you fear that she would rebuff you?'

'I didn't think about whether she would rebuff me or not.'

'And in the early evening you sailed back to Cannes, arriving around dinner time?'

'Yes.'

'Did you suggest dinner?'

'Yes.'

'Did she accept?'

Jordan felt hot, hotter than he had when he'd first stepped, his mind blank, on to the witness stand. 'No.'

'What were her precise words?'

'As best as I remember, she said she was not hungry after the lunch.'

'What else do you remember her saying, Mr Jordan?'

'That she was tired.'

'And?' demanded Beckwith, the frown deepening.

'That she wanted to go to bed.'

'And...?'

Jordan did not immediately reply. Alyce was still looking at him without any expression whatsoever.

'Mr Jordan?' demanded Beckwith.

'But not by herself,' Jordan blurted.

'Mrs Appleton told you she wanted to go to bed but not by herself?' insisted the lawyer.

'Yes.'

# Twenty-Four

'You stalked her, didn't you!' demanded David Bartle, loudly. 'You sought out Alyce Appleton in the South of France and pursued her until you got her into your bed!'

Totally unaware of any of the detailed evidence that Appleton's enquiry team might have assembled to incriminate him, Jordan recognized that under cross-examination he had to test every word and innuendo, to avoid stumbling into traps. And never lose his temper. No danger from this first, exaggerated opening. 'No, I did not.'

'You knew Alyce Appleton was a married woman?'

Too easy to be caught, Jordan thought. 'She wore a wedding ring.'

'And a particularly obvious engagement ring, given to her by her husband.'

'I did not know from whom she obtained the engagement ring,' qualified Jordan, believing he saw a safe avoidance. 'I believe widows – divorcees even – still sometimes continue to wear their rings.'

'She told you she was married?'

'Yes.' He needed to repeat that he and Alyce had parted without any intention to meet again, one of the several points with which Beckwith had concluded his examination, minutes earlier.

'But not until after you'd seduced her!'

'Not until after we'd slept together,' said Jordan, qualifying again.

'At your persistent urging!'

'I have already told this court the circumstances in which the affair began.' Very slightly, although not easing any of his self-imposed safeguards, Jordan began to relax. He didn't think Bartle was a particularly good interrogator but very positively refused to lapse into any false security.

'You're telling the court that Alyce Appleton was prostituting herself up and down the French

321

Riviera?'

Jordan felt the burn of anger but quickly subdued it. 'I am telling you nothing of the sort and you – and the court – know it!' He should have stopped after the initial denial! Shit!

'Before this examination is over I shall know a great deal about everything,' threatened the lawyer. 'Did you find Alyce Appleton attractive?'

Jordan hesitated, trying to anticipate the subsequent question. 'Yes.'

'Did you fall in love with her?'

Jordan managed to avoid the hesitation. 'No.'

'Did you think she might fall in love with you?'

Too obvious, thought Jordan. 'No.'

'What would you have done if she had indicated that she was falling in love with you?'

'It wasn't that sort of situation.'

'Answer the question,' Pullinger ordered, sharply.

'I would have made it clear that the feeling was not reciprocated.'

'But gone on sleeping with her?'

'No,' insisted Jordan.

'What would you have done?' persisted Bartle.

'Terminated the situation.'

'Are you sure?'

'Quite sure.'

'You are no longer married?'

'I am divorced.'

'How long were you married?'

'Four years. I have provided the court with all the legal documents and evidence.'

'Were there children from the marriage?'

'No.'

'Are you the father of any children out of wed-lock?'

It was a re-run of his first meeting with Daniel Beckwith, Jordan remembered. Wrong to regard that as a useful rehearsal. Alyce hadn't known he had been married, he remembered. 'No.'

'It is customary for you to vacation every year in the South of France?'

'Yes.'

'Always at the Carlton at Cannes?'

'I move along the coast.'

'Until you find a woman to pursue?'

Fuck you, thought Jordan, not responding.

'I asked you a question, Mr Jordan,' pressed Bartle.

'I inferred it as a totally fallacious and mis-leading statement, which, being both untrue and ridiculous, did not require an answer.' Jordan thought he detected the slightest of facial expres-sions, a wince maybe, from Beckwith.

'Indulge me with a comment, Mr Jordan.'

He shouldn't have opened himself to the mockery, Jordan acknowledged. And the ques-tion could be the feared mantrap if they'd dis-covered previous holiday affairs. 'I do not tour the Cote d'Azur seeking women to seduce.'

'How many years have you vacationed in the South of France?'

Jordan genuinely had to pause, to calculate the period. 'It's not a figure I've ever bothered to record. I would estimate about ten ... twelve, possibly.'

'How many holiday romances have you had during the course of those possible twelve years?'

The trap was gaping open in front of him, feared Jordan. At once came a contradiction: why was it so much of a trap? He could even cover himself if they had discovered some of the other woman, before Alyce. 'Three, I think.' He hadn't spent a single holiday alone.

'Were any of them married?'

'I don't know.'

'Did any of them wear wedding rings or engagement rings?'

'I don't remember.'

'Does it matter to you if the women you pursue are married?'

Surely the lawyer would have pounced by now if he'd found a previous conquest! And so what if he had, Jordan asked himself again. 'Every liaison in which I have been involved has been consensual. I do not, to use the word you persist wrongly upon using, pursue women.'

'You didn't know if it would or would not endanger Alyce Appleton's marriage when you first went to bed with her, although you knew she was married!'

Jordan seized the ineptly presented opportunity. 'Neither Alyce Appleton nor I regarded our time together in France as anything other than what it was, an adventure that would end with no attachments on either side. We parted, as the court has already heard at the end of my earlier evidence, without any intention of ever meeting again. I did not alienate Alyce Apple-

324

ton's affection from her husband. She no longer had the slightest affection for him.'

'She told you that?'

'She told me that papers upon which she had been working – signing – the day we met were divorce papers.'

'Why did she extend her holiday in France for a further week?' persisted Bartle.

Jordan shrugged and immediately regretted doing so. 'We didn't discuss it at any length. I was not returning to England for another week. She had no pressing reason to come back here to America.'

'Wasn't it that she was falling in love with you?'

'Absolutely not. As I've told—'

'But that you told her you didn't love her?'

'I repeat, absolutely not,' denied Jordan.

'You gave her a ring, did you not?'

'A what?' frowned Jordan, incredulous, conscious of Beckwith's sudden jerk of attention.

'During your stay in St Tropez didn't you buy her a ring and put it on the finger upon which Alyce Appleton by then no longer wore her wedding or engagement rings?' demanded Bartle. 'And celebrate, as people do upon engagements, by drinking champagne?'

'*What?*' exclaimed Jordan, blocked on the same word in his astonishment.

Bartle beckoned the usher, handing the man a sheaf of photographs and itemizing their recipients. To Pullinger the lawyer said, 'These were taken in St Tropez, your honour. The date clearly shown upon the prints coincides with that during which Alyce Appleton shared a room with Harvey Jordan at the Residence de la Pinade.'

Momentarily Jordan stared bewildered at the two photographs he had been handed. One showed him and Alyce walking arm in arm by what he recognized to be the Place des Lices and the other at a table at the Mouscardins restaurant at the edge of the port. He was clearly holding her left hand, putting a ring on her wedding finger. There were half filled champagne glasses on their table, the bottle in its cooler alongside. And then he erupted into laughter. Alyce, at whose courtroom table another set of prints had been delivered, sniggered, leaning sideways to her lawyer. Reid didn't laugh.

'Perhaps your client would share the joke with the court, Mr Beckwith?' said Pullinger, who wasn't smiling either.

'There's an open air market on the Place des Lices in St Tropez on two days of the week, Tuesdays and Saturdays,' explained Jordan, patiently. 'It caters for tourists as well as local residents, selling all sorts of things: cheap clothing and a lot of local produce, cheeses and meats. And there are bric-a-brac stalls. From one of them, at a Tuesday market, I bought a plastic ring, in imitation marble. It was a joke between us. Play-acting, the way people do.'

'Play-acting the way people do when they feel they are falling in love?' said Bartle.

'*No!*' refused Jordan. 'It wasn't like that.'

'Like what, Mr Jordan?'

'A serious declaration of love: a declaration of anything of the sort you are trying to make it into.'

'Why didn't you mention it, in your written statement?'

Hold your temper, Jordan told himself. 'Because it was so inconsequential: so meaningless. I had totally forgotten the incident: didn't even remember it when I first saw the photographs.'

'You claim it was a joke?'

'It *was* a joke: a silly, harmless joke.'

'People laugh at jokes,' said Bartle. 'You and Alyce Appleton look very serious at your restaurant table, with your celebratory champagne.'

'This is a ridiculous attempt to create a situation where no situation existed,' insisted Jordan.

'Did Alyce Appleton continue to wear your meaningless plastic joke ring after that day in St Tropez?'

There'd be more photographs, Jordan guessed. 'She might have done. I don't remember her doing so. As I have tried to make clear, it was totally inconsequential, something over in a moment and forgotten.'

'Alyce Appleton doesn't appear to have forgotten it,' said Bartle, summoning the usher to distribute another selection of photographs.

The second batch was thicker than the first and Jordan was surprised that his initial reaction at flicking through them was not apprehension at the questioning they were going to prompt but the briefest moment of nostalgia.

'Do you recognize – remember – these photographs?'

'Of course I do!' replied Jordan, unthinkingly.

'Of course you do,' again mocked Bartle, as he

looked up to the bench. 'I would particularly invite your honour to look at the ring upon Alyce Appleton's finger as I go through the numbered sequence. Here – dated as they all are – is Mrs Appleton boarding a yacht to another sailing excursion, this time to the Iles de Porquerolles. And print five shows Mrs Appleton and Mr Jordan at Cagnes. Print six has them at the Hermitage Hotel in Monte Carlo and this,' declared Bartle with the enthusiasm of a conjuror groping into his top hat for the rabbit, 'is the photograph of Alyce Appleton passing through Nice airport for her return to America...' Bartle paused, to create his moment. 'Each of the photographs before you, your honour, very clearly show Alyce Appleton wearing the joke, inconsequential plastic ring so seriously slipped upon her finger by the defendant, the gesture celebrated with champagne.'

And he hadn't once been aware of it being on Alyce's finger after that one fun lunch at the Mouscardins restaurant, thought Jordan.

Alyce walked unaided but with her lawyer attentively close at hand to the witness stand, her doctor tensed forward from his chair behind, took the oath in a controlled voice and settled herself demurely in her seat, knees discreetly covered by her mid-calf skirt, hands crossed in her lap. Despite the lack of make-up, there was a tinge of natural colour to her cheeks. In a steady, controlled voice she went through the identifying formalities before looking expectantly to Daniel Beckwith. On her trip to France, she

328

agreed, she had had an affair – the first in which she had engaged after her marriage to Alfred Appleton – with Harvey Jordan. She could not recall a time in her life when she had felt so lost, so abandoned. Having initiated the divorce proceedings after discovering she had a sexual disease and undergone successful treatment, she had tried to distance herself as far away as she could from a husband she despised and for whom she no longer had any feeling other than contempt. When she'd got to France she'd realized it was not the good idea she had imagined it would be. She was lonely, her confidence gone: there'd been days – specifically two, she admitted, under Beckwith's questioning – when she hadn't bothered to bathe or even get out of her hotel bed. Harvey Jordan had been kind. At no time had his attitude towards her been that of a predatory seducer. She'd been intrigued by his invitation to what emerged to be the prison in which the man in the iron mask had been held, never for a moment considering the possibility of his making a sexual advance. Which he didn't. Feeling as she did because of her personal circumstances – the circumstances of being betrayed and abandoned – she had been deeply moved at seeing the cell in which someone had been shut off from the world, as she at that moment felt herself to have been.

'What happened after you disembarked from the catamaran back in Cannes, to return to the hotel at which you were both staying?' asked Beckwith.

Looking directly at the man, her voice even

and clear, Alyce said, 'Harvey asked if I wanted to have dinner. I told him no, that I was tired after being at sea all day and that I wanted to go to bed. But not alone.'

'Had Harvey Jordan made any sort of sexual approach, any sexual advances, prior to your telling him that?'

'No, none whatsoever.'

'So the approach came from you, without any encouragement or pressure from him?'

'Yes. Although when I said it I didn't think of it – imagine it – as a sexual approach. I'd been too long alone, like the poor man who'd spent his life in jail for an offence that has never been positively known. I just didn't want to be alone that night.'

'But that night you and Harvey Jordan made love?'

'Yes.'

'Were you a willing partner to the lovemaking?'

'Yes.'

'Did Harvey Jordan force himself upon you?'

'Absolutely not! I had only ever known one man, sexually, before Harvey, who was the most gentle, considerate man I could ever have imagined. Sex with my husband had been close to rape. Sex with Harvey was what I'd always imagined love to be, but never known.'

The reactions stirred through the court. From the Appleton table there was anger from the man himself, but a smile of satisfaction from Bartle. Beckwith irritably tapped his finger against his leg.

Quickly Beckwith said, 'Did you imagine yourself – believe yourself – falling in love with Harvey Jordan?'

'Of course not! Neither of us, from that night until I left to return here, to this divorce, had any illusions or fantasies about what was happening. We were having an affair, for my part a wonderful affair. But it ended with my flight taking off from Nice.'

'You did not intend – plan – ever to see him again?'

'Never.'

'What was your reaction at learning that Harvey Jordan had been cited as a co-respondent in this divorce? And that a damages claim for criminal conversations had been filed against him?'

'Great distress. I do not deny the affair in France. But according to my understanding of the damages accusation Harvey Jordan is not in any way responsible for me divorcing my husband. By the time I met Harvey Jordan there was not the slightest affection remaining to alienate me from my husband. There hadn't been, for a very long time.'

As he sat, Beckwith leaned close to Jordan and said, 'Better than I'd hoped.'

Apart from the actual moment of admitting that she had made the first sexual move, Alyce had avoided looking at Jordan. He thought she might have returned to him when her examination switched from Beckwith to Bartle, ready to give a smile of both thanks and encouragement, but she didn't. She did shift on the witness stand, sitting more positively upright, as if preparing herself for the attack that was to come. But it was with an attitude of defiance – forced defiance maybe – not the lassitude under which she had appeared crushed throughout most of the hearing.

'You went to France still considering another reconciliation with your husband, didn't you? That's why you took the final irrevocable documentation with you instead of signing it here, in America.'

'I had no intention whatsoever of entering another attempted reconciliation with a husband who had given me venereal disease. The final documents were not signed here in America because they weren't ready when I went to France. They were sent to me, for signature, while I was there.'

'In France you fell in love with Harvey Jordan...' Bartle paused, searching for the quote from his notes. '"The most gentle, considerate man I could ever have imagined".'

'No.' Her face was more flushed now, with what Jordan inferred to be anger.

'You were so much in love with him that you couldn't wait to get into bed with him, could you? So eager, in fact, that you actually invited him to sleep with you?'

'After enduring the life to which I was sub-jected by my whoring husband I welcomed gentility and kindness.'

'Is that why you were happy to settle with a plastic token of love!'

'I would...' started Alyce, but stopped. Instead

she said, 'It wasn't a love token. As Harvey has already told you, it was a joke, a silly joke that meant nothing.'

'A silly joke that meant nothing but which you continued to wear throughout your time together in France, even on the plane coming back here for your divorce action that you didn't finally initiate until you met Harvey Jordan?'

'I've answered your question,' said Alyce.

'Not quite,' argued Bartle. 'You began answering but changed your mind about what you were going to say. What was that, Mrs Appleton, that you originally intended to say?'

'I said what I intended to say,' insisted the woman.

'Did you set yourself a time limit, to take a lover in France?'

'My purpose in going to France was to get as far away as I could from a man of whom my contempt and disgust was absolute, not to take a lover.'

'She's holding up well,' Beckwith leaned sideways to whisper to Jordan. 'He's trying to run her down like a truck but she's not letting him.' Beside his lawyer Jordan was burning with fury, hands tightly gripped together beneath the court table.

'You do not like love – sex – do you, Mrs Appleton?' persisted Bartle. 'From the very moment of your marriage you were reluctant to share your husband's bed.'

'It was not until I met Harvey Jordan in France that I learned the joy of sex. What I did not like was rape, which is how I came to regard my

333

sexual encounters with my husband very early on in my marriage.'

'You loved your husband, though, didn't you?'

'I imagined I did, at the very beginning. It did not take me long to realize that was all it was: imagination. Which is why this action against Harvey is so ridiculous. How can a man alienate affection when no affection exists?'

'You've rehearsed your story well, the two of you, haven't you? Practically the same phrases, the same denials?'

'There has been no rehearsal, no preparation, between Harvey and myself to defend this preposterous accusation. There didn't need to be. All we both needed to do was to tell the truth. Which we both have.' The flush was going from her face; Alyce even appeared to have resettled, more relaxed, in her seat.

'Where's the ring you wore throughout your time with Harvey Jordan in France?'

'I've no idea.'

'You've no idea of the whereabouts of the love token that was so precious to you?'

'I have no idea where the joke ring is, no.'

'Isn't it somewhere at home, in one of those boxes in which women keep things, trinkets, that they treasure more than diamonds or gold? Things of the greatest sentimental value?'

'I do not have such a box.'

'You do remember him buying it and giving it to you in St Tropez, don't you?'

'I had forgotten, until I was reminded by your photographs.'

'But now you do remember?'

'Yes.'

'What did he say when he took your hand and slipped it upon the finger from which you had so recently discarded your husband's wedding ring?'

'I don't remember.'

'Did he say it was a token of his love?'

'I don't remember.'

'Did he ask you to marry him, when you were divorced and free to do so?'

'I think I would have remembered, if he had. I don't remember.'

'Surely he didn't say something like: "this is a plastic ring I want to put on your wedding finger as a joke!"?'

'I really don't remember,' repeated Alyce. 'It is you attaching such great importance to the ring. We didn't.'

'Except that you wore it all the time you were together.'

'Look at your own photographs,' invited Alyce. 'You'll see in most of them that I wore the sun hat and sandals I bought there. It was very hot. That was all I thought them to be, a hat and a pair of sandals.'

There was an isolated snigger from Dr Harding, from behind the rail.

'I can see that you did, Mrs Appleton,' agreed Bartle, resuming his seat. 'But as you've just told the court, you bought the hat and sandals yourself. Harvey Jordan bought the ring for you and you didn't wear that *most* of the time. You wore it *all* the time.'

\* \* \*

335

Beckwith waited until Alyce got back to her table to sit beside her lawyer before rising, and as he did so the judge said, 'I trust this will not be a lengthy concluding submission?'

'I see no reason for it occupying very much more of your honour's time, because I believe the evidence you have heard speaks for itself,' responded Beckwith. 'This was no instant love match, the stuff of fiction and movies. This was a brief, adult affair between two people, one a single, unattached man on vacation, the other a lonely woman about to divorce a husband for whom affection, if it had ever existed, had long ago died. Mr Bartle has attempted, with very obvious desperation, to make much of the giving of a ring as proof of his client's claim against Harvey Jordan. Both Harvey Jordan and Alyce Appleton have described the ring episode as a silly joke, which was all it was. I submit to you, your honour, that Mr Bartle's efforts to make it appear otherwise is an even sillier joke and an indication of his desperation, although far less sinister than the efforts to which the other side appeared prepared to go with the medical evidence of chlamydia. About which I will say nothing further, knowing as I do that your honour has reserved judgement upon it. What I do invite you to find upon the evidence is that under Section 1-52(5) of the North Carolina statute Harvey William Jordan is not guilty of alienation of affections, nor of criminal conversations, and dismiss him from the proceedings.'

Judge Hubert Pullinger had listened to the

submission slumped back in his chair, not appearing to make any notes. He remained that way for several moments before coming forward over his notation ledger, his throat rumbling, as it had earlier, to clear it before making a pronouncement. 'You have, Mr Beckwith, forcibly made a submission of some substance – some passion even – which I would be ill treating with a snap ruling, without the benefit of proper reflection: a snap decision which might, even, provide you with ground for an appeal. I choose to remind you of the legal application open to me on charges of alienation of affection and criminal conversation, between which there is an important division. The date of separation of the parties is important to prove alienation of affections and I have yet to hear sworn evidence to prove the depositions that have already been provided to the court. Essential to that is the malicious conduct of your client, Harvey Jordan, in contributing or causing such loss. The parties to the marriage must still be together in order to prove this claim. I have yet to hear further about that, although there is every indication that by the time Mrs Appleton met and engaged in admitted adultery with Harvey Jordan the contesting parties were not together.

'The action of criminal conversation, however, is more complex. It is a lawsuit sounding in tort – an injustice to the person – based upon sexual intercourse between the defendant, your client, and the plaintiff's spouse, Mrs Appleton. Further to define the law, a criminal conversation is a strict liability tort, because the only thing the plaintiff, Alfred Appleton, has to establish is an act of sexual intercourse, the existence of a valid marriage between the plaintiff and the adulterous spouse, and the bringing of a lawsuit within the applicable statute of limitations. It is not a defence that the defendant did not know his sexual partner was married, which indeed, Mr Beckwith, you did not advance. Nor is it a defence that the adulterous partner consented to the sex, which again you have not advanced. Nor is it open to you to plead that a separation already existed, that the marriage was unhappy or that the defendant's sex with the spouse did not otherwise affect the plaintiff's marriage. Most important among other caveats, which I will not at this stage explore further, is that the plaintiff had also been unfaithful...'

There was the familiar pause, for further throat clearing. Beckwith, expressionless, was sitting tensed forward, leaving the judgement to be recorded by the court stenographer. Bartle was doing the same but there was already a satisfied smile settling on his face. On that of Alfred Appleton, too.

'None of which diminishes the submission that you have made before me today. It is my function to interpret and administer the law, as it has been proscribed. Even before the full and proper beginning of this action, matters arose which greatly disturb me and upon which I have yet to adjudicate. I do not believe that I would be properly administering the law, which is my duty, if I found for your submission and dismissed your client from this matter. As I have, in the matter of the medical evidence, I intend to reserve my judgement, pending the full hearing.'

'Fuck it!' Jordan heard his lawyer say. It was what Jordan thought, too.

# Twenty-Five

After granting David Bartle's instantly sought, and unopposed, application on behalf of Appleton for the divorce hearing to be in closed session, Pullinger adjourned until the following week, citing his need to use the intervening days to 'tidy the loose ends of this wholly unfortunate beginning', and once more Jordan and the two lawyers gathered in Reid's Raleigh office to review the judge's rejection.

'We should have known about that goddamned ring,' complained Reid at once, openly accusing.

'If I'd remembered it I would have told you,' said Jordan, no longer deferring to either lawyer, although glad now that he and Beckwith hadn't split after their earlier disputes. 'It was exactly as Alyce and I told the court: a stupid joke thing that was totally unimportant. And I can't – and won't – believe Pullinger refused the dismissal because of it. That would be ridiculous.' He looked at Beckwith. 'I thought you made a convincing submission. Thank you.'

The lawyer inclined his head in acknowledgement and said, 'It was annoying, being caught out about the ring, but I don't think that was why Pullinger found against us, either. I think he was thoroughly pissed off by what the other side tried to pull and didn't want to protract every-thing further with another possible plea on Leanne's behalf. This way he's tied it up in one bundle.'

'You still estimating any finding against me as high as you did in the beginning?' asked Jordan.

Beckwith shook his head. 'We're way down the scale now. We've got to be!'

'I agree,' said Reid.

'Alyce stood up well, until it was all over,' said Jordan. When she'd been invited to the review conference she had pleaded exhaustion and Dr Harding at once confirmed, after examining her, that medically it would be too much for her to go through any analysis, actually administering some medication in a court ante-room before yet again smuggling her from the building.

'Now you're going to be centre stage,' Beckwith reminded Reid. 'You think she's going to be strong enough to stand up to it all? Today wasn't even a taste of what she's going to face from Bartle when we get to the full case.'

'I'm glad of the adjournment,' admitted Reid. 'I'm seeing Harding first thing tomorrow. After what's already happened I don't want to throw any more medical stuff at Pullinger but I might ask for some relaxation in her attending if Harding tells me it's necessary.'

'You intending to have him on hand all the time?' queried Beckwith.

'Another reason for seeing him tomorrow,'

expanded Reid. 'I'm hoping his function at the Bellamy clinic is more administrative than actually practising. If it is he might be able to spend more time than someone with a patient list.'

'He looks young to be the administrator of an entire hospital?' suggested Jordan.

'Local boy made good,' said Reid. 'Very good indeed.'

'What do I have to do now?' Jordan asked his lawyer. 'Do I have to be in court the whole time?' There was a lot more use to which he could put the New York bank accounts.

'I'll think about that as things take their course,' said Beckwith, cautiously. 'We're pretty much at the back of the bus in the immediate future. But certainly you should be in court in those early days. I'm sure we're still ahead, as far as our part of the case has gone. But I don't want to upset a spiky old bastard like Pullinger by making a move he'd consider disrespectful. And after his reaction to how you make a living I wouldn't like to argue pressure of business.'

'I don't think much of Bartle. Or Wolfson,' prompted Jordan. Or Reid, for that matter, he mentally added.

'We knocked both of them way off course,' said Beckwith. 'Bartle did the best he could with what he had. Which was why the ring was a nuisance. Without it he really would have been floundering.' He looked at Reid. 'Don't underestimate him next week. He's got a lot of court ground to recover. Wolfson, too. Alyce is going to be put through a lot of hoops and she already needs a doctor on standby.'

'That's what I'm going to talk through with Harding tomorrow.'

'Shouldn't there be a specialist on hand, as we had over the chlamydia business?'

'I told you, that's what I'm seeing Harding to decide,' insisted Reid. 'And I think these after-court discussions are useful. I'd welcome the input continuing.'

I bet you would, thought the unimpressed Jordan. He said, 'You're going to need more than discussions like this if your enquiry people don't move their asses more than they've done so far.'

'The planning conference with them is scheduled for tomorrow afternoon. They're making promising noises. I'll bring Dan up to speed before we start next week.'

And I'll bring myself up to speed on Trojan horseback, thought Jordan.

But not here in Raleigh, he decided, recognizing the opportunity again to get back to New York, which he already knew his lawyer intended to do on the first available flight the following day.

Dinner was Jordan's first reflective opportunity on the outcome of the day and he accepted, without admitting it to his lawyer, that he'd been too optimistic of Pullinger's dismissal. But as objective as he always was, Jordan at once recognized that there was a potentially protective benefit from him being officially detained in America instead of remaining there of his own volition, which he'd already decided to do if they'd won the day. This way there could be no suspicion of him in any way being responsible or involved in the intended retribution against Alfred Appleton, remote though any such suspicion might be, so carefully – and so far undetected – had Jordan evolved his unfolding attack. But he would be restricted in expanding that attack if he had constantly to attend the Raleigh court. This fact created an uncertainty – a hindrance – in the mind of a man who didn't like initiating anything about which there was the slightest doubt or difficulty.

Jordan was glad he wasn't able to get a seat on the same flight as Beckwith, able to travel alone back to New York. So accustomed to working and being always alone, responsible only for and to himself, that, objective again, Jordan acknowledged that the constant presence of Beckwith and Reid – of so many other people – had caused something like claustrophobia in him in Raleigh. It might not have been so bad, he supposed, if things had been different with Alyce: if he'd been able to see her, be with her, sometime during the adjournment. Fragile though she was, she had been magnificent on the witness stand, doing everything that she could to prove he wasn't guilty or responsible for her marriage collapse under ridiculous Dark Ages laws enacted by Puritans who believed in witches and burned them at the stake. He wanted – needed – to thank her: thank her for enduring the humiliation of actually admitting that it was she who had come on to him before he'd hit upon her, which he'd intended to do the night they'd got back from the prison island visit anyway. Was Beckwith right, that what Alyce had gone through the previous day was a soft prelude to what she was going to be subjected to by Bartle the following week? He didn't want to be excused the court when Alyce was on the stand. He'd be there every day, supporting her if he could, letting her know if he could that he was there for her. As he would be. Counting. Counting every humiliation, every shitty trick or device that Bartle and Appleton imposed upon her. And by every notch in that count he'd increase the humiliation and shit he'd already started to dump on Alfred Jerome Appleton. Not just an eye for an eye or a tooth for a tooth: he'd figuratively dismember the man organ by organ, limb by limb, until all that was left for people to laugh at would be a hump-backed, flush-faced head on a spike.

He'd advised the Carlyle the previous night of his return to Manhattan and his retained suite was predictably immaculate, his intrusion detectors in the suit closet and dressing-room drawers undisturbed. He held back from unstabling his Trojan Horses at once, deciding that there was so much he had to cover that he needed to create a reminder list to avoid him overlooking anything. It took him an hour to compose and he was surprised at its length when he finished.

He assumed that Bartle and Wolfson would have returned as he and Beckwith had – maybe Appleton and Leanne, too – but there would have been little opportunity for the lawyers to have updated their computer case files. Working his way patiently through his reminders, Jordan decided that with the exception of DDK Investigations, Reid's enquiry agency, within whose computers he had so far not embedded a see-all spyhole, he'd probably be premature accessing any of his already burgled sites until the following day.

Jordan was on the point of quitting the hotel for West 72nd Street and whatever mail might be waiting there for him in Appleton's name when his telephone rang.

'I wondered if you'd be back here,' said Alyce.

'You're in Manhattan?'

'I couldn't stand being in Raleigh any longer. And there were television and cameramen all around the estate.'

'How are you?'

'It's just the court. Once I'm out of it, not in the same room with him, I'm OK.'

'What are you doing?'

'Just here, in the apartment. You?'

'Just here, in the suite. There's still time for a late lunch.' West 72nd Street could wait.

'That would be nice. Do you know Enrico's, on 57th and 3rd?'

'I can find it.'

She was there, looking through her heavy-rimmed glasses at the menu while she waited, when Jordan entered. The black sweater showed off her blondeness and she'd covered the courtroom pallor with more make-up than she normally wore and Jordan thought the lipstick was too bright, almost as bright as Leanne Jefferies' has been in court. She was drinking mineral water. She seemed to sense his presence before he reached the discreet side booth, shadowed even more than the already deeply shadowed restaurant, and looked up, smiling. 'Hi!'

Jordan lowered himself opposite her and said 'hi' back. She hadn't completely managed to hide the dark rings beneath her eyes.

'I know I look a mess,' she said, as if reading his thoughts.

'You don't look a mess and you know it.'

'I feel a mess.'

'You've no reason to feel a mess, either.'

She smiled again, shaking her head. 'I don't believe you. But thanks anyway. The hotel in Raleigh told me you'd gone away until Sunday, so I guessed you'd come back here.'

Jordan said, 'I'm glad you got me. I want to thank you for everything you said in court.'

'It was the truth. That's what you're supposed to do, isn't it? Tell the truth. Why didn't you?'

'What!'

'About having once been married?'

Jordan shook his head. 'All part of the venture capitalist nonsense, too busy for a normal life.'

'How did it go wrong for you?

'Rebecca found another guy she liked better.' She had, but not until he'd tried to drown himself at the bottom of a bottle.

Alyce humped her shoulders, dismissively.

Jordan ordered a gin martini from an enquiring waiter. 'It still can't have been easy for you, standing there in front of your husband, saying what you did.'

346

'I'm sorry about the ring.'

'Turned out to be a pretty bad joke, didn't it?'

'It was nice at the time. Everything was nice at the time.'

Jordan hesitated, curious at the remark. 'I thought so, too. I really didn't notice that you went on wearing it.'

'I know you didn't.'

'Why did you?'

'I wanted to. I wouldn't have done it, though, if I'd known everything we did, everywhere we went, was being watched as it was. Alfred's a bastard; a one-hundred-and-ten-percent bastard.'

'But we fucked him with the chlamydia lie. Him and Leanne.' Jordan suddenly remembered that Reid hadn't made his promised application to the judge for the medical records, if any still existed, of the dead Sharon Borowski. He supposed that it wasn't so important now.

'I hope we can catch him out in all the others.'

'What others?' demanded Jordan, alertly.

'I wish I could guess. There'll be a lot more, believe me.'

Jordan did and wondered if he'd get any leads from the following day's phishing trips through the computers. 'We've agreed to have daily, after-court conferences, Dan, Bob and me. There's a lot of us on your side.'

'I'm glad you are,' Alyce said, smiling at him across the table.

From her study of the menu before he'd arrived Alyce immediately asked for spaghetti with clams when their waiter returned. Jordan, who hadn't bothered with the menu, said he'd

347

have the same, as well as a bottle of Chianti, eager to get rid of the man.

'What happened to the ring?' he asked.

'I took it off on the plane. Left it there when I got off. We'd agreed it was over, remember?'

Jordan hesitated. 'Didn't you want it to be?'

Alyce shrugged, awkwardly. 'It was best that it was. Except that it wasn't over, was it?'

'Isn't,' insisted Jordan, correcting her tense.

Alyce shook her head, positively. 'Let's not walk this route any further. You're still a defendant, possibly going to lose a lot of money.'

'After showing up their medical reports as we did, Dan doesn't think it's going to be anything like as bad as it might have been.' He was shortening the man's name, he realized.

'I don't see the connection, but that isn't what I want to talk to you about. I ... I mean the family will pay back whatever's awarded against you. As well as your costs. What's happened to you is my fault ... nothing to do with you...'

The offer silenced Jordan for several moments, his reactions colliding between anger and gratitude and settling somewhere in between. 'I don't want that. Thank you, but no.'

'It could be a lot of money.'

'I know. I can afford it.' How much he wished he could tell her that it would be her husband who paid and in a lot more ways than just money.

'You're offended,' she accused.

'I told you no. And mean it.'

They were both glad of the arrival of their food. The wine was better than Jordan had expected but Alyce limited herself to half a glass. Seizing the abstinence as a weak excuse to break the embarrassment that had come between them Jordan said, 'Aren't you supposed to drink with whatever medication the doctor's given you?'

Alyce didn't reply at once. 'It was just a tranquillizer yesterday. And it's not regular medication.'

'You're going to be under a lot of stress, a lot of pressure, next week.'

'I know.'

'Have you talked to the doctor about it?'

'He says there are things but I don't want to slow myself down, certainly not when I'm giving evidence. I don't want to give the bastard the slightest advantage.'

'Surely...' started Jordan, his mind on the previous day's after-court discussion. 'I've forgotten his name...?'

'Walter,' she provided. 'Walter Harding.'

'Is there a guarantee that Walter will be able to be in court every day?' persisted Jordan, not trusting Reid to be as thorough as he should be.

'Bob says he's going to try to get me excused some of the time.'

Jordan decided against referring to the conversation with the two lawyers. Instead he said, 'What if Pullinger refuses?'

'Maybe then I'll have to take something.'

'Dan seems to want me there most of the time.'

Alyce gave a half smile. 'That'll be something, having you there.'

'When are you going back down to Raleigh?'

'Sunday, I guess. It's not something I particularly want to think about.'

'We could spend some time together here at the weekend.'

'Maybe,' Alyce said, doubtfully.

'Why don't I call? We could drive up into the Catskills.'

'I don't want to pick up where we left off in France, Harvey. Not...' She stopped. 'I just don't, OK?'

'I'll call,' insisted Jordan.

Jordan went several times through virtually every word of their conversation, eagerly analyzing every inference and meaning, sure of his final conclusion. The most important of which was that Alyce hadn't wanted their affair to end in France, which he'd been too stupid then not to realize. But now he did realize it. And decided it wasn't too late for him to recover. She'd clearly reconciled herself to it being over, her only consideration now the impending turmoil of the coming weeks. But that's all it would be, just weeks: days and weeks when he'd be with her, doing everything he could to help and support and protect her. And when it was all over ... What about when it was all over? he demanded, halting the fantasy. All it could ever be, a fantasy. How could it be anything else, doing what he did, existing every day of his life as he did? *Darling, there's something I've got to tell you. I'm not a professional gambler, any more than I was an investment financier. I'm a crook. I steal people's identities, rob them –*

*never stripping them clean; just as much as I think they can afford to lose, apart from your ex-husband, who, by the way, is paying for everything it's going to cost me – I've already got close to $140,000 of his money – but we can have a wonderful life together if you can overlook where the money comes from.* Impossible, Jordan told himself. He lied to everyone else but never to himself, which was what he was doing – trying to do – now. It was time he woke up from the daydream: remembered who he was and what he did and accepted France for what it had been, a nostalgically recalled but passing, thank-you-and-goodbye affair. Except that he didn't want it to pass, not now. For the first time since Rebecca – unthinkingly, unintentionally – he had developed a feeling, an emotion, he'd never imagined himself capable of again. Still impossible. But not totally dismissable, not quite yet. There were still the next few weeks, a period during which he had no alternative but to stay where he was, with Alyce as much and as closely as possible. Looking after her.

The outstanding loan invitation was waiting for him at West 72nd Street, along with acceptances, with the money already deposited in his account, for each of his four earlier applications. There was still time for Jordan to complete it and personally deliver it before moving along Wall Street to draw upon those already agreed, swopping the amounts between the various safe-deposit boxes to keep the value in each below the legal reporting levels.

351

Back at the hotel he picked his way meticulously through the trading accounts and internal email stations of Appleton and Drake, the first task always to pick up the slightest indication of suspicion or discovery, before making further transfers to the banks he had so recently visited. Again he travelled further than the already plundered currency trades, moving that late afternoon through the company's metal division, drawing predominantly from already agreed copper and aluminium futures.

Jordan was at his laptop, showered and with room-serviced coffee beside him, before eight the following day, trawling through his illegal computer emplacements roughly in his order of establishing them. He saw that Beckwith had written himself an aide memoir to bring to the attention of the jury, before whom the full divorce would now be heard, what he labelled 'a determinedly attempted deception over the initially incomplete chlamydia findings'. On the systems of both Boston venerealogists, in email exchanges and in an already partially written defence to the Massachusetts medical licensing authority, Jordan found written confirmation that the inadequate reports had been prepared under pressure from Appleton as well as David Bartle. There was also a series of email's between Appleton and Bartle in which the lawyer complained of having to defend Mark Chapman free of charge before any disciplinary body and of the difficulty he might have getting Chapman back into court for the full divorce hearing. One note contained the phrase: 'your stupid interference that could get the whole lot of us in serious shit, which puts a lot of strain upon our friendship'. Jordan discovered, and saw them as a potential gold mine, some incomplete but hostile emails between Bartle and Wolfson from which the most obvious conjecture was of a falling out between Appleton and Leanne Jefferies. In one message Wolfson wrote of the chlamydia dispute: 'seriously endangering the agreement our two clients have reached and led me to question my own professional position, as perhaps you should question yours'. That had caused Bartle to write back that: 'I think any further consideration of this particular aspect should be very strictly restricted to one-to-one, unrecorded discussions between the two of us.'

It was mid-morning before Jordan returned to the communications between his own lawyer and Reid, which were intriguing but again frustratingly incomplete. Reid wrote of his enquiry agents' investigation being 'much better late than never' and of it being couriered to Beckwith, who'd replied, obviously after reading whatever had been uncovered, that Reid might encounter difficulty introducing it into the forthcoming hearing on grounds of 'applicable admissibility unless you can manage it during cross-examination'. Encouraged by the notes between the two lawyers Jordan broke off from accessing his already established sites to get into his newly established Trojan Horses in the computer system of Reid's investigators. He was frustrated once more by what had passed between the two of them. There were apologies for delays and appreciation of Reid's patience but it was obvious that the findings had been provided on hard, paper copy, not transmitted over an Internet link. Knowing that the master copy had to be somewhere on a hard disk, Jordan spent almost two hours – as he had earlier trying to locate the other obviously couriered documents saved on other hard disks – but failed to find it without the necessary in-house, dedicated file name.

Jordan failed, too, to find a possible link when he went back a third time into Reid's system, but did locate further interchanges within the previous hour with his own lawyer about Alyce. The planned morning meeting with Walter Harding had been delayed, reported Reid. The hospital administrator diagnosed Alyce's problem to be psychological stress, compounded by having contracted the venereal infection from the man she was now divorcing; although the condition had been completely cured her gynaecologist had found considerable fallopian tube scarring, which made it unlikely that she would ever be able to carry a child full term. Harding had undertaken to attend the court for the majority of the hearing, certainly during the times that Alyce was on the witness stand, both when she gave evidence or faced cross-examination. Alyce's gynaecologist was prepared to appear to give evidence about the fallopian scarring, and Harding to support any application for her to be excused court attendance. He could also recommend a psychiatrist if the court demanded corroborative evidence about stress, although he knew Alyce to be reluctant to call such an expert witness – 'because she doesn't want to sound mentally unbalanced, which she isn't' – as she was reluctant to be prescribed tranquillizers throughout the duration of the case. Beckwith had responded recommending that Reid do the best he could to get women on the jury during its selection process and to 'do everything you can to bring out the fact that because of what Appleton did to her Alyce can't ever have kids'.

Jordan worked through lunch, not finishing his final computer invasion until gone five. A useful phishing trip, he decided, particularly discovering the disarray among the opposition. But there was far too much at the moment that was incomplete and needed expanding. He'd done well, ingratiating himself with both Beckwith and Reid. It was essential he kept it up – made the sort of practical suggestions that his hacking had already produced – to ensure he was always included in the after-court conferences. There should be enough, from what he'd come up with today.

There was no reply when he telephoned Alyce's apartment and he held back from leaving a message that would identify his voice if anyone other than Alyce accessed the machine. There was still no answer when he called again an hour later, nor at eight the following morning. On that call he said, 'It's me. Call me back,' and waited in his suite until noon. It was just after when his phone rang, his smiled expectation seeping away when Beckwith said, 'You all set for tomorrow's flight?'

'All set,' confirmed Jordan.

'How's your weekend been?'

'Not as good as I'd hoped it would be.'

# Twenty-Six

The first day of the full divorce hearing was largely technical, dominated by the painstaking jury selection which, to the judge's quick and obvious irritation, became protracted by Reid's determination to follow Beckwith's advice to pack the eventual adjudicating panel with as many female members as possible. The manoeuvre succeeded in a jury of seven women and five men, achieved largely by Reid's persistence in objecting to anyone who admitted prior, and therefore possible biased, awareness of either the social or historical standing of the Bellamy or Appleton dynasties.

For his part, Pullinger opened his court cleared of that jury and any of its impending participants, to rule to the briefly admitted media that the hearing was to be conducted strictly in camera as allowed by every free speech caveat available to him under the First Amendment of the Constitution of the United States of America, including, as well as written words, any current or past television or newspaper images.

It was during their exclusion that Jordan had the first, although limited, opportunity to talk to Alyce, who'd already been in the court – and scarcely acknowledged him – when he'd arrived that morning. For Pullinger's publicity-banning statement both sides were separated in different ante-rooms. Dr Harding, who had accompanied Alyce for the opening day, was also excluded, but instead of joining them in the ante-room, he hurried off to telephone his hospital. Beckwith and Reid huddled together at the larger of the two available tables, discussing various court documents set out upon it. Alyce went to a window, her back to the room.

'You OK?' Jordan asked, coming up behind her.

She half turned, smiling wanly. 'That's not the most intelligent question you've ever asked, is it?'

'I called over the weekend, like I told you I would,' said Jordan. He thought the lipstick was still too heavy.

'I know. I was there.'

'Why didn't you pick up the phone?'

'We talked everything out in Enrico's.'

'I'm not sure that we did.'

'I wanted to talk about the money. That was all. It went on beyond that.'

'I believe I misunderstood a lot of things in France. I don't think I do now.'

'Stop! Please stop! What's happening now – going to happen now – is all I can handle.'

'It's going to end. You're going to win, be rid of him, and we'll be back where we were.'

'We *weren't* ever anywhere!'

'I told you I misunderstood. Let's talk about it again when this is all over.'

'There's nothing to talk about! I got you entrapped and I hate myself for getting you caught up in it and I want you to change your mind and take the money, however much it might be.'

'Stop talking about the damned money! I'm not interested in that. I'm talking about us.'

'You two OK over there?' called Beckwith.

'Just chatting,' Jordan called back, not realizing that he'd raised his voice.

'I'm not,' said Alyce, lowering hers as well. 'All I want to think about – get through – is this case. I can't think – won't think – about anything else.'

Jordan saw she was shaking, hands clenched tightly by her sides. 'Hey! Let's calm down. That's what we'll do, get through this. Then we'll talk some more.'

'But not now! Nothing more now! Promise me. Just promise to be here, doing what you've been doing,'

The shaking had worsened and Jordan reached out towards her. Alyce hesitated and then came into his arms, although keeping her own at her sides. He said, 'I promise.'

'You got a minute, Harvey?' Beckwith called again, from across the room.

When Jordan reached the lawyers, leaving Alyce at the window, Reid said, 'What was that all about?'

'She's wound up tighter than a spring,' said Jordan. 'No reason why I can't talk to her now that the judge has ruled against my dismissal, locking me into the case, is there?'

'I guess not,' allowed Beckwith. 'But let's leave the physical support to the doctor, shall we? The huggy stuff wouldn't look good outside this room.'

'How did your meetings go after the adjournment?' Jordan asked Reid directly, anxious for his inclusion to be automatically accepted.

Reid hesitated and it was Beckwith who answered. 'Bob's people think they might have something about what you picked up on – Appleton's withdrawal from that Olympic selection, remember?'

'And why he seemed to drop out of Boston's social life,' added Jordan, building on the reminder. 'What was it?'

'They haven't fully pinned it down, not completely. But a woman, a girl, seems to have been part of it.'

Alyce had talked of something involving a girl, Jordan at once recalled. What he couldn't remember was when and then he did: when they'd first met in New York with neither of them sure whether or not it legally endangered them. Cautiously he said, 'That's not going to impress Pullinger, from what I've seen so far.'

'That sort of observation is not why you're being included in these conversations to provide,' dismissed Reid.

Those words of Reid's echoed in Jordan's ear like the clearest of warning bells. Too softly for her to hear from where she stood at the window, he said, 'Ask Alyce.'

'I already have. She says she doesn't know what it could mean.'

'Ask her again,' insisted Jordan.

The pony-tailed Beckwith let out an exaggerated sigh. 'We going to have to beat this out of you, Harvey?'

It had to remain vague, Jordan decided. 'Alyce told me something that sounds familiar, about Appleton and a girl, before she and Appleton got together.' Jordan was conscious of his lawyer looking pointedly at him as Reid walked across to the window at which Alyce stood.

Beckwith said, 'You got something more to tell me, just the two of us?'

'No.'

'I don't want to be caught out again, like I was with that fucking ring.'

'I explained that! You agreed it wasn't important.'

'I accepted how it might have happened. I won't accept getting caught with my pants down a second time. You and Alyce got an agenda I don't know about?'

'No!' denied Jordan, again. He was walking backwards into a cul-de-sac, he decided.

'Where did Alyce talk about this? In France? Or here?'

'Here.'

'When?'

'Before the dismissal application.'

'A meeting you also forgot to tell me about! After I'd told you – Bob had told you, as well – to stay away from each other!'

'It's in the past! Over!' said Jordan, inadequately. 'Now it could help.'

'You want to do me a favour, Harvey? I want you to stop thinking – behaving – like a gambler and more like a defendant in a court case that could still cost you a whole bunch of money. You've contributed a lot and I recognize that. Appreciate that. As Bob does. Don't risk losing everything we've so far won by trying too hard.'

He had to capitulate, Jordan accepted, reluctantly. And was relieved, too, that Reid was walking back across the ante-room towards them. Jordan said to his lawyer, 'I'll tell you every time I piss, too,' and wished he hadn't the moment the words were out.

'Make sure you do it in the pan and not all over your feet,' scored Beckwith, easily, increasing Jordan's regret.

'She doesn't know much more,' announced Reid, getting to them.

'How much more?' demanded Jordan.

'Alyce thinks the girl belonged to the same yacht club as Appleton, in Boston. And that she lived in Lexington: it's a suburb of Boston with a lot of history,' said Reid, continuing on. 'I can get that enquiry underway before the court resumes.'

More than Alyce had volunteered to him, thought Jordan. But then he hadn't pressed her very hard on it. 'Should be a good enough lead,' he remarked to Beckwith. He didn't add that he'd started to discover the story of other people's lives from much less.

Jordan, who was walking behind, was conscious

of Alyce looking anxiously around for her doctor as, rejoined by Reid, they filed back into court. Jordan couldn't see Harding either and before they passed through the gated rail he came as close as he conveniently could and said, 'He'll still be on the phone. Don't worry.'

She gave no indication of having heard him. The Appleton group followed into the court directly afterwards and virtually as they sat Pullinger began addressing the recalled jury. As was in his power, the judge said, the court was to be closed to reporters and photographs, either old or new, forbidden from publication until they had reached their verdict. For that reason they were prohibited from discussing with anyone outside the court anything they heard in evidence, including members of their families or friends. If they were approached by strangers seeking information they were to obtain as best they could – a telephone number, for instance – the identity of that stranger and report it at once to a court official. Their sworn and therefore legally required function, having heard his concluding directions, was to decide which of the petitioning parties was primarily responsible for the breakdown of the marriage. Their second function, according to a law which North Carolina remained one of the few states within the Union still to observe, was to decide the financial culpability of the two co-respondents, separately cited by each of the petitioning parties. Here again, insisted Pullinger, the jury was to be guided by his very specific concluding guidance, before retiring to reach their verdicts.

If there was anything whatsoever that they did not understand, or by which they were confused, they were immediately to contact a court official, for those doubts and uncertainties to be resolved.

Turning to Appleton's attorney, the judge said, 'At last, Mr Bartle!'

Jordan was reminded, within minutes of Bartle opening, of his own lawyer's remark that Bartle had a lot of court ground to recover. Jordan's biggest surprise was that there was no attempt to apportion or admit blame to either Alyce or Appleton. Marriage was a solemn but often difficult undertaking, intoned Bartle, its failure always regrettable and too often acrimonious. They would hear of such acrimony. They would hear of adultery, to which the judge had already referred. From the care of its selection, Bartle acknowledged each member of the jury to be men or women of the world and as such, on behalf of his client, he accepted that theirs, after his honour's guidance, would be a properly considered and well founded verdict.

'Clever opening,' insisted Beckwith, unasked, bending sideways to Jordan. 'Not talking down to them but *to* them, as equals not to be frightened of a court or what they've got to do in it.'

Coming sideways to meet the lawyer, Jordan was briefly aware of Walter Harding resuming his seat just behind the separating rail and of Alyce's brief, snatched look of relief.

Returning to what was happening in front of him, Jordon decided Alfred Appleton appeared even more overpoweringly large when he took the stand, trying – but failing – to refuse his earlier thought of the incongruity of such a gross man being in bed, making love, to someone as fragile as Alyce. There was a studied politeness, though, in the way Appleton responded, even voiced, to his attorney's lead, talking not to Bartle but always between the jury and the judge. He was proud, declared Appleton, to be a descendent of one of America's oldest and most respected families. And had been even prouder when, by his marriage to Alyce, there had been created the link to another similarly respected, country-founding family. He had never – nor ever would – take lightly the privileges and responsibilities of his birth. He worked – worked hard – for his living, hoping in a small way to give back something of the benefits that he'd inherited from his forefathers' building and development of the great country that was the United States of America. He'd hoped his marriage to Alyce Bellamy would be a contribution towards that ambition. So hard had he followed the American ethos of working to build up his Wall Street practise that, stupidly and now regretfully, he'd neglected Alyce in the early years of their marriage. But he'd hoped to have realized that neglect in time, trying to balance the demands of business with the responsibilities of his marriage.

His fervent hope had been that they could start a family, to seal the joining together of their dynasties with children. But they did not materialize. Knowing that his wife preferred a country to a city life he'd suggested she live in a family house on Long Island, from which he'd commuted every day of the week to Manhattan. Commodity dealers worked to a twenty-four-hour clock, meaning that he needed to be in the city around six in the morning and felt rarely able to leave before seven at night and after a few months he was warned by his doctor that he was risking a nervous breakdown. He changed his routine, splitting his week evenly between their two homes. His wife became unresponsive to him and he, in turn, became convinced that she was having an affair. Stupidly, rejected by a wife he loved, lonely in Manhattan, he became involved in two quickly terminated affairs, one of which, to his great and abiding regret, had resulted in Leanne Jefferies appearing with him in court as a defendant in a damages claim brought against her by his wife.

He believed his conviction that his wife was having an affair was confirmed when he discovered he was suffering a venereal disease. Despite which, after treatment, he made a determined effort to save his marriage by attempting a reconciliation with his wife after she demanded a divorce. Shortly afterwards, his wife announced that she was suffering a venereal infection and blamed him for giving it to her, which he categorically denied then and still did now, believing it was she who had given it to him, for him, in turn, unwittingly, to give it to Leanne Jefferies.

Despite the difficulties they had experienced – the venereal infection being the greatest – he still loved his wife and was willing once more to try yet another reconciliation. He had made that clear to her but she had said she wanted to go away to France to consider it. But from France, where he later learned she had formed an association with an Englishman, Harvey Jordan, she had instructed her attorney to initiate the threatened divorce that had brought them to court that day.

Beckwith began scribbling a series of notes to Alyce's attorney as Appleton's evidence-in-chief drew to its close, with Reid hunched in what appeared to be virtually permanent conversation with a head-shaking, red-faced Alyce.

'How would you describe your being here in court today, confronted with the end of a marriage in which you held so much hope and expectation?' asked Bartle, finally.

'A tragedy I shall regret for the rest of my life,' replied Appleton.

Reid appeared in no hurry to get to his feet, to begin his cross-examination, and even when he stood he fumbled, without apparent success, through his disordered papers. And then he needed to use an asthma inhaler before he could speak. Finally he said, 'I apologize, your honour. And to you, Mr Appleton.'

'Do you need a short recess?' asked the judge.

Jordan, concentrating upon Appleton, caught the briefest exchange of satisfied looks between the man and his lawyer.

'No, your honour. But thank you for your consideration,' said the attorney, no indication of difficulty in his voice. 'But I would seek your understanding in an application, even before beginning my examination, to recall this witness at a future time.'

Jordan was aware of Appleton's face tightening. Bartle's, too.

'Do you wish to approach the bench?' invited Pullinger.

'No, your honour. The jury has heard of the plaintiff's admission of two adulterous relationships, but been introduced to only one, that with Ms Leanne Jefferies, a defendant in the secondary action of criminal conversation.'

'Your honour!' interrupted Bartle, coming to his feet. 'Perhaps it was remiss of me not to have brought to the jury's attention the death of the second woman to whom my colleague is referring. And if you find it to be so, I apologize. But –' he turned, to include the jury – 'the person concerned, Ms Sharon Borowski, was the victim of a fatal automobile accident. As such she cannot feature in any way in this hearing. This surprise intercession therefore has no purpose or part in these proceedings.'

Reid took his inhaler from his pocket, considered its use, but then replaced it. 'Your honour, in the required exchange of material before the commencement of this case –' he moved his hand through the papers on the table before him, coming up with a single sheet – 'numbered thirty-five in your bundle, your honour, I advised the other side that I required the medical records of Ms Borowski?'

'To which I replied that none were available, the unfortunate woman being dead,' came in the opposing lawyer, again.

'Indeed Mr Bartle did,' agreed Reid. 'It's numbered thirty-six in your bundle, your honour. Two other people died, in the accident involving Ms Borowski, a mother and her son. The fatality is the subject of a civil action, against Ms Borowski's estate by the husband of the other woman who died. From enquiries I have made, after Mr Bartle's dismissal of my request, I believe there was a toxicology analysis carried out upon Ms Borowski. That would have included blood samples. I have applied to the coroner for a copy of that analysis, relevant as certain medical matters would appear to be in this case and to which the plaintiff, Mr Appleton, has already given some evidence...' Turning very slightly towards the jury, Reid went on: 'And I would stress some evidence, to the matter of transmitted infection. It is for that reason, in the hopeful expectation of a reply from the coroner during the course of this hearing, that I am making my recall application.'

'I find no problem with this,' said Pullinger. 'Mr Bartle?'

'I know of no precedent for such a course to be admissible,' argued Bartle. 'The dead cannot provide evidence from the grave.'

'It would not be Ms Borowski providing evidence from the grave,' disputed Pullinger. 'It would be a coroner or medical examiner, both of whom could be called to give evidence before this court, on oath, of their findings...' He paused. 'A course, a provision of evidence, that Mr Reid opened to you by his original request.'

'I am at your honour's discretion and disposal,' capitulated Bartle, with no alternative.

'Which is that I shall allow Mr Reid's application, as I now invite Mr Reid's initial examination.'

Beside him Jordan saw that Beckwith had created a virtual army of exclamation marks upon his legal pad. Aware of Jordan's attention, his lawyer scribbled, 'Absolutely Brilliant!!!' and immediately blacked out the words to make them unreadable. Jordan saw that Alyce was sitting with her head sunk so low upon her chest that she could have been asleep.

'Mr Appleton,' began Reid, still with no catch in his voice. 'You are giving evidence to this court under oath?'

Appleton looked for guidance to his lawyer, who did not respond. The man said, 'Yes.'

'Which requires you to tell the truth?'

There was still no protest from Bartle. Appleton again said, 'Yes.'

'Do you intend telling the truth, Mr Appleton?'

Bartle at last rose in protest. 'Your honour! Isn't this risking your court being brought into disrepute?'

'A question I am still considering from the hearing that preceded this one,' replied Pullinger, at once. 'I will allow it but would recommend restraint, Mr Reid.'

'Are you telling the truth, Mr Appleton?' repeated Reid.

'Yes.'

'You admit two affairs, one with Sharon Borowski, the other with the defendant, Leanne

Jefferies?' demanded Reid.

'Yes.'

'Which was the first, that involving Ms Borowski or Ms Jefferies?'

'Ms Borowski,' replied Appleton.

Appleton was trying to protect himself with clipped, one-word answers whenever possible, Jordan recognized.

'When did the affair with Ms Borowski begin?'

'I'm not sure of a precise date,' said Appleton.

'You can surely remember the month!'

'I think it was March.'

'March last year?'

'Yes.'

'Which part of March, the beginning or the end?'

'I said I'm not sure. More towards the end than the beginning.'

Reid again made the pretence of consulting his disordered papers. 'Ms Jefferies is a commodity trader, like yourself?'

Appleton was shifting uncomfortably on the stand, gripping and ungripping its bordering rail as if needing physical support. 'Yes.'

'What was Ms Borowski's occupation?'

'I don't believe she had an occupation.'

'You don't *believe* she had an occupation? You had an affair with her! Surely you knew whether she had a job or not?'

'It was a very brief affair.'

'How brief?'

'A matter of weeks.'

'How many weeks?'

370

'Four. Five.'

'How did you meet?'

'At a party, in Manhattan.'

'I asked you how?'

'Your honour!' interjected Bartle, once more. 'What possible relevance has this to do with the current case?'

'Mr Reid?' invited Pullinger.

'If I am allowed to continue, with the expectation of receiving the toxicology and blood analysis findings upon the deceased Ms Borowski, I hope to show that it is of crucial importance to the outcome of this matter, particularly the transmission of disease,' insisted Reid.

'Then it will continue,' decided Pullinger.

'I asked you how you met Ms Borowski,' repeated Reid.

'I told you, at a party.'

'That was *where* you met her. *How*?'

'I was introduced to her, by a mutual friend.'

'Towards the end of March, last year?'

'Yes,' replied Appleton, too quickly.

'Was that when your affair began, that night?'

Appleton re-gripped the edge of the witness stand. 'It might have been.'

'*Might* have been! Was it or wasn't it, Mr Appleton?'

'I think it was.'

'You think it was,' echoed Reid. 'You did know Ms Borowski before you were formally introduced to her at the end of March last year, didn't you?'

'I didn't know her,' insisted Appleton.

'But you'd seen her before? Been to parties

371

where she was?'

'I may have done.'

'May have done,' echoed Reid again, going unerringly into his tumbled papers to bring out a neatly prepared, individually separated batch of papers, beckoning the usher to give him the majority to distribute, but personally delivering their packages to Beckwith, Bartle and Wolfson. 'I would ask that these be placed before the jury and yourself, your honour.'

'These are copies of newspaper cuttings!' objected Bartle. 'These can't be admissible!'

'What's the purpose of this introduction, Mr Reid?' demanded the judge, stopping the usher before he reached the jury box.

'They feature photographs of Ms Borowski, in the diaries and social columns of certain New York newspapers, some with caption references to her which might give some indication of the occupation of which Mr Appleton appears un-sure,' said Reid.

'I object to their introduction,' insisted Bartle. 'This court was given no indication or warning of their being presented.'

'We've already touched upon your dismissal of Mr Reid's enquiries concerning this lady,' reminded Pullinger. 'I will not recess the court but read them here at the bench. Attorneys will read them, too, but not yet the clients they represent or the jury.'

There were shuffles throughout the court, mostly from the jury. Alyce remained head bent. Behind her, Dr Harding was leaning solicitously forward.

The three lawyers were still reading when Pullinger finished. He said, 'Mr Beckwith?'

'I have no objection to their introduction,' replied Jordan's attorney.

'Mr Wolfson?'

'I have no objection,' said the man.

'I will allow them, Mr Bartle, but warn you, Mr Reid, to be extremely careful in whatever it is you have to say,' ruled the judge. 'The usher will deliver the copies to the jury and to the plantiff.'

'From the photographs Ms Borowski was obviously an extremely attractive girl, Mr Appleton?'

'Yes,' agreed Appleton. The copies fluttered slightly from the tremor in the man's hand.

'In the copy number one, in the *New York Daily News*, Ms Borowski's age is given as twenty-three. Was that how old she was?'

'I did not know her age.'

'Or her occupation,' reminded Reid. 'If she was twenty-three that would make her younger than you by almost twenty years?'

'Your honour!' protested Bartle.

'Quite so,' agreed the judge. 'Careful, Mr Reid.'

'My apologies, your honour,' said Reid, with no obvious apology in his voice.

'The *Daily News* suggests an occupation for Ms Borowski, does it not? On the marked line it describes her as "a party girl", doesn't it?'

'Yes.'

'And there is something similar in the *New York Observer*, isn't there? On the marked line of the cutting, numbered two, she is described as "a regular party person", isn't she?'

'Yes.'

'What do you take "party girl" and "regular party person" to mean, Mr Appleton?'

'I don't know. I don't think it means anything.'

'That is you in the background of the cutting from the *New York Observer*, isn't it, Mr Appleton?'

'Yes.'

'The date of that cutting is February eighth last year, isn't it?'

'Yes.'

'So you were already aware of Ms Borowski before you formally met in March?'

'Yes.'

'And that affair with party girl Sharon Borowski began the first time you met her in late March, presumably at yet another party?'

'Yes.'

'Would you agree with me that "an affair" is a consensual relationship – a sexual attraction – between two people?'

'I suppose so.'

'You suppose so,' mocked Reid. 'You had sex with Ms Borowski on the first night of your meeting, that's right, isn't it?'

'I've already told you that I did,' said Appleton, his temper flaring for the first time.

'Did you envisage a long-term relationship?'

'I do not intend letting this continue much longer, Mr Reid,' warned the judge.

'I...' started Appleton, but stopped. Then he said, 'I don't know.'

'But you do know – remember – that you continued to sleep with Ms Borowski – and have sex with her – over the course of four or five weeks?'

'Yes.'

'Did you pay to sleep with Sharon Borowsk, the regular party girl?'

Bartle rose to protest yet again but before he could Appleton said, loudly, 'No, I did not pay her! She was not a hooker!'

As Bartle sat, Pullinger said, 'Have we laboured this point sufficiently, Mr Reid?'

'I have just one further question on this particular matter, your honour. Tell the court, sworn under oath as you are to tell the truth, Mr Appleton, did you give Sharon Borowski any gifts? Jewellery, for instance? A bangle, perhaps?'

'I think...' stumbled Appleton. 'I gave her a bracelet, that's all.'

'Let me move on to another part of your evidence-in-chief,' said Reid. 'You were working hard to establish your new business – despite apparently having time to party – your wife was living in the country, which she preferred but you were trying for a baby, were you not?'

'Yes.'

'But without success?'

'Yes.'

'Were you saddened, disappointed, that your wife did not conceive?'

'Yes.'

'Your wife suggested adoption, did she not?'

'Yes.'

'But you argued against that. Why?'

'I wanted our child to be biologically ours. To carry the bloodline of our two families. It was important.'

'Your wife also underwent medical examinations and tests to discover if there were some medical or physical reason why she was incapable of bearing children, did she not?'

Appleton had precariously lodged the newspaper cuttings on the corner of the witness stand and in reaching out yet again to grip its edge he knocked them off. Some fell inside, others outside, of the box. 'I'm sorry,' he said, stooping to recover those inside as the usher collected those beyond. Having retrieved what he could Appleton stood uncertainly with them in his hand until the usher reached out to take them.

'Mr Appleton?' urged Reid.

'Yes,' agreed Appleton, rigidly maintaining his minimal script.

'But you refused to undergo any medical examination, didn't you?'

'Yes.'

'Why?' demanded Reid, matchingly short.

'There is no biological or physical impediment in my becoming a father!' insisted Appleton.

Reid strained the maximum silence from the remark before saying, 'Without undergoing any medical examination you know there is no biological or physical impediment to you becoming a father?'

Bartle was sitting with his head bowed, although not as deeply as Alyce and Appleton stood flushed on the witness stand, washed away by a tide he couldn't fight against. Eventually he said, 'That is what I believe.'

'Believe because of some internal conviction?' pounced Reid. 'Something of which this court is unaware? Or because you have already been the father of a child?'

'Your honour!' exploded Bartle, coming finally to his feet.

Before Pullinger could respond, Reid said, 'I am finished for the moment, your honour.'

'What in the name of fuck was that?' demanded Jordan, as they settled in Reid's office. There were glasses and a bottle of Jack Daniels on the desk. Once more Alyce had insisted she couldn't withstand a review.

'I'll tell you what that was,' offered Beckwith. 'You remember me telling you that courts were theatres, in which people performed? You've just witnessed a performance deserving more Oscars than there are Academy Award categories. You were brilliant, Bob. Absolutely fucking brilliant.'

And I never believed the man capable of opposing a speeding ticket, thought Jordan, still needing time to properly assimilate it all. 'We never discussed any of this! I never knew you had so much to throw at him!'

'I don't remember our agreeing to talk about – to discuss – everything,' said the resistant Reid, pointedly.

Looking between the two of them Beckwith sniggered and said, 'You play a lot of poker, Harvey, as a professional gambler?'

'Some,' allowed Jordan, further confused.

'Then you know about bluff.'

Jordan looked from one lawyer to the other. 'Will someone – either of you – tell me what the hell you're talking about?'

'All Bob had were the newspaper cuttings,' explained Beckwith. 'We don't expect there to be any surviving toxicology evidence from Sharon Borowski. Which was why Bob delayed until the last minute asking the coroner for it, because we didn't want to be told there isn't any. It gives Bob the chance to recall Appleton, with whatever might arise during the hearing. Appleton and Bartle will be shitting rocks that we know more – have something – which was what I meant by Bob's Academy Award performance.'

'What about Appleton already having fathered a child?' persisted Jordan.

'Who knows whether he has or he hasn't,' shrugged Reid. 'He's admitted to not undergoing a fertility test. What more did I need?'

'But you knew about a bracelet?' persisted Jordan.

'No I didn't,' denied Reid. 'I just tossed it into the pond to see if I could make ripples. And I did.'

'You mean there wasn't any evidence for any of the inferences and innuendoes you spread around in there today?' demanded Jordan.

'Every question was justified from the evidence available before the court,' insisted Reid. 'We can't be caught out, like the other side was caught out with chlamydia. And the opposition don't know where we're coming from next.'

Jordan wasn't sure where he was coming from next, either. He'd been too confident of being dismissed from the case and had even more grossly misconceived how fully he'd thought he was being included by the two lawyers. He wasn't the driving force any longer, he accepted. And then he further accepted that perhaps he never had been.

# Twenty-Seven

'Body language,' said Jordan, his approach – and hopeful recovery – mentally rehearsed from the ill-tempered email exchanges he'd read between Bartle and Wolfson. And he did have to restore himself in the lawyers' judgement, Jordan decided: recover a lot and not allow his overconfidence to imply – the overconfidence verging on conceit – that he could do Beckwith and Reid's job better than they could.

Beckwith frowned and looked up from his Jack Daniels, with which they'd both continued at the hotel after the initial celebration in Reid's office. 'You want to help me with that?'

'You asked me earlier if I played poker. There are two essentials to win at the game. You need to be able to memorize every discard, to narrow down what your opponent might be holding. And read his body language.'

'And bluff, which Bob did so well today,' added the lawyer.

'I've been watching Leanne Jefferies,' said Jordan, doggedly. 'All day today she's actually sat as if she's trying to distance herself from Appleton.'

'Are you surprised?' exclaimed Beckwith. 'If the jury finds against her she's going to go down for big bucks. She's got every reason to hate the guy. Certainly to despise him.'

'Which I think is a new hate,' urged Jordan. 'Her lawyer's from the same firm as Appleton's and she went along with using a Boston venerealogist, both of which has got to be under pressure from Appleton. My impression is that she didn't realize the shit he'd dropped her into until she ended up in court. She doesn't know yet which way Pullinger's going to go with what they tried with the venerealogists, and today she heard, my guess is for the first time, that before her Appleton was screwing a hooker whose infection she caught.'

Beckwith, whose cross-examination of Appleton was to begin the following day, appeared to consider the argument. 'Could be you're right.' He smiled. 'Maybe an idea to widen the rift a little, before we get her on to the stand?'

'Better to widen it a lot.'

'Trust me, Harvey,' sighed Beckwith.

He was trying too hard again, Jordan accepted. Quickly he said, 'There's something I don't understand.'

'There's a lot I still don't understand,' remarked Beckwith, gesturing for refills.

Jordan hoped the lawyer wasn't getting drunk on the basis of that day's success. 'Why did Appleton *volunteer* his affairs with both women, actually providing Alyce with the grounds for divorce? And for the claim against Leanne?'

'I'm there ahead of you,' insisted Beckwith, vaguely mocking. 'It's on my reminder list for tomorrow. But thanks.'

'Why didn't Bob go for it, today?'

Beckwith sighed again. 'Because it's not the strategy we're following.'

Which he didn't know about, acknowledged Jordan, wondering if it had been decided when he'd been at the ante-room window with Alyce. 'Which is?'

'Re-examination,' disclosed Beckwith. 'Bob achieved it today on a limited point. If something comes out tomorrow, he can stretch – or try to stretch – the remit. As I can if Appleton slips between his replies to me and the replies he's already given to Bob. And we can do it all over again with Leanne when we get her on the stand.'

'What about Alyce?' demanded Jordan, at once. 'Won't she be exposed to a double act, from Bartle and Wolfson?'

'If they work out our game plan,' agreed Beckwith. 'As you will.'

'Were you going to warn me, if I hadn't asked?'

'Of course.'

Jordan didn't believe the other man. 'Is Bob going to warn Alyce?'

'It would make good sense to do so. I don't

like how shaky she is.'

Neither did he, thought Jordan. 'Bob should try to get her excused from the court.'

'Too soon,' insisted Beckwith. 'Pullinger will have seen a lot of women break up in pieces far worse than Alyce has done so far. Divorce is never a walk in the park.'

He had all his illegal sites still to access, Jordan remembered. And he hadn't yet helped himself to that day's tranche of Appleton and Drake's money. That thought prompted another. He said, 'Are things going more slowly than you anticipated?'

'Largely because of what the other side tried to pull,' said Beckwith. 'With Pullinger's adjournment built in, an entire week has been added.'

'So are we still looking at a month, from now?'

The lawyer shrugged. 'How the hell do I know? When I gave you that estimate I didn't imagine us encountering anything of what we have so far. You got a problem?'

Yes, thought Jordan. On his current rate of the Appleton embezzlement, he could possibly amass a further half a million by the end of a month, but that was to offset any damages that might be awarded against him. But he didn't imagine he could continue for a month without some financial controller or individual trader realizing Appleton and Drake was being milked like a milch cow. Which wasn't the most pressing problem; even after it was suspected or proven by a snap audit it would still take at least another month – maybe even two – for an official criminal enquiry to begin, by which time he would have distanced himself untraceably from all the illegally established Appleton bank holdings, leaving only their existence as evidence of Appleton's theft and money diversion from his own company. But Jordan intended far more. And an in-house investigation could very easily – and badly – impede his next move. To avoid his plans being disrupted he had to siphon off – although to different destinations – larger sums than his usual daily collection. But by increasing those amounts he correspondingly increased the danger of earlier discovery. Another week of simple bank transfers, Jordan decided. After that he had to begin, much more aggressively, undermining Appleton's very foundations.

Belatedly responding to Beckwith's question Jordan said, 'No real problem. I undertook to stay until everything was over if we lost the dismissal and I will. I just don't want everything to limp on, open-ended, which it seems to be doing.'

'Pullinger won't let anything that he controls "limp on, open-ended",' declared Beckwith. 'If he suspects for a moment he's being manipulated – as he clearly thinks he was with the venereal disease business – there'll be hell to pay.'

How, wondered Jordan, could he create a situation that would appear to the judge to be precisely that, motivated by Appleton? He didn't, at that precise moment, have the remotest idea. But he was confident he'd be able to think of one. Confident, Jordan at once qualified: not *over*confident.

'You employed a lot of people to watch your wife in France, didn't you?' demanded Beckwith.

'I engaged an enquiry service,' said Appleton.

'But not specifically for France?' insisted Beckwith. 'You'd engaged them long before that, hadn't you?'

'Yes,' conceded the commodity dealer.

The man had reverted to his single-word answers, Jordan recognized, although Appleton appeared more at ease in the witness box than he had the previous day. Alyce did, too, despite Dr Harding not being in court. Leanne looked strained, her face drawn.

'Why?' asked Beckwith, matching the brevity.

'I told the court yesterday,' said Appleton, determined against saying too much.

'Not to my recollection,' refuted the lawyer. 'Why did you put your wife under surveillance before she went to France?'

Appleton's face flushed, very slightly. 'I wanted to discover the man with whom she was having an affair. The man from whom she contracted the venereal disease that I caught.' His voice had risen, too.

Beckwith was proving as good as Reid, the previous day, thought Jordan. Within minutes he'd irritated Appleton out of his attempted stonewalling answers, which he guessed Appleton now realized, and by so doing unsettled the man. The lawyer stoked the unease by letting Appleton's reply settle in the minds of the jury before saying, 'What was the outcome of that surveillance here in the United States?'

'Nothing,' Appleton was forced to admit.

'I didn't quite hear that,' said Beckwith, settling into his performance.

'They didn't discover the man.'

'They didn't discover the identity of *any* man with whom your wife was having an affair,' expanded Beckwith. 'How long was your wife under surveillance here in America?'

'I'm not sure,' Appleton tried to avoid.

'Of course you're sure!' insisted Beckwith. 'You employed them: paid them money for the period during which they tried but failed to find anyone with whom your wife was sleeping. How long was your wife watched here in America before she went on vacation to France?'

'A month.'

'Your enquiry agents will be called, to give evidence,' warned Beckwith. 'Do you want to think again how long a period it was?'

'Maybe six weeks. It ran on, over into the time they spent in France. It may have been six weeks here.'

'Are they experienced enquiry agents?'

'Yes.'

'Yet over a period of six weeks, they failed to discover the lover with whom you were sure your wife was sleeping?'

'Am sure!'

Beckwith let Appleton's blurted, angry answer hang in the air for several moments before asking, 'Your investigators failed to find any evidence of a lover here. What other evidence – other source – do you have to make that assertion?'

'The infection I caught.'

'That's your proof?'

'Yes.'

'How much did six weeks unsuccessful surveillance here in America cost you, Mr Appleton?'

'It wasn't broken down in the bills I have so far paid.'

'All right. Then tell the court the amount you have so far paid.'

'Two hundred and twenty thousand dollars.'

There was a stir among the jury and Beckwith waited for it to subside. 'A huge sum of money, the majority of which I assume to have been incurred on air fares and expenses in sending your investigators to France?'

'Yes.'

'Where they discovered the affair between my client and your wife?'

'Yes.' Appleton smiled.

'Were you relieved?'

Appleton moved to speak but stopped. 'I don't understand.'

'A reputable investigation agency had failed after six weeks of twenty-four-hour surveillance to find that your wife had a lover in this country. In France they found my client. Your suspicions were vindicated, weren't they?'

'It proved she was promiscuous.'

'Did it?'

'Of course it did.'

'Why?'

'Don't be ... it did. What else could it prove?'

Appleton was almost shouting when he finished.

Today was unfolding just like yesterday, thought Jordan. And without the slightest input from him. He saw Alyce was leaning forward in her seat, head slightly to one side, her entire concentration upon her husband. Leanne Jefferies' attention was also focussed intently at the overpowering commodity trader.

Instead of responding to Appleton's demand Beckwith said to Pullinger, 'With your permission, your honour, I would like to introduce into the court the birth certificate of Harvey William Jordan, the copy of the passport of Harvey William Jordan and a venerealogist's report upon Harvey William Jordan prepared by an American specialist, Dr George Abrahams.'

To Pullinger's nodded agreement, the court usher collected the itemized material for distribution; as Reid had done the previous day, Beckwith personally handed the individual packages along the attorney tables.

'The first document before you, numbered one, attests the birth of Harvey William Jordan in Paddington, London, England, on June tenth, 1966, does it not?'

'Yes,' agreed Appleton.

'Will you turn to the final page of the copy of the United Kingdom passport, numbered two on its attached sticker, and read aloud to the court the surname on the first line of the man photographed in it?'

'Jordan.'

'And the given names on the next line?'

'I am being lenient here, Mr Beckwith,'

cautioned the judge, making his first interruption.

'Which I appreciate while asking your honour to accept the importance of this pedantry to my client,' said Beckwith.

'Keep it within bounds,' ordered the black-robed man.

'The given names, Mr Appleton?' prompted Beckwith.

'Harvey William,' dully responded Appleton.

'Go now, if you will, to the front of the document, in which are recorded the visas and entry dates into countries outside the European Union,' guided the lawyer. 'What is the last entry stamp that you can find for an entry into the United States of Harvey William Jordan, a copy of whose passport you now hold?'

'January thirteenth, 2004.'

'Endorsed for what period of time?'

'Ninety days.'

'From which it is beyond question that Harvey William Jordan could not have remained in the United States of America beyond April thirteen, 2004?'

'I suppose so.'

'Will you now go to the diagnostic page of the medical report prepared by Dr George Abrahams, numbered three, that you hold. Does that conclusion read that Harvey William Jordan does not, nor ever has, in the opinion of Dr George Abrahams, suffered from the sexually transmitted infection chlamydia?'

'Yes,' sighed Appleton.

'You spent the majority of $220,000 having

your wife followed more than three thousand miles to the South of France to find her with the lover your detective team had failed to identify after six full weeks of surveillance here in this country, didn't you?'

'It proved she was promiscuous.'

'It proved she engaged in one, brief and immediately terminated affair after contracting a venereal infection from you, who admits to at least two extra-marital relationships, doesn't it?'

'I did not infect my wife.'

'Neither could Harvey William Jordan, could he, from the irrefutable evidence you hold there in your hand?'

'She did not contract it from me!' In his shouted anger Appleton leaned forward over the rail he had the previous day needed for support.

'Who did she catch it from?'

'Her other lovers,' insisted Appleton, wildly.

'Other lovers your detectives failed to discover.'

'She's very clever: knew I was having her watched.'

'How did she know?'

'Because I told her!'

Jordan was aware of David Bartle shifting noisily at his table to attract Appleton's attention, the only way possible to warn the man of his loss of control. Jordan saw, too, that for the first time since she had been in court that Alyce was smiling.

'When, how, did you tell her?'

'I don't remember.'

'You don't remember when you told a wife

with whom you wanted a reconciliation that you were having her watched!' spelled out Beckwith, spacing every word to stress his incredulity.

'We were arguing.'

'Over what?' seized Beckwith.

Appleton shifted, too late realizing the trap snapping closed behind him. 'When she accused me of infecting her.'

'Which you did, didn't you?'

'No!' denied Appleton, loudly again. 'She infected me!'

'Go on.'

Appleton shrugged. 'That was it.'

'No it wasn't *it*, was it, Mr Appleton? You were arguing about who had infected whom and you told her you were having her watched. Tell the jury of that occasion.'

'She said I'd given her a complaint and wanted a divorce and I said I'd got it from her and that I was going to find out who her lover was and that I was going to have her watched. And she said she was having me watched.'

Jordan saw Alyce suddenly come close to Reid as Beckwith said, 'Was going to *have* her watched? Not that you already *had* her under surveillance?'

'I don't remember the precise words.'

'What was the date of that confrontation?'

'I don't remember that, either.'

Beckwith paused as Reid passed him a note, smiling up from it. 'Can I help you with the date? It was April fifth last year, wasn't it?'

'It might have been.'

'You really can do better than this, giving

testimony on oath, can't you, Mr Appleton?' persisted Beckwith, sorting through papers and material in front of him. He came up, a diary in hand. 'April fifth was a Saturday. You would have been home in Long Island on a Saturday – a weekend – trying for your much sought reconciliation with your wife, wouldn't you?'

'It could have been April. I don't know the actual date.'

'You can't remember the date when you still wanted a reconciliation with your wife?'

'No.'

'How many days are there in the month of March?'

Appleton looked anxiously to his lawyer, who shook his head. Appleton said, 'Thirty-one.'

'And April?'

'Thirty.'

'Yesterday you admitted to the court that during March – the precise date you couldn't remember it starting – you were in a sexual relationship with Sharon Borowski?'

Appleton nodded.

'The court requires an audible reply,' said Beckwith.

'Yes,'

'For six weeks?'

'Yes.'

'So at the same time as desperately trying for a reconciliation with your wife, you were committing adultery with the party girl, Sharon Borowski?'

'I'd ended the relationship with Sharon Borowski when we agreed to a reconciliation.'

'Yesterday you told his honour and the jury that your affair with Sharon Borowski extended over six weeks.'

'That was a mistake. I meant we slept together maybe six times, all during March.'

Beckwith didn't hurry shuffling again through his papers, all the time keeping the note that had been passed to him by Reid very obviously in his hand. Beckwith finally stopped at something among the documents. 'Sharon Borowski was the first of the two women with whom you admit adultery. The second is Ms Leanne Jefferies, who is a defendant in the criminal conversation claims brought by your wife?'

'Yes.'

'I really do need your help in establishing a time frame, as I am sure the court does,' said Beckwith, once more consulting the note that had been passed from the adjoining table. 'Even giving you the benefit of your corrected recollection that your sexual relationship with Sharon Borowski began and ended in March, we've still got your confrontation with your wife on April fifth. At which you each accused the other of transmitting a sexual disease to the other. When, exactly, did you fit in your affair with Ms Jefferies?'

'It's wrong!' shouted Appleton.

'Something is very definitely wrong,' commented the lawyer. 'What, very exactly again, is wrong, Mr Appleton?'

'All the dates. All the dates are wrong. It all didn't happen in as short a period as you are suggesting.'

'Suggestions to which you have agreed, under oath, Mr Appleton.'

'I was confused. Am confused. Not thinking properly.'

'Isn't the confusion caused by you lying about the sequence of events and trapping yourself into a time frame that is too tight for you satisfactorily to fit in two separate affairs at the same time as supposedly trying a reconciliation with your wife?' demanded Beckwith.

'No!'

'And isn't the only way to make it work to tell the truth, that there was no sequence but that you were conducting your affair with Sharon Borowski and Leanne Jefferies not separately but simultaneously? And at the same time as you claim you were attempting a reconciliation which your wife rejected because she contracted chlamydia from you?'

'No!'

'And isn't it also the truth that trying to suggest that my client, Harvey Jordan, gave your wife chlamydia is blatant nonsense, because at the time that you, she and Leanne Jefferies suffered the infection, Harvey Jordan – who is not a sufferer of the disease – had not even met your wife!'

'It proves she is promiscuous.'

'And isn't it also blatant nonsense that Harvey Jordan caused the breakdown of your marriage, which by the time he met your wife had already irretrievably broken down?'

'No!'

'You were honest, when you admitted affairs

with Sharon Borrows and Leanne Jefferies, weren't you?'

Appleton didn't reply, genuinely confused on this occasion.

'The court requires an answer,' insisted Beckwith.

'Yes,' Appleton finally said.

'Why?'

'I don't understand what you're asking me.'

'Why did you tell the truth about those two affairs before you had been accused of them?'

'Because ... it's the truth ... I believed I had to.'

Beckwith glanced at the paper that had been handed to him and which he still held. 'Isn't it that having contracted chlamydia your wife told you at that confrontation on April fifth that she already had *you* under surveillance? That you knew you had been caught conducting your simultaneous affairs and decided to admit to them in the hope that those two admissions would be sufficient and you wouldn't be accused of any others?'

'No!'

'So, before being challenged, you told the truth.'

'Yes.'

'The truth with which you are having so much difficulty now.'

'Your honour!' said Bartle, rising at the first available protest.

'It is for the jury and myself to decide the truth or otherwise, Mr Beckwith,' rebuked Pullinger.

'Quite so, your honour. I withdraw the comment, with apologies,' said Beckwith. 'I believe

I have taken my examination as far as I am able at this stage but I would refer to the submission that Mr Reid made yesterday. To my understanding there has still not been a response from the coroner who conducted the enquiry into Ms Borowski's death. I would, therefore, officially request your agreement to me resuming my examination of Mr Appleton in the light of whatever that response may be.'

'In principle I agree, subject to the arguments upon admissibility that might be made by either Mr Bartle or Mr Wolfson upon the contents of the coroner's reply.'

'I would also ask your honour's agreement to my approaching the bench upon the subject that occupied this court before the swearing in of the jury.'

'No!' refused the judge. 'I will, instead, see all four attorneys in my chambers.'

The court stenographer, together with her machine, was positioned directly alongside the judge, still in his robes, and again Pullinger kept them standing, extending the schoolboys-to-headmaster analogy by not speaking for several moments. When he eventually did he said, 'My court – this court – is being reduced to a vaudeville parody against which I have already warned. I will neither tolerate nor allow this to continue unchallenged. What I will permit is this one final – and I mean final – application from Mr Beckwith. I will also consider any belated applications from the rest of you here before me. Which – and make no mistake of my seriousness and determination – will be the end of the nonsense to which I suspect myself and my court to have been subjected. All four of you know my disquiet at what emerged during the closed hearing. Already in my mind is the possibility of me reporting each of the four of you to your respective bar authorities, which is why a verbatim record of this meeting – and this warning – is being made. Do any of the four of you have the slightest misunderstanding or doubt about what I am saying?'

Led by Beckwith, each lawyer recited, 'No, your honour.'

'Mr Beckwith?' invited the cadaverous man.

'I believe it is incumbent upon me to recall Dr Abrahams, to provide in open court his expert testimony in the defence of my client. It was therefore equally incumbent upon me to advise the court to give Mr Bartle and Mr Wolfson the opportunity to recall their expert witnesses who gave evidence before you in closed court, your honour.'

'This is preposterous after what happened earlier, your honour,' protested Bartle, at once and without being invited to speak.

'What happened earlier was equally preposterous,' responded Pullinger. 'Are you objecting to the application?'

'I am, most determinedly,' said Bartle.

'Mr Wolfson?'

'No, your honour. I am not objecting, anxious as I am for my client's case to be opened before you.'

'Mr Reid?'

'Not to the recall of Dr Abrahams, your honour. But I also seek to call on behalf of my client both Dr Walter Harding, the administrator of the Bellamy clinic, and her gynaecologist, neither of whom are on my original witnesses' list.'

'Which leaves you the odd man out, Mr Bartle?' the judge pointed out.

'After the misunderstanding during Mr Beckwith's failed dismissal application, your honour made observations concerning Drs Chapman and Lewell which surely makes their recall impossible,' argued Bartle.

'Not to recall Drs Chapman and Lewell would surely provide you with grounds for appeal against whatever verdict and judgement is returned by the jury, would it not?' disputed the judge. 'And legally it is not open to you to offer – nor for me to accept – an assurance at this stage that you will not seek to appeal,' said Pullinger.

'This is manipulation of your court!' accused Bartle, looking sideways to Beckwith.

'About which I opened this meeting with what I hoped to be sufficient and serious warning,' said Pullinger. 'It is my opinion that without matching expert witnesses for both Alfred Appleton and Leanne Jefferies they would be appearing before me at a disadvantage, which I will neither countenance nor permit. I am suspending the court for the rest of the day, although I intend remaining on the premises. You, Mr Bartle, and you, Mr Wolfson, are to approach your respective medical specialists and invite them willingly to return tomorrow. If they refuse, because of the earlier episode, I will subpoena them, which I give you permission to warn them of when you speak to them.'

'I am obliged, your honour,' said Beckwith, formally.

'No,' refused Pullinger. 'None of you are obliged. All of you continue under warning, the last any of you will receive. Do not try my patience or expect any further allowances of the law. None is any longer available to any of you.'

Harvey Jordan felt disconcerted, without having a positive focus for the feeling. He was not sure, even, if disconcerted properly described *how* he felt. It was a combination of things, he supposed, none greater than the other but each forming part of a whole, like a snowball getting bigger and bigger as it rolled down a winter hill. After wanting Alyce to be part of the after-hearing discussions he was disappointed that today, when she had finally attended, it hadn't been at all as he'd imagined it would be, although there had been some benefits. Chief among them had been the admission from Beckwith that only the April fifth date had been written upon the note that Reid handed to him but that – theatre again – he'd used the paper itself as a prop to convince Appleton it held more incriminating questions.

Jordan was curious – as well as pleased – at Alyce's apparent recovery, asking more questions and offering more opinions than he had himself. In contrast Beckwith and Reid had seemed to hold back, as well, volunteering very little – too little – of what had been discussed and ruled in the judge's chambers. The more he thought about it the more Jordan came to the conclusion that their reticence had resulted from Alyce's presence for the first time. There had been positives, though. The consensus had been that Beckwith had performed as well as Reid, the previous day. And that Appleton had emerged a bumbling and obvious liar. Another surprise – a question that they hadn't resolved before the analysis conference ended – was Wolfson's easy agreement to Dr Lewell being recalled, which prompted one of the few contributions Jordan did make, trying in the limited way available to him to pass on what he'd learned from his Internet burglaries by reminding his lawyer of Leanne Jefferies' body language implying a rejection of her former lover.

Alyce had accepted without any visible regret the calling of her doctor and gynaecologist and insisted that she could remember telling Appleton during their April fifth confrontation that she already had him under surveillance, which in fact hadn't begun until after she'd engaged Reid as her divorce lawyer.

When the after-court conference ended Jordan hesitated, on the point of suggesting that he and Alyce spend the unexpectedly free afternoon together, only pulling back at the awareness that he had more arrangements to make for his planned moved against Alfred Appleton.

Back in his locked hotel suite Jordan patiently surfed the net for hedge funds based throughout the Caribbean – uncaring that what he intended breached US financial regulations – and selected two in Grand Cayman, one in the Turks and Caicos Islands and the other in Aruba. To each he wrote, from his position inside Appleton's personal computer, in Appleton's name and giving Appleton's genuine passport details, Social Security identification and asked for opening deposits required to establish a portfolio.

He did not expect immediate responses – imagining a delay possibly as long as a week – but within an hour he received an acknowledgement from one of the Grand Cayman funds, stipulating $25,000 as a minimum, and another from Aruba setting the figure at $10,000. He notified each to expect contact from Alfred Jerome Appleton within the coming month.

Beckwith was waiting for him when Jordan got to the bar, delayed by the hedge fund enquiries and still with some of his sites unchecked. The lawyer announced that he'd taken the chance of Jordan agreeing to their going to a restaurant that Reid had recommended, about ten miles out of town.

'A change from here would be good,' accepted Jordan.

'Abrahams has confirmed his arrival tomorrow,' said Beckwith. 'So have the other two.'

'I didn't expect that, did you?'

'It's getting difficult to anticipate anything,' said Beckwith. 'All these delays must be boring the hell out of you?'

'I manage to fill in the time,' said Jordan.

When they got back from the restaurant, which they'd enjoyed and decided to use again, Jordan declined Beckwith's offered nightcap, anxious to complete his nightly computer check.

He'd been at his screen less than an hour when he came upon the query from a Chicago broker and accepted that the hunt to find the Appleton and Drake intruder had begun.

# Twenty-Eight

There was the briefest stomach lurch at his detection: if there hadn't it would have meant he had become complacent, which Jordan had always regarded as the greatest sin possible in his profession. But that was all it was, brief, as quickly acknowledged and just as quickly compartmentalized because there was not the slightest risk of the investigation that would now laboriously unfold ever connecting him to what had already happened or with what was going to continue happening until, Mr Invisible once more, he chose to disappear at the split-second click of a computer key. A gambler, which Jordan most very definitely was not, would have bet upon it taking two months from this moment for Appleton and Drake to go thoroughly through their back office trades for them to begin to recognize how completely they had been invaded and by how much they had been looted. Jordan set himself a month to complete what he had started. Even if, by the sort of miracle in which Jordan did not believe, the investigation within a month traced the intrusion to Darwin he was still not in any personal danger. The Trojan Horse in the Darwin cut-out system was in Appleton's name and contained all Appleton's identifying details, none of Jordan's.

Jordan was nevertheless disappointed – and irritated – at being discovered. He'd been particularly careful not to siphon money from any 'wash trades' – buy-and-sell futures purchases upon which an immediate profit was likely, sometimes within the space of twenty-four hours – but those instead intended to be held for a longer period for the price to go up. Jordan's mistake, which he at once and fully acknowledged, was not sufficiently following the market movement in all the commodities through which he'd moved collecting, figuratively with his basket in hand. He'd concentrated upon metals, the primary trading activity of Appleton's company. The five-hundred dollars he'd skimmed from the order placed by a Chicago-based broker named David Cohen was for pork belly, predictable from the Chicago exchange being dominated by meat trades, the movement of which, unlike metals, he hadn't consulted daily and in which there had obviously been a sudden upward price jump to trigger the sell. Like all objective men, Jordan accepted it as a lesson to be learned and a mistake not to be repeated: from now on he had daily – even twice daily – to monitor the price shifts of every commodity deal he raided.

A month then, Jordan rationalized. More than sufficient time in which to achieve everything – more maybe – that he wanted. No reason, yet, for him to break the American financial regulations by opening, in Appleton's name, the intended hedge fund portfolios. His only current pressure was to move the visible money from the New York bank accounts into the safe-deposit facilities to make available space for fresh infusions from the Appleton and Drake client list. During the four weeks Jordan estimated he could accumulate between $500,000 and $750,000 to offset any court award and lawyer costs; possibly more if his monitoring of the impending investigation disclosed that it was moving more slowly than he'd estimated. No! Jordan warned himself, at once. To go beyond his time limit would be to risk the gamble he had already decided against.

Jordan awoke by six, wrongly believing the Chicago challenge to be the only leftover surprise of the day. There had been insufficient movement over the preceding three days to prompt profit selling in either copper or steel and he decided to restrict himself entirely in both, going through previously untouched accounts and distributing a total of $5,000 between the five New York accounts. The transfers completed, Jordan came across a letter from the Chicago broker, which was not addressed to Appleton but to a junior partner in the firm, John Popple, who had carried out the futures purchase, smiling at the confirmation of its tone. It was not phrased as a complaint but as an enquiry, inferring that the five-hundred-dollar disparity was a bookkeeping or accounting mistake, which was the manner in which Popple replied, promising a records check of the back office buy and sell comparisons, with the undertaking to get back to Cohen within days.

He'd underestimated the time it would take for a proper investigation to get underway, Jordan decided, upon reflection. It was far more likely to be three rather than two months. But he'd stick to his schedule. Unless, that is, something came up that he hadn't anticipated.

How long would it be before Appleton learned of the Chicago enquiry? Jordan wondered, gazing fixedly at the hunched, dour-faced commodity trader as the court assembled. Certainly not this week. Maybe not until a full blown criminal enquiry, by which time the divorce case could be over and he, conceivably, back in England evolving another, overly delayed new operation. Or would he be? Wrong question, he corrected himself. Did he *want* to go back to London directly after distancing himself both from the divorce and the retribution against Alfred Appleton? All of it had been – and would continue to be – work: unaccustomed work far harder and more demanding than that upon which he was normally engaged. And in between which he usually allowed himself a recovering break, if not a proper vacation. Didn't he deserve a period of rest, just he and...? Jordan stopped the drift, very positively refusing it, turning to the other side of the court for the first time that day. Alyce was in black again, her paleness accentuated, and she had turned back to the separating bar towards which Dr Harding, in turn, was stretched forward in nodded conversation, along with a greying, bespectacled woman. In the same row, although not directly alongside, sat the three venerealogists. Because of how she was twisted to look behind her Alyce became aware of Jordan's look and turned to smile, briefly, at him. Beckwith and Reid were also stretched between their separated tables in huddled discussion and as they rose for the familiar opening ritual of the judge's entry Beckwith muttered, 'Could be another good day.'

Reid remained on his feet as the rest of the court settled and to Pullinger's enquiring look said, 'I wish to inform your honour at this earliest opportunity, and prior to the expert medical evidence for which this court was adjourned yesterday, that I have received this morning, by courier, the requested medical examination report on Sharon Borowski, after her fatal automobile accident. I have had that report duplicated for distribution, with your honour's permission, before the calling of today's medical experts, whose interpretation I believe will be necessary.'

'You are not seeking yet another adjournment, are you, Mr Reid?' demanded the judge, threateningly.

'Subject to any representation from other counsel – and of course to your honour's guidance – I am prepared to ask doctors Abrahams,

Chapman and Lewell to respond from the witness stand. If it would further assist the court, there are also present today Dr Walter Harding and Mrs Appleton's gynaecologist, Dr Brenda Stirling, whose addition to my witnesses list I have already advised.'

Instead of addressing the other lawyers individually, Pullinger looked between the three of them and curtly said, 'Well?'

Bartle was first on his feet to agree, followed by the other two and while the medical examiner's report was being circulated Beckwith said, quietly, 'Shit!'

'What's the problem?' Jordan whispered back.

'If whatever's in the report on Sharon Borowski goes against Appleton, there's room for a mistrial appeal – intervention at least – on the grounds of insufficient consultation.'

'Why didn't you object?'

'It's better as far as you are concerned to go ahead. You're the guy I represent, remember?' said Beckwith, rising as George Abrahams was called to the stand. Because it was the first time the jury were to hear the evidence referring to the chlamydia, the beginning of Beckwith's examination was a virtual repetition of the previous closed court hearing establishing that Jordan was clear of any such infection.

Beckwith got as far as: 'Can we now turn...?' before Pullinger's interruption.

'Not yet,' stopped Pullinger. To Abrahams he said, 'I require you to answer in the briefest manner possible some questions I wish to put to you, which have to be introduced into the public

406

record. You have already given evidence before me, in the absence of a jury, upon chlamydia, have you not?'

'Yes,' confirmed the venerealogist.

'During the course of that evidence you were asked to comment upon the findings of two other expert witnesses, Drs Chapman and Lewell?'

'Yes.'

'What were those comments?'

As he had in the closed session the man shifted uncomfortably, looking at both other specialists. 'That they were inadequate.'

'With what result?'

'They were reconsidered and resubmitted.'

'What did those resubmissions prove?'

'That Alfred Appleton and Leanne Jefferies had in the past suffered from chlamydia.'

'Which the initial reports did not indicate?'

'No.'

'Thank you,' said Pullinger, nodding for Beckwith to continue.

'I am going to impose upon your expertise with the continuation of my questioning,' apologized Beckwith, in advance. 'You have before you the medical findings upon the late Sharon Borowski, with whom Alfred Appleton has admitted a sexual liaison. I seek your correction, if it is appropriate, in suggesting that the listed injuries in that report – a skull fracture, compression of the left rib cage, burst aorta and spleen – is consistent with injuries sustained in a head-on collision between two vehicles, one of which, according to the report before you, was driven by the late Sharon Borowski?'

'Consistent also with the deceased not wearing any seat restraint,' agreed the doctor.

Beckwith nodded his thanks to the qualification. 'Can we now turn to the other findings, particularly the serological discoveries? Can you explain those to the jury, Dr Abrahams?

'The blood alcohol level is two and a half times beyond the legal driving limit. There is also a substantial amphetamine reading.'

'So Sharon Borowski was driving under the influence both of drink and drugs?' broke in Beckwith.

'Unquestionably.'

'Are there any other analyses?'

'There is reference to unidentified antibodies which were not judged medically relevant to the particular autopsy.'

'What are antibodies, Dr Abrahams?'

'A body – a substance – formed within the blood either synthetically or by the immune system of the body to fight a toxin.'

'A disease or an infection?'

'Yes. But which is not specified.'

'What is the recognized treatment for chlamydia?'

'Treatment by one of a number of antibiotics.'

'Which would result in antibodies in the blood?'

'Yes.'

'Could Sharon Borowski have been suffering from chlamydia?'

'I have already testified that the antibodies are not specified, by analysis. It could have been one of a number of diseases or infections,' refuted

Abrahams.

'One of which could have been chlamydia?' persisted Beckwith.

'Or not,' the venerealogist continued to refuse.

'I think you have pursued the point sufficiently, Mr Beckwith,' said the judge.

None of the other three lawyers chose to cross-examine Abrahams. Forewarned by the judge's previous intercession Beckwith did not directly question Dr Chapman about his first attempted medical submission during the closed session, leaving it to Pullinger to extract the admission from the specialist that his first medical assessment had needed substantial correction and clarification. Despite Beckwith's pressure, when he resumed after the judge – pressure matched by Reid when he took up the questioning – Chapman doggedly refused to go beyond his closed court insistence that his initial failure to disclose chlamydia antibodies in Appleton's blood had solely been because of his strict adherence to the instructions he'd received from David Bartle. Chapman even more insistently refused to speculate on the presence of unidentified antibodies in the blood of Sharon Borowski.

Jordan expected the same monosyllabic repetition from Dr Jane Lewell when she was called to the stand, his mind more upon what he was going to do outside the court in the coming month, until Pullinger yet again broke into Beckwith's examination to put the closed court dispute before the jury and into the public record of the case.

'Your first submission before me had to be

substantially corrected, did it not?' Pullinger asked the identical question he'd put to Chapman.

'Yes,' replied the woman. 'Because I had been pressured to omit the presence of antichlamydia IgG in the blood of Ms Leanne Jefferies, which professionally I should not have done and now deeply regret and for which I now publicly apologize.'

The court resumed after thirty minutes, although without the jury. At Pullinger's insistence Peter Wolfson remained standing beside Dr Lewell, although in the well of the court, not directly in front of the bench for the exchange to go unheard.

To the lawyer, the judge said, 'Have you fully advised your client of the constitutional protection against self-incrimination?'

'I have,' assured Wolfson, dry-voiced.

'Have you understood everything you have been told by Mr Wolfson about self-incrimination?' the judged asked the woman.

'Yes,' replied Dr Lewell.

'Have you fully advised your client of the penalties available to me if perjury is committed?' Pullinger asked the lawyer.

'I have, you honour,' replied Wolfson. 'Although I would remind your honour that the evidence my client gave under oath during the closed hearing was entirely truthful concerning the chlamydia infection contracted by Ms Leanne Jefferies.'

Pullinger looked unwaveringly at the lawyer

for several moments before turning to the venerealogist. 'Did you fully understand what you were told by Mr Wolfson about lying under oath in a court?'

'I fully understood,' said the woman.

'Then you will return to the witness box and although you are already sworn you will be sworn for a second time to remind you that everything you tell me must be the absolute and complete truth.'

As the jury filed back in Jordan leaned sideways towards his lawyer, but Beckwith raised a forbidding hand, as well as shaking his head. As he withdrew Jordan saw Bartle similarly refuse Appleton's approach. The commodity trader wrote hurriedly on his own legal pad, pushing it towards his lawyer, who gave no reaction to what was written on it.

'Dr Lewell,' began the judge. 'I want you to explain the remark you made before I adjourned the court.'

'I apologized for not including in the original venereal report upon Leanne Jefferies the presence of antichlamydia IgG in her blood.'

'What would the presence of antichlamydia IgG have established?'

'That she had been treated for a chlamydia infection.'

'That she had, in fact, suffered such a disease?'

'Yes.'

'Did you treat her for a chlamydia infection?'

'No, I did not.'

'Do you know who did?'

'I believe it was her gynaecologist.'

411

'Were you aware of the reason for examining Leanne Jefferies?'

'Yes, I was.'

'In the report upon Leanne Jefferies that you originally submitted, but which you did not swear to in court, you omitted to record that in Leanne Jefferies blood you found antichlamydia IgG?'

The woman frowned, uncertainly. 'That's what I have already told you.'

'If you had submitted and sworn that original report, what would it have conveyed to the court?'

'That she was not suffering chlamydia, which medically she no longer was. She had been cured.'

'If that original report had been accepted, could it not have conveyed or been inferred by a jury that Leanne Jefferies had *never* suffered from chlamydia?'

Dr Lewell hesitated. 'Yes.'

'So the intention was to deceive the court that neither Leanne Jefferies nor her admitted lover, Alfred Appleton, had ever suffered such a disease and that therefore Alfred Appleton's wife must have contracted it from a lover?'

'At the time I prepared the report I did not know it was for presentation in a court. I only learned that when I received a witness summons.'

'Why didn't you prepare a fuller, more accurate report when you did receive the witness summons?'

The woman looked to her right, where Appleton was at last in whispered conversation with his lawyer and Wolfson was leaning back towards the separating rail to talk to Chapman. 'I suggested it. But was told it wasn't necessary; that all that was necessary was to establish that Leanne Jefferies no longer had it.'

'Told by whom?'

There was another hesitation, as she again looked to the plaintiff's side of the court. 'Dr Chapman.'

'That's not true!' shouted the other venerealogist, standing at the rail.

'Sit down!' ordered Pullinger. 'You'll get your chance when I recall you.'

To the woman he said, 'At the closed hearing your lawyer, Mr Wolfson, admitted giving you the remit to restrict your report. Now you are telling me it was Dr Chapman.'

'It was Dr Chapman first. Then it was reinforced by Mr Wolfson.'

'Didn't that strike you as odd?'

'It was the first time I had been asked to prepare this sort of report for a court. I did not know the procedure. I sought guidance from Dr Chapman, whom I knew had experience. He told me what to do.'

'Is what you're telling me true?'

'You ordered that I retake the oath,' said Dr Lewell.

'Which isn't the direct answer to my question.'

'It is the truth,' she insisted. 'I also want to make it clear that if I had been called to testify upon the original report I would have corrected it verbally.'

'You were called before me at the closed hearing. Why didn't you tell me then what you have told me today?'

'I was bewildered by what happened at the closed hearing ... the challenge about the report ... your telling me you were going to report me to my licensing authority. The reports had been corrected and the fact established that Leanne Jefferies had been infected. I just wanted to get away.'

'But today you weren't in so much hurry to get away?'

'I wanted to apologize. And I have.'

Pullinger did not adjourn for the second time but from the bench lectured Mark Chapman himself on the American constitutional protection against self-incrimination and of the criminal offence of perjury, before having the venerealogist sworn. Again it was the judge who conducted the examination, putting to the man practically the same questions that he had posed to Dr Lewell. Chapman's replies were remarkably similar. The man insisted that he, too, had not believed he would be called as a witness but that the purpose of his examination of Appleton – and the way in which he had prepared the discredited report – was solely to attest that at the time of the examination Appleton did not have chlamydia, not that he had never been a sufferer.

'Would you have corrected it in court?' demanded Pullinger.

'It had already been challenged and corrected.'

'Answer the question you have been asked,' demanded the judge.

'Of course I would have corrected it.'

'What advice did you give Dr Lewell when she asked about preparing a venerealogy report to be submitted to a divorce court?'

'That she had to be very specific in her answers to the questions set out by the lawyer representing Leanne Jefferies.'

'Did you tell her to omit any reference to there being any antichlamydia IgG in Leanne Jefferies blood, indicating that although no longer a sufferer she had, in fact, once had the infection?'

'No,' denied the man.

'What did you tell her when she asked you?'

'That she should stick very specifically to the remit from Leanne Jefferies' lawyer.'

'And I want you to be very specific in your answer to this question,' insisted the judge. 'Did you ever tell Dr Jane Lewell to omit her finding of the antibodies in Leanne Jefferies blood?'

'No, I did not,' replied Chapman.

'How do you account for Dr Lewell telling me that you did?'

'The only explanation that I can offer is that she misunderstood the advice I gave her and inferred I had told her to omit it when in fact I had not.'

'Will you stand, Dr Lewell?' said Pullinger. 'Did you misunderstand what Dr Chapman told you? Or did he specifically tell you not to include your finding.'

The woman remained silent for several moments before saying, still haltingly, 'I could

415

have misunderstood.'

Beside him Jordan could see that Beckwith had paraded another battalion of exclamation marks on his legal pad. Jordan looked startled at the man when Beckwith declined Pullinger's invitation to take up the examination. Reid did, though, coming up hurriedly at the judge's first gesture.

'Would you describe yourself as one of Alfred Appelton's oldest friends?' asked Reid. There was no indication of any tightness in his breathing.

'I believe myself to be one of them,' responded the medical specialist, cautiously.

'From college days?'

'Yes.'

'My recollection from the closed hearing which preceded this case was that your friendship began at Harvard, through a mutual interest in sailing?'

'Yes.'

Jordan was aware of Beckwith poised to add more exclamation marks. Alyce was tensed forward, her entire concentration upon the man in the stand, unlike Leanne Jefferies who was actually looking away from the man, as if her mind was upon something else.

'Would you describe Alfred Appleton as a man of integrity?'

After the briefest of pauses, Chapman said, 'Yes.'

'An honest man?'

'Your honour!' interrupted Bartle. 'Is there anything of relevance in this exchange?'

416

'I am as curious as you to find out,' said Pullinger. 'Mr Reid?'

'I sincerely hope so,' replied the lawyer. 'Far more relevant than an uncorrected, inadequate medical report.'

Beckwith stood five exclamation marks to attention.

'I look forward to reaching it in the shortest possible time,' said the judge, although not aggressively.

'I asked you if Alfred Appleton, one of your oldest and best friends, was an honest man.'

'I believe him to be.'

'As you are an honest man of integrity, giving evidence under oath, having been warned of the dangers of perjury?'

Chapman's pause was longer this time before he finally said, 'As I believe myself to be.'

'Were you an honest man of integrity, bound by a medical oath as you are by a legal oath in court today, when you carried out your medical examination of Alfred Appleton for presentation before this court?'

'Yes,' insisted Chapman, unable to prevent the hint of uncertainty in his voice.

'Had you ever medically examined Alfred Appleton before the report intended for presentation before this court?'

Chapman looked towards Bartle, who remained expressionless and unmoving.

'Dr Chapman?' prompted Reid.

'Not to my recollection.'

'Before you specialized in microbiology, and more specifically in the study and treatment of

417

sexually transmitted diseases, did you practice as a general medical physician?'

Chapman's uncertainty was even more obvious when he said, 'I served a period of hospital internship. I never practised generally.'

'That period of internship was at the Massachusetts General Hospital, situated on Fruit Street, Boston, was it not?'

'Yes.'

'During that period of internship you were a fully qualified hospital physician, able to reach diagnoses and, if necessary, to authorize admissions and prescribe treatment?'

Chapman did not reply. Jordan saw that Appleton was sitting statued at his table, both hands extended upon it as if to prevent himself falling forward.

'Dr Chapman?' again prompted Reid.

There was still no reply.

Pullinger said, 'Dr Chapman, you will answer the question.'

Finally Chapman said, 'Yes, I was.'

'In November, 1991, were you attached to the accident and emergency department of the Massachusetts General Hospital on Fruit Street, Boston?'

'I was working at the hospital in 1991.'

'In November of that year, in the accident and emergency department?'

'I worked in a variety of departments.'

'Including accident and emergency?'

'Yes.'

'Do you recall an admission that you authorized into the emergency department of Massachusettes General Hospital on November third, 1991? And the diagnosis you reached upon that emergency admission?'

'Your honour!' protested Bartle. 'I again ask the relevance to this case of something that occurred so long ago. How can Dr Chapman be asked to remember such a specific event?'

'The point you are seeking to establish, Mr Reid?' enquired the judge.

'Points,' enlarged Reid. 'Those of honesty, credibility and possible collusion to pervert the course of justice.'

'You will answer the question, Dr Chapman,' insisted Pullinger.

'No, I do not remember,' said the man.

Reid let the pause build, finally inhaling deeply for the breath he needed. 'You do not remember admitting Alfred Jerome Appleton – your old college friend with whom you so often sailed and whose integrity you so much admire – to Massachusetts General Hospital on November third, 1991, after a traffic accident in which a car plunged into a lake, a car from which Anthea Elizabeth Bell, a girl of twenty-three, could not free herself from her seat belt and therefore drowned, resulting in the death not only of herself but of an unborn child!'

'No, I do not remember,' repeated Chapman, the reply only just audible in the sudden noise.

# Twenty-Nine

The Jack Daniels bottle was on the table again, although this celebration was more muted than its first appearance. The judge had upheld David Bartle's protest at the inadmissibility of the fatal accident, refused any further reference to it and rejected Reid's application to call DDK investigator Jack Doyle to give supporting evidence, at the same time as instructing the jury to disregard any inference when considering their final verdict.

'They won't be able to disregard it,' Beckwith told the other lawyer. 'It's in their minds and you put it there. Where it will stay when they get around to reaching a decision.'

'I could have done so much more,' complained Reid. 'We even had proof of the $500,000 payoff Appleton's family gave Anthea's parents to avoid charges being pressed; the mom and dad broke up because of the accident and mom changed her mind about it being hushed up. She actually wanted to be called to give evidence that Appleton made her daughter pregnant and that he'd started out only offering $100,000.'

'How did the kid die?' asked Jordan.

'He was drunk, after some yachting event,' said Reid. 'Missed a turning and drove instead into a lake. Managed to get himself out and swim ashore. The driver of a following car called emergency and got Appleton to hospital. Appleton didn't say anything about the kid in the car until the following day. By then it was obviously too late but a medical examiner said if she'd been gotten out she and the baby would have survived. Chapman swore Appleton was too concussed to have remembered anything – that he couldn't even remember the accident – so no prosecution was brought.'

'And there was Chapman again with all the necessary qualifications willing to help out with venereal disease and pressure another specialist to go along with it,' completed Beckwith. 'How the hell did Appleton think he was going to get away with it!'

'Arrogance of the rich and spoiled, I guess,' said Reid. 'It worked once, with the same guy. And let's be honest, Appleton was within a whisker of getting away with it again now.' The lawyer raised his whisky glass in silent acknowledgement to Jordan's contribution.

'Alyce didn't do so well today,' said Jordan. After Chapman's release from the witness stand Reid had cleverly ignored the attentive Dr Harding but called Alyce's gynaecologist, Brenda Stirling, to testify to what Jordan had already read in the intercepted email correspondence, that Alyce now only had a ten percent possibility ('and that's being extremely optimistic') of conceiving a full term birth because of the fallopian tube scarring caused by the chlamydia infection. Alyce had wept openly throughout the testimony and Reid hadn't bothered to invite her to that evening's conference.

'I've got to call her to give evidence tomorrow,' said Reid, unapologetically. 'And Leanne, directly after, for the jury to compare the two of them literally side by side. And Alyce can cry as much as she wants.'

'That's cynical,' protested Jordan.

'That's practical,' dismissed Reid. 'Don't worry about Alyce. Worry about yourself and the hook you're still on.'

'It's because I'm still worried about myself that I'm worried about Alyce and wondering how she'll stand up to a full examination and cross-examination. Bartle's got to destroy her to give Appleton any sort of a chance, hasn't he?'

'I don't see how he can damage her,' said Beckwith. 'I actually don't see how Appleton and Bartle could have believed they had any chance of pursuing the case they're attempting.'

'Arrogance of the rich and spoiled,' echoed Jordan.

Beckwith shook his head. 'There's got to be more than that. So far Appleton doesn't have a damned defence. '

'On the subject of defence, let's not forget Pullinger's lecture about rebuttal of criminal conversation, as far as you two are concerned,' warned Reid. 'The law, the way Pullinger interpreted it, comes down pretty heavily against any logical defence.'

'You can't be serious!' argued Beckwith.

'Logically you looked to be home free at the dismissal hearing. But Pullinger didn't find for you,' reminded Reid.

'We discussed it,' reminded Beckwith, in turn. 'Pullinger's an ornery old bastard. Look how far everything has turned in our favour since then. Harvey can't possibly be found guilty.'

'No one ever said the law was fair, any more than life.'

'Can we take pause here!' urged Jordan. 'The jury can't find against me, not on what they've heard.'

'I don't think they should, nor am I saying that they will,' insisted Reid. 'But Pullinger *is* an ornery old bastard and he's still got to sum up and guide the jury. I wouldn't like to place bets, not yet.'

'He finds against us I'll appeal,' insisted Beckwith.

'How many more months – and how much more money – could that cost?' demanded Jordan, genuinely shocked. Confronting Reid's caution, Jordan acknowledged that although he'd begun raiding Appleton's firm to build up the necessary insurance against having a financial penalty imposed against him, he had increasingly begun to regard the money as the fitting punishment against Appleton for the inconvenience and upheaval Appleton had caused him; precisely, in fact, the sort of compensation people sought from insurance.

'Anything up to a year to get a hearing before the North Carolina Supreme Court,' answered Beckwith, to Reid's vaguely nodded agreement. 'Costs would be open-ended. If we won, which we would, minimal; the majority would go against Appleton.'

'And if we failed, double whatever I'd have to pay now, plus whatever is awarded against me in the first place!' challenged Jordan.

'I said we'd win,' repeated Beckwith. 'And you wouldn't have to hang around here, while you waited. You could go back to England and only need to return here when we got a hearing date.'

He wouldn't come back, was Jordan's first thought. And then just as quickly realized that he wouldn't have a choice. There was still the danger of limited publicity and of his identification at the conclusion of this case. That publicity – and identification – would be far greater if he failed to return for an appeal, with the inevitable photographs and the even more inevitable recognition. This would blow open the identity thefts he'd carried out in America in the past, and almost certainly at the New York banks in which he had opened the accounts in Appleton's name and with whom he would be publicly linked in an appeals procedure. And during Beckwith's estimated year, the attack he'd mounted against Appleton and his firm would be very actively under investigation. 'What can we do?'

Beckwith actually laughed at the facile question. 'Go on expecting to win, of course! That's why we're all here. There's nothing more we can do, unless you've got a better idea.'

Jordan didn't have, although he spent much of a disturbed night trying to think of one: to think of anything. He finally decided, ignoring the pun, that Alyce's lawyer was playing devil's advocate to their over-confidence, which he'd admitted to himself the moment Reid had spoken. It would be wrong to regard it as anything more than a cautious touch on the brake. Jordan still wished Reid hadn't created the doubt and that Beckwith hadn't been so flippant dismissing it.

Despite trying to dismiss it himself, the doubt remained lodged in Jordan's mind as he scrolled through his illicit web hideaways. There was nothing more on the Chicago query, nor any additional questions on any of his other raids. Prices remained virtually static on copper and Jordan limited himself entirely to that one metal for the day's pilfering.

On their way to court Jordan said, 'I didn't like Bob's doom and gloom last night.'

'Forget it,' Beckwith continued to dismiss. 'Bob's a pessimist. That's why he always dresses in black, like a funeral director.'

Funeral director to Dodge City cowboy, thought Jordan.

He was surprised that Dr Harding, who knew it was Alyce's day on the witness stand, wasn't in court when they entered. She was already at her table, nodding to whatever Reid was saying to her. She looked up, through her thick-rimmed, and now shaded, glasses, as Jordan and Beckwith took their places, but didn't give any response to Jordan's nodded smile. She was again in funereal black, matching the pessimistic Reid, without any noticeable make-up, and as she stood to take the oath, her left hand on the rail of the witness stand, Jordan was further surprised to see that for the first time since that initial day in France she was wearing her wedding and engagement rings.

'Where would you rather be today than here in a divorce court?' opened Reid, creating an immediate stir throughout the court.

'Practically anywhere,' replied Alyce, at once. 'Most of all in my own home, with a family of my own.'

'Including children?'

'Of course including children. A family isn't a family without children. How can it be?'

'Children which, until you contracted a sexual disease, you were – according to your gynae-cologist who testified yesterday – medically capable of bearing?'

'Yes.'

'How do you feel now at having less than a ten percent chance of bearing a child full term?'

Alyce didn't reply at once, bringing to her face a handkerchief Jordan hadn't been aware of her taking from her purse 'It might not properly explain how I feel ... what I mean ... but I feel empty. Inadequate. Not a proper woman.'

'And now never able to *be* a proper woman?'

'He's pushing it right to the edge of the cliff,' Beckwith whispered to Jordan, who saw that so far there were no exclamation marks of approval on his lawyer's legal pad.

'I'm no longer a proper woman.'

'How important to you was having children?'

'It was everything to me, beyond just being a woman. My marriage, as the court has already

426

heard, was the bringing together of two of the oldest families in America. I have no brothers, no sisters. There is no direct bloodline. It will die, with my death. I believe that is important, a loss. Not to other people, I wouldn't think. But to me it is.'

'Of course,' said Reid. 'Your marriage wasn't happy before your infection, was it?'

'No.'

'How – what – did you feel about that?'

Alyce again hesitated. 'Inadequate, like before. Which again I guess other people, other women, might not understand.'

'Didn't you think of divorce then?'

'Of course I *thought* about it: how could I not have done? But I never actually considered it as an option. I hoped the separation might help.'

'Help what?' seized Reid.

'My husband.'

'In what way?'

'Help my husband to love me.'

Jordan saw Beckwith was at his legal pad at last, although he was assembling question marks, not approving exclamations.

'If you didn't believe he loved you, why did you marry him in the first place?'

'I believed he did, when we got married. It was not until afterwards that I thought differently.'

'Why?'

'I very quickly came to believe that what I thought had been love was really pride on his part: pride at me, a Bellamy, being his wife. It was as if I was a trophy. He kept cuttings, in a special book, when we appeared in social

427

columns or magazines. He agreed to a television programme being made about us.'

'Didn't you like that?'

'I hated it! I knew who I was: who my family were. I didn't believe we had to prove it. It seemed...' She paused, seeking the word. 'Arrogant, I suppose.'

'Did you talk to him about it?'

'I tried to ... told him I didn't want any more television programmes because after the first there were other approaches ... but he told me I was being stupid. That it would bring clients to the business; prestige by association, he called it. He told me I was being unreasonable.'

'Did he want to accept some of the other TV approaches?'

'Yes. I refused to take part, so they never happened.'

'Was he upset?'

'Very. He said it didn't reflect well on our marriage.'

'But you didn't talk of divorce?'

'Not over something as stupid as a television show. Divorce is a failure, isn't it? A lot of people stay together unhappily, for the sake of the family. I thought that if I had a child it would be all right: that he might change but that if he didn't it wouldn't matter ... I'd have a child, hopefully more than one child, and that would be enough for me.'

'Would it have been?'

'I never found out. Now I never will.'

'Did you ever suspect he was being unfaithful?'

'Not in the beginning, although after the first few months he invariably came home late. He said it was how it had to be in his business. I thought there might be other women when I went up to Long Island and he stayed in Manhattan. He was rarely in the apartment when I called.'

'Did you ever challenge him?'

'No.'

'And you didn't have any proof?'

'He was disinterested in me when he did come home.'

'Sexually, you mean?'

'Yes.'

'Your husband engaged a private enquiry agent to watch you. Did it ever occur to you to do the same, to watch him?'

'No. When we finally did, appointing DDK, it was at your suggestion. I didn't have to, before then. He'd admitted it, hadn't he?'

'I'm not sure I understand that remark. Or that the jury will,' complained Reid.

'When I told him he had given me chlamydia there was the big argument – he'd been drinking. When I said he'd obviously been sleeping with someone else he said not one. Two. And laughed. He later tried to deny it, when he sobered up and realized the mistake he'd made.'

Jordan saw Reid's frown. 'Do you think that's why he admitted it, in his statement?'

'I don't know. When I told him I wanted a divorce he said I wouldn't win. That he'd destroy me.'

'How was he going to destroy you?'

'Begin divorce proceedings against me, first. And make my life a misery.'

'The lover you never had: the lover his investigators failed to find?'

'Yes.'

'Did your husband ever physically attack you?'

'He actually hit me twice. Once was at that time, during the argument. He slapped me, across the face. Told me to pull myself together.'

'Were you bruised? Marked in any way?'

'Not really.'

'You didn't need hospital treatment?'

'Oh no!'

'When was the other occasion?'

'Soon after, when I told him I was going to France and that he would be hearing from you, my lawyer, about the divorce. That I was finally getting away from Long Island and the marriage and from him. He punched me ... said...' Alyce stopped.

'Said what?' pressed Reid. 'The words he used?'

'Told me to fuck off, right then. Never to think of coming back. He actually said crawling back, like the sad bitch I was.'

'Were you hurt when – and how – he punched you?'

'I wasn't expecting it. I fell over, hit my leg and side against a table.'

'So you were hurt?'

'I was bruised.'

'Did you need hospital attention?'

'Dr Harding looked after me. I left Long Island

right then. For the last time.'

Beckwith had started taking proper notes but stopped when Reid said, 'You told your husband that I was going to initiate divorce proceedings *before* you left for France?

'Yes. I took the papers I needed to sign with me'

'Weeks before you met Harvey Jordan, the defendant in your husband's claim under the criminal conversation provisions in the alienation of affections statute in force in this state?'

'At least six weeks before. Which is why the accusation against Mr Jordan is so ridiculous.'

'What was the likelihood of your crawling back, after discovering you had contracted venereal disease from him?'

Alyce snorted a laugh. 'As ridiculous as him citing Mr Jordan. Only one person is responsible for the breakdown of my marriage to Alfred Appleton. And that is Alfred Appleton.'

'You're not telling the truth, are you, Mrs Appleton?' demanded David Bartle.

'I am telling the truth, which I swore to do when I took the oath.'

'He never hit you, did he?'

'He slapped me when he was drunk and I told him I was beginning divorce proceedings. And threw me over, as I have just told the court.'

'Neither of which needed any medical treatment?'

'Dr Harding looked after me after I was punched. There was bruising, as I told you. Some grazing.'

'Yet Dr Harding, who has attended you remarkably closely so far because of what is claimed to be the stress of these proceedings, is not in court on the day of your major evidence?'

'I did not want to take them but he prescribed some pills when he knew he would not be able to be here today.'

'Your honour,' broke in Reid, rising before Bartle could continue. 'Dr Walter Harding is not in court today because of something that unexpectedly arose at the hospital at which, as you know, he is the administrator. I could make contact to see if the situation at the hospsital has been resolved, for him to come here, if your honour wishes.'

'I think it is essential, in view of your questioning, don't you, Mr Bartle?'

'I would have thought it essential for him to be here in the first place,' complained Bartle, tightly.

'Quite so,' said the judge. 'We find ourselves with another lapse in the presentation of the case. But it can easily be remedied. You are excused the court in the hope of bringing Dr Harding to us before we end today, Mr Reid.'

Jordan saw Beckwith had arranged question marks on his pad. Some were at an angle instead of being upright.

'Your husband didn't admit to two affairs, did he?' resumed Bartle. 'You told him you'd had him under surveillance, because you suspected he was being unfaithful. And that you were going to cite Sharon Borowski and Leanne Jefferies?'

'That is not the correct sequence,' rejected Alyce. 'It was as I have described it. I had not organized surveillance and had no idea who the whores were with whom he was sleeping: I just knew he was sleeping around because that was how I had become infected. *That* was what I told him.'

'It was you who first mentioned the divorce statute of criminal conversation here in North Carolina, not him,' insisted the lawyer.

'Until I engaged Mr Reid – and learned the totally unfounded case brought against Harvey Jordan by my husband – I had no idea of any such law or divorce provision. How could I have done?'

'Yet you initiated proceedings against Ms Jefferies!'

'I was advised by Mr Reid that it was a course open to me. And that it was one that I should take.'

'You had suffered a disease, which you claim your husband gave you. You had told him you were divorcing him. Yet you took the papers with you to France, instead of signing them here. You were still unsure about the divorce, weren't you?'

'No!' denied Alyce. 'The papers weren't complete, particularly the criminal conversation claim against Leanne Jefferies. They were posted to me in France. I took what was already prepared. I was going to be by myself. I had time to read everything very thoroughly.'

'But you weren't by yourself, were you?'

'I wish I had remained so, not for my own sake

but for Mr Jordan's. I very much regret his entrapment by my husband.'

The exclamation marks on Beckwith's pad were all upright now.

'Your husband is a wealthy man, the president of one of Wall Street's leading commodity brokerages with a multi-millon dollar turnover?'

'My husband never discussed business affairs with me, only in the beginning when he borrowed a million dollars from me.'

'A million dollars that you have no proof of drawing from any of your accounts.'

'It was how he wanted it done, in cash.'

'Not only is there no traceable record of it having been withdrawn from your accounts, there is no recorded entry of such a sum in the company books. How do you explain that?'

'Easily. I told you he asked for it in cash, to avoid it showing in the books. If it were recorded it would have been taxable. Maybe it was to spend on the women I then didn't know about.'

'You had a Manhattan apartment costing well over a million dollars. The Long Island house is valued at four million. You had staff. A $10,000-a-month allowance. Luxury cars. All provided for you by your husband.'

'He said the cars were part repayment of the loan, which meant I was buying them for myself.'

'What about the rest?'

'I would have exchanged it all for a loving husband home before ten every night. And children.'

'Your husband paid for all those homes and

luxuries, didn't he?

'To which I made a one-million-dollar contribution.'

'Did you love your husband when you married?'

'I thought I did. I thought he loved me. Now I know I was wrong on both counts.'

'Families – dynasties – were more important to you than love, weren't they? That's what your marriage was, the creation of an American royal family, and you knew it, didn't you? That's what you've already told the court today. You didn't expect love.'

'Of course I expected love: love and respect and a family. One of the most important factors in a royal marriage is the provision of an heir, don't forget.'

'Which was why your husband wouldn't consider adoption, because it wouldn't have provided a proper bloodline.'

'If that is the explanation you are offering for his refusal to adopt, it is total and arrant nonsense,' rejected Alyce, as Reid returned to the court.

'As your denial that you had a sexually infected lover is total nonsense,' challenged Bartle.

At last, despite her robustness so far, Alyce broke into tears, at which Reid hurried to his feet and said, 'You honour! My client should surely be allowed the protection of the court.'

'Which I am allowing her and which you must observe, Mr Wolfson,' warned Pullinger, as Leanne Jefferies' attorney got to his feet.

'The shouted, violent confrontation with your

husband that you have described to the court followed your discovery that you had chlamydia?' began Wolfson.

'Yes,' agreed Alyce, dry-eyed now.

'As far as I understand your evidence, your marriage to Alfred Appleton was already profoundly unhappy? Your living in Long Island and his living most of the time in Manhattan was virtually a separation, wasn't it?'

'Yes.'

'But the chlamydia was the final, irreparable breaking point?'

'Yes.'

'You did attempt a reconciliation, though?'

'Yes.'

'Did it work?'

'No.'

'If you hadn't been infected, would you have filed for divorce?'

'Yes, I think I would.'

'Just think?' pressed Wolfson.

'Not just think. I would have filed for divorce. My marriage – our marriage – was a sham.'

There was a line of upright exclamation marks on Beckwith's pad, Jordan saw.

'When you had that final, irreparable breaking-up fight with your husband did you know of Leanne Jefferies?'

'I knew he had a mistress. I didn't know her name.'

'When did you learn her name?'

'When the proceedings began ... when my lawyer received the papers from my husband's lawyer.'

'Until that time, did you have any intention of claiming financial damages from Leanne Jefferies for criminal conversation, for being the cause of the collapse of your marriage?'

Jordan turned, at the shift in the jury box, and saw Walter Harding sliding into his accustomed seat beyond the separating rail.

'No,' Alyce replied to the question. 'I've already given evidence that I did so because of the law in this state ... of the availability of the provision.'

'Did Leanne Jefferies cause the end of your marriage? Wasn't your marriage already over before you ever learned her name?'

During the woman's hesitation Beckwith leaned sideways and said to Jordan, 'Good try – his only try – but it isn't a defence.'

Finally Alyce said, 'Yes, it was, I suppose.'


'Bruising,' identified Harding, from the witness stand in a bland, even, bedside voice. 'To the upper right thigh and lower ribs. Some contusions, but no actual skin break by the time I examined Mrs Appleton. I suspected there might be internal rib bruising, too.'

'How did you understand Mrs Appleton received those injuries?'

'She told me she had been violently punched by her husband earlier in the day, at their Long Island home, that her ribs had been particularly painful on the flight back here, to Raleigh.'

'Did you not consider having Mrs Appleton X-rayed at your hospital to establish whether her ribs were actually broken? Or fractured?'

437

'From the external bruising I did not believe either to have happened. If either had occurred there is no medical procedure – no plastering or binding support – that could have eased the healing or reduced the pain beyond the palliative medication I prescribed.'

'Were the physical injuries on Mrs Appleton's body consistent with her being violently punched to the ground?'

'The specific injuries we are discussing were consistent with a fall. But on her upper left shoulder, extending maybe three or four inches down her upper chest as far as her breast, there was further bruising, marked in such a way to indicate knuckle separation. This was consistent with her having been punched. There was another, separate bruise on her right shoulder, which could have been caused by a thumb being heavily pressed in her at this point.'

'Violently punched?' pressed Reid.

'It would have to have been a heavy blow, to have resulted in the bruising I am describing. And to have knocked her to the floor.'

'And the pressure that caused the other mark, on her right shoulder?'

'Substantial.'

Harding agreed, under intense questioning from Bartle, that he had been in Raleigh, not Long Island, where Alyce claimed to have sustained her injuries and repeatedly agreed that he had no way to substantiate that they could have been inflicted in the way she had described to him.

'So, she could have received the bruises and

contusions by the simple act of tripping, falling, from her own clumsiness, not by being attacked?' demanded the lawyer.

'The bruising and contusions to her upper right thigh and side, yes,' agreed Harding. 'But most definitely not the bruising to her upper left shoulder and breast that was clearly imprinted with the method of its cause, a heavy punch. And it's not possible to punch yourself to leave that severity of imprint. She was hit – hit hard – by somebody else.'

The practice was for Jordan to wait in the corridor outside the court to be collected by his lawyer and Reid to go on to their after-hearing conference and assessment but that night Beckwith emerged alone to announce there wasn't going to be one.

'Why not?' demanded Jordan.

'Wolfson wants a meeting with Bob.'

'What about?'

'Bargaining's my guess,' said Beckwith. 'That's the usual reason for opposing lawyers to get together during a hearing.'

'To whose benefit?'

'It's got to be Alyce's. It's Wolfson who's come to Bob.'

'You think the case is collapsing?'

'Something's shaking, at least.'

'Did you notice Alyce was wearing her wedding and engagement rings?'

'And kept them visible all the time,' expanded Beckwith. 'Oldest trick in the world in a divorce hearing. A constant reminder to the jury of what they're there for and the punishment the wronged wife has suffered. And don't tell me it's cynical. I know it is. But if I'd been representing Alyce that's exactly what I would have told her to do. Don't forget...'

'...the theatre,' accepted Jordan. 'Why the different, sometimes angled, symbols today?'

'Yesterday Bob was brilliant. I wasn't completely sure of the questioning tactics, although unless there's any re-examination I think Bob got away with it.'

'Got away with what?'

'Didn't it strike you as curious how well Alyce stood up to everything, only showing the slightest weakness, a few tears, at the very end?'

'Harding had given her something. She said so from the stand.'

'She didn't seem much under the influence of anything to me,' said Beckwith.

'She did her best in front of the jury for you.'

'You think from the way it's going it could all be over quicker than you imagined?'

'Very little has come out the way I imagined, apart from our part. And that's come out better than I imagined.'

Which was what Jordan thought until he turned on his computer.

# Thirty

There were two more challenges, both from Manhattan brokers this time, both highlighting shortfalls, one on a $200,000 copper disposal, the other on an aluminium trade that should have resulted in a $130,000 profit. The combined deficit for which Jordan was responsible – both one of his early hits – was $3,400. As with the Chicago query, the approaches from both brokers imagined a miscalculation and the Appleton dealers' replies promised immediate enquiries.

It was the internal email correspondence upon which Jordan concentrated.

In sequence they began between the two metal dealers but within the space of three messages grew to include John Popple, the dealer to whom the Chicago complaint had been made. Popple's pick-up to his two colleagues was that the initial back office investigation had failed to discover the disparity in his sale, to which the copper broker, George Sutcliffe, replied suggesting the three of them immediately report the situation to their financial control division. The third man, Colin Nutbeam, warned against an over-reaction before making their own essential enquiries. 'We'll look fools if there's a simple explanation like a misplaced digit or a dropped decimal point, with no cause for panic.'

Popple countered that he was going to bring it before his section leader. 'I've been trying to track it down for days and can't. It's time I made it official.' Both the other traders asked Popple not to mention their problems until they'd had the chance to make their own checks. Popple wished them luck.

Still no cause for him to panic, Jordan judged. There was no way, short of a professional electronic sweep, of discovering his illegal presence within the Appleton and Drake computers. And when that eventually happened, weeks away from now, the embezzler's name uncovered would be that of Alfred Appleton, not Harvey Jordan. But before that there would have to be a full scale and individual trader audit to establish the embezzlement in the first place and after that a criminal investigation mounted to trace its source to Appleton.

It was still moving faster than Jordan had expected. But then, although he knew his way through the labyrinth of computer hacking, he hadn't actually worked such a complicated scam as this before. So he didn't precisely know *what* to expect. Except, of course, to win. Which he would because he always did.

Jordan phished Appleton and Drake's trades with the delicacy of an angler dancing a fly on a trout stream, taking his time, undecided between gold or silver, eventually choosing to split between the two. He raided three gold holdings and two silver, switching a total of $18,500 in bank transfers. The tranche brought him close to his self-imposed banked limit, making essential withdrawals from all the accounts into the unrecorded safe deposits. In which, including the $18,500, his profit currently stood at $195,000.

He hadn't confirmed the possibility of their meeting that night but decided there was a need, suggesting by telephone to Beckwith that they go again to the out-of-town restaurant to get away from the incarceration of the hotel. Both stopped, momentarily startled, at the sight, already at a table although not yet eating, of Appleton and Bartle. Both, briefly, seemed equally surprised.

It was the bejeaned Beckwith who recovered first. He gave a stilted half wave, to which Bartle awkwardly responded, told the bell captain they needed their reserved table to be at the opposite side of the room and as they walked towards it said to Jordan, 'It's a free country and there ain't any law against it.'

They ordered martinis in preference to the heavier Jack Daniels and a recovered Jordan said, 'You know what baffles me? How someone as –' he had to pause, for the word – 'as delicate as Alyce could have shared the same bed with someone like him. I've never actually seen one, but with that funny hump of his he reminds me of that bison on your belt buckle.'

'You've got the inside track to make that sort of comparison, which I guess makes you biased,' said the lawyer and smiled. 'But he sure as hell doesn't give Tom Cruise any competition,

443

does he? It make you uncomfortable, being in the same room?'

'Not at all,' said Jordan, meaning it. At that moment, he reflected, he knew more of the inside workings of Appleton's business than Appleton himself.

'Miserable looking son of a bitch as well,' said Beckwith. 'But then at the current state of play he's got every reason to be. I'd still like to hear what they're talking about.'

'What Leanne's going to say would be a good guess,' suggested Jordan. Coming to the first reason for his invitation, he went on: 'You heard from Bob, about what he and Wolfson talked about?'

Beckwith shook his head. 'Didn't expect to. We're hugger-mugger about everything involving you and Alyce because of the obvious mutual interest. Anything concerning him and Wolfson – and Leanne, I guess – is outside the loop.'

'What bargain has Wolfson got to offer Bob?'

Beckwith shrugged again. 'Beats me. The only purpose of bargaining meetings is mutual co-operation and I can't imagine what there is to co-operate about between Alyce and Leanne.'

'Wouldn't it also be...' Jordan has to pause again, for the word. 'Illegal, unprofessional maybe, for them to talk like this?'

'It's coming pretty close to the fence,' allowed the lawyer. 'But it's not forbidden. And if you can't stop the express train coming at your client at 100 miles an hour – which Wolfson can't – it doesn't hurt to negotiate.'

'About what?'

'I just told you,' said Beckwith, with a flare of impatience. 'I don't know! And can't think of a reason.' He looked across at the other table. 'They're really not very happy to see us.'

Jordan followed his lawyer's concentration across to the other table, from which both Bartle and Appleton were looking at them and talking at the same time. Bartle took a cell phone from his pocket, dialled and abruptly slammed the lid shut. Appleton half rose but sat when Bartle held out a restraining hand.

Jordan said, 'Looks like an argument. As well as a telephone call that didn't connect.'

'I'd say so,' agreed Beckwith.

Jordan turned away at the arrival of the wine waiter. As the host he tasted and agreed to the Nappa Valley burgundy, although he would have preferred a French wine. Coming to the second point he wanted to establish, he said, 'Let's talk about something you might be able to speculate on. The way it's going I don't think it'll get anywhere near your estimate.'

'No way,' agreed Beckwith, at once. 'We've got Leanne tomorrow. Maybe some recalls, although I'm not going to apply for any at the moment. I don't think Bob has got anyone else, now that his enquiry people have been cut off by Pullinger. I don't think he needs anyone else.'

'So what's your new estimate?'

'Middle of next week, tops.'

Everything was definitely moving faster – coming up to the speed of light – than he'd expected, acknowledged Jordan. 'I know it will

445

only be a ballpark figure. That's all I'm asking for. Keeping everything else out of the equation, how much am I into for costs?'

Beckwith waited for their meal to be served, cut into his inevitable steak but held it on the fork before him, as if examining it. 'We got a problem here, Harvey?'

'Absolutely not, apart from moving necessary funds across from England,' assured Jordan. 'Which is why I'm asking the question. I may need to go back to withdraw some more ... make plane reservations, stuff like that.'

'Ballpark?' heavily qualified Beckwith.

'Ballpark,' confirmed Jordan.

'Two hundred and fifty thousand,' estimated Beckwith. 'And don't even think of anything extra for an appeal.'

From his conversations in London with Lesley Corbin, Jordan had imagined it would be much higher. 'Maybe I won't need to go back to England.' Just hit Appleton far harder, after making room in the open-mouthed accounts, he thought.

With a better view of Bartle's table from where he was sitting, Beckwith said, 'And baby makes three!'

Jordan turned again to see Peter Wolfson approaching Bartle's table. At something Bartle said the other lawyer looked across towards them before he sat. Beckwith gave another hand gesture, which Wolfson did not acknowledge.

Beckwith said, 'Like the wise man said, shit happens! They go to all the trouble of finding a little, out-of-town hideaway for their council of

446

war and we walk in. No wonder they look so pissed off.'

'You think Wolfson's come straight from seeing Bob?'

'Hardly need the help of Sherlock Holmes, do we?' said Beckwith. 'I can hardly wait for tomorrow.'

But they had to, longer than they'd expected. After rigidly sticking to his early morning routine, which produced nothing beyond what he'd already read on Appleton and Drake's computers, Jorden went down for breakfast to be told that by the time Beckwith called him, Reid had already left to collect Alyce from the Bellamy estate.

'Earlier than usual?' queried Jordan.

'Two hours earlier than usual,' agreed Beckwith. 'They obviously had things to talk about.'

And they were still talking, already at their table, when Jordan and his lawyer arrived at court. There was only the briefest moment, before the judge's entry, for any conversation between Alyce's lawyer and Beckwith, before Peter Wolfson called Leanne Jefferies to the stand. Jordan managed eye contact with Alyce as the other woman was being sworn. Alyce looked back at him blankly. On his pad Jordan wrote, 'What?'

Beckwith scribbled back: 'Leanne's ours!'

Led by Wolfson, with Appleton and Bartle both intently forward over their separate table, Leanne confirmed her age to be thirty and described herself as a senior partner in the Wall

Street commodity firm of Sears Rutlidge. Not once looking at him, Leanne testified she had known Alfred Appleton by reputation over a period of five years as the senior partner of Appleton and Drake, a rival firm of commodity dealers. Thirteen months earlier she and Appleton had begun a brief relationship, which she estimated to have lasted no longer than two months. At that time she had understood Appleton to be coming to the end of an unopposed divorce. Her relationship with Appleton had ended when she contracted a sexually transmitted disease, which Appleton told her he had, in turn, caught from his wife during a failed reconciliation before their relationship began. She would not have engaged in such a relationship if she had known that divorce proceedings had not, at that time, even been initiated. She had not regarded their affair as a serious commitment on either side and now deeply regretted it.

'How many commodity firms are there in Wall Street?' demanded Reid, as he rose to cross-examine. As always, when he was on his feet in court, there was no trace of asthma in his voice.

'I'm not sure.' There was a discernible uncertainty from how she had responded to this questioning.

'Ten? Twenty? Thirty?' suggested Reid.

'I really am not sure,' Leanne insisted.

'Would you say it was a comparatively limited community, most dealers knowing other dealers?'

'Not particularly.'

'But you knew Alfred Appleton for what,

almost four years, before your affair began?'

'Yes.' When she wasn't talking Leanne had her lips drawn in tightly between her teeth.

'Wasn't he someone particularly well known in Wall Street because of his family antecedents?'

'Not particularly,' she repeated.

'Did you know of the family history?'

'I may have heard something of it.'

'Did you or didn't you?' demanded Reid, brusquely.

'I'd heard something about it,' conceded Leanne, defensively.

'What about the historically well known Bellamy family?'

'I didn't know anything about a Bellamy family,' protested the woman.

'You didn't know that your lover, Alfred Appleton, was married to Alyce Bellamy, uniting two of the best known families in America's founding history?'

'No,' said Leanne. Before every answer she looked hopefully towards Wolfson although still steadfastly refusing to look at Appleton, so close at the adjoining table.

'When did you discover the identity of Alfred Appleton's wife?'

'I don't remember. Not until we became close, I don't think.'

'How did you become close? When did it happen? Who approached whom?'

Leanne took several moments to reply. 'It was at a seminar in New Jersey. Went over two days.'

'When did it begin, the first night or the second

night?'

There was another pause. 'The second night.'

'Before you went to bed with Alfred Appleton the second night, you knew he was a married man, didn't you?'

'He told me he was divorced.'

Appleton thrust sideways to talk to his lawyer at Leanne's answer.

'*Was* divorced? Or *getting* divorced?' pressed Reid.

'Was divorced,' insisted Leanne. 'Just waiting for the decree to become absolute.'

'That's exactly what he said, that he was waiting for the decree to become absolute?'

'Yes,' blurted Leanne, before seeing Wolfson shaking his head. 'I mean ... I think ... yes...'

'By then you knew who Appleton was ... the history, didn't you?'

'Something had been said ... I had an idea,' the woman stumbled on.

'You saw yourself as the second Mrs Appleton, didn't you, marrying into one of America's oldest families?' pounced Reid.

'No!' Leanne denied, flustered. 'That wasn't how it was ... what it was ... I told you, it wasn't a commitment.' She looked at Alyce, beside her interrogator. 'Like hers wasn't a commitment. Didn't mean anything. Just something that happened...' She twisted, looking for the first time to Appleton and managed, 'You ... you bastard...' before collapsing back into her chair, sobbing.

To Jordan, Beckwith finally said, 'If I can only get the chance!'

450

* * *

First Bartle and then Wolfson objected to Beckwith taking up the cross-examination, Wolfson even pleading that Leanne was incapable of continuing despite her obvious recovery on the witness stand, but Pullinger dismissed both arguments that further questioning was unnecessary.

'You did believe Alfred Appleton's marriage was over, didn't you?' began Beckwith, softly encouraging.

'Yes.'

'Because that was what he'd told you?'

'Yes.'

'So he lied to you?'

'Your honour!' Bartle tried to protest but Pullinger gestured him down.

'Yes,' said Leanne. She no longer appeared uncertain.

'As he lied about catching chlamydia from his wife?'

'I suppose so ... from what I've heard here, in court.'

'Why didn't you go to a doctor, a venerealogist, in New York?'

'He said he knew people in Boston who could help ... that he had influence there.'

'Alfred Appleton persuaded you to go to Boston because he had influence there!' said Beckwith. 'What did you understand he meant by that?'

'I don't really know ... that they were good doctors, I suppose.'

'Why weren't you treated by the same

venerealogist who treated him, Dr Chapman?'

'He said it would be best if we were treated separately.'

'Did you ask him why?'

'No, not really. I was very upset, at having been infected. He said I wasn't to worry. That he'd fix everything.'

'Your honour,' objected Bartle, again. 'I really must protest at this! My client—'

'Is here, in court, able to refute anything that this witness says if you choose to call him,' stopped Pullinger. 'As you are to cross-examine in an attempt to obtain contrary evidence if you choose, Mr Bartle.'

'He told you he would fix everything,' picked up Beckwith. 'Is Alfred Appleton a dominant man, Ms Jefferies?'

'Very much so.'

'Who dislikes opinions contrary to his own?' finished Beckwith.

'Who *refuses* opinions contrary to his own,' said the woman. She was sitting forward in her chair now, looking directly at Appleton.

'When was the first time you heard of a person named Sharon Borowski?'

There was a falter from Leanne Jefferies. 'When I was served with the court papers, ordering me to appear here.'

'You hadn't expected them? Been warned to expect them?'

'Of course not!' replied Leanne, indignantly.

'Because you believed the divorce was already resolved: over?'

'Exactly!'

452

'What did you do?'

'Called Alfred. Asked him what was happening.'

'What did he say?'

'That there had been a mix-up: a mistake. That he'd fix it.'

'That he'd fix it,' repeated Beckwith, for the second time. 'How did he say he was going to fix it?'

'He made me go to his lawyers in Boston who said—'

'Stop!' sharply ordered Pullinger, from the bench. 'Do you intend pursuing this, Mr Beckwith?'

'In view of the suit that has been brought against my client I believe it is incumbent upon me *to* pursue it, your honour,' said Beckwith.

'Mr Bartle?' asked the judge.

'I would respectfully submit that this is far beyond any grounds of admissibility,' said Appleton's lawyer.

'Mr Wolfson?' repeated Pullinger.

'With equal respect, your honour, I would make the same submission,' said Leanne's lawyer. 'And would further seek to approach your honour either at the bench or in chambers if your honour feels there is benefit to your court or to yourself from such discussion.'

Pullinger slumped reflectively into his high-backed chair, leaving three of the four attorneys on their feet. Leanne looked around her, confused. Alyce stared directly ahead, unmoving. Appleton's bison's head was forward, over his table. There were the sounds of shifting from the jury box.

Pullinger came slowly forward, further than he normally sat, immediately bringing to Jordan's mind the imagery of a watchful predatory vulture. 'To permit the continuation of this examination, while permissible within the bounds of law, would seriously invite the possibility of my having to dismiss this jury and declare a mistrial upon the grounds of undue and prejudicial bias. To deny its continuation provides Mr Beckwith with the opportunity to seek an appeal on behalf of his client, as indeed it does Mr Bartle and Mr Wolfson on behalf of theirs. So be it. This has been the most contentious and most unsatisfactory hearing I believe I have ever been called upon to adjudicate. I further believe, however, that at this stage it is still possible for me to direct the jury, subject to consultation with the respective attorneys about further potential witnesses, to a fitting and legally satisfactory conclusion. Which it is my intention to do. It is also my intention to release the jury from their responsibilities for the rest of this day, be available in chambers for individual or combined discussion with counsel about witnesses to whom I have already referred and, subject to those representations, address the jury at the opening of the court tomorrow.'

'We've won!' declared Beckwith.

'There can't be any doubt,' agreed Reid.

They'd gone together to see Pullinger in chambers, to announce neither had any remaining witnesses nor objection to the hearing being closed and waited back at their tables to be recalled by the judge if the separately attending Bartle and Wolfson had raised a question needing a fuller discussion, which seemingly they hadn't. Reid telephoned his office from the courtroom corridor, before helping Alyce into his car, and the ordered champagne – French, not American – was waiting when the four of them arrived.

Alyce hesitated at the toast and said, 'You heard what Leanne said, about his always needing to dominate. Which I'd already told you he does. Alfred will appeal. The judge actually invited him to!'

'Not even a control freak like your soon-to-be ex-husband could risk having paraded in open court, to be reported every day, what's come out here,' insisted Reid. 'And it would come out, if you retained me to appear on your behalf at an appeal. I'd object to any closed hearing and make that clear to whatever attorney he engaged. And it wouldn't be David Bartle. I don't think he would take the case even if he were offered it. Which I don't think he would be able anyway because I think Pullinger is going to report both him and Wolfson to their bar council for professional misconduct. Which in my opinion Wolfson's move last night definitely was.'

'I'm still waiting to hear what that was!' protested Jordan.

'He offered a deal, an out-of-court damages settlement of $500,000 to Alyce from Leanne if we agreed not to call her. She'd told Wolfson, who'd told Bartle, that she'd be a hostile witness because of the crap Appleton dumped on her.'

'But I said no,' added Alyce. 'I didn't – don't – want her money. I want Alfred just once to be shown he's not God.'

Which she would, although not immediately, thought Jordan. 'Where was Leanne going to get $500,000?'

'Appleton, I guess,' said Reid. 'Wolfson insisted the money was there, if we agreed.'

'She wouldn't have done,' said Alyce. 'The bastard would have cheated her, like he cheats everybody.'

'Are we going to get around to drinking to victory?' complained Beckwith.

They finally drank, Alyce hesitantly. She said, 'Thank you. Thank all of you. I can't believe it's virtually all over. And it is, isn't it? Virtually all over? We can behave like normal people again?'

'All over but for the formalities,' promised Reid, bringing out the Jack Daniels from his desk drawer in preference to the champagne.

Alyce shook her head against her glass being refilled, as Jordan did, moving with her away from Reid's desk.

'What are you doing this afternoon?' asked Alyce.

'I haven't thought about it,' lied Jordan. He'd already calculated that at only just past one he had more than sufficient time to get to Manhattan to empty the overflowing bank accounts to make room for more transfers and be back in Raleigh long before tomorrow's court opening.

'Why not spend it back at the house?' invited Alyce.

'I'd like that very much,' accepted Jordan. The bank accounts could wait, overflowing or not.

# Thirty-One

Jordan and Beckwith had alternated between cars to move between the hotel and the court building and that day they had used Jordan's hired Ford. Beckwith accepted with a frown, although nothing more, at being told he'd need a taxi for his hotel return and within fifteen minutes Jordan and Alyce were driving in the opposite direction to the Bellamy estate. Jordan followed Alyce's route directions from the civic centre court avoiding any possible media interference, isolating none, but Jordan quickly recognized the surroundings, and as they passed it nodded towards the previous night's restaurant. 'That's where we saw them, after Wolfson made his pitch to Bob.'

'Bob told me,' said Alyce. 'They must have thought you were having them watched, knowing where they were, when you walked in.'

'They certainly reacted as if they had been caught doing something wrong,' laughed Jordan. It wasn't difficult for him to laugh – to be very happy – alone with Alyce driving through the low, undulating North Carolina countryside.

'I can't believe they thought I'd go for the offer, legal or otherwise. Bob doesn't think they ever expected you to fight the case in the first place; that you'd be too frightened of losing and simply stay away.'

'I still might wish I had stayed, after tomorrow.'

'I'm not as confident as either Bob or Dan,' Alyce admitted. 'They don't know Alfred like I do. He doesn't lose, ever: doesn't know how. He'll appeal if there's the slightest room for him to do so.' There had been no building, no sign of any habitation at all, for the previous fifteen minutes and Alyce raised her arm, gesturing to his right. 'Just around this bend there's a turning to the right that suddenly comes up. Take it.'

Jordan did and almost at once found himself on the edge of a plain that stretched out in all directions as far as he could see. He said, 'That's incredible! The world's flat and we're right at the edge!'

Alyce shifted in her seat. Quietly, as if she were embarrassed, she said, 'It's all Bellamy land, as far as the horizon and as much – more than as much – again beyond.'

'That's ... I don't know ... it must be...' groped Jordan.

'A lot of land,' helped Alyce. 'And there's more, way over to the south right up to the coast. We've leased a lot of it: long, hundred year leases, but we still own it.'

'*You* own it,' qualified Jordan.

'Ultimately, I guess,' agreed Alyce. 'It's all

tied up in trusts and foundations and charities and God knows what. It was all here for the taking when the first ships landed, all those years ago. And a man named Hector Bellamy took it. At least, unlike most of the other early settlers, he didn't annihilate the native Americans who already lived here. Maybe he should have done. According to the history they rose up against his settlement and killed him. But not until he had sons...' Almost inaudibly, she said, 'Which I can't now have.'

Jordan wasn't sure if she'd intended him to hear and pretended that he hadn't. They drove on for what Jordan knew from the car's speedometer trip to be a further ten miles, passing through an unexpected neon-lit township – which Jordan thought of as an unwelcome intrusion – before Alyce gestured another right turning on to a private blacktop. Within yards there was a CCTV-monitored gatehouse with a further camera-mounted identification speaker grill, into which Alyce leaned across him to announce their arrival. A huge, electronically-controlled barrier that filled the entire gate space began to open. From both sides of the gatehouse spread a high fence in front of which, at intervals, were printed warnings of its electrification. About twenty yards behind the fence began a thatch of even higher trees seemingly planted without any design but which, in fact, formed a straggled forest beyond which it was impossible to see from the outside. No house was immediately visible but there were several flocks of faraway sheep as well as a herd of nervously attentive deer. When the buildings came into view Jordan realized that there was not one house but several, a complex dominated by the central, columned and veranda-encircled white clapboard original with separate, two- and three-storey constructions grouped around it, completed by a single storey, L-shaped stabling to one side. Around it all was looped a stand of very tall and long-established shading trees. Jordan was surprised, when he stopped, to see that they had only been driving a little over an hour.

As the towering front door opened to their approach Jordan said, 'It'll be a uniformed butler!'

'House manager,' corrected Alyce, although it was a man in a black suit and tie waiting for them at the entrance. 'We'll eat something when I've got out of these court clothes.' To the man she said, 'We'll use the garden room, Stephen. Take Mr Jordan through, will you?'

Alyce's instinctive authority he remembered from that night at the Carlyle – but only occasionally in France – had returned, Jordan recognized, following the man as Alyce mounted the wide stairway winding around half of the circular entrance hall. From its panelled walls were displayed a portrait gallery of whom Jordan guessed to be Alyce's ancestors. The garden room fulfilled its title. It was a vast glass-walled and roofed conservatory stretching out into sculpted and fountain-flower displays on three sides, with long-leafed plants and vases of more flowers inside. Jordan declined the offered drink, looking out beyond the neatly bordered and colour-coordinated beds in which two gardeners were working.

When Alyce entered she was wearing a V-necked sweater, light blue jeans that Jordan was sure he'd seen in France and was barefoot. He nodded in the direction in which he had been frowning and said, 'What looks like a long red flag, way beyond all the buildings? It's a wind sock, right?'

'An airstrip,' she agreed. 'Flying is the quickest and most convenient way to commute up and down from New York. There's a helicopter as well as a Lear. Both owned and run by the Bellamy Foundation.'

'I didn't guess it was anything like this ... as extensive as this ... an empire.'

Alyce shrugged. 'Stephen offer you a drink?'

'I thought I'd wait.' Jordan saw that while he'd stood with his back to the room a table, glass topped to fit its surroundings, had been laid with cutlery, goblets and tumblers.

'Lunch is scrambled eggs and smoked salmon.'

'Sounds good.'

Alyce, totally comfortable in her own accustomed environment – the creator of her own environment – went to a side cooler Jordan hadn't seen and said, 'How about a drink now?'

Jordan saw at once that it was the white burgundy he'd ordered for them in France. 'Now I'd like one.' His conflicting – unaccustomed – feelings were colliding. At that precise moment he knew himself to be confused. Seeking a

461

balancing plateau, he said, 'I thought your mother would be here?'

'She likes the beach house at this time of the year. She paints. Actually paints quite well.'

Faraway in another part of the mansion there was the distant sound of a telephone and almost at once a louder summons from a multi-lined console on a side table. As Jordan gestured that he was leaving the room he heard Alyce say, 'Hello? Hi... Sorry ... Yes, he's here now ... I'm fine ... no problem ... OK...' He was at the door when he heard, 'Hey, come back.' And when he re-entered the room she said, 'Thanks for the politeness but you didn't have to do that. It was Walter. He's coming over when he's finished.'

'Walter?'

'Walt Harding. He can guide you back, later.'

Jordan hadn't thought about later; hadn't thought about anything, not wanting to anticipate anything more than a minute ahead. Now he felt disappointed. He said, 'I could have found my own way.' He admitted to himself the hope that he wouldn't have needed to. At least it took away the uncertainty.

Alyce didn't reply, rising instead at the re-entry of the butler. He was pushing a flame-heated serving trolley from which, as they sat, he ladled eggs and fish on to plates and topped up both their glasses.

Alyce said, 'I guess by this time next week you'll be back in London?'

'I haven't thought about it. Let's get tomorrow over, first.'

'Wondering why I invited you out here this

462

afternoon?'

'No,' lied Jordan.

'It's about tomorrow. Like I told you, I'm not as confident as either Bob or Dan. Even if there's no damages awarded against you, you've still got a lot of costs and—'

'Stop!' demanded Jordan, loudly. 'We've done this too many times and I've told you no too many times. It's still no. Always will be, so let's forget it once and for all, OK?'

'No, it's not OK!' she argued. 'You're going to be out a lot of money, whatever happens. That's not fair.'

Jordan swept out his arm, encompassing the house and beyond. 'So you brought me here to show me you could afford it more than I could!'

'That's not fair, either!'

'Tell me it isn't true then.'

'I wanted to talk to you, by ourselves. The court break was convenient. I wasn't trying to impress you. This is just how it is.'

'I am impressed,' finally conceded Jordan. 'But not enough to take your money. It's no longer a conversation between us.' He'd never imagined himself uninterested in anyone else's money, Jordan further conceded. But there had been a lot of other things – attitude changes – over the last few weeks that he wouldn't have imagined possible, either.

'Never again,' Alyce promised. She sniggered. 'Promise you won't get mad if I say something else, though?'

'I'll try.'

'You know who you reminded me of, yelling

463

at me like that?'

'You tell me it's Alfred and I'll yell louder,' he said, joining in the game.

'It was Alfred. How he used to speak ... talk to people ... talk to everybody...' She hesitated at Stephen's return with a black uniformed woman to clear the table apart from their wine and water glasses. Allowing time for them to get out of hearing, she said, 'People never worked for us, either in Manhattan or Long Island, beyond a few weeks, because of it.' She physically shuddered, at the recollection.

'In the land of the laid-back, why on earth does everyone automatically refer to him as Alfred, never Al!'

Alyce's laugh this time was more spontaneous. 'Call Alfred Al! You've got to be joking! He was always Alfred and even then only to a very few people.'

'How the hell did you ever get involved with such a...' Jordan paused. 'A man.'

'Monster would have done,' she said. 'You wouldn't believe how many times and in how many different ways I've asked myself that same question. But he's very good at hiding himself, when he needs to ... when it's necessary. And it was very necessary with me and the family and all that we'd created. It was only when it didn't work, as he'd intended it to work, that it all started to go wrong. That the punishments started...'

'You're losing me,' complained Jordan. 'Maybe we shouldn't even be talking about it, now that it's virtually over. There's no point.'

'You know what I now realize Alfred really

felt about me? About me and all the historic bullshit and where we, the Bellamys, are now?' said Alyce, too engrossed in her own reflections to heed Jordan's caution. 'It was resentment. It was right, what Bob suggested in court, although he never brought it out like it truly was. It wasn't me that Alfred loved. I don't think it's possible for him to *love* anyone, probably not even himself, although I think I said that he did. What Alfred really did love, which Bob challenged him with, was the idea of being the king in an American royal family – a king who could have as many mistresses as he wanted, like kings once did: like some still do, maybe. Marrying me gave him the combined lineage but to make it really work he needed the court and the country to rule. Which didn't exist. But the Bellamy Foundation existed; the foundation on which I was a working chief executive until he persuaded me to resign, as I told the court. Except that it wasn't because he considered it ill-fitting for me to be a working woman. He manoeuvred that to vacate the throne for himself. But he miscalculated, as Alfred so often miscalculated. The Bellamy Foundation is a charitable organization, with all the responsibilities that were explained in court. But there's nothing charitable about the board that runs it. They're hard-assed professionals who were the first to see Alfred for what he is, long before I did. Getting on to it wasn't the shoo-in he thought it was going to be. He couldn't get the necessary board member vote, certainly not when mother, who's got the controlling vote structure, wouldn't back him.

That's how the punishments started...'

'Punishments?' queried Jordan.

'I believe that's what the loans were, Alfred Appleton's personally imposed financial penalties. And the neglect and the whoring, although I don't think infecting me as he did was an intended humiliation, because to do that he had to contract it first and not even he would do that.' Alyce abruptly laughed, although nervously. 'Jesus, I've really run off at the mouth, haven't I? Turned you into my therapist.'

Jordan laughed with her, anxious to lighten the mood. 'I had a free afternoon.'

'I know...' she started, but then stopped.

'Know what?'

'I'm not going to talk about money, I promise. But I know from Bob what a hell of an input you made. I want to thank you and apologize for you getting caught up in it and I promise never again to mention any of that, either.'

'You think I could have a moment or two to talk?' asked Jordan, sure he knew what he wanted to say but not at all sure how to say it.

'Depends what it is,' qualified Alyce, cautiously.

'None of what's happened...' Jordan started awkwardly, stopping at the sound from the far door of the garden room.

'Hi!' greeted Walter Harding, emerging from the foliage.

'Hi!' said Alyce.

Shit! thought Jordan.

When they came to be delivered Jordan's initial

reaction to the verdicts was that of an anti-climax – despite, even, his total exoneration – because that was how he regarded the conclusion of the previous afternoon at the Bellamy house, anxious at its end to quickly leave a place which, until Harding's intrusion, he'd hoped desperately *not* to leave that night. Hopefully not for many nights. So occupied still was he by that disappointment that at the opening of the court proceedings Jordan actually had to force his concentration upon Pullinger's summation and guidance to the jury, which strictly obeyed Pullinger's insistence on the priority of its required judgements.

This meant Appleton's criminal conversation claim against him was the first to be dealt with and totally dismissed. Immediately following the verdict, Pullinger ordered that Appleton should pay three quarters of Jordan's total costs for initiating such a flagrantly insupportable action, in part for which he held Bartle responsible for providing the inept legal advice. The jury found against Leanne Jefferies but again following Pullinger's instructions limited the award against her to $50,000 in Alyce's favour. They also found in Alyce's favour on her cross petition against Appleton.

After discharging the jury Pullinger declared he had considered a bench order alleging perjury against Appleton but held back from doing so in the event of the man appealing upon the grounds he'd offered the previous day. He definitely intended an enquiry into alleged perjury against Mark Chapman and to carry out his already indicated decision to report both venerealogists to their respective Massachusettes licensing authorities for professional misconduct. On the same grounds he was going to report David Bartle and Peter Wolfson to both the North Carolina and New York State bar associations.

'In addition to which,' Pullinger told the two attorneys, whom he'd ordered to stand before him, 'I shall refuse ever again to have either of you appear before me on any legal matter, which I shall make clear to both bar associations I have nominated. I further order, upon the possibility of both or either of your clients being held in contempt of my court, against making comments or assisting in any way the media, either electronic or print, beyond what this court provides about any of the defendants or claimants in these proceedings. I want your assurance, which will be recorded by the court stenographer, that you fully and completely understand the order I have just issued.'

One by one the two attorneys, Appleton and finally Leanne Jefferies, acknowledged that they understood.

'This hearing, the most disgraceful ever presented before me, is now closed,' Pullinger concluded.

Reid's office was judged both inadequate and inappropriate for the celebration and at a loss for an alternative they went back to the all too familiar hotel where a hurriedly arranged private room was hired and food and drink ordered while Alyce telephoned her mother to relay the news and Jordan returned to his suite to make an earlier-than-usual computer check that there had been no movement upon the existing shortfall enquiries, nor any new challenges. As an afterthought as he was actually leaving his suite, Jordan quickly dialled Lesley Corbin in London, who said she'd never had any doubt of the outcome and whom Jordan didn't believe.

Jordan was back in his anti-climax depression when he got to the celebration, by which time Walter Harding had arrived and Alyce had passed on the court verdict. Also there were the DDK enquiry team who had never been called upon as well as some support staff from Reid's office.

Harding approached Jordan the moment he entered the room and said, 'Didn't I tell you this was exactly as it would turn out!'

'You certainly did,' agreed Jordan. As well as a lot of other I-can-predict bullshit by which he'd become so irritated the previous afternoon that he'd switched off any attention to the man's constant outpourings.

'How's it feel?' demanded Harding.

'I'm not sure it's settled in.' Jordan wished Alyce would break away from Reid so that he could excuse himself from the hospital administrator.

'It was obviously nonsense from the beginning,' insisted the man. 'I guess you're now going back to reality and England, where everything and everybody is normal?'

He'd never ever lived in reality, thought Jordan. Always the opposite, the unreality of living

469

– being – somebody else, with somebody else's name and persona. He said, 'I'm not sure that's an apt description, either.' He saw Alyce had moved away from her lawyer and immediately excused himself to join her.

Alyce said at once, 'I didn't realize Pullinger was delaying the media release until tomorrow.'

'Neither did I.'

'By which time I shall be back at the house, beyond any camera lens.'

'Is that what you're going to do?'

'There's no better place to hide.'

'For how long?'

'For as long as I choose, although the judge put a pretty effective lid on it becoming a long-running saga, didn't he?'

'So what after you come out of retreat?' pressed Jordan.

She smiled at the expression. 'Regain my life. I've already arranged to get my place back on the board of the Bellamy Foundation.'

'As well as?'

'That's as far as, for the moment,' said Alyce. 'There was something you were going to say, just before Walter arrived at the house yesterday?'

'Maybe later,' said Jordan. 'Not now.'

'Call me.'

# Thirty-Two

Jordan tried the moment he got into his Carlyle suite the following morning, before even bothering to unpack after a delayed New York arrival from Raleigh. At the Bellamy North Carolina estate, Stephen – after having established who Jordan was – told him Alyce wasn't there and that he didn't know when she would be returning; she hadn't given a date or a location, although he didn't think it was Manhattan. Jordan told the butler where he was – even stipulating his suite number – and to pass on a message for Alyce to call if she made contact. And did the same when, despite the butler's doubt that Alyce was in New York, he got the answering service at her West 84th Street apartment.

During the returning flight Jordan had scoured as many newspapers as were available at Raleigh airport. Both the *New York Times* and *Wall Street Journal*'s coverage was relegated to deep into the inside pages, boosted beyond the strictly limited factual release from Pullinger's court by photographs of both Appleton and Alyce and the inevitable historical background of both families. Jordan was named only once, without either a photograph or an indication, even, of his English nationality. There was nothing in any international edition of any English newspaper collected for him by the hotel's customer service department. He'd alerted Lesley Corbin during his earlier call from Raleigh and when he telephoned again she confirmed there was no reference either to the case or to him personally in any of that morning's London editions. Neither had there been on any national British television or radio bulletin or any Internet news source she'd accessed.

'Why should there have been?' she asked him, rhetorically. 'You were found not guilty of any involvement in the case.'

Jordan waited until after he'd unpacked before mounting his daily monitor of the Appleton and Drake computers. There was a further challenge, again from a Manhattan broker, to a shortfall on another of the earliest copper trades he'd raided, and evident growing alarm in the continuing email conversations between the two earlier questioned metal traders at their inability to discover the cause of their individual problems through any of the personal enquiries they had so far conducted. One, Colin Nutbeam, complained of not being able to look any further or differently than he already had and his colleague, George Sutcliffe, agreed that if they didn't identify the cause of the disparities in the next twenty-four hours there was no alternative but to officially report it to their respective financial supervisors. From the now extensive communications between the originally challenged John Popple and his financial controller there were gaps indicating either personal interviews or internal telephone conversations, culminating the previous day in the latest email from the fiscal manager, not to Popple but to Alfred Appleton, asking for the earliest possible meeting upon his return from Raleigh to discuss an apparently inexplicable financial discrepancy in an onwardly traded pork belly future. In an attempt to trace the error before the requested meeting, the controller intended conducting an audit of every buy and sell contract in which Popple had been involved in the preceding six months. Until the matter was resolved it was suggested that a specific accounting be made of every buy and sell trade in which Popple had engaged.

Jordan unsuccessfully tried Alyce's number again before leaving the hotel, delaying any more raids upon Appleton and Drake holdings until he had made room in the five bank accounts. Even though the banks were comparatively close to each other it took him almost four hours to move between them, keeping to the same strict routine. He first withdrew all but between $2,000 to $3,000 from each account, carrying the cash to the separate securities divisions, where in the locked seclusion of their individual private rooms he emptied the already well filled safe-deposit boxes into the two briefcases he carried with him.

Both for continued security against the unlikely irony of a street mugging and to necessarily relieve the physical strain of carrying the two now very heavy cases, Jordan hailed a taxi when he emerged from the last bank to take him back to the Carlyle hotel. There he re-entered the computers of Appleton and Drake and spent almost a further hour plundering previously untouched accounts, moving a total of $22,000 into the five banks in which he had been earlier that afternoon. There was no new correspondence in any of the Appleton and Drake sites he accessed, including the personal station of Alfred Appleton.

Jordan again got Alyce's answering service when he tried the Manhattan apartment and Stephen insisted there had been no contact from her since Jordan's previous call, promising to pass on his message and location the moment there was.

The low table in the suite's sitting room was substantial, running virtually the entire length of the two couches it divided, but it was still too small to accommodate the money when Jordan tried to tip out the contents of both briefcases, even though he had mostly stipulated $100 notes every time he had made a cash withdrawal. Jordan worked carefully and with practised professionalism, assembling the money in individual, one-thousand-dollar bundles before moving the piles from the table to the floor to make room for what was in the second case. At that moment the haul amounted to $530,0000, which meant that after Pullinger's reduced costs decision in his judgement that Jordan had more than sufficient to settle his account with Daniel Beckwith, even if the final bill exceeded the attorney's ballpark figure of $250,000. Jordan managed to fit $10,000 in the suite safe, concealed inside the bedroom closet. Neatly stacked as the money now was it was easy to assemble in envelopes of $10,000 each to transport it all in just one briefcase to the cashier's office, where he rented three more safe-deposit boxes in addition to the two already in his genuine name.

Jordan resisted his impatience to telephone the Manhattan apartment too early the next morning, waiting until just before ten before calling Alyce again, not bothering to leave another message when he again got the answering machine.

Why had she suggested he call if she hadn't intended to be at either of the numbers she'd given him?

It wasn't until his settlement meeting with Daniel Beckwith, after a further two days without any contact from Alyce, that Jordan learned Alyce had changed her mind about hiding in North Carolina and flown instead to Antigua.

'According to Bob she didn't want to be kept a prisoner there by the media: they've set up camp outside, despite Pullinger's warnings,' said Beckwith.

'You know where in Antigua?'

'No,' frowned the lawyer. 'Why?'

'I didn't properly say goodbye,' improvised Jordan.

'When are you going back?'

'In a day or two,' said Jordan. He really did need to go back to England, he told himself. There could be a lot of correspondence at the

475

Hans Crescent flat, quite apart from what might be waiting for him in Marylebone.

'I guess it's still possible that Appleton might appeal, despite Pullinger's warning,' said Beckwith. 'He could, I suppose, apply for a retrial *because* of the comments. Or argue separately against the costs apportionment. Whatever, I don't see how or why you should be enjoined, apart from the matter of costs, but if anything comes up that you need to know about I'll liaise through Lesley, OK?'

'Fine,' agreed Jordan. 'What are those costs?'

'Exactly what I gave you as a ballpark figure,' said Beckwith. 'But by the judge's order, your liability comes down to $50,000.'

'Cash OK?' questioned Jordan. He could settle what remained outstanding of the Carlyle bill the same way and still have a lot left over, he calculated. Enough, even, for a short detour to Antigua.

'Cash is always OK,' smiled the lawyer.

When Jordan called the North Carolina house yet again, Stephen insisted he did not know where Alyce was staying in Antigua – know even that she was on the island – and repeated that there had still been no contact. Jordan decided against telephoning Reid in Raleigh for the number at the same time as realizing he was verging upon making himself appear ridiculous pursuing the woman as he was doing.

When he'd explored Appleton and Drake before leaving for his appointment with Daniel Beckwith there had been no new email exchanges but it was very different when he entered again that afternoon. There were two fresh broker enquiries on discrepancies on metal trades, as well as the decision to alert their financial managers by the two traders who'd failed to solve their individual shortfall problem. And a blizzard of correspondence to and from Alfred Appleton, including four of increasing animosity, between Appleton and his partner, Peter Drake, demanding to know why an in-house investigation had not been initiated earlier. It was difficult for Jordan to assemble a fully comprehensive understanding of everything that was unfolding in the Wall Street office, because of the obvious breaks in the sequences by telephone or personal meetings, but towards the end of the day Jordan knew Appleton had ordered a total internal audit of their previous six months business upon every trader, in addition to imposing supervision upon every future trade until the cause of the apparent errors was traced. There were also emailed instructions – with the assurance of personally signed letters to follow – against allowing anything of the problems leaking outside the office to undermine the reputation or confidence of the firm. Any such disclosure would be investigated with the tenacity with which the financial irregularities were being pursued. Any uncovered whistle-blower would face civil litigation for commercial infringement of the confidentiality clauses of their contact, as well as instant dismissal.

It was time to close down, Jordan concluded. It was still short of the time he'd originally allowed himself and far shorter still of the inevitable outcome that would engulf Alfred Appleton. Jordan's decision had nothing whatsoever to do with any belated regret. And certainly not pity, for how badly the outcome of the case had gone for the commodity trader. Appleton had set out to damage and inconvenience him as much as Appleton would eventually be damaged and inconvenienced in return. Nor was it Jordan's fear of discovery, because after today's final closure the risk of his being caught would no longer exist. It was, rather, that Jordan had lost interest, virtually to the point of boredom, in any future retribution. Jordan believed he had his priorities in their carefully arranged order and Alfred Appleton no longer featured on the list.

Except for this one last, explosive time.

From a selection of Appleton's personally held but unmoved trades Jordan switched a total of $12,000 into the account he'd taken out in Appleton's name in the Chase Manhattan and in which $2,000 still remained, although the safe-deposit box was now cleared. Directly after that he ordered by email that $10,500 be transferred into the Caribbean hedge fund that had advised him their minimally acceptable opening invest-ment was $10,000, well aware, too, that the Chase were required automatically to report the transfer and that such reporting would just as automatically trigger the sort of official enquiry – and attendant publicity – that Appleton was so anxious to avoid.

Jordan then patiently severed all connection and trace of his Trojan Horse stables throughout every computer and ancillary link-line in the

Appleton and Drake system. After electronically ending the lease on the West 72nd Street apartment and settling all out-standing bills, electronically again, he telephoned the concierge at the Marylebone flat and Lesley Corbin just off Chancery Lane, advising them of his return the following day, leaving until last his final call to North Carolina, leaving with Stephen the message that he was going back to England and would call Alyce from there sometime in the future. He managed to book a conveniently timed mid-morning flight to London the following day and that night, after dinner, took a taxi to the 23rd Street marina and seaplane port into which Appleton had flown during his daily commute from Long Island, enjoying the irony when, judging the moment, he dropped the much-used and incriminating laptop into the East River.

As he settled his outstanding and substantial bill in cash the receptionist said, 'We hope you'll be coming back soon to stay with us again.'

'So do I,' said Jordan, meaning it.

# Thirty-Three

It was a Tuesday, a month after Jordan's return to London, when his retribution against Alfred Appleton became public knowledge with headlines in the *New York Times* and *Wall Street Journal*, both of whose websites Jordan monitored daily, doubting that the announcement of a police investigation into the affairs of Alfred Appleton would be carried in English newspapers. It was, though – in the *Independent* and the *Daily Telegraph* – when the FBI were called in after the additional discovery of the apparent hedge fund application, and even then the coverage was based more upon the recent divorce that had broken the ten-year bond between two of America's oldest historical families. The *Telegraph* even carried a wedding day photograph of Alyce and Appleton. There was a second photograph of Appleton being escorted from Appleton and Drake's Wall Street building by Federal agents, above a company statement denying any knowledge or involvement in alleged embezzlement of client funds and attempted illegal monetary transfers into offshore funds. The English coverage was short lived and Jordan relied upon the continuing coverage in the American newspapers, extending his monitoring to the *New York Daily News* as the initial story grew with the uncovering of the five New York bank accounts in easy walking distance of the commodity dealers' building and the West 72nd Street apartment leased in Appleton's name. Jordan's concentration remained upon any reference or comment concerning Alyce, which he found towards the end of the first week. An unnamed spokesperson from what was described as the Bellamy North Carolina compound was quoted as saying that Alyce was out of the country at an undisclosed location on an extended vacation from which she was not expected to return for several weeks. She would have no comment to make upon that return.

Jordan had made four unsuccessful attempts to contact Alyce from England, in between working to restore the far too long neglected routine in his life, although stopping short of actively selecting a new persona to adopt. There remained, of course, the already researched operation as Paul Maculloch, in whose name the Hans Crescent apartment was leased and whose every personal detail he knew. Also existing, in the Maculloch name, were the Royston and Jones bank accounts and the unbreakable rule against carrying over from one job to another an already established facility. Jordan accepted that he was stretching the protective rule to its breaking point but that's what restraining rules were: protective. And for this reason they had to be strictly observed.

That decision made long before the eventual Tuesday revelation about Appleton, Jordan moved both to guard his existing savings as well as severing all links to the little used Maculloch identity, even though in doing so he breached another forbidden barrier.

Within two days of his return from America he loaded half the money in the Royston and Jones deposit boxes into a crammed suitcase, far more than he had ever moved before, and went directly from Leadenhall Street to the Jersey ferry port to put it beyond any discovery or court power in the bank secrecy haven of St Helier. Two weeks later – far more quickly than any previous asset transfer – Jordan risked the repeated trip and crossed the English Channel again with the remainder of the London money. Jordan closed the Leadenhall Street facilities and the Hans Crescent flat rental the same day and spent the majority of his evenings in casinos in which, over the course of the four weeks he lost close to £20,000 of his total £70,000 stake which, although he refused to admit to any gambler's superstition, not regarding himself as one, he regarded as a bad omen, although he still collected the necessary winning receipt certificates on the £50,000 that remained.

Dinner with Lesley Corbin on his first week back was a highlight, largely because he had so much background to recount of the Raleigh hearings – during which she pointedly reminded him there'd been a loose, unfulfilled arrangement for her to attend as a legal observer, adding that she'd already heard from Beckwith how much he'd contributed – but he'd declined her invitation to a nightcap when he delivered her home to her Pimlico flat. He paid Lesley's bill, in cash, by return the following week and she telephoned to thank him and Jordan responded as he knew he was expected, with another dinner invitation. Afterwards he took her to a Mayfair casino and overrode her protests to stake her with five hundred pounds. She doubled it and he lost £2,300. He declined the nightcap invitation that night too. She promised to call if there was any contact from Beckwith about an appeal by Appleton and Jordan said there was a message service with which he kept in contact if he wasn't at the Marylebone flat, lying that there was a possibility of his soon going on a gambling sweep through Europe. He did actually go to Paris for the Arc de Triomphe race meeting, briefly sorry that he didn't invite her but regretting more losing £5,000.

It was the publicity of the Appleton investigation that brought Jordan out of denial to confront the fact that he'd done virtually nothing whatsoever constructive to re-establish anything like a proper working regime but that, to the contrary, he was positively avoiding doing so.

Jordan used the excuse of that publicity to telephone Daniel Beckwith, who responded at once with the demand, 'Would you fucking believe it?'

'Never in a million years,' said Jordan, wondering the colour of the other man's cowboy shirt that day. 'You heard anything about an appeal?'

'With the shit he's now covered in! Forget it!'

'You think he really did it?' asked Jordan, to justify the conversation.

'The story is they're running book on Wall Street. You should get back over here, win yourself some easy money.'

With what he knew he could probably do just that if what Beckwith said was true, reflected Jordan. 'You heard how Alyce is reacting? Spoken to Bob maybe?'

'Don't expect to,' dismissed Beckwith. 'I'd imagine she's turning cartwheels and setting off fire crackers in celebration. I'll keep in touch, if there's anything.'

Jordan mulled over the idea for almost an hour before calling Reid in Raleigh.

As Beckwith had done, the North Carolina lawyer took the call at once, although more controlled. 'There's a guy with a whole bunch of trouble,' the lawyer agreed. 'The late night talk shows are competing for the best jokes.'

'I've tried calling Alyce, to see if she's OK,' said Jordan, honestly. 'I read in one of the papers that she's abroad and won't be back for some time.'

'A smokescreen,' dismissed Reid. 'She's mostly down here on the estate just outside the city. Best place to be if she wants to hide, which she does. And she can fly in and out when she wants from the airstrip they've got there.'

'You speak to her a lot?'

'Not a lot. No reason to, now it's all over.'

'If you do, will you do me a favour? Tell her I've tried to call, to see if she's OK. That I'd like to hear from her.'

There was a pause from the other end of the line. 'I'll pass it on, if we speak again.'

Jordan's phone rang two days later.

'I've tried to call,' said Jordan.

'Bob told me.'

'And before I came back.' He thought her voice was flat, as if she were depressed.

'Stephen told me that, too.'

'How are you?'

'Pissed off with all the media hanging around again, since Alfred's arrest.'

'I guess he's in deep trouble.'

'I guess,' she agreed, disinterestedly.

'I'm thinking of coming across.'

'What for?'

'Just a trip,' Jordan pressed on. 'I thought maybe we could meet up?'

'I told you, I'm under siege again down here.'

'Bob said you could get in and out by air when you wanted to. We could get together in New York, if they haven't found your apartment there.'

Alyce didn't respond.

'Alyce?'

'I am going up for a foundation meeting next week. It'll be the first time since my re-establishment on the board.'

'It was next week I was thinking of coming over,' improvised Jordan. 'When will you be there?'

'Tuesday onwards.'

'I'll be at the Carlyle again. I'll call you from there.'

'Wednesday,' said Alyce. 'Make it Wednesday.'

'Wednesday,' agreed Jordan.

485

*  *  *

Remembering his jetlag Jordan caught a week-end flight. The Sunday edition of the *New York Times* reported in a front page story that the FBI had encountered some 'unusual features' in the Appleton investigation.

Jordan didn't once leave his Carlyle suite on the Sunday – eating from room service – and only walked as far as Central Park the following day. It was in the park that he read that day's *New York Times* and *Wall Street Journal*, both of which reported, without much more detail, that the Justice Department were possibly convening a Grand Jury to investigate the Appleton affair.

He reached only Alyce's answering service on his two Tuesday calls, asking her on both occasions where she wanted to eat, to enable him to make the reservation, but it wasn't until the Wednesday morning that she finally answered, personally, suggesting lunch, not dinner, and at the hotel.

'What's wrong?' Jordan finally asked. She was as flat voiced as she had been when she'd called him in London the previous week and since then he'd thought about little else but her obvious lassitude.

'You really do sometimes have the strangest aptitude for asking the most stupid questions!'

'As you sometimes have the strangest aptitude for responding with the most confusing answers.'

'You want to call it off?'

'No!' said Jordan, urgently. 'The last thing I want to do is call anything off. I want to see you.

Talk to you.'

'At lunch,' Alyce insisted.

'I'll make the reservation; we can have a drink first. I'll be waiting in the lobby again.'

Which he was, a table booked in the bar as well as the restaurant, the half bottle of champagne already in its cooler. Alyce came into the hotel with the same commanding confidence as before, attracting the same attention as before, although Jordan judged it to be because of how she was dressed – a long coated white trouser suit with a floppy-brimmed matching white hat – and so perfectly made up, the too bright red lipstick replaced by paler pink, the colour to her face more natural than applied. She accepted the champagne and extended the flute for the glass-touching toast and said, 'I almost didn't come again but now I have I'm glad and it's good to see you.'

'And I'm even more confused than ever,' said Jordan.

'Which I guess I am, too. And don't want to be, not any longer.'

'Then I'm glad I made the trip here because I don't want any more confusion or misunder-standings,' said Jordan. 'From this moment on I want both of us to understand everything, know everything about the other, although I'm not sure it's going to come out as straight as I want it to.'

'You sure about that, my darling?'

Jordan smiled at the word, the relief surging through him. 'I think so ... I think I know so.'

'And I think I should speak first, before—' started Alyce.

487

'No!' refused Jordan. 'You spoke ahead of me when we said goodbye in France and I stupidly agreed because I didn't understand ... didn't know ... and I'm not going to let it happen again. Nothing's going to be easy, because of what and who you are and because of what I am, although what I am – really am – isn't going to be any barrier because I'm all set for another career change that's going to get that out of the way. I love you, which is something I never thought I'd ever tell anyone again. I want us to be together. Married together, although God knows how that's going to happen but I'll make it happen. I guess you'll want to continue living here – working here – which is fine. And I don't want you to imagine I want to live off you and your money and your position. I've got a lot of money ... enough money ... and we can give all yours to yet another charity. And—'

'Stop!' insisted Alyce. 'Please stop! I don't want you to go on misunderstanding ... saying things I don't want to hear you say, although I do want to hear you say them—'

'You're not making sense,' halted Jordan, in turn.

'Then let me,' pleaded Alyce. 'Let me talk, try to explain as best I can, without stopping me. Without stopping me and hating me because I never want you to hate me, not now and not ever. I know who you are, Harvey. Know *what* you are. Which means I know what you've done to Alfred. How I guessed you paid all the bills and didn't want my money...' She stopped, gulping too deeply at her drink and having to cough when it caught her breath.

'I tricked you, my darling,' she started again. 'Tricked you and now I am so very, very sorry. I never intended it to happen, none of it. I never imagined Alfred would invoke that stupid fucking criminal conversation claim; never thought I'd ever see you again, which made everything worse, because I wanted to, so much, after France.'

'You're not—' Jordan started again but sharply she interrupted him.

'No! I've got to finish because I don't think I can say it all a second time. Of course I knew Alfred was having me watched here because I was having him watched long before he put his private detectives on to me. I knew all about Sharon Borowski and Leanne Jefferies, and had two other women if I needed to cite them. But here, in America, he was getting too close. He had to be diverted, get the co-respondent he needed for the divorce. Which is why I went to France and found you. You were only ever supposed to be a necessary name to get him to pull his people off. I didn't even know of something called criminal conversation. Or guess in a million years that you would fight it. Never thought I'd ever see you again although by the time I flew back I wanted to, so very much...'

Jordan took advantage of another gulped drink. 'How do you know what I do?'

'That extra week, when I extended the vacation? That was to get my own enquiry people to France: those I'd personally employed to watch Alfred, not the DKK agency that Bob engaged.'

489

She sniggered a humourless laugh. 'You know why I did it? I did it because I really didn't want you to get in the situation you ended up in. But you confused us so much, back in England. Changing from Harvey Jordan to Peter Thomas Wightman. It didn't take long to work out why, though. Then we thought you'd caught us out, all those evasion tricks when you went back to your own apartment...' She raised her hand towards him. 'Don't worry, darling. What you did when you got back to England wasn't breaking any American law, not that I'd have blown the whistle on you if it did. And I'm certainly not going to tell anyone about what you've done to Alfred.'

'You keep calling me darling.'

'Why do you think I wore that stupid plastic ring all the time, after you gave it to me ... even wore it back here on the plane? I loved you by then ... like I love you now. Which is why I'm going to end it now and marry Walter, who's kind and gentle and who I came to France to protect from Alfred's people. And who I think I love enough, just enough, to marry.'

'No!' refused Jordan. 'We could make something work. I don't know what or how but there'll be some way...'

Alyce shook her head. 'It might have worked, maybe, if Alfred hadn't sued for criminal conversation. And if you hadn't beat him in court, as you did. Somehow, somewhere, it would come out if we got together. And when it did Alfred would have every grounds for appealing the court's decision. Alfred would employ every private detective he could, although he wouldn't need many to show your photograph to the banks in which you opened the accounts in his name and the realtor from whom you leased the apartment on West 72nd Street that all the newspapers have identified, would it? And then you'd go to prison – which I couldn't bear – and all the Bellamy Foundations and trusts would be disgraced because I'd be linked – possibly even charged with complicity with you – and I couldn't expose the family to that, as much as I love you. It's over, my darling. It's got to be over. We got too clever, both of us. And ended up beating ourselves.'

Jordan reclined the back of the First Class seat and adjusted the eye shades against being disturbed by the cabin staff, even though he'd already told the supervisor he didn't want anything to eat or drink, just to be left alone. Which he was, he acknowledged; alone again, with only himself to consider or think of, which he'd once considered the perfect way to be, but didn't any more.

Alyce was right, of course. He'd known that all the time he'd argued with her – close to pleading with her – that they could work out a way to stay together, be happy together, to her head-shaking adamant refusal that they'd end up hating each other, unable to hide from Appleton. Which meant, he supposed, that in a way Appleton had won, after all. Too convoluted, Jordan corrected himself: too much self-pity. He had to accept what had happened – not yet, but eventually – and move on, as he'd eventually moved on after that other long ago collapse into self-pity.

Except that he didn't want to. The sudden awareness surprised Jordan; confused him even and he forced himself to confront exactly *what* it was he didn't want any more … To go on as he was, doing what he did, he answered himself, further surprised at another potential, self-imposed upheaval in his life. What life? he asked himself, continuing the personal analysis. What – where – was the life in becoming someone with a different name every two or three months, turning some poor bastard's existence on its head as his had been turned by what had just happened to him? Compartmentalizing everything between himself and Alyce, Jordan recognized he'd been lucky escaping as he had, remaining undiscovered for what he was by Appleton's surveillance team. Harvey Jordan, the man who never gambled, acknowledged that his luck couldn't last.

What could – would – he do then? Not a decision to be rushed, although he'd once done well enough running his own legitimate computer programming business and there was more than sufficient money squirreled away in Jersey to start again. There was no need or reason to rush the decision, he thought again. Maybe something to think about, refine in detail, on another vacation. But then again, maybe not: the vacation that is, not the detailed consideration on his future. The weather in the South of France was uncertain in October.

He slept dreamlessly and undisturbed during

492

the flight and disembarked in London actually excited at the thought of doing something new. The immigration officer was a blonde girl who reminded him vaguely of Alyce. She looked between him and his passsport photograph and said, 'Harvey Jordan?'

'Yes,' he replied, to his own satisfaction. 'Very definitely Harvey Jordan.'